AN UNQUIET LIFE

ODYSSEY OF A WHISTLEBLOWER

Also by Herbert H. Keyser M.D.

Women Under the Knife

Prescription for Disaster: Healthcare in America

Geniuses of the American Musical Theatre: The Composers and Lyricists

Two Drifters: Off to See the World

A Chautauquan Searches Paris For The Best Tarte au Citron

AN UNQUIET LIFE

ODYSSEY OF A WHISTLEBLOWER

Herbert H. Keyser M.D.

Cogent Publishing NY
Imprint of The Whitson Group, Inc.

THE WHITSON GROUP, INC.
COGENT
PUBLISHING NY

Published by Cogent Publishing NY
Imprint of The Whitson Group, Inc.
3 Miller Road, Putnam Valley, NY 10579
(845) 528-7617 • www.cogentpub.com
cogentpub@aol.com

This is a work of fiction. Names, characters, businesses, places, events and incidents are the products of the author's imagination. Any resemblance to actual events, locales or persons, living or dead is entirely coincidental.

ISBN: 978-0-925776-41-9
1 2 3 4 5—18 17 16

For Quentin Young (1923-2016)
No one ever gave more of his life to ensure
quality healthcare for everyone.

Acknowledgments

$\mathcal{I}$ grew up in the 1930's in a family struggling for survival in the Depression. My parents' plight was especially difficult. Besides the general poverty faced throughout the community, they had the added disadvantage of being handicapped, having both been born deaf.

We lived next door to my maternal grandparents. The exposure to those two individuals, who in the midst of all their problems were kind, generous, charitable, loving and community-minded had a significant effect on me. I grew up grateful for whatever I had.

After five relatively unsuccessful years attempting to be a star in the theatre, my parents were more than thrilled when I was accepted to Medical School. Thrilled is not the best word... try ecstatic!

From the very onset I knew that, coming from significant poverty I had been given the opportunity of a lifetime. I believed that there was much I needed to give back.

The nine years after college, being in training left little time to give back as I was deeply into preparation for my life's work. During that time I began to meet mentors that would direct my life forever. The first was Dr. Joseph Seitchik. I had never met a person before of such brilliance and compassion. I am certain that the fact that he was an Obstetrician, among other things, led me to enter that field.

During my internship and residency, exposure to greatness in the form of Dr. David Spain and Dr. Isadore Snapper further propelled me to the desire to accomplish something of value.

I met many physicians who commanded my respect due to the fine work they performed, but at the same time I began to realize there were others who acted quite differently. The entire system of healthcare appeared to me to be flawed. So over the next decade I began writing articles and reports about the things I believed needed to be changed in order to make health care safe and available for everyone. That writing did not sit well with much of the medical community.

During this time I discovered something else—there were a number of highly moral physicians who too were trying to expose these problems. I looked more deeply into the work they were doing and found something very disturbing—these medical whistleblowers were having their lives destroyed by the medical establishment. So, more than twenty-five years ago, I started to write a novel about their plight. This novel has been written and rewritten multiple times. I found that although I was writing and getting non-fiction published over the past three decades, I faced the marvelous catch 22 of the publishing world—it is almost impossible to get a novel published without an agent, and no agent will work with you until you have had a novel published.

I must thank two people who kept reading and editing my book during those years, my wonderful wife Barbara and my brilliant writer son Chris. But all their valuable work could not help me get it published. Finally, two very special people, Ivor and Ronnie Whitson, who run a publishing house, Cogent Publishing NY, read the book and wanted to publish it. They placed it in the hands of an amazing editor, Ann LaFarge, who was a joy to work with.

Though this will be my sixth published book, none can even touch what this book means to me, as changing America's health care system has been my life's work. I will be forever grateful to those who helped bring it to fruition. Though this is a work of fiction, within its pages is a back story that exposes the real world of medicine, together with some thrills and twists that makes it an enjoyable novel. Also revealed is the true nature of the human female sexual response. And beyond all this it reveals a story, though fictionalized, of the courage that a number of very fine physicians have exhibited over the years in the effort to make our health care system better.

Prologue

*I*t was an experience not to be forgotten. The television set rested tilted on a broken table in the corner. One of its legs had vanished during the two decades of its life and as a result the TV rocked off balance whenever the set was accidentally touched. When that happened, the picture suddenly developed multiple white horizontal stripes and became distorted. Rabbit ears extended from the worn imitation wood surface as I watched a CBS special, "The Soviet Union: Seven Days In May."

A lamp sat on the floor of the sparsely furnished living room. It was not meant to be a floor lamp, but there was no table for it. There was no shade either. The remainder of the apartment had the same empty eerie feeling. A chartreuse colored shag rug originally purchased as a remnant that the store was thrilled to sell covered the floor. In the spartan bedroom there was a single bed, a small chest with drawers that were all off their tracks, and a miniature painted table. It was chipped in multiple places where the different colors of previous paint jobs could be seen. The only lamp had a shade with a hole punched out on one side.

As in every other room, the walls were absolutely bare. Cold, barren and lonely, it was my home for ten days. On the bedroom table sat the most beautiful item in my temporary dwelling—a phone. It was used frequently to touch any support system I could find. My name is J. D. Brown. Through most of my adult life as an obstetrician I've been called, simply, Jay.

I had dinner that evening at a local Italian restaurant. A nurse suggested, though not enthusiastically, that it was about the best food that could be found in this small community. Cooked with a very heavy hand, it came with a guarantee that heartburn would follow. I ate sparingly, and left most of the offering behind on my plate.

My waitress had told me, with a southern drawl, "My name is Betsy and I'll be serving your dinner."

She was as sweet as the sugar cane grown locally and devastated by the volume of food I left behind.

"Sugar, ain't you gonna take the rest of that home in a doggy bag?"

It took whatever diplomacy I had accumulated over the years to assure Betsy that everything was fine, and that I had no way to use the food once I left the restaurant. It was a white lie. But the last thing in the world I wanted to do was eat that meal again.

What am I doing here? I thought to myself.

There was not a single moment that my mind did not wander through thoughts about how all this could have happened. But this night in particular put a strain on my ability to cope with the events of the last few years.

The television special evaluated a possible change in Russian society.

The journalists asked, "Was it in fact becoming more open?"

In the process they confronted issues such as the fairness of its legal system. I listened as they indicated that Russians were not granted the same legal rights that were available to all American citizens. I had not the slightest doubt that the infringement of rights in Russia, to which the commentator referred, truly existed. But I felt total frustration in the knowledge that I had experienced things which were not that dissimilar. I felt a sour taste in the back of my throat, but couldn't be certain whether my gastric juices had backed up due to my anger or as a reminder of the meal I had just partially consumed.

Were the producers of this documentary aware of the problems physicians like me had confronted in the past few years?

The question was rhetorical. Actually, some members of the media had made efforts to expose the type of problems I had faced. They had experienced little to no success. *Could I expect to achieve what they could not?*

I knew there was little support for my philosophy. But I actually wasn't very concerned. The purpose was so clear, too obvious and too important for the public not to rally. My naiveté knew almost no bounds.

I soon found that I did not stand alone. Many others had fought the battle to correct abuses within the medical profession before, but they were unknown to me because they had lost and been buried in the mire of their cause. Some wished never again be identified with their struggle. When I learned of that, I had some concern about what might happen to me. After all, why would I be able to do what so many others before me had found impossible?

The problems that resulted from the actions that I took bore no relationship to this small rural community. This was merely an aftermath. This was what I was relegated to, as a result of what I had done. This small town represented for me one thing only—a way to earn some immediate cash to sustain myself. Here I had a new title. I was a *locum tenens*.

The words represented an anglicized latin phrase used in medicine to describe temporary traveling physicians. Doctors, such as I, filled vacuums in medical care. Those positions were not likely to be found in a major metropolis where replacements could easily be found locally, but small rural communities did not have that opportunity. Their missing doctor had no local backup. Thus came the demand for replacements.

In this particular rural community, in which many of the residents were impoverished, it was the care of the needy that was not provided. I was one of a series of obstetricians, each of whom had come in for a short stretch of time to handle an extremely heavy work load. In the first week I worked, on two occasions, for thirty six hours straight. Newspapers had written articles about such unacceptable schedules. Editorials questioned the safety to patients. But, the choice to be working here was mine. I worked whatever schedule was required to fulfill my obligation to the agency that had sent me here.

At the age of twenty five I spent five grueling years in that type of rigorous schedule during my training. I found it somewhat humorous, now that I was fifty four years old, no one seemed to care much about my work schedule. For the hospital, turning out the work was the only issue. Here I was, looking my age, and though I was in reasonably good physical shape, the workload was taking its toll on me.

On my seventh day a young woman had shown up in the labor and delivery suite in pain and vomiting. I went to evaluate this poor soul who would punctuate this horrendous ten day stay. In time I came to be very fond of her and also of her mother, but definitely not on that first night.

The patient had received some prenatal care, but it was very sparse. Even that was much better than most of the patients from the lower economic strata of this town. It was common to have patients enter the hospital in active labor, never seen by any physician or midwife during the pregnancy. In this poor community prenatal care was supplied primarily by midwives, who were limited to caring for the less privileged. The midwives had no private patients. By this mechanism the local obstetrical community rendered the midwives non-competitive with the local practicing physicians.

My new patient was obese, not an uncommon finding among the indigent, whose limited finances required that they consume a diet over weighted in carbohydrates. They had little knowledge of proper nutrition.

Though physicians like to see themselves as being nonprejudicial, it always seems easier to relate to a patient who makes an effort to conform to what the physician perceives as "proper behavior." At that initial meeting, neither the patient nor her family made any great impression on me. In retrospect I would like to forgive my lack of compassion based on a plea of utter fatigue.

Her mouth was a battlefield of broken and infected teeth. Her gums were a periodontist's delight. Her hair was a mass of dirt. I cannot adequately describe how physically unattractive she was.

I came to realize that my evaluation of her demeanor was grossly distorted by other factors. That night her mental faculties were at the very low end of normal due to her pain.

Her name was Julia Benson. For her, this was a return visit to the labor and delivery suite where she had initially appeared earlier in the day. At that first visit, a diagnosis of false labor had been made. The midwife, who had seen her both times, called me on the patient's return visit. Mrs. Benson's abdominal girth had increased significantly in the intervening hours.

The patient moaned in extreme pain. It was constant and in no way similar to the pain of labor. The size of her abdomen was what one might expect from a patient at full term with a twin gestation. Like so many of the patients with inadequate prenatal care, the history of her menstrual cycles was quite vague. The determination of an accurate due date would necessitate the use of other modalities such as ultrasound. But ultrasounds were not very accurate when used for the first time near the end of the pregnancy.

Julia was a little shy of full term according to the examination done earlier in the day. By my examination, the size of her uterus was much smaller than it should have been. It was comparable to that of a woman 7½ to 8 months pregnant. With poor prenatal care it was not unusual to see growth retarded babies, who were smaller than expected size.

If the baby was near term and growth retarded, I knew it would be much better off outside the uterus. Babies like this were poorly nourished when they stayed in the uterus.

Obviously Julia's increasing total abdominal size was due to another problem. For some reason her intestines were not functioning. The clear message was that emergency action had to be taken. I immediately called for a nasogastric tube.

I was well aware that patients considered the passage of such a tube to be worse than the disease.

With the patient fully conscious I would pass a plastic tube through her nostril down into her throat, and from there into her stomach.

I had often wondered how I managed to do this procedure. After all, I am the one who gags the very moment a physician places a tongue blade in my mouth to look at my throat. It is I whom the ophthalmologist can't reasonably check for glaucoma as I constantly blink the moment his instrument gets near my eye. Yet I was about to inflict all of this on this wretched patient.

Painstakingly, before initiating the process, I explained the absolute urgency of the procedure. The patient needed to understand how important it was that the tube remain in place, attached to a suction apparatus to relieve the pressure building up in her GI tract.

For whatever reason, illness or basic slowness of thought, she was not altogether with us as we proceeded. The nurses, the midwife and I moved with all due speed to prepare for the process.

"Get me the water and straw. Make sure it's ice water."

"Mrs. Benson, please listen to me! I need to pass this tube. And

I need you to absolutely continue drinking that water, without a stop, once I tell you to start."

A deep sigh of relief was my response, once the tube was passed. I continuously uttered words of reassurance to the patient.

"You WILL get used to it, Mrs. Benson. It won't feel nearly as bad in a little while. Try to take just slow deep breaths. You WILL become accustomed to it and it will make you feel so much better in the end."

But Mrs. Benson continued to gag on the tube in her throat. There was no way possible for her to believe that shortly she would become accustomed to that terrible sensation. To her it would never be acceptable.

On the other hand I knew how important it was. She would be temporarily out of trouble until we determined why nothing moved through her G.I. tract.

Another call came from the emergency room. I was responsible for every obstetrical patient who came through the E.R. twenty four hours a day, seven days a week. It was bearable only because I understood that it was only for a ten day duration.

In the background, while we talked I could hear the sounds of my patient as she made all sorts of guttural primitive noises. Within minutes a nurse came out of Mrs. Benson's room. She looked, for all the world, like a lost soul at the end of her rope.

"She's pulled it out!"

"Oh hell!" was my forlorn retort.

Step by step the torture was repeated. There was no place for a compromise.

She begged us to stop, but we proceeded, with pity and anger, with sympathy and annoyance. We wanted to help her through this terrible time, while we secretly wished she had wandered into someone else's delivery room.

"The tube must stay in!"

"I don't want it. I want to go home. Let me go home."

Her mother stood by her side in anguish. She understood that her daughter's request was impossible, but felt helpless to get her to comply.

I paused, slowly brushed my hand backward across my brow to a hairless head, and then, with total determination, said,

"No! No! Absolutely no! Do you understand me? No! You cannot go home and you WILL have this tube in your stomach, if I have to put it back a hundred times."

Once again we began.

The patient was obviously in the midst of a serious general surgical problem. Pregnancy in itself could not account for such symptoms. What we had accomplished up until this time was merely a stopgap measure. A general surgeon would have to make a decision about what action needed to be taken.

Mrs. Benson was not in labor, but in the midst of all the work with the tube, we had applied a fetal monitor to her abdomen. It indicated that she did not have any contractions. The evaluation of the fetal heart rate gave us evidence that the baby was not in any acute distress, but certain patterns that we saw on the monitor recording did not reassure us about the baby's condition. Decisions needed to be made. Should we allow her to continue to carry the pregnancy, irrespective of her surgical problem? If a surgeon planned to operate to correct her bowel problem, I decided I wanted to deliver this baby by Cesarean Section at the same time. The first step, however, was to get a general surgeon to see her immediately.

I understood why I was in this community. No one wanted to care for these indigents. The local physicians had made the decision to no longer provide that care. They were tired of the work without any significant remuneration. They did not want to assume the responsibility for patients who were noncompliant, who didn't show up for appointments, and who presented constantly as high risk problems without prenatal care.

Ultimately, that risk created the possibility of a resultant malpractice case. The threat drove even the most ethical of them to the decision not to provide care. I soon learned what this environment had in store for me, to say nothing of this poor patient who had come under my care.

After I checked the E.R. roster, I called the surgeon on first call and explained the situation to him. There was a prolonged silence on the other end of the phone.

"Doctor I need you to come see this patient NOW! I need an immediate surgical consultation."

"I don't do obstetrics."

"What are you talking about! I do the obstetrics. I didn't ask you for an obstetrical consultation. I need a surgical consultation... Now!!!"

"I've never had a case like this in a pregnant woman."

"Listen here, doctor. I haven't got the time, the patience or the inclination to play games with you. Are you coming here right now or do I get somebody else?"

"Under the circumstances I think it might be advisable for you to consider getting someone ..."

I slammed the phone down and turned to the nurse in charge of obstetrics with fire in my eyes and ice in my voice.

"I want the nursing supervisor, NOW!"

In the background was the constant growl of my gagging patient. My frustration had reached the boiling point when the supervisor arrived. She suggested that I call the surgeon on second call. I told him the complete story about the patient and the problems I had faced in my conversation with the surgeon on first call.

"I'm not on call," he told me.

"I was last night and I worked. There is absolutely no reason why the surgeon on first call should not respond. I don't want to come in just because he is negligent."

I hung up the phone. The nurses looked at me and waited for a response. My right hand rested against the lower half of my face, as I stared out into space. I sighed, very deeply. I felt powerless in this institution that had legitimized the rejection of care for the weak and least fortunate in our society.

"Get me the operating room," I said. The call yielded worthwhile information. A young surgeon had just completed an operation. I spoke to the Operating Room supervisor and told her that I had a major emergency. I asked if she could prevail upon him to come to the labor and delivery suite as soon as possible. Meanwhile, I arranged for immediate Xrays to be obtained in the labor suite.

Within fifteen or twenty minutes the young surgeon arrived. But, just moments before, she did it again. The tube had been yanked out.

He methodically examined her. He went over her abdomen carefully and listened to hear if there were any bowel sounds at all. He then told her in no uncertain terms that the tube needed to be reinserted a third time. She emphatically insisted she would not agree to have that done. The young doctor approached the matter in an entirely different manner than I had done.

In a calm voice he said, "That's O.K. You can go home and in a little while you will be dead."

Unfortunately, it didn't work.

"I don't care. I'd rather be dead."

He realized he had accomplished nothing with a sane, calm rational approach. With the helpful encouragement of her mother, we semi-forcibly put the tube back down into her stomach.

Together, the surgeon and I analyzed the situation and discussed a differential diagnosis to explain what had happened. Like me, he was certain of one thing: She had no bowel function. There was either an obstruction or the bowel no longer functioned due to some other intraabdominal abnormality. He decided to wait and see if the presence of the tube might improve her condition overnight.

A condition called volvulus is a rather rare one. It almost always follows some previous surgery in which adhesions, intraabdominal scarring, cause a loop of bowel to become twisted. The result is an obstruction. Mrs. Benson had had surgery for appendicitis as a child. Volvulus became the primary diagnosis.

We both left the suite and I felt somewhat more secure with the knowledge that someone else shared the responsibility with me. Another mind, besides my own, now considered what complications our patient faced. Several hours had passed when I called in to check on her progress.

The nurse said I had just beaten her to the punch. She was about to call me. The tube was out again and our patient had vomited fecal material. It was now obvious that the block had originated well down into the length of the bowel.

In a matter of minutes I was there. Her abdomen was even larger than before. The sound of her vomiting over and over pounded in my ears. It was obvious that her problems had compounded. No one I had ever treated before could have wished to be dead more than Mrs. Benson did that night.

Though it was hard to believe, at the very moment I instructed the nurse to get our young general surgeon back to the hospital, the emergency room called me to come as quickly as possible to see a patient they believed to have an ectopic pregnancy. That diagnosis—a pregnancy located outside the uterus—if correct, would necessitate immediate surgery. Fortunately, they were wrong.

There was no second call behind me. I was first call, second call and any number beyond, as the night progressed. One more acute emergency came to the E.R. later—a patient who had bled profusely from a miscarriage.

The young surgeon and I took Mrs. Benson immediately to the operating room. When we opened her abdomen the findings boggled my mind. We initially did a Cesarean Section to deliver the baby. It was extremely difficult due to the massive displacement of everything by her intestines. Our ability to work with our view obstructed by her bowel was the major problem.

After the delivery was completed, we discovered that volvulus was the correct diagnosis. The enlargement of her uterus had pushed the intestines into a position in which they became twisted, probably due to scarring from the appendectomy. The involved portion of the small bowel, normally an inch or an inch and a half in diameter, had distended to the size of an automobile tire inner tube. The walls were so thin that on lifting the loops of bowel, I could actually see the surgeon right through them on the opposite side of the operating table.

Inside the bowel there was a level of fluid. It was like looking through a clear glass with water in it. That a loop of bowel this distended had not just ruptured was miraculous and life saving to her. We removed several feet of her intestine

Through the wee hours, I got to my other emergencies and collapsed into bed just before 7 A.M.

Over the next few days, Mrs. Benson and the baby did very well. We no longer had to fight to keep the gastro-intestinal tube in place. I saw her as she was normally, without physical distress—a caring and loving mother. All day long she walked the hallways as she was instructed to do. She toted her I.V. pole, a tube hung out of one nostril, and she carried a full bag of urine like a purse. It was attached to the catheter in her bladder.

Whenever I came to visit her, she stopped everyone in the hallway to tell them "He saved me and my baby." My face reddened with embarrassment. But I knew she did it out of love.

————

Those ten days were definitely a time not to be forgotten. I was, for all intents and purposes, no more than a young obstetrical resident. When I originally left that stage of my life, many years before, I never expected to be back in that status once again. This is the story of how I got into this situation. It is also the untold story of many others who failed in the same quest that I undertook, and whose outcome was even less fortunate.

Chapter One

Rhonda's Revenge

*J*ay Brown found himself somewhat isolated in this world he had now created. Resisting the establishment, even in a manner which he believed to be rather benign, had significantly changed the environment in which he practiced medicine.

It wasn't just in his position as Chairman of the department of Obstetrics and Gynecology at Northwest Community Hospital on Long Island that life had changed. In his own office there was a different mood. Marvin Green who was one of the finest obstetricians Jay ever knew, or would come to know, was mildly annoyed at the rumpus Jay had raised. Never a harsh word had passed between the two of them in the fifteen years they had practiced together, but they were as different as night and day.

Patients liked the personality Jay exhibited when non-serious matters were discussed. It was light and friendly. Yet they knew another side of him as well. When the situation called for it, he was warm and serious. Critical matters were not to be treated frivolously. Jay spent untold amounts of time talking, reassuring, teaching and supporting the medical and emotional needs of his patients.

Yet when a stranger walked past a delivery room, she might be startled to hear a voice singing old show tunes to a new mother with her legs spread-eagle as he sewed up her episiotomy.

But there was another Jay Brown. He had less compassion and acceptance of human frailty when he saw that frailty in other physicians. As a professional he visualized nothing in shades of gray. He applied stringent demands on himself and on others. Jay looked down upon those who, for any reason, were not able to maintain the standards he had set. He had little patience for those who fell short. Jay Brown's tolerance level for those who did not meet his professional standards was zero.

It never occurred to Jay that he was insensitive in his dealings with those who were less than perfect. On the other hand, the physicians around him saw that unpleasant side of Dr. Jay Brown quite clearly.

Marvin Green, who was almost twenty years Jay's senior, and the original builder of this well established and highly respected practice, was the charmer of the world. He was as honest as any physician who had ever sworn to the Hippocratic oath. Jay thanked God for that part of Marvin Green's personality. In appearance, Marvin was damn near a Greek god. He fit the standard description of tall, dark and handsome with a gift of gab that could talk you out of your house, business or last penny if he had wished. Every patient adored him.

Marvin Green never did a single surgical procedure that Jay thought was unnecessary. But medicine still was definitely a business from Marvin's perspective. While Jay spent what Marvin Green thought was an excessive amount of time talking to patients about all their concerns, Marvin saw patients in rapid fire. But he had a way with them that was so special, not one ever felt that she was being rushed.

"Mrs. Storch, if I had a wife as lovely as you, I wouldn't let her out on the streets alone, not even to see her decrepit old obstetrician."

"Oh, Marvin, you are so sweet, but I don't believe you for one minute."

Jay heard conversations like that for years in the corridors of their office. He was never certain whether they believed Marvin or not.

However, in the relationship between them, Jay always knew when his bon vivant partner was a charmer and when he was sincere. Jay trusted him never to lie. More than that, he would entrust the care of any woman, patient or family member into his hands.

To Jay, Marvin's hands worked like magic. He believed that he learned almost everything he knew about obstetrics from Marvin Green. Though Jay considered himself well trained when he joined Marvin, directly out of his residency, he saw an obstetrician who was as gentle as any he had ever known. Jay learned things from Marvin about the delivery of newborns that he had never seen before. Green made difficult forceps deliveries seem like a piece of cake. It was a finesse and style in the delivery of a child which impressed Jay for all the years that they worked together.

But Marvin knew there was a business end as well. He was impatient with Jay's constant struggle with other physicians about the quality of their care. Marvin wanted Jay to devote himself to being a good obstetrician and make a fine living as well. Jay did not pull his weight when it came to how much income he produced for the practice. The result was that Marvin was not happy.

Life at home for Jay was not much better. He and his wife Rhonda had grown farther and farther apart. The children went off to schools in other parts of the country. He and Rhonda slept in separate bedrooms and at best were cordial to each other. They had dinner together. That was the extent to which they were still married. Neither as yet had any inclination to establish any other relationship.

Somewhere along the way, Rhonda came to the conclusion that Jay had time for all his patients, but not for her. She had a deep seated anger for what she believed was an emotional desertion. She accepted this as just another phase in her life she had to tolerate. She saw Jay as only a source of permanent financial security. On the surface she functioned as if nothing at all disturbed her about their relationship. Deep within her, that was far from true. Jay, on the other hand, quietly sank into a deep depression about what was happening in his private life.

———

It seemed to Jay that he had had intermittent vague symptoms of soreness in his back for at least five years when he awoke on that May morning of 1973. A glimmer of sunlight shone through the separations in the bedroom draperies as he flipped over in his bed when...

"Aaahhhhh!!!"

The scream was like a cannon shot that shattered the walls and could be heard clear across the house. But it was like the tree that falls in the forest. No one was there to hear him. Rhonda had been gone for several days in Chicago, attending a Women's political rally. Jay was alone.

If he remained absolutely motionless, there was a vague but definite pain, but even a deep breath caused the sensation of a dagger stuck through his back and down his left leg.

"Oh hell. Now what am I going to do?"

He lay perfectly still trying to decide on a plan of action as he lifted an arm to see whether he could reach the telephone. The pain shot through again.

"Oh shit!" he yelled.

The pain had to be pretty severe because Jay Brown never uttered even benign curse words.

He twisted his body just slightly and slid across the smooth sheet. He pulled himself like a worm stretching its muscles to slowly gain a minimal amount of distance to get closer to the edge of the bed. He finally extended his arm far enough to reach the telephone as he gasped "Aah!" with the last effort. As carefully as possible he dialed.

"Marvin," he took a deep breath, "you're not going to believe what's happened to me. I'm lying here in bed and I can't move. My back has gone out completely."

"OK Jay, OK!" Marvin said with a not too hidden tone of annoyance. "Does that mean I've got to see all those patients in the office alone today?"

"Damn it, Marvin! So cancel my patients. I'm lying here in pain and you're worrying about whether we're going to lose a few bucks."

Marvin didn't hear a word he said. "Will you be back tomorrow?"

"Marv, I don't even know when I'll be able to get out of bed."

"Oh hell, why does everything happen to me?"

"You, you, what do you mean, you? I'm the one here in pain."

"OK, don't worry I'll take care of everything. Call me when you feel better." Click!

Jay couldn't believe it. Marvin had hung up.

Call me when you feel better. I could be undergoing brain surgery and he'd ask me whether it was going to upset the schedule.

Jay realized he was overreacting and suddenly stopped the conversation he was having with himself.

"Ha. . . Ha" he began laughing. "Ha. . . Ha, Ha, Ha, Ha. . . Ha," and then suddenly another, "AHHHHH!"

He laughed so hard about Marvin's reaction that he moved his back a fraction too much and the knife thrust returned. Jay took a long breath, but not too deep, and lay still for a few moments. He was calmly assessing his next move, when a disastrous turn of events occurred.

He began to feel a sensation in his penis, associated with another in his groin. It said to him, *"I need to be emptied, NOW!"*

As if he was in direct conversation with his bladder, Jay shouted, "Now, now…. How?"

He tried not to panic, and slowly slid himself toward the edge of the bed. Each move caused considerable pain, but he knew that he must somehow get to the bathroom. Cautiously he slid his legs down the side of the mattress. *Would they ever reach the floor?*

"Let me call you sweetheart. I'm in love with you. Let me…"

He sang to himself as he did frequently, especially when a crisis arose. *Why had he come up with this old standard?*

"Let me hear your whisper… Ohhhhhhh shit!"

The pain shot through him as his foot struck the floor. Now gradually, as he clung to the sheets on his bed, he slowly lowered his trunk over the edge of the bed onto the floor. Finally, he was flat on his back. He tried not to think about what he felt. Should success not come very quickly, he might have to swim to his toilet through the volume of urine he would release beneath himself.

Jay slowly rolled his body over to his stomach and began a long, slow crawl to the bathroom. It astonished him how close the bathroom had always seemed before. That was, of course, when he was a member of that species which had learned to propel themselves on their hind legs, alone and in an upright position. Now that he had joined the lizard family, he covered distances much more slowly.

At last, he reached the door to the toilet. Stretching his right arm to its absolute maximum, he grasped the knob on the door and gave it a jerk. Unfortunately, the strength and direction of his tug was so great that he pulled the knob right off the door, but Jay hardly noticed it. He had misjudged the arc of the door's swing to his position on the floor and, "Ouch!" The corner of the door cracked against his raised forehead.

In a slightly dazed state Jay looked at the doorknob he held in his hand and just flipped it across the room. Then he cocked his head and shoulder slightly off to one side. He felt the electric like shocks in his back with each movement and pulled open the door past his prostrate body. He had reached his goal.

Jay pulled himself in front of the commode. There was no way he could possibly stand up to empty his bladder. He slowly pulled his body up against the side of the commode while on his knees, until his groin reached the edge of the toilet bowl.

The toilet seat and cover were both down. He realized that the width of the toilet seat would be too great a distance for him to get the end of his penis beyond it, so that he could empty into the bowl. So instead he just lifted the cover and the toilet seat with one motion of his left hand. He held them against the back of the commode as he pulled his penis out through the fly opening of his pajamas and laid it across the edge of the bowl, put his right hand up against the wall to support himself, and began to urinate.

Jay had not even seen the new addition to his commode. He was so preoccupied with his immediate problem that he had not noticed that Rhonda had added a plush fabric cover to the toilet seat cover. It created a problem that Jay had seen at times with other toilet seats, but never his own. An addition like that could cause the seat and cover to be at the wrong angle when raised against the back of the commode and unable to remain upright.

In his brain what followed was almost like a slow motion sequence of his life flashing before him. It began with the recurrence of the excruciating stabbing pain in his back. As Jay shrieked, he unwittingly lifted his left hand off the toilet seat and cover he had been leaning against and thrust his left arm up against the wall.

With a look of horror he saw the seat and Rhonda's new cover slowly make their way forward from the back of the commode.

As the pitch of the seat came further forward he realized that his manhood rested in the line of fire. It was about to be crushed by the falling object.

Just before that very moment of horrifying contact, Jay found the energy to push his two hands forcefully against the wall. As his body thrust back, he sprayed urine on the back of the commode, up against the wall and then freely into the air. As Jay hurtled backwards, he felt the moisture across his face as it gravitated to the ground.

For a moment he lay absolutely still. He had twisted his back in a strange series of contortions. He lay flat on his back. The significance of the new toilet seat cover finally struck him. In his state of somewhat disoriented thinking he concluded that Rhonda had done him in. Now, what was he to do about his back? He slowly raised his head and pushed his arm out for support as he attempted to raise his body. Something strange had happened. There was no pain. His body rose and. . . there was no pain. Up to his knees he progressed, and. . . there was no pain. Could it be? Could the phenomenal backward twist he had just performed reset his back like a chiropractic maneuver? Jay's version of the renowned Fosbury Flop of high jump fame had just been discovered.

Jay Brown stood and looked at himself in the mirror. He was standing straight and tall with no difficulty as he said to himself, "Orthopedic textbooks will now have to add to their armamentarium the Brown Phallic Flip."

"Tell Dr. Green I'll be in the office on time," he called in to his secretary.

Chapter Two

Confrontation

*T*he Department of Obstetrics and Gynecology selected the second Tuesday of each month at noon as the optimum time for their regular meeting at Northwest Community Hospital. It never began at noon, and this was not likely to be a regular meeting.

It was 1974 and Jay Brown, as Department Chairman, decided that April was just the right month for this particular topic. He had carefully checked the attendance rosters over the past several years and found the April meeting to be the one best attended. It was typical of the way Jay approached everything in his life. Though every effort of his was well planned, he was not devious. He simply wanted to be certain that nothing unplanned overtake the scheduled events.

An event could be as momentous as the April meeting or as inconsequential as what he would do in the afternoon of the third day of his vacation. He thought of it as being organized. Rhonda, who was no longer his wife, called him compulsive.

Jay was a master collector of information, such as the attendance schedules for these monthly meetings. Whether it was significant medical research data, the earned run averages of the Mets pitchers, or scraps of paper in his pocket with information about meetings or appointments, he stashed it all away in steel file cabinets or in the very well organized file within his skull.

His choice of April for this particular meeting, in fact, made great sense. In the winter a large portion of the medical staff traveled to the beaches of the Caribbean or to ski country. The hospital cancelled all meetings in the summer.

The meetings were usually deadly dull. Though the hospital was fairly large, it was not academically oriented. That was especially true of the Department of Obstetrics and Gynecology and was typical of hospitals in large urban or suburban communities with nearby medical training centers. As its stated purpose, Northwest Community Hospital provided care for the community of patients. Less clearly understood by the public, it was the location where physicians applied their skills and earned a very substantial living.

Northwest provided respectable care for its patients, but its physicians generally had little interest in education or research. Those motivated to learn and keep up their skills were on the staff of the local medical school hospital. All that one needed to, or cared to, learn was available at the school on a regular basis, but only a very small minority of Northwest's obstetricians made use of the school and its frequent conferences.

It was much the same all over the country. The great mass of physicians were private practitioners. They learned their skills, some quite well. A portion of them remained current through medical journals. But for many of these physicians, the journals ended up in a pile on their office desks. It looked great to the patients. Every few months they got stored or thrown away. Then another stack was begun. The physicians rarely cracked the pages. Even the outer plastic mailing envelopes would remain in place if it were not for a nurse who watched over the best interests of her boss. She realized that having journals in view of patients, with the plastic left on, was worse than not having them there at all. She removed the covers.

It wasn't that information didn't reach these doctors, but most of it came from a biased source. "Detail" men and women informed physicians about their employers' own drugs and equipment. They provided information on what the latest research recommended in relation to the product they hyped. The accuracy of their data was certainly swayed in a positive direction for their product. Possibly, a few years down the line it might turn out that claims of efficacy might be disputed, but that was an issue to be dealt with later. Now, the primary concern was the volume of sales. Unexpected complications might begin to appear sometime after wide use had been achieved. When that occurred, evidence of such a possibility was often traced back to the earlier research, ignored in the rush of getting the product to the marketplace.

Fortunately, the number of true major changes and advances in care were few and far between. The "treat them, flying by the seat of your pants" technique really worked quite well, most of the time. Dr.

Katz at Yale wrote about it negatively, probably with great accuracy. But Yale was Yale, and this was the real America, from one small town to another, and even in the heart of major urban communities.

For the most part these physicians worked quite diligently. That's why the noon scheduling of the meeting of the Ob-Gyn Department at Northwest didn't make a lot of sense. Those physicians who held Tuesday morning office hours scheduled to end at noon were never done by that hour. Even if the meeting scheduler didn't know that, Sid Schultz's patients certainly did. Sid, Jack O'Rourke and Ned Spitz, his partners, always still had at least a half dozen patients in their outer office as it approached the noon hour. Sometimes they didn't get to the meeting until a quarter to one or later. Even that was only possible because their office was directly attached to the hospital. But, there was a reason why they almost never missed the meeting, no matter how late they turned out to be.

The hospital understood what some of the physicians didn't. Although the level of education provided at those monthly sessions might be inconsequential, level of attendance was not. Among the mass of data the Joint Commission on Accreditation of Hospitals would collect, in its biannual evaluation of Northwest was the attendance of the staff at meetings. So, the hospital followed the dictum that "the way to a man's heart was through his stomach." The spread of food that the hospital kitchen provided was always very, very special. So Sid, Jack and Ned never missed it. The same was true for much of the staff.

Attendance from the Krollberg group was not quite as good. They had no Tuesday morning office hours. They had selected Tuesday as one of their primary days of elective surgery. It was not unusual for them to be in the operating room for a portion or all of the meeting time, which officially ended at 1:30 P.M. But this particular Tuesday, Jay wanted them, more than any of the others, to be there. Though the hospital was in a neighborhood that was primarily Catholic, it seemed to have little effect on the makeup of the medical staff. Well over half the staff, and even half the department heads, were Jewish. In the Department of Obstetrics and Gynecology, beyond the three of the Krollberg group, the Jewish doctors included Berg, Stein, Abramowitz, Hirsch, Fisher, Gold, Weiner, and the two Cohens, who were unrelated and didn't even like each other. Finally, there were Jay and Marvin Green, Jay's partner for many years.

Jay was 6'4" and slim with strong angular facial features. He had long, straight blond hair that barely dropped below his collar. It remained always at that length, not long enough to make him look in any way unprofessional, and not short enough to appear to be too much a part of the establishment. His eyes were a vivid blue. Not strikingly handsome, he had a look of authority and of the gentry. From his physical features one would guess that his origins were from northern Europe, possibly Germany or Scandinavia. He had a penetrating smile and a softness in his eyes. which deflected any possible thought that he was haughty or arrogant. By his features and his name, J. D. Brown, had he wished, no one would know that he was a Jew.

Jay, however, had a deep connection to his faith. It made him uncomfortable, on this particular day, although no one except himself knew that the primary direction of his assault was toward the Krollberg group. It was in the front of his mind, and it angered him. He was ashamed of the fact that they were Jewish.

It was approximately 11 A.M. when Jack Stein and Norm Abramowitz arrived in the delivery suite. They had been called by Alice Crain because of changes she noted on the fetal monitor strip that was running on their patient. Alice was as good an obstetrical nurse as could be found anywhere. She had already worked at the County Hospital and the private obstetrical facility at the medical school. Alice possessed every ingredient necessary to be at the top of her profession—except tact and political sense. Her outspoken behavior continually kept her from achieving positions of authority. But nothing detracted from her brilliance as a nurse. Alice had accumulated a vast store of knowledge in medicine within her field. No physicians on the staff had superior intelligence or a greater understanding of the practice of obstetrics.

Alice had been married to a physician, divorced, and involved in several very unpleasant affairs with other doctors. Those sexual encounters, as well as confrontations with powerful and unethical physicians, had led to her being relieved at one institution after another. Her level of frustration with the quality of care she saw frequently led her to leave hospitals, generally by mutual consent. But every doctor knew that if their patient was being watched by Crain, there was no cause for anxiety about the care that patient received.

Alice had great compassion and patience for women in labor. Though she had never had a child, she did have a sixth sense about what these women were going through. Even though she never experienced childbirth, she was able to feel the pain herself. Other nurses and doctors at times became impatient with laboring women who would not, or could not, follow instructions because of a loss of control of their emotions. Alice never reached even the slightest level of annoyance. No scream, no curse, no invective, no vulgarity, not even a swinging arm, could arouse Alice to chastise these women.

"Was I terrible in labor?"

"No, no! Well maybe a little when you bit the doctor on his arm" always brought a laugh that made the new mother put the last few hours out of her mind as she bonded with the new miracle.

Alice never ceased to be overwhelmed by the sight of a newborn squeezing its way through such a small opening as it greeted the new world with a lusty yell.

"I'm here, and I started from two little cells to become the spectacular creature that I am."

For Alice, the miracle was not the delivery. It was how this new human being had come to be.

She saw mothers as part of a divine process of bringing new life to the world. Whatever the tremendous stress of that moment caused them to do, these women were to be excused—unconditionally—for their actions in labor. None was to be judged during that interval of time.

But Jay made judgments about Alice—judgments of deep admiration. He constantly came to her defense. At Northwest Community Hospital she was simply a staff nurse. Jay was repeatedly offended when some physicians mockingly referred to her as the department "head." It resulted from her reported sexual proclivity which had been bantered about with meanness by some of the men with whom she had had affairs.

Stein, and even more so Abramowitz, were not the finest obstetricians in the department. They were particularly shaky on reading fetal monitor strips, while Alice was the best. Only two years had passed since the monitors were introduced. Northwest had sent Alice Crain and Jay Brown to special programs organized by the March of Dimes. On their return, Jay and Alice assumed responsibility for the in-service training of the other physicians and nurses. Not everyone learned quickly.

"The important thing is the relationship to the contraction when the baby's heart rate drops," Alice explained. "Just having a decrease in the rate doesn't necessarily signify that the baby's in distress."

"But it's my neck if you're wrong."

"I'm not wrong, Dr. A," Alice responded to Abramowitz with frustration. The patience she had with women bearing down on their rectums did not always extend to those physicians, whom she considered to be comparable to that part of her patients' anatomy.

She knew it was to no avail. They would go through this game every time. Stein or Abramowitz raised the flag of the malpractice threat. Alice agonized as she tried to persuade them that the baby was in no distress and then, in frustration, be forced to prepare the patient for an unnecessary C-section. The babies came out pink and yelling, while Abramowitz or Stein, whichever one Alice would be "fortunate" enough to have in the labor and delivery suite at that time, would quote verbatim the same trite statement they repeated in every similar case. It was like a catechism learned in childhood.

"Well I never had a case where I was sorry that I did a C-section. Buuut, I had a few when I was sorry that I didn't."

Alice always felt guilty about her participation in the surgery.

Abramowitz and Stein would be late for this Tuesday monthly meeting.

————

The conference room was not particularly large. Although the total number of obstetricians in the department ranged from twenty two to twenty five over the years, Jay considered an attendance of fifteen quite good.

As opposed to actual eating tables, the hospital purchased modifications of old schoolroom desks. Each physician sat in a very comfortable seat, with their meal during the conference.

Jay Brown was at his desk by 11:30 A.M. He nervously awaited the arrival of the staff members as he flipped through a sizable stack of papers.

It was earlier than he usually arrived, but this was not a usual day. The hospital kitchen staff worked at the large buffet table in the back of the room where all the food, trays, utensils, etc. were set up in preparation for the department members who began to arrive about ten minutes before the hour.

One by one the dietary staff greeted Jay with a "Hi Doc!"

The men and women, multi-racial and multi-ethnic, were always warm and friendly to Jay, but he could never make up his mind as to whether they even knew his name or not. He believed that they had great respect for him, but some emotion, deep within him, made him sense that he would feel so much better if, just once, one of them had called him Dr. Brown. It would even be fine if someone said "Hello, Jay." But that would never happen. He hated the feeling that the dietary staff thought he was better than they were.

Jay's eyes darted back and forth from his papers to his watch, like a cat eating a meal while continually glancing to see if some other animal were coming to confiscate part of it. He didn't need this much time to prepare. He was as fully prepared for this conference as any he had ever run. Jay realized he was the picture of anxiety and wondered whether it resulted from his need for the conference to begin or his concern about what its outcome might be.

The meeting began, as he had planned, with the usual dull reports of the monthly statistics of the number of deliveries, the Cesarean section rate, the live births, the stillbirths, the multiple births, and so on down the line. Then Jay presented the gynecological statistics and tediously reviewed the numbers of each type of surgery. Most of the staff found this to be a fine time to be filling their jowls with food that was better than almost anything they could obtain in restaurants in the area. It bore not the slightest resemblance to the food being served to the patients in the hospital. It definitely fulfilled its primary purpose— to draw a large number of physicians to the monthly meeting.

Some of the obstetricians leaned across to the seat of a colleague to discuss a television show, or a movie, or even better, some inner hospital gossip. In the middle of the statistics loud laughter was heard. It was not a reflection on something Jay was saying, but the result of some other conversation. It was not meant to be rude. It merely demonstrated the total lack of attention that was given to the numbers being rattled off. Almost no one wasted time listening to the same litany month after month. They soon realized that they would be caring more in the future.

Jay's inner self shook as he spoke, but not so much that anyone noticed. Beneath the surface of his totally cool composure existed a less than totally secure persona. All who knew Jay saw him as a strong and decisive man with leadership qualities, but he never saw himself that way. He had much less difficulty believing in the principles for which he stood than in himself. There was always the feeling, shared with no one, of how inadequate he was to the task at hand.

"If only I possessed the intellect and the ability to motivate others," he thought to himself, *"how very much more could be accomplished. And they know, they really know, how shallow I am."*

Now Dr. J. D. Brown began the critical portion of this meeting with a bare-faced lie. He didn't normally do that kind of thing well. As the very words came out of his mouth he imagined his colleagues thinking, *"Does that asshole think I believe the bullshit he's telling me?"*

"With the evaluation of our hospital by the Joint Commission on Accreditation approaching very rapidly, I've been notified that they will look very closely at our rate of D&Cs to determine how well we monitor that. They will be specifically looking at our indications for doing such procedures."

"So who the hell cares?" chimed in Nat Farber from the back of the room, while he filled his tray from the assorted platters that had been set up by the dietary staff. Farber still had his back facing the physicians who were seated when Jay looked up to see who had responded to his opening thrust.

As he looked to the back of the room, he realized with mixed emotions that the Krollberg group had arrived. Though he wanted them there, he knew it would mean head to head conflict. But Jay had made the choice many weeks ago, so there was no turning back. And, with his adrenalin high, he really didn't want to.

Jay responded, "The JCAH, THEY will care! And they can make us so uncomfortable, we'll wish we had cared more. . . and sooner."

Al Krollberg entered the conversation for the first time. He was the most senior in years of service in the department. There were a few still older who were occasionally seen around the hospital, but they had almost ceased to practice. More than that, Al Krollberg had the largest practice at Northwest Community Hospital. Nat Farber was about ten years his junior, with Aaron Asher almost twenty five years younger than Al. That Krollberg ruled the group with an iron hand was a fact of which everyone was aware. Nat Farber was something of a comic character. He did what he was told and repeated Krollberg's dictums verbatim. Aaron, on the other hand, was young, fresh out of training, and brighter than either of his partners. He now had the opportunity to reap the financial rewards of a huge practice established before him, once the years passed and he achieved seniority. Until that time he worked harder and got paid considerably less than either of his partners. The economic possibilities for his future were enormous and certainly sufficient for him not to buck the system and challenge the manner in which his partners practiced. Though he knew better, he was not about to jeopardize his future position.

Al Krollberg not only had seniority, he had poise and stature. He spoke in the manner of a Shakespearean actor. Deep, clear tones reverberated through the room when he made his utterances, which were delivered as if they were sent down from above. His patients adored him. None would have the temerity to question what they were told when Dr. Krollberg said, "My dear, the course I am recommending for you is the ONLY sensible approach. I will gladly send you for a second opinion. But don't you think that would be a terrible waste of your time and money when no other choice of treatment makes sense for you? I hope you will agree that it is needless for you to do that."

Jay knew very well that he faced that kind of challenge when he made the decision to confront the staff on this issue.

"I believe that every member of the illustrious staff of this institution functions at a level far beyond what one sees in evaluations of the hospitals in this area. We should be commended. Through the diligent work of our Credentials Committee, we have selected only the highest level of obstetric and gynecologic specialists, highly trained and exceptionally ethical," Krollberg bellowed.

Jay thought for a moment that his bullshit tolerance had almost been exceeded. The hospital had accepted every single obstetrical applicant for as many years as he could recall. The major requirements had been breathing and the completion of a residency program... anywhere. The quality of that training program or any recommendations were non factors. The ability to admit patients to the service, on the other hand, was a major factor.

The hospital had not been specifically unethical. It had not encouraged physicians to increase their level of admissions. It merely encouraged the doctors to make whatever admissions there were to Northwest, rather than to some other hospital in which the physician had staff privileges. However, much more importantly, the hospital never challenged the physicians as to the propriety, or possibly the impropriety, of some of those choices for hospital admission and surgery.

"The Audit Committee has been a constant and vigilant watchdog over the quality of care which is being provided in our wonderful hospital, and of that we should be extraordinarily proud," Krollberg continued.

The Audit Committee had met sporadically and did not take action in one single case over the years since its inception before Jay assumed the Chairmanship of the department. No one else in the department really cared to discuss or even think about it. Jay knew it would be best to allow Krollberg to finish his bombastic remarks. It was the least of what was certain to come.

"I believe, JD... " *and now he'll say "old friend"*... "old friend. *You could bet your last nickel on it*... that you are overreacting to the Joint Commission's review. They will see that, as in the past, the standards of this hospital are exemplary. Our very fine care will clearly shine through when they make their inspection."

Unfortunately, in a sense, everything that Al Krollberg had dramatically stated would really be true. The quality of care at Northwest had not diminished in recent years, and the hospital was never cited for any significant insufficiencies in the ObGyn Department for as long as Jay could remember. Jay had contacted the Commission once in the past to discuss the type of review they were doing, unrelated to Northwest. In Jay's superficial evaluation of what happens in many hospitals, he wondered why so few actions were taken by the JCAH. By chance, he had contacted, in his inquiry, Ira Rauch.

Ira had worked for the Joint Commission on Accreditation of Hospitals for the past eight and a half years since his retirement from private practice. He was a successful urologic surgeon who had burned out. Discontented with some of the things he had seen in his years as a physician, he believed this was a great opportunity to change his life style and do something about the disturbing practices he had seen.

Unfortunately, his discontent followed him. Ira found that the process of evaluation was severely limited by the totally insufficient number of personnel available to do the job adequately. It became rather simple for hospitals to cover up their weaknesses and defects.

But, worst of all, he soon realized that political machinations within the profession made it extremely difficult, for one at the level of a hospital inspector, to have any clout with large and powerful institutions. Real changes could not be made. In Jay's conversation with Ira, Jay realized that Ira had psychologically "thrown in the towel" in his effort to have any significant impact about the abuses in health care.

Jay was not surprised by the response at the Department meeting. He proceeded straight ahead as if he had heard not one word from Al Krollberg.

"I've made an effort in the past few months to establish a standard by which we might measure, in the future, our indications for D&Cs."

The constant hum and babble of separate conversations between department members that had been going through the room, and which was the common background noise for these sessions, suddenly ceased. Jay wished it had not.

"It appeared in our review that certain questionable indications were commonly seen. As an example, we looked at the age group for cases in which the indication was to rule out a malignancy, to determine if too many were being done on young women, where the risk of cancer was slight."

Not a sound was heard in the room other than Jay Brown's voice.

"We examined the records for women who had D&Cs for postmenopausal bleeding while they were taking estrogen replacement therapy, which most likely caused the bleeding. We were surprised to find out how often no effort was first made to determine if stopping the hormones alone might stop the bleeding. In most of these cases, a D&C was done without any interval to see if the problem could be resolved non-surgically, or at least with just an office biopsy."

The silence was now deafening. Cross looks were bound to be followed shortly by angry words.

"There were a number of cases where we found the D&C was combined with a polypectomy. In these cases, the presence of the polyp was listed as the primary indication for the operation. Unfortunately, in a number of these cases the polyp was so small it could easily have been removed in the office without hospital admission and surgical intervention under anaesthesia."

The "we" Jay referred to was not the royal "we." He had worked for months in the Record Room, almost under cover, with Alice Crain. For years they had complained, privately between themselves, about the way medicine was being practiced at Northwest Hospital.

It was not easy. Even as the Chairman of the department he butted heads with a lot of people. The Administration was not very supportive as it was bad for the bottom line of the hospital.

That left no one but Stanley Roth to come to Jay's aid. Stanley was only thirty nine years old, two years younger than Jay. Though their basic goals in life were quite different, they were good friends. While Jay never demonstrated the slightest interest in accumulating wealth, Stanley had become a multimillionaire at the age of thirty-one. A boy wonder, with a Harvard MBA by the time he was twenty three, he became the controlling force in a number of manufacturing enterprises. By his middle thirties he felt that he wanted to achieve greater respectability in the community at large. He undertook major philanthropic positions, beginning with large contributions and then moving into positions of activism. By virtue of his innate leadership qualities, three years after he joined the lay Board of the Hospital, they elected him Chairman of the Board. He was Jay's ace in the hole.

It was a Sunday afternoon during the Christmas holiday season when Jay had first contacted him about his plan. Jay wanted to build up enthusiasm in the young dynamo for achievements at a higher level than other hospitals. And it worked. The excitement of this project pulled Stanley not just in line, but out front. When Jay followed the initial approach with the information about his lack of ability to obtain the necessary support to obtain the records, total assurances came forth from Stanley that everyone would be instructed to cooperate. He and Alice were on their way.

With determination Jay continued, "There were other cases in which patients were admitted for D&Cs when they had an intra-uterine device in place for contraception, which apparently caused abnormal bleeding. In a number of cases, instead of removing the device to determine whether the bleeding would stop, a D&C was done immediately in very young women. We had hoped..."

"Who the hell gave you permission to go through all our cases and come to these asshole conclusions?"

There was nothing polite or friendly in the outburst by Nat Farber. But he spoke not just for himself; the same thoughts probably streamed through the minds of almost everyone in that room. Farber came to the support of his partner's original comments. It was easy for him because he didn't particularly like Jay Brown. The feeling was mutual.

Others made public outbursts like "Yeah!" and "What right... ?"

But Sid Shultz had too much class for that. He leaned over to Jack O'Rourke and whispered, for his ears only, "Fuckin' Jew trouble maker."

For the next forty-five minutes, Jay revealed the support and direction that came from the Board of Directors itself. He gave his fellow obstetricians detailed information about his findings. He told them that there was no intention to embarrass anyone. All data would be presented without identifying the physicians involved. The point was to demonstrate the existence of these kinds of problems. He touched a nerve when he said certain unspecified doctors were responsible for the largest portion of the surgical excesses.

In recent years Jay had read the work of Dr. Eugene McCarthy of Cornell University Medical School. In addition to his research concerning surgical excesses, Dr. McCarthy had come to the conclusion that physicians who were made aware of the fact that someone was watching, changed their patterns of practicing medicine. He called this the Sentinel Effect. Jay hoped to achieve success through McCarthy's method. With his speech he naively believed he could decrease the number of unnecessary D&Cs in his hospital.

At the end of his presentation, which received increasing hostility as the hour went on, Jay told them that no action was being taken at this time. However, for the next six months the same study would prospectively continue. The Department expected to provide a follow-up report at a subsequent meeting for each member of the department. It would have code numbers for each physician, to determine whether improvement had been accomplished.

Jay believed they could all recognize themselves in the statistics, even without a name being affixed. He had a strong feeling that McCarthy's theory would work. Jay wasn't such a purist that the change had to occur by appealing to their moral standards. Shame was a satisfactory modus operandus for him.

———————

On that Tuesday in April of 1974 the ObGyn staff believed that life at Northwest would never be quite the same again. They were right.

Jay Brown believed he had embarked on a small effort which, whether successful or not, would have little effect on his career or his life. He was very wrong.

Life certainly changed for Alice Crain. She was an easier target than Jay. As the staff became aware of her role in the new atmosphere of the institution, the effort to rid themselves of her—an ally of Jay—seemed more and more attractive. Before the year was out she was gone.

Gone, for Alice, meant the attempt to put a lot of distance between herself and many years of personal pain inflicted almost exclusively by physicians who had either married her, bedded her, worked with her, disliked her, or used her. Although her exposure entitled her to the anger she felt, her perspective of the medical community was in fact a distortion. She had helped create the world in which she lived. At times she was able to see it with more clarity. She'd look in a mirror and say to herself, *"Alice, if you were in the world of lawyers, architects or dentists, they too would be clever and witty and conniving and find a way to take advantage of you."* Then she would always stop, smile in the mirror, and mumble to herself, *"Well, maybe not dentists!"* It was a little game that helped her through the day.

Before 1975 was over she established a new life for herself in Austin, Texas. Things would get much better. She knew she would be happier. If she had made a misjudgment, it wouldn't be the first time.

Chapter Three

Alice Crain

*D*r. Jack Marsh had reached his climax only a few moments earlier, but he was already in a deep sleep. Alice Crain, bare breasted and covered with a flowered sheet up to her waist, sat in the darkness. She smoked a cigarette while she day dreamed. She was past forty five and in reasonably good physical condition. Nevertheless her normal concerns about aging made her look for, and find on a regular basis, pockets of cellulite in her thighs.

Alice was neither beautiful nor unattractive, neither striking nor exceptionally plain. But the package that she brought with her of intelligence, warmth and above-average features was sufficient for her to find no difficulty in attracting men.

She married James Crain when she was only twenty two. Crain was a medical student while she was a nurse at the hospital. The combination of the minimal number of hours he had available to meet people outside the school environment, and his economic inability to establish much of a social life, made the attraction of a nurse at the hospital a logical alternative.

The relationship solidified rapidly. He was among the brightest of the students while not so narrowly focused as many medical students were. Their late night talks included subjects other than medicine. To Alice he was exceptionally appealing. One evening the talk turned to a kiss and then a touch here and then there. Jim was relatively shy with relatively little sexual experience when they met, but not so for Alice. They were quickly into bed together and Jim realized the tremendous advantages, after a long stress filled day, of having someone who sexually relieved all his frustrations. For most people of Jim's age the physical aspect of a relationship was paramount. For him it became everything. Somehow he never seemed to get past that in their courtship or marriage. Alice, meanwhile, never lost sight of the power of her sexual prowess. No one had ever gone down on James Crain before. It was not Alice's first time.

Her father was a very successful psychiatrist. Alice's childhood, with the economic advantages the family had, should have been quite pleasant. To the contrary, it was extremely unhappy. All of her recollections were centered upon the meanness of spirit that was basic to him. Alice did not then, nor even now, comprehend how someone with her father's psychological hangups functioned adequately as a psychiatrist. She came to realize, as she spent her professional life in health care, that psychiatrists frequently had dysfunctional families.

Alice's father was a wiry, thin-lipped man, of less than average height, with a small mustache he curled into a fine point at each end. His narrow eyes had a look of contempt as he spoke with you. He never raised his voice, but ruled the household like a dictator. The primary object of his power was her mother, an extremely beautiful woman. Unfortunately, Alice's mother's self-esteem was better characterized as non-existent rather than weak. She did exactly as she was told by her husband without fail or any discussion. It would be the role model provided to Alice as she grew up.

Alice believed, though she had no specific proof, that her parents had either no sexual relationship, or an unpleasant one. The purpose of that, she imagined, was exclusively to satisfy him. In actuality her suspicions were correct. Alice suspected that he was unfaithful to her mother as well, although she had no evidence of such a situation. She was right about that also.

A rather strange psychiatrist, he disliked most people. While in his private life he considered women to be only sexual objects, he perceived the male sex as universally desirous of taking advantage of the weakness he attributed to women. The dominating idea he fostered in his relationship with his only child, Alice, was his mistrust of men. From a time before she was even ten years old—she could not remember exactly when—he filled her with thoughts about the "evils and filth" of sexuality. He repeatedly attempted to implant in her brain the concept that she must always protect herself from being used by the opposite sex.

Around the age of eleven or twelve, her girlfriends began to have co-ed parties. They invited boys from their class or preferably one grade higher. Her father would not allow her to go, though a kiss and a giggle was the extent of the sex at these events. The following day at school Alice would listen to her girlfriends talk about the party she had missed. The irony of her father's narrow-minded approach was that the wonder Alice experienced in listening, but not attending, caused major sexual tension for her.

The months went by and secondary sexual characteristics, her breasts and body hair, became apparent. Her sexual maturity, though denied by her father, could not be ignored by her. The budding sexuality of her classmates resulted in rather average early experimentation of no major consequence. Alice, on the other hand, was under constant restriction due to her father's phobia about the loss of her virginity. In retrospect, she often wondered how a psychiatrist could have so little insight into the harm he inflicted.

Alice's natural instinct to obtain the forbidden fruit, regardless of how horrifyingly it had been painted for her, was resolved in the summer of her fourteenth year. She had gone with her parents to a resort on the coast of Maine.

Among the young people Alice met down by the docks was an eighteen year old college student. He worked at a local restaurant as a waiter. Alice looked older than her years and she intentionally dressed and acted beyond them. It was a reaction to her father's overbearing surveillance.

"Would you like to go out with me some night?"

"I might,…" Alice coyly responded in a manner befitting her age. Then, after a pause, "… but I don't think so. My Dad makes sure that I'm back at the hotel by 10 P.M. sharp, before night falls."

"That's OK," he said. "We could meet at 8:30, when I'm through at work."

Alice to this day remembered the fear and bump in her heartbeat. She could barely believe she heard herself saying, "We'll have to meet someplace where my father can't see us, someplace not near the hotel."

They arranged to meet at a location about a quarter of a mile from the hotel, down the road by a large strangely shaped tree that everyone in the area knew by the name Crooked Oak. He waited there in his car. She arrived at the agreed time and they drove off. Alice was almost overwhelmed by anxiety and apprehension. Her new friend's primary emotion, however, was anticipation. In subsequent years Alice could remember nothing of the conversation between them as they drove to a secluded area. He parked the car and made slow gentle advances. No one had ever touched her breasts before. After an initial gasp she seemed to relax slightly.

There was never anything forced or rushed or overly aggressive about what happened subsequently. As he removed each item of her clothing there was no resistance and no assistance. She was frightened, but felt compelled to go ahead. She knew it was a subconscious effort to punish her father.

Alice's date lifted her nude body and they both giggled as they half climbed and half fell into the back seat. He removed his clothing from the waist down and attempted to enter her, without success. He was not inexperienced and she was not making it more difficult, but for the first time in his sexual life, he was unable to penetrate a vagina, though he was extremely aroused with an erection that was quite adequate. Her nervous laughter came to a halt as she began experiencing some pain from his effort.

"Is something wrong?" she murmured tremulously.

He kept his composure, but didn't answer. She became anxious and he reassured her. She vaguely remembered that he stopped and turned on the overhead light in the car. Night had not yet fallen, but tucked underneath the trees the natural light in the car was somewhat dim. The one thing she would never forget for the remainder of her life, was the sight of his erection which appeared unbelievably enormous. Though she had untold numbers of sexual encounters in the years that followed, in her mind's eye she never saw a penis that large again.

With their bodies lit by the interior light, Alice was amazed to watch him clinically examine her genital anatomy. What surprised her, even as much, was her compliance as she lay there and watched him proceed. His touches were gentle, not meant to stimulate. He had a serious concern about whether the problem was his own; nevertheless it aroused her. She had masturbated before but had never reached a climax. She found herself reaching a level of excitation higher than she had ever achieved previously, when suddenly he stopped.

"It's not me." And then, after what seemed like a very long pause to Alice, "It's you," he said in a sympathetic tone, as he felt reassured about himself. "Your hole is so small I can barely see it. I can't even get my pinky finger in."

She was in a state of panic, wondering if she was abnormal, when she heard him say, "Please do something."

She was both horrified by her inadequacy and totally confused by his request. He lifted her up to a sitting position and kissed her again, softly and gently. She put her hands on the sides of his head and held him tightly, seeking some sign that he was not angered by what had happened. Then he gradually pulled his lips away from hers as he slowly brought her head down to his penis. She learned that summer night the tremendous power she could exert over a man. Alice was a novice that evening, but she was committed to learn how to become an expert. Fellatio became the chosen part of her sexual stock and trade. Even with all she accomplished professionally as a nurse, she believed, as the years passed, that sex was her only source of power.

Over the years, on many occasions. Alice thought about that early evening in Maine. Somewhere along the way the recesses of her mind lost the boy's name.

———

After one last long puff on her cigarette, Alice looked down at her body which was quite clearly outlined in the rather bright moonlight. Because Alice had never been pregnant, her breasts were still reasonably firm, but not the way they had been in her twenties. She checked the lines in her face on a regular basis, constantly threatening, in her private thoughts, to have a face lift. Overall she felt fortunate to have someone share her bed, but sometimes she wondered whether it was better to have no one than some of the lovers she had known.

'I could have done worse than Jack,' she thought. Marsh was the Chairman of the Department of Ob-Gyn. No matter what else it provided for Alice, one thing was certain, as long as she was his lover, she would never find her job in jeopardy again.

"Crain, you'all got a nice ass," was the most tender sentiment she could expect from Jack Marsh. But she never minded hearing him say that, though she rather he'd say something about her intellect. In actuality Jack was really not crude at all in his language. She saw him in conversation with other members of the Department. While some had constant four letter words as a part of their vocabulary, it was not so for Jack Marsh. He came from a rather rigid Baptist background and lessons of the Church had been drummed into him, but he had a strange mixture of values. The work ethic was pre-eminent in his philosophy and demonstrated very clearly his devotion to medicine in general and to his own patients in particular. It was at least partly due to that diligence that he rose to the position of Chief. He was only of average intelligence and had accumulated whatever knowledge he possessed about obstetrics through hard work all during his training. Once out in practice, his outgoing personality and concern for his patients allowed him to develop one of the largest practices in Austin. The effort involved in that process left him with little time to actively keep up with medical literature and changes within his own field.

Although he was not stupid, he had little taste for anything intellectual. He was big, strong and handsome. A letterman in high school in Austin, that was the image he maintained even though he was well past forty and graying at the temples. He played golf, tennis and hunted with his old classmates who were now lawyers, bankers and businessmen in Austin. Jack was a "good ol' boy."

Alice was glad he had chosen her "ass." There were other nurses there who would have jumped at the chance. She also knew that she wasn't the first. But Jack had a strange set of values when it came to marriage and women. He had been married for many years. When he got married it was forever, just as he had sworn to his God. But, somehow, he never remembered swearing about fidelity.

Jack's wife Claudia knew about his affairs; their strange relationship was common knowledge to the entire community. The stage of embarrassment, for her, had long since passed. There was an understanding that they would remain married with no further discussion about his other life. Most nights he did not come home. Mainly they were spent in the delivery suite with a patient in labor, but there were never any questions about whether he had been at the hospital, or someplace else.

Within Jack's moral code he was completely loyal. He was a one-woman man. During the years he used Alice's body at his will, he never touched Claudia, because he saw that as being unfaithful to Alice. Claudia, on the other hand, retreated into a world of abstinence, because she knew the law was clear, the natural law of Texas. For them to remain married, she could never shame him in this community. No ol' boy's wife would be unfaithful and live to tell the tale. Jack Marsh had never physically abused her, but she had no doubt of what he was capable of doing should she ever compromise his manhood.

"By my way of thinkin', you'd be a lot better off if you stopped puffin' on that weed," Jack mumbled as he looked at Alice's silhouette in front of the dimly lit window.

The sky was overcast and Jack saw only the outline of Alice. She had gone off so deeply into her daydream that for the moment she forgot where she was. Hearing his voice and his concern brought her back to reality.

"Thanks Jack. I know you're right. One day I'll break this damn habit. Even then I think I won't want to pass up that one cigarette after we've made it together."

"You keep doin' that and you'll have a lot less years of makin' it at all."

Jack's concern for her made her feel especially good. As far as she could tell, this relationship had a non-ending run. There was not the slightest doubt in her mind that he would stick by her. The security felt so good, it never occurred to her that anything would ever make her jeopardize this safest place she had ever known in the world. She was at last at home, at home in Austin. On rare occasions she would think of Jay Brown, the physician she had most respected in her entire career in medicine. But she was determined to put behind her the crusader traits which he encouraged in her over the years.

For the first year after she left New York, Alice had dated no one. A fantasy, involving Jay, which she had held in abeyance for many years, came into the frontal reaches of her mind. Like many others at Northwest Community Hospital, she was aware that Jay Brown did not have the best of marriages. But neither Jay nor Rhonda had ever violated their marriage bonds. So for Alice, though she did love him in every other sense, there was never the attempt to become part of his private life.

During that first year in Austin, when Alice practiced masturbation for the first time since her teens, Jay was the image she fantasized as she lay in the dark fifteen hundred miles away from him. Fantasy was the only way she had ever shared her body with Jay. And when Marsh took her to his bed, Alice thought it was to be the last time that Jay Brown would ever enter her sexual thoughts.

Chapter Four

The Krauses

*R*ebecca Celia Krause had never forgotten how and why the Alliance began. While she had lived her entire life, until 1953, in Morocco, she always considered herself to be French. But her feelings about France were schizophrenic.

Whatever she wanted to believe about the honor and purity of the French democracy, she could never find it within herself to deny the innate feeling that anti-Semitism lurked under the surface. At times, when historical incidents were rekindled, those emotions came powerfully to the forefront of her thoughts. She shared the desire of so many of her French compatriots to believe that their democracy was above that. It was that belief that made the incidents stand out. Everyone knew of the Dreyfus tragedy and, as the years passed, even more details of France's despicable role in the Nazi treatment of French Jews. But somehow, the Mortara case in Italy, which was the impetus for the establishment of the Alliance in France, was not so widely exposed. That incident struck her deeply.

Rebecca had heard of it first from her father, as a child. He constantly emphasized to her that the incident, though Italian in origin, could just as easily have happened in France. In later years she recalled the fear she had experienced when, in the deep hours of the night, she thought about it while lying alone in bed. At times she wondered why her father had subjected her to that depth of anxiety, when their relationship was characterized by such deep mutual love and respect. Eventually Rebecca came to understand that it was his way of involving her in what had been the driving forces of his life—the survival of the Jews and the creation of a homeland where they could be safe even from his own people, the French.

The story of Edgardo Mortara went back to the night of June 23rd, 1858 in Bologna, Italy. He was a Jewish child less than seven years of age. Some five years previous to that date, in his infancy, a Christian domestic servant of this affluent Jewish family, who believed that an illness was about to cause Edgardo's death, had baptized him. When a younger sibling became ill the nursemaid did not have the opportunity to baptize that child. Feeling guilty, she revealed the details of the earlier baptism she had performed on Edgardo to her local parish priest. With that information in hand, on that June evening in 1858, Edgardo was abducted by Papal police and taken to Rome. The incident was not unprecedented. However, due to the importance of the Mortara family, efforts were made in their behalf even by Napoleon III and Moses Montefiore. All their pleas went unheard.

Over the years Edgardo became a brilliant student within the Catholic Church. At the age of eighteen he was finally given the opportunity to make a personal choice—to accept Catholicism or to return to Judaism and his family. With eleven years of exposure to and education by the Church, he obviously abstained. Subsequently he became a professor of theology, and received a number of important appointments at the Vatican.

The horror of the incident for the Mortara family was the driving force that initiated the Alliance Israelite Universelle in Paris in 1860. Its purpose was to defend the civil rights of Jews throughout the world. Though geo-political issues were the driving force of the Alliance, an educational arm began to assume great importance at the end of the nineteenth century. It was in that area that most of Rebecca's efforts were directed.

While teaching in Morocco, Rebecca met Duvid Krause, a young Jewish engineer who was deeply involved in Jewish thought and politics. Rebecca's love for him was, in a sense, a reflection of the great admiration she had for her father. He and Duvid demonstrated remarkable similarities in their ideas, and their ideals.

Rebecca and Duvid married in 1929 and had two children. Their first, Label, was born just after Rebecca's father died in 1933, and was named after him. Rebecca somehow believed that, had Label grown up knowing his grandfather, things would not have turned out as they did. In reality it was unlikely that that was true. The forces that shaped Label emanated from Rebecca and Duvid, his parents. Their second and last child, born four years later, was Esther.

Rebecca shared in all of Duvid's dreams and concerns. Though they had great individual strengths, the two of them seemed to mesh beautifully.

As part of a new growing middle class in Morocco, she felt no great personal threats. She recalled how the rumors had spread to her community in August of 1942 about what was happening to Jews in southern France. Word had reached them that in mid-July the Vichy government had turned over its Jews to the Nazis. She understood very clearly that living in Morocco was the one thing that enabled her family to survive the Holocaust. But life for many other Jews in Morocco was horrendous. There was rampant poverty. Her family, like most of those in her class, had become less and less religious and probably would have been assimilated into the non-Jewish Moroccan society were it not for the unceasing anti-Semitism of the French North African middle class. Rebecca remembered that in the eyes of the non-Jews who surrounded her, she was a Jewess.

As opposed to her early lifetime Rebecca understood much more clearly what it meant to be a Jew after 1940. Once the Holocaust began the family was constantly in fear that it would spread to Morocco. They survived, but suffered terrible indignities. The government crowded Rebecca, Duvid and the young children into the mellah, a ghetto with minimal food rations. Epidemics raged from the crowding. But the information that came through underground sources about what was taking place in Europe made her thank God for the survival of her family. Her empathy created a burning desire to reverse the pain that other Jews were feeling.

Duvid, on the other hand, dealt less with emotions than with reality. He combined a love of his people with a wit and a shrewdness that enabled him to plan and organize, even if at times he needed to be deceptive in order to achieve his goals.

The fate of genetic transfer had seemed to play a queer trick in the conception of their two children. Esther was endowed with the deep feelings and compassion that both her parents brought to her. Label captured the anger, shrewdness and deception, without the love. He would learn well to use them, and even at times to overuse them.

Label was almost through his university studies and on his way to becoming a physician in Morocco, a rather uncommon accomplishment for Jews there, when Rebecca and Duvid decided that the climate had become even more dangerously anti-Semitic. Alliance schools were set on fire. They made plans to leave their homeland and move to France. The choice was a wise one. The upcoming years found Jews facing greater difficulty as they desperately tried to get to Israel. Emigration, usually illegal, went on for the next fifteen years.

All these factors drove Rebecca and Duvid into an even stronger commitment to Judaism. But Label felt that his unchosen birth as a Jew was a cross he was forced to bear. As a result, in 1961, when Rebecca, Duvid and Esther made *aliyah* to Israel, Label said good-bye to them for the last time. He remained in France to advance his medical career, never again to see his parents, or Esther, he believed.

In 1971 a crack appeared in his armor. Neither the total separation from his mother and sister, nor the death of his father in Israel, caused the slightest distress. Even the death of his wife, at the hands of an intruder into their home, did not appear to have a devastating effect on him. Associates knew that he was having an affair at the time, but no one at the University particularly cared how he ran his private life. They really didn't care much about Label Krause in any way. While all that adversity did not get Label off the track he had set for himself, a misjudgment in his professional life accomplished what none of those personal disasters had.

Label Krause, in his paranoia, always believed that his very slow ascendancy within the University of Paris' Department of Obstetrics and Gynecology was due to senior members' knowledge of his familial affiliation to Judaism. That belief was baseless. If such anti-Semitism did exist, it was not possible there. So many members of all the different specialty departments were Jews. In fact, within Label's own department other Jews had already achieved considerable success, though they had in no way hidden their religious affiliation. Nevertheless, Label's lack of advancement was true. What he did not perceive was the general dislike most of his peers had for him. It extended as well to the residents who had been assigned to him. They were the greatest source of his problems. On several occasions a few of the more courageous residents had actually taken the liberty of speaking to the senior department members concerning their feelings about Label Krause's inadequacy as a gynecologic surgeon. They pointed out errors in judgment and technique they had witnessed in his cases, including a number of episodes in which there had been excessive blood loss during an operation. And worst of all, they were concerned about the number of his patients who had to be returned to the operating room due to complications that developed during the first few days post-operatively. Since there had been no major disasters, no one was inclined to take any action. But neither was there any inclination to promote rapid advancement for Label Krause.

In 1969, Label arranged with one of the largest drug firms in France to do primary testing on a new contraceptive device. The company, rather small, had some difficulty in the earliest testing. It related to high expulsion rates of the device from the uterus and the inability to control irregular bleeding. Label surreptitiously made arrangements with some mid-level executives of the drug firm. He would utilize their product exclusively on his patients.

In the agreement, though not in writing, the company supplied him with an unlimited number of their devices without charge. Label, nevertheless, charged the patients for the device and the insertion. Beyond that the company paid him a fee for "expenses" of seven thousand and five hundred francs every month. In return, he promised that he would report excellent results of his "research."

In 1970, his article appeared in a major journal. It stated exactly what he had previously promised he would report. Unfortunately, several other researchers had tested the product independently and raised serious questions about his reported results. The Chairman of Label's department felt compelled to request the data from which the paper had been produced. An internal investigation followed which revealed major irregularities in both the information and the methods of collection of data that had been utilized. Finally, collusion between Label and the drug company was suspected.

In his panic, Label Krause arranged a deal with the director of the Department; he agreed to leave the country. He was allowed to resign from the staff rather than being dismissed. Dr. Jean LaRouche, the head of the Ob-Gyn service, was anxious to get rid of Label as a member of his Department and saw his offer to resign and move to America as a good way to avoid any scandal that might arise from a dismissal. They agreed that Dr. LaRouche would provide generic recommendations, neither favorable nor unfavorable, and the deal was set.

Label discarded Marianne, his mistress before and after his wife's mysterious demise, without a moment's notice. He had no anxiety about the abrupt disruption of their affair. He had never allowed her to be privy to any of the corruption within his professional life. The relationship never had any significant meaning to him which was not surprising, in view of the fact that no human bond in his life had ever held any great importance for him. For Label she was nothing more than a warm body, replaceable by another across the ocean.

The French had exported much finer products than Label Krause to the United States in the past. Whatever rudeness the French might have perceived in Texans who visited France, it seemed to be cruel and unusual punishment in return when they sent Label Krause to Austin in 1971.

From that day forward Label was known as Louis Crown, a non-Jew. His perfect English combined with his beautifully flowing French accent provided the immediate image and assumption of a superior intellect. In this new land his dialect was associated with importance both by his patients and the less astute of his medical associates. Even after all the years had passed since his arrival in America, his French accent remained as definitive as the day of his arrival. His name was always pronounced Louie, and from his very first day at the hospital, he achieved an appearance of authority he had never approached in all his years in Paris. In this environment his personality disorder found the opportunity for considerable growth.

For the remainder of Louis Crown's life no individual ever knew that he was Jewish, not even Monica Kreutzer whom he would meet and ultimately marry. Monica, who came from Austria in the late 1940's, grew up in a deeply anti-Semitic family. Her parents were supporters of the Third Reich, but with no positions of any consequence. They found life in Austria hostile after the war. Monika was nine when she came to America. She was married for three years, in the middle sixties, to a man of considerable affluence and received a significant financial settlement in her divorce. She had no difficulty living in high style without the need for a new husband to support her. As a bright, stunning and wealthy woman, she became a semi-socialite in Austin. She developed a reputation of being rather free with her body among the unattached rich men in the city. She had no interest or intention of establishing a permanent relationship with any of them, until Louie Crown swept off her feet. After all, he was the extremely charming new physician and academician from France.

They immediately sparked for each other. Both had a haughtiness typical of European aristocracy, though neither had such a background. They shared a love of the arts and most definitely had similar philosophies of life. "Opposites attract" had no place in their relationship for they were more like twins than if they had been born into such a relationship. There was an ease of deception and dishonesty that each one had developed through the years. One might think that such a realization, by either party, would have created anxiety about the ability to trust one another. The thought never occurred to them. They understood exactly what the other was. They jointly supported the deceptions of their mate in all dealings with the other world, the one surrounding them with all the rest of the people. As opposed to the powerful bond between each other, they had no commitment at all to other people.

In their primary world—the one of Louis and Monika alone— the only deception that ever existed was Louis' true origin. Otherwise they kept faith with each other in every way. One of their favorite common bonds was a basic contempt for Jews. For them it was not a casual belief. The community had a significant number of Jews, and in the circles in which they traveled, especially the art world, Jews were frequent acquaintances. Monika and Louis provided a joint public perception of a gracious non-prejudiced couple. But they derived boundless pleasure from their private aside conversations about the Jews in their immediate circle. As they slipped into bed, after an evening spent in the company of the many Jews who were a part of their circle, the late night pillow talk was frequently punctuated by the joint laughter over whatever disparaging remark the other might make in reference to those "disgusting" people.

Chapter Five

A New Beginning

*J*ay walked slowly down the long wide basement corridor that paralleled the operating suite. Patients on gurneys were being pushed back from the X-ray unit to their floors. The Radiology Department occupied the greater portion of that floor on the opposite side of the corridor from the Operating Rooms. Lab technicians in white coats moved rapidly to their labs with specimens just drawn from patients on the floors above. Among all these employees were several nurses, primarily from the Operating Room staff.

A man from the Housekeeping Department positioned large red cone-shaped markers, which looked like megaphones, to indicate where the floor was wet from his washing. The hospital didn't need to be sued by someone who accidentally slipped on the freshly mopped floor. Jay thought it looked clean enough to eat on, even in the areas the porter had not yet cleaned.

It was extremely common, in Jay's experience, for hospitals to have their surgical suite below ground. It was no different here in Texas and it struck a funny note for him. He smiled as he walked.

Those who passed saw the broad grin and thought he looked rather strange. They couldn't possibly know that while he was completely oblivious to them, he was in the midst of a daydream he had experienced in the past. Originally it had occurred at night while asleep. It had been quite frightening and had varied endings before it aroused him abruptly. Jay believed that the dreams were manifestations of the anxiety he had experienced in confrontations with his peers. Now Jay found himself recreating the nighttime scenario with a humorous conclusion whenever he was in a hospital whose operating suite was underground.

In his fantasy, Jay stood at an operating table when suddenly a flood came pouring into the underground area. The level of water in the operating suite continued to rise. In his dream, nurses and doctors scampered out of the rooms for survival. Patients jumped off tables in gowns that left their rear ends exposed as they chased after the escaping staff. In the daytime version of the scene, the visual picture in his mind brought the corners of his mouth to a significant curl.

Jay smiled and laughed easily. Somewhere along the way, possibly even in his childhood, he became a constant punster. Words never seemed a challenge to him; he played with them naturally. Even Jay could hardly deny that generally the puns were pure corn. A stop at the photography shop, when his films were not yet ready, would result in "some day my prints will come".

Rhonda, his wife in name, had found it a lovable trait when they first met in their twenties. She would laugh even when, during lovemaking, he would sing out, "I'll be comin' Rhonda mountain, when I come."

As the years passed, the puns yielded groans rather than smiles. For that matter, so did the entire marriage. There were no more children at home. There was no pillow talk. Their bodies became silent as well when they reached their beds. They were now sleepwalking through the years.

––––––––

At the hospital Jay was collecting material that indicated surgical abuse within his department. But now other obstetricians on his staff were undermining him with members of the lay Board of Directors. Stanley Roth, who, as Chairman of the Board, had been so helpful in supporting him when he began his efforts to improve the Department, no longer held that position. Now the obvious targets of Jay's research were threatening to desert the hospital and take their patients elsewhere. That concerned Board members. For them, anything that affected the hospital's bottom line was a cause for worry. Actually they were empty threats. No other hospital of quality, that was geographically reasonable in relation to the location of their offices and their patients' residences, existed for these physicians. Nevertheless, the constant undercurrent was beginning to get to Jay. The underground Operating Suite dream became more frequent and more frightening.

Several years had now passed since Alice Crain had been forced out of the hospital. There had never been a personal relationship between them, much to Alice's sadness, but Jay missed his strongest ally.

His frustrations had extended even beyond the walls of the hospital. Jay's research, reading and conversations had led him to a piece of information which was extremely disturbing. Although it was generally recognized that patients should be receiving a recommendation to have a Pap smear performed on an annual basis, many obstetricians were instructing their patients to have the procedure performed twice a year, and in the case of some physicians, even more frequently. Jay had no way of knowing, in the mid-seventies, that subsequent data would reveal how much overkill that involved, but he was certain that twice a year in normal women, in such a slow-growing disease as cervical cancer, was an abuse.

How to make changes in such a wide group of doctors, many not even obstetricians, seemed an almost impossible task. The problem went far beyond the borders of his hospital and seemed impossible to solve. The answer struck him like a two-by-four whacked against his brain. In the entire county there were only six hospitals of any significance, he was one of only six Chiefs of Obstetrical Departments. Because of his stature he need only obtain support from the county Ob-Gyn Society. They had to be shown that it was imperative for such an important organization to make a formal policy statement about Pap smears to the staffs of their hospitals.

––––––––––

At an Executive Committee meeting of the Society he presented his plan. It was then for the first time that he realized that the Society was nothing more than a hollow veneer representing the wishes of its membership. In its own right it stood for nothing. It wasn't just without a backbone; it functioned without a brain or a heart. In a sense it was a quasi-union that met for its monthly dinner and drinks among friends, and nothing more. They would usually have a speaker, sometimes dull and sometimes less dull. Everyone would enjoy the evening away from the usual routine, and out with their peers. It was sort of the medical version of a "night out with the boys." There was an open bar, but very few of the physicians abused that, except of course for Jack Simms.

Though Jay had never seen the incident, he laughed every time he heard the story told. This group of physicians all knew it by heart, yet repeated it frequently to the sound of great laughter between themselves during bull sessions.

Simms had gotten quietly drunk at every meeting of the Society for as long as anyone could remember, without any consequence. He would get thoroughly soused, then sit at his dinner seat, finish his meal, and slowly doze off during the presentation. On this particular occasion, the speaker had to make a quick plane connection out of town after his speech. As a result he was allowed to begin speaking as the meal was being served.

Following in the tradition of the past, the guest speaker was sufficiently dull to allow Jack to quickly fall off into dreamland while leaning forward over the table. Waitresses, meanwhile, brought bowls of clear chicken broth as the first course to each of the Society members. Suddenly Jack's elbow slipped off the edge of the table and his face slid into the bowl. So deeply inebriated was he that he did not raise either the lips that sometimes quivered when he spoke, nor the nose which had become reddened over the years. Realizing what had happened, several of his nearby dinner partners pulled his head out of the bowl, lowered him to the floor, and began resuscitation. A delay of more than fifteen minutes, while they were caring for Jack, caused the speaker to leave before the completion of his talk. The evening ended with the membership absolutely certain that it had been the best meeting the Society had ever held. True or not, it brought a smile to Jay's face whenever he thought of it.

But Jay found nothing to smile about at this meeting. The Executive Committee hemmed and hawed and stated they would find it difficult to take such action. He understood what that meant. If the obstetricians wanted to abuse the system, their friends and associates weren't going to blow the whistle on them.

Jay decided that the only alternative would be to take drastic action on his part. There was no way the organization would want to face the publicity that a head of an obstetrical department in one of the largest hospitals in the county would resign from the organization. The reports in the press would be very unpleasant.

"Gentlemen, I sincerely didn't want to take this action. However, if the Society is not willing to take a simple stand on such an important issue for our patients, by making a policy statement about the use of Pap smears, then I'll be forced to resign as a member of this prestigious group."

"Jay, would you give us a moment to discuss this issue in Executive session?" asked Francis O'Rourke, the present Society President.

"That's fine. I'll wait out in the restaurant lounge."

Not more than five minutes had passed when they summoned him to return.

"Jay we all have a great deal of respect for you, and. . . we've been friends for many years…. That's why it's with sadness… we regretfully accept your resignation."

Jay stared at O'Rourke. Flashing through his mind were all sorts of responses. None left his lips. He glanced around the table at the other members of the Executive Board, stopping specifically with a long look at the visage of Al Krollberg, from his own department. Jay felt certain that he saw the slightest sign of a smirk on his face. He then slowly turned away and walked out of his last meeting of the Society.

––––––––

The state of his marriage, his position at the hospital, his relationship to his peers and, most significantly, the resultant general depression he was experiencing, made him an easy target when he received an unexpected phone call from Alice Crain. She told him in the most effusive terms how happy she was in her new environment in Austin.

"They really need more obstetricians here, Jay."

"Hey Alice, I don't know about Texas, but I know we're really suffering a Crain drain since you left."

"Boo! You can come up with better puns than that."

"Don't you miss the excitement and hub-bub of New York?"

"Jay, just before I left there I was visiting a friend in the city. She walked me over to her local subway station and as I walked down the steps I heard her say, 'I hope you get home safely.' Hell Jay, that's what my Mom said to my brother when he left for Vietnam."

With a broad grin on his face, Jay thought, *"Why not? It was 1976, a good year to assert one's independence."*

By the end of 1977 he would be leaving New York for a new life in Texas.

———————

"Excuse me, are you lost?"

"No, uh, yes," Jay was startled as he came out of his daydream with a broad smile in that hospital corridor and saw an attractive young nurse talking to him. "Could you tell me where the O.R. dressing room is please?"

"Sure, just go straight ahead and turn left at the end of the corridor and it will be the first door on your right."

There was a twang, a warm Texas twang, to her voice.

"Thanks an awful lot. See you around."

He believed that Alice was right. There was going to be a warmer friendlier attitude down here. Life would definitely be different from the crowded, and at times hostile environment of the northeastern part of the United States, where he had spent his entire life up until now. He was simply going to practice obstetrics and gynecology here. He would turn away from goals and challenges. There would be no proselytizing. Jay was going to enjoy life and start fresh, professionally and personally.

He thought, *"Maybe I'll even date a pretty young nurse like the one who stopped to talk to me, especially if she has a Texas twang."* He was sure he was going to like it here.

Jay knew how Alice felt about him, but decided that he wanted her to be a friend, and only a friend. He was certain that romance would come back into his life, but he wanted to find it with someone new and totally separated from his professional life.

"O. R. STAFF LOUNGE"

There it was on the door. Jay pushed it open and found a large room filled with sofas and chairs. They were all empty except one seat in the corner. Sections of newspapers, which had obviously been read earlier in the day, were strewn all over the chairs and tables. He looked toward the fiftyish-year-old man in a business suit, his head bent toward the Wall Street Journal he was reading.

"Hi! My name's Jay Brown."

The man looked up and with a slow drawl said, "John Candless."

His head nodded back to the newspaper. If Jay were ever to subsequently describe the vibrations of that initial greeting, it would be remembered as one quite far from the friendly spirit he had been expecting from Texans.

He continued past the lounge area through an open doorway labeled "Dressing Rooms." There Jay found multiple rows of metal lockers. Most of them had padlocks already on them, obviously taken by the permanent members of the staff, but one group of three were unlocked. These were obviously meant for the use of visitors and other less-frequent users of the hospital.

Jay had opened his office less than one week previously, but the standard grapevine was in operation and his arrival had been noted by all. It was something he had expected as a result of the credentialing process for staff privileges, which had included a lengthy interview with the head of the Credentials Committee. It was no cause of concern to Jay. He knew it was almost unheard of to be rejected.

Randall Royal, head of the Credentials Committee, seemed to be a fairly decent fellow, and Jay would come to know him as an honest physician. But unlike Jay Brown, Randall Royal had grown up here and knew everyone. Like it or not, Randall was an "ol' boy" and Jay never would be. Jay came close to understanding, but not for a long time, that there was no closer tie in this part of the country than being an "ol' boy." Even if he wished it, Jay could never fit that description.

———

This was Jay's maiden voyage into the O.R. He had received a telephone call from Dr. Ralph Tyson.

"Doctah Brown?"

"Speaking."

"I understand you've recently opened yo' practice heah in Austin and that yo' credentials are quite excellent. I like to help new people who have come to the community to get stahted. So, I wondered whether you'd have the time and would be willin' to assist me in an operation this week. I'm doin' a hysterectomy on a woman who has lahge fibroids and has been bleedin' profusely with her periods for the past yeah. She..."

Tyson went into a long and detailed history. Jay thought that he was going to be quite pleased with this early welcoming hand. It certainly would be a great help in the management of his bills when there were almost no patients and a definite negative cash flow on his books.

"If ah like the way you work..." and then a strange sort of "huh, huh... there'll be lots more opportunities like this."

––––––––––

Jay grabbed a set of scrub pants and tops from a shelf and had started getting dressed in front of one of the empty lockers when he heard the door to the doctor's lounge swing open and then shut.

"Hey John, you asshole, you still wastin' your money in that stock market?"

"Ja-a-ck, Ah don't mind bein' an asshole, 'cause wheah ah work, ah look at assholes all the time. But let me tell ya. Ah ain't seen a one yet thet ain't better lookin' than you."

Jack Marsh laughed and responded, "You sound like you're in high spirits."

"Ah ain't feelin' too bad. The news from Nawthtown Hospital is lookin' pretty damn nice. Befo' the month is out, theah gonna fiah that Jew bastard pathologist. We're gonna get a good ol' boy in thet spot."

Jay stared at the lockers. He could pass for anything. *"They probably don't know I'm Jewish.... Maybe they know and just don't give a damn. I've never experienced any prejudice in my professional life. Every place I've worked the Jews were in the majority.... Am I in for some culture shock? ...Is this what I'm going to face with most of the doctors here? ...or is this an isolated incident? But Ralph Tyson did call me to assist.... I wonder if he knows that I'm Jewish."*

Actually Ralph Tyson didn't know that Jay was Jewish. But had he, it would have made no difference. Tyson was an ol' boy to the nth degree and a WASP of so many generations that he could not identify when his family first came to Texas. Nevertheless, Jay Brown could have been a black, half Jew, half Catholic or a card carrying Communist, and it would have made no difference. If Jay was willing to close his eyes to the quality of care provided by Ralph Tyson, and provide him with the night and weekend coverage that Tyson sought, he could be anything he wanted and earn a significant amount of money while at it. It was a technique that Tyson had utilized for a number of years with new physicians arriving in the community. At times the system worked quite well.

Tyson was a large man who could have easily looked slovenly, but he handled his obesity well. Whatever defects existed in his personality, he still possessed the ability to mingle among the old money, the country club set and the ol' boys of the community. To maintain that position a certain level of style was a prerequisite. To his good fortune, however, there was no requirement to maintain any level of medical expertise or even competence. Over the next few years Jay would come to be astonished that affluent, and even extremely bright individuals, who were a part of that society, would accept second rate medical care. He could only assume that they were so emotionally tied to their social community that the connection did not allow them even to consider the possibility that the care was inadequate or, worse than that, dangerous.

Jay Brown stood on the patient's right side, watching Tyson prepare to make the initial incision. Ralph Tyson provided an illusion of total confidence. He was an impressive figure, Jay thought as he looked across the operating table.

It wasn't possible, however, to miss the shakiness of the hand as the knife slipped through the skin in the lower abdomen. The thin red stripe which immediately appeared was slightly jagged. Jay had a small clamp in his hand in order to begin clamping the superficial vessels as the depth of the incision was increased. As he clamped and reached his hand out for the scrub nurse to snap another clamp into his fingers, he could not help but be concerned about what he saw. Tyson also had taken a clamp from the scrub nurse. He was grasping the tissue blindly and missing the vessels repeatedly. Although the nurse had passed another instrument to Jay, he stood motionless watching Tyson continue to grope roughly, tearing away the superficial fatty tissue where the small superficial vessels were found. Jay felt a sense of moderate panic about the question of Tyson's technical ability and what might happen subsequently when they arrived at more critical stages in the operation. It suddenly struck him that he might have been the recipient of kindness from Ralph Tyson because no one else was willing to work with this surgeon.

But why does the hospital continue to allow him to operate?

"Here, Dr. Tyson, let me sponge off this area and see if I can find this little sucker that seems to be hiding from us."

The operation progressed and Jay Brown was to find that the initial concern about this apparently inept surgeon was to be the least of his problems today.

Jay, of course, had never seen this patient previously. All he knew about her was that she was undergoing the surgery as a treatment for her large fibroids.

"Two pickups," Tyson mumbled, even as they were being held out by the scrub nurse to each doctor.

All the abdominal layers down to the peritoneum had been opened and this last incision would reveal the abdominal contents. Without difficulty Tyson snipped between the two pickups that were holding up the peritoneum. The incision was then enlarged to reveal multiple loops of bowel. Jay watched Ralph Tyson slide his hand through the loops and down into the pelvis and waited for him to lift up the significant pathologic entity which had brought them to this O.R. table. He waited patiently as Tyson's hand, no longer visible from the wrist down, immersed in abdominal organs, remaining fairly still.

At first it caused Jay Brown no concern, as not infrequently abnormal pelvic findings would be associated with significant adhesions from one structure to another. The operating surgeon would frequently spend a few moments trying to blindly feel what the present anatomical configuration might be. It was even possible that Tyson was making an effort to separate some of the adhesions bluntly with his fingers before attempting to open up the area to direct visualization. Once that was done, they would be able to pack away, out of the operating field, the loops of bowel that were presently obstructing any possible view.

Jay finally said, "What've we got?"

He heard from Tyson a sound that rang a bell in his brain.

"Huh, huh."

It was the same strange noise Tyson had made in the first conversation on the telephone. It was apparently Ralph Tyson's choice to say nothing when expressing himself would not be in his best interest.

"Lap packs and an O'Connor-O'Sullivan retractor," Tyson snapped at the scrub technician.

Jay Brown stood silently as Tyson somewhat roughly packed away the bowel into the upper abdomen and inserted the self-retaining retractor. The metal blades of the side panels of the retractor were pulled laterally to hook under all the layers of the abdomen. It contained a ratcheting mechanism which increased the lateral stretch by small increments with each stronger pull. The visible field enlarged considerably. Then the separate blades for the upper and lower parts of the incision were inserted. In a similar manner they were pulled to their maximum stretching point. The lower abdominal contents could then be clearly seen.

Jay looked down and saw a tiny uterus, even smaller than average, with two apparently normal ovaries lying alongside.

It is amazing how little one can tell about a person when a cap is placed across his forehead immediately above the eyebrows, while a mask covers everything from the lower eyelid down past the chin. Certainly it is impossible to determine the facial expression behind those shields.

As Jay leaned slightly across the table and whispered, almost in a growl, Tyson may have suspected what he would have seen had their faces been uncovered.

"Where is the pathology you described on the phone?"

Although Jay's comments were heard by no one but Tyson, Ralph spoke out in a voice heard by all, as if he were simply making a comment about the case, unrelated to the question.

"Well this patient was havin' excessively heavy periods that we just couldn't control. This operation ought to make her a perfect wife. No more 'not tonight John.'" He followed it with a laugh that was not so much dirty as dumb.

The O.R. staff was used to Ralph Tyson and just went about its business. They knew him to be inadequate, crude and dishonest in his dealings with patients. It was not their responsibility. They had a job, and they did it. They understood very well that keeping their jobs meant keeping their mouths shut and their noses clean.

Jay, on the other hand, felt sick to his stomach. As ligaments and vessels were cut across and tied one by one, pelvic organs were being removed which he knew to be completely normal. Instead of the polite supportive words he had used in the beginning of the operation when Tyson was demonstrating some lack of technical ability, he said no more. When Tyson seemed to flounder, Jay would rudely push Tyson's hand aside while assuming more and more responsibility for the procedure. As the minutes went by Jay could hear himself screaming inside, *"God damn son-of-a-bitch!"* His anger was as great toward himself as toward Tyson.

The final wound dressing went on the incision and Jay waited in the operating suite until Ralph Tyson was ready to leave, and walked out behind him.

Just as the door closed behind them, "Dr. Tyson that will never happen to me again. If you're in some drastic emergency situation and I'm the only one around, I'll come to your assistance, or should I say to the patient's assistance. But don't you DARE... do you hear me... don't you ever dare to call me again to assist you at some elective surgery."

Jay began walking away but his fury was growing rather than subsiding, so he turned and came right up to Tyson's face with his finger.

"If you ever put me in a situation like that again, I'm gonna kick the fucking shit out of you, you asshole!"

It was language that Jay Brown never ever used. It was his participation in unnecessary surgery that was so painful. He felt shame and guilt for having been a part of it.

———

As the weeks and months went by Jay had no reason to believe that that type of behavior was pervasive within the department, but he wasn't certain what the quality of surgical care was at that hospital. He didn't have the kind of access to records as he had in the past. Due to his previously horrifying experience he subsequently asked a number of specific questions in advance when a gynecologist requested his assistance. At the time of surgery the findings were not anything like his first experience, but the frequency of invitations dwindled down to almost zero and Jay suspected it was due to his thorough questioning about the proposed operation. Nothing beyond the initial case gave him any clear impression about the quality of care at Sam Rayburn Community Hospital. But he had an uneasy feeling.

Chapter Six

A Bond

*A*lice Crain and J. D. Brown needed to have warnings posted on themselves. DO NOT ALLOW THESE TWO PEOPLE TO COME IN CONTACT. THEY WILL DAMAGE SURROUNDING PROPERTY AND SELF-DESTRUCT AS WELL.

In reality the risk should have been quite small. There was no sexual chemistry between them, except in Alice's case. In the past, even that was sort of an intellectual sexual attraction.

Some things, however, are inevitable. Too much time spent with a person one greatly admires begins to affect the hormones. The physiognomy of a platonic friend, which appeared rather unremarkable at first, begins to change in the synapses of the brain. Somehow that person becomes more and more appealing. Jay and Alice had a strong mutual respect for each other's knowledge and compassion for patients. In time that changed into other types of emotions.

Their backgrounds were extremely dissimilar. Alice came from affluence, but the Greene family was the epitome of dysfunction with a father who dominated her mother, Bea. The pathological image of sexuality Alice's father created for her was only a part of the cause of Alice's anger. On a daily basis she witnessed him demean her mother. She could not recall a single incident of overt affection between them. Alice's dislike of her father never abated and she spent less and less time with her parents as the years passed.

An extraordinary revelation for Alice about her mother came to pass shortly before Bea died. Alice could not recall her mother ever mentioning a single word about sexuality. But her mother aged prematurely and the changes in her mental processes were quite evident. Memory loss became more obvious. Bea's ability to concentrate on any matter at hand changed markedly. But all thoughts by Alice, and by Bea as well, about Alzheimers were blocked out. As long as her mother managed from day to day, there was no need for Alice to deal with the reality of the situation.

Like every other human being, her mother learned from infancy that certain types of behavior were unacceptable. The range of such rules varied widely, depending upon one's environment and social class, but whatever the standards might be, they became the basis for the establishment of inhibitions in behavior. Alice's mother underwent changes that not only did not allow her to remember a conversation held a half-hour previously; she forgot what her mind had taught her was acceptable and what was not. In the case of her sexuality it was not necessarily all bad. The inhibitions she had learned had not served her that well during her lifetime.

It was a brisk fall day and Alice came home for one of her rare visits. She remembered quite clearly the strange behavior her mother exhibited as they prepared to leave Bea's house for an appointment with her internist.

These trips frustrated Alice, as Bea's physician had relatively little to offer. Bea was in excellent physical condition beyond the gradual mental deterioration. The visit was at the end of her doctor's office hours. By the time Alice and Bea left the office and were in the car, traffic barely moved. It was the witching hour of five when everyone headed home.

They sat in a long line of cars and moved only a few feet at a time with each light change. Immediately to their right, and just a short distance from Bea's window a rather large nondescript mongrel was now firmly implanted on the back of a smaller black dog which looked like a cocker spaniel except for its strange color pattern. The inferiorly positioned animal was obviously in heat. She appeared to be totally compliant and rather oblivious to the fact that her lover for that day was furiously forcing his weight upon her back and in quite a dither. Due to the stationary nature of the line of traffic, both Alice and Bea had a ring side seat at the mating. Alice felt a combination of being slightly uncomfortable with a twinge of vicarious pleasure. But she was suddenly brought out of her partial trance by Bea.

In the rather flat, monotone speech pattern which had become the norm for Bea, she said, "For forty years sex was the most unpleasant part of our marriage. No matter how I felt, or what I wanted, I had to take part in some form of sex almost every day. I didn't feel we ever made love since shortly after we were married. It was just something I had to do, like having a bowel movement."

Bea quietly and sadly recalled the past. Then there was a long pause for Alice to regain her composure following these revelations.

"Didn't you ever have any pleasure, Momma?"

It was a name Alice hadn't called her in more years than she could remember. But it flowed from her comfortably as she felt tremendous pangs of compassion.

"He made me do things that I hated."

Only Alice's imagination provided her with any knowledge of what those "things" might be. Her mother would go no further with the conversation that day, or ever again for the short remaining time in her life.

When her mother was gone, and all the talking was over, what had been called "unpleasant" fit a different description in Alice's vocabulary. She would never think of it again as anything other than spousal abuse. It would never cease to be a part of the image of her father. Alice sometimes thought she would never have a healthy relationship with a man. How could she ever feel good about herself with such a disturbing role model and a father with a distorted sense of morality?

Who will I be… my mother the second time around?

Alice certainly had the intelligence, knowledge and desire to break that pattern. But deep inside a powerful voice continued to say, *You can't escape the past, no matter how hard you try. You will be your mother.*

"I don't know whether it's genetic or environmental. I can't separate myself from her," she painfully revealed to psychologists over the years.

Whatever strength Alice possessed, she derived from the efforts to overcome her pathologically deficient self-esteem by accomplishments within her professional life in medicine. Love and respect emanated from the women she cared for in labor. Nevertheless it did not carry over into the world of her personal relationships.

Deep in her psyche Alice disliked and distrusted most men. It was easy for her to remember the terrible world her father had created for her. She despised him then as well as now. In the subsequent years communication between them had become less and less frequent. After Bea died that communication became almost non-existent. Finally, when he died, Alice did not even attend the funeral and felt no guilt whatsoever. Every psychologist she had known had given her the same trite advice: "Alice," with a tone reflecting grave concern, "now is the time for you to go back while your father is still alive and resolve all those deep inner feelings before it's too late. You will NEVER forgive yourself, or find peace, if you don't come to terms with your innermost anger. Otherwise you will never learn to love yourself."

Not only were the words always the same, there was a rhythm to the phrasing that made it almost impossible to differentiate one psychologist from the other. Alice thought that loving herself was less difficult than tolerating the same rote advice.

More than any other memory of her father was the one she never revealed to anyone, including all her therapists. It was a recurrent dream that was hazy and shadowed. In it a small child was fondled by a man whose face she could not see. The child sobbed. She could not remember any physical abuse in her childhood, but the dream made her wonder. After her mother related her experiences that day in the car, the dream seemed to recur more frequently and its aura became more sinister and forbidding.

He died. Alice never looked back for one moment. She felt no guilt nor regret for the non-resolution of her anger. Alice didn't believe the advice she received from therapists about resolving the relationship. She was happy with her decision because the dream died with him.

————

Jay Brown never knew a world like the one Alice had experienced. He grew up in poverty with first generation Americans. They came to the United States from Russia with nothing but hope and a dream. They struggled through the devastation of the Depression with three surviving children; another had died of rheumatic fever.

Jay remembered his childhood very well. His recollections were of constant love and caring. He felt no need to block out memories. He had absolutely no concept that he had lived in a Jewish ghetto. As a child he was certain that almost everyone in the world was Jewish.

There were Irish, Italian and Black people that he saw occasionally in his neighborhood; their ghettoes, just as large as the Jewish one, surrounded his. In the 1930's and 40's those other groups were given demeaning names in his society's vocabulary. His contact with them was very limited.

By the time he was seven or eight, Jay's mother allowed him to walk the one city block past the very modest row houses to one of the major streets in his neighborhood. He began to realize that the world was larger than his small Jewish community. Sometimes he would greet a person sitting on one of the small porches connected from one house to the next. Frequently a dog tied up on a porch and dying to have a small boy play with him, would attract Jay sufficiently to delay his daily trip to his appointed role at the corner of the street. But, should he begin his trip later than planned, neither human nor beast would slow down his rush to his assignment. He would not fail to reach his goal at the appointed time.

On these trips Jay arrived at the corner where his father would disembark from the trolley that brought him home from a hard day of work.

When he reached the corner, Jay sat down on the bottom concrete step of the corner building. It was his reserved seat. But if it was raining or if there was snow on the ground, Jay had to stand and wait. Sit or stand, the only thing that mattered to Jay was that he be there in time to greet his father at the end of the day.

Two separate trolley lines passed that corner. They originated at different sites, but at the location where Jay waited they shared a common track. Jay knew that his special passenger would be on line number 19, not line number 14.

The actual data were very clear. The same number of 14's and 19's passed that stop every evening when the rush hour traffic brought workers and shoppers home. But the schedule was not so perfect that they arrived alternately. Depending on the traffic where they originated, it was not uncommon for two or three of one line or the other to come consecutively. But Jay could never be persuaded that there were as many #19's as #14's. He felt certain that was very unfair.

A hill, about half a block from where he waited, allowed Jay to hear the trolley before he could see it. Like a puppy dog, his ears perked up when he heard the sound of the metal wheels as they rolled along the track. If Jay had been seated, he jumped up to see the first sign of the long wand that reached up to the electric wire which powered the trolley. His heart pounded as he waited to see the sign on the top of the trolley as it appeared over the horizon of the hill. Would it be a #19 or a #14?

Since Jay always arrived early, on most days 20 or 30 cars passed before the one where the conductor opened the door and Jay saw his father.

Jay would run to the curb but no further. His instructions were quite clear. Never set foot into the street.

Jay smiled and called out to his father. In the midst of his fatigue his father could not help but yield a broad smile in return as he slowly walked with his heavy tool box from the trolley to the curb. On his arrival, he placed the box on the ground for a grand hug and a kiss and words repeated more than once on the walk down that single block to their house.

"Daddy, I love you. I love you."

Jay could not possibly know the effect his presence and unbridled affection had at the end of a very long and arduous day.

"Daddy, so many more #14's came before the #19 you were on."

"Zeesa kind" his father would say referring to Jay in his Yiddish for "sweet child," and then try to explain why it might appear so.

"No Daddy, no! There really were more number 14's"

His father would then agree, as he had so many times before. Once again hugs and kisses and terms of endearment between the two followed.

Even when Jay grew to adult life, he would laugh at his inability to control the outcome of how some events, like which trolley would come first, would unfold. Whenever he stood in a supermarket checkout line, he was certain that the line he had not chosen moved faster. With a quick adjustment he would slide into the other queue, only to find that it had now stagnated. His original line, of course, sped up once he had left it. Whether he stayed or changed again there was one thing of which he was certain: Those at one time behind him, now passed through the checkout desk and left the store while he still waited.

It was no different when he drove. He knew for certain that the lane he changed into suddenly slowed down. No matter which lane he tried, it slowed to a snail's pace. Fortunately it never angered him... just made him smile.

The experience on the street corner was typical of life in his family, filled with love and devotion. Though there was a strong Jewish identity, rituals were practiced in a very limited way. Jay and his siblings went through the expected formal Jewish education in their childhood, but now they were only seen at the synagogue on the two major holidays—Rosh Hashanah and Yom Kippur. But no matter where they lived, every member of the family returned home to celebrate the Passover Seder.

Jay never knew why the active practice of the religion had diminished in the family. There was never any conversation among them to explain it. When he got older he had the distinct impression that there was a relationship to the tragic death of his young brother. It had burned a hole in the hearts of his parents, especially his mother. It never seemed to completely heal.

As a child Jay's name seemed perfectly normal to him—Jehudah Davidovitch Bronozovsky. Before he even entered school, his family legally changed their surname to Brown. His father persuaded his mother that it was a step to the goal they sought, to be Americanized in this grand new country. But it was actually Jay's kindergarten teacher who had the most significant effect on his name. She said it would be easier to just call him J.D. His childhood friends shortened his name to Jay. From that early time he used the signature J.D. and answered to Jay.

Jay often thought about how his strong sense of right and wrong had come to pass. His parents were simple people, essentially without formal education, but they were highly respected within the local Jewish community. As a boy he sat for hours at his father's work bench in the dingy basement of their house. A cabinet maker by trade, his father made beautiful pieces of furniture for the family during the rare hours he was not at work. Jay remembered his father building book shelves especially for him.

More than anything else from that time he recalled the constant emphasis, as he watched his father work, on the importance of doing all work with aim toward excellence. The work ethic message was not just about working hard. It was a message of being true to oneself.

"Jehudella, ich dof machen dus geet."

"Poppa, you can talk English. Say it in English."

He went into detailed descriptions of how to dovetail the sections of the drawers so that the fit was perfect. Each similar section was crafted to exact specifications so that every drawer slid perfectly. Everything was glued with the finest available products. There were no nails. And, of course, he painstakingly applied the finish in multiple applications.

He repeated the conversation on many occasions, always as if it were the first time the words had ever been spoken. It was the gold standard by which Jay's father and mother lived. An honest day's work, an honest day's pay, mixed with love and sharing fairly well summed up the entirety of their philosophy of life.

From Jay's mother there were lessons of kindness and love. Jay saw her provide for the poor who came to the door. He saw her place whatever small change she could save in the small blue and white box which was brought to the synagogue on the High Holidays. From all these small actions Jay assumed that he grew up among the well to do. It was only as he grew older that he realized that they were the poor, and that his mother still understood that there were those who were even less fortunate. The love his parents felt so strongly for each other was the complete antithesis of what Alice Crain experienced in her family. And the valuable lessons he learned subliminally from both of them were to stay with him long after they died.

Jay was fiercely loyal to ideals that he believed were basic to his way of life. Even as his marriage disintegrated over the years, he was never unfaithful. When he found that he could no longer remain within the relationship, he ended it and did not look back.

If there was a theme to his life, it was defined by that decision. He rarely wavered. Once he made a firm decision to take action, no forces stopped his momentum. Fortified with a powerful self-image, he tenaciously made every effort to accomplish the goals he had set for himself. His determination like almost all personal characteristics was a double edged sword. For some who knew him, it meant he could be trusted to see a problem out to the end, no matter what difficulty arose. To others it was seen more as stubbornness and the inability to backtrack, even if the course taken was a misjudgment.

———

With no similarity either in their past or in the way they viewed the world, there was one force that magnetically pulled Alice and Jay in the same direction. It was their love of medicine. For Alice it was the source of respect. And Jay believed that everything worthwhile in his life had come from the opportunities the profession gave him.

Here in Texas their paths crossed once again. Neither suspected that this reunion was anything other than an opportunity to renew a professional relationship with a person whose standards and performance were a source of admiration. Both were determined not to fight the system again.

While Alice found Jay extremely attractive, she was never certain whether it was her view of him as a physician or a man. Though she would have been a willing mistress for him in New York, she knew he would never be available.

Once she became a part of Jack Marsh's life she was certain it was permanent. Alice believed she would never have another lover for as long as she was capable of sharing her body and her mind. She had no expectation of marriage, but felt certain that her love of Jack would never end.

For Jay it was now the time and place to find a new love. That new love would not be a casual one night stand, and it would not be a non-Jew, like Alice. He believed that people could never leave the cultural background they came from and be truly happy. He was certain that he would soon start a new life. He would find someone with whom he could share those experiences which had been an integral part of his life from his childhood to the present.

With all that as a backdrop, there need be no fear that Jay and Alice would take any action that would have a significant effect on the lives of one another.

Chapter Seven

Two Joans

*S*am Rayburn Hospital was a large sprawling facility which was the most important hospital in Austin, other than the Medical School. Rayburn was built in the same large complex as the school, two smaller hospitals, and a number of medical office buildings. The choice of the site for this centralized medical center was the crux of a battle, now long forgotten. Those who had no financial ax to grind pushed for it to be located closer to the lower economic area of the city, in order to provide access to the medical school clinics for the poor. But big money was to be made in this project, and ultimately the land developers who held most of the property around the present location of the health facilities prevailed. The building projects started with the Medical School and Hospital. Following that, Rayburn and the office buildings went up, and finally the other hospitals. The poor of Austin made the long trek to the clinics when they could find the transportation. And when they couldn't, it was the same as in many other major urban areas: they went untreated.

A few physicians on Rayburn's staff had ties with the Medical School. The hospital itself was loosely tied to a religious denomination in order to maintain its status as a not-for-profit hospital, but essentially it was in competition with all the other local private institutions. Comparable in size to the local Baptist Hospital, it was far enough away geographically for there to be no competition between them.

The hospital functioned for the benefit of its staff members and the local community. It was a symbiotic relationship which was not unfamiliar to Jay Brown. There were no training programs for residents or interns. Basically as long as they increased the size of their staff, gradually increased the number of beds and services they provided, and faced no interference from the ivory tower, their Administration was satisfied.

The ivory tower, a name applied to the medical school primarily by those who were not admirers, was always thought of as a threat.

Its staff, recruited from every part of the country, had a much higher proportion of Jewish doctors than any other segment of the medical community in Austin. As a result it was not uncommon for physicians in any of the other voluntary and private hospitals in the city to refer to it as the Jew school.

At Rayburn the feeling always existed that they were looked down upon by the members of the medical school faculty. At least a portion of the important leaders at the school recognized that the accusation was accurate and that corrective action needed to be taken. It was difficult to get the teaching staff at the School to realize that they did treat physicians, who were not part of the academic center, in a supercilious manner. It was not easy to persuade them that the correction had to come mainly from their side of the fence.

Jay knew some of the faculty members from the New York area and immediately started to attend conferences at the school. It set him apart from most of the obstetrical staff at Sam Rayburn, who were almost never seen at the school, though it was only a short walk away. It was all very reminiscent of his days at Northwest and Jay soon learned learn how small the world was; how little difference fifteen hundred miles made.

Jay had made several trips to Austin while still practicing in New York to prepare for his move. The transition was time consuming. He needed to find office space, go to hospital interviews and search for new employees. He questioned every physician he met for leads on how to find qualified staff for his new office. These were chores he performed happily. There was an excitement about starting a new life.

————

Joan Nordstrom did everything. She was an unbelievable find. But it wasn't accidental. She was five foot ten and damn near as big around as she was tall, with short dark hair, dark eyes and singularly unattractive features, she looked more like a prison guard in a 1930's movie than a caring nurse.

But Joan was even more caring than most people wanted her to be. Predominant among those people were obstetricians. She had been a delivery room nurse at Sam Rayburn Hospital for almost ten years.

"I'd like to know how you'd feel about leaving the hospital environment and working with one doctor in an office... I'm just beginning here. I'd need you to do everything to start. You'd be the nurse, receptionist, bookkeeper and..."

"Hold it a second," Joan responded. "Are you looking for a nurse or a Mother Superior? Just kidding. I don't suppose a Jewish doctor is going to have a Mother Superior in charge."

"I knew with a name like Nordstrom you wouldn't be Jewish. But that doesn't mean you couldn't be a Jewish mother. That description is non-denominational. Even some men fit into that mold." Jay continued, "I've been told you're the most outspoken, outrageous to some, and progressive obstetrical nurse in the city. I'm also told that many obstetricians would love to see you anywhere but in their hospital, challenging their decisions. I just thought I'd give them a break and get you out of their hair."

"That's darn noble of you. But I'm really just a big pussy cat."

"What I liked, from what I was told, was that you were a pussy cat with the patients and a tiger with the docs."

"Oh I really wasn't that tough on them."

"Well that's a shame. Guess I'll have to look elsewhere.... No! Just kidding. Let me tell you what I had in mind. You know better than I, that except for the school, there are NO prepared childbirth classes in this town. I want to establish my own, or how about this— our own. And I want you to be the one who teaches it to our patients. I'll train you to be an instructor and we'll provide the only such service in town."

"You are either very dumb or very gutsy, or maybe both."

"You think that's going to present problems?"

" No... no problem at all. These docs around here are going to be thrilled with you setting that up and stealing their patients."

"I don't want to steal anyone's patients."

"Well you're going to."

"You mean if I'm going to practice here, I'm going to have to practice like everyone else? I can't do that."

"That's O.K. with me Dr... Dr..., How about if I call you Dr. B and you call me Joan? I think the patients would like that."

"Would you feel more comfortable calling me Jay?"

"I sure would, but I think the patients will feel more secure if I call you Dr. B."

Joan paused for a moment and gave Jay a great big smile.

"I like what you want to do and I'd like to work with you," she went on, pausing again before adding "if you want me?"

"You've already punched your time card. You're checked in for today. Your salary started the minute we began talking."

They looked at each other and saw the first glimmers of respect, trust and admiration starting to flicker. These two already knew they were thrilled with this new adventure.

———

It was well past one o'clock and the office had begun to crowd up slightly. More than a year had passed, and it had been a very gratifying one for Jay, and for Joan as well. That wasn't difficult to understand. Jay had made her feel that the practice was as much hers as his. Word spread about the level of care and compassion that could be found in their office.

The natural childbirth classes had done just what Joan expected; create some havoc within the obstetrical community. But Jay got lucky. Times had changed rapidly. The hospital decided, shortly after his example, that they should be enticing patients in the same way. They organized a fine program which was then utilized by a number of the other obstetricians. So the brief firestorm that Joan had warned about came to an end.

Some of the more conservative, and less adaptable, obstetricians didn't utilize the hospital's program. They were unhappy that all this "nonsense" about a new way to have babies had ever started. They remembered who the culprit was who started it all. For one reason or another, a number of obstetricians were less than thrilled with the new guy on the block.

The practice grew well. It had reached the point that if Jay was late for office hours, it quickly became overcrowded. Joan knew that he had gone into the hospital sometime during the middle of the night for two labor patients.

Mrs. Mercado was seven weeks early and Jay managed her conservatively for almost a week before she spontaneously went into labor. He felt lucky to have already gained an extra week of maturity, using the new tocolytic, terbutaline, to stop the contractions. But late the night before, she broke through the ability of the drug to control the contractions. Terbutaline had given him good results in the past, but there were forces in the onset of labor that no one understood clearly. At times there was nothing that could stop the mechanisms from progressing.

Jay had switched drugs. He jumped to magnesium sulfate. On occasion, when terbutaline failed him, he found success with the use of that drug. This time it appeared to be a losing battle. The momentum of labor built. He faced the prospect of a thirty-three week gestation— seven weeks premature.

Joan was well aware of what happened, as Jay had spoken with her in the morning and brought her up to date. By the time office hours were to start, she and Jay had spoken, and Mrs. Mercado had already delivered. Joan Jason, another patient who had come in during the night, and a favorite of both Jay and Joan, was well into labor.

The Mercado baby was in the neonatal intensive care unit. She came through with flying colors. Her expected weight had been about four pounds. No one was happier than Jay that this preemie was quite well nourished and tipped the scales at almost four and three quarter pounds—four pounds and eleven ounces to be exact. Best of all, it was a girl. Everyone knew that females had an increased advantage when it came to the stresses faced by premature newborns. In the back of his mind, when Jay thought about that phenomenon, he always remembered one of his favorite books on anthropology—Ashley Montague's *The Natural Superiority of Women*.

Mrs. Jason, as opposed to Mercado, was at full term. She progressed in labor quite nicely considering it was her first baby. Jay had told Joan (Nordstrom, not Jason) that he expected the labor to carry all through the afternoon office hours. He assured her that once everything was stable with the Mercado baby he would come to the office, but not on this day.

He was barely ten feet away from the back door of Sam Rayburn when he heard, "Dr. Brown, Dr. Brown, stat to the delivery room!" the voice droned over the hospital paging system.

He turned and ran back down the corridor and pushed his way past several nurses and visitors who were slowly ambling in the same direction. It was about 12:45 P.M. as he burst through the swinging doors and into the labor suite.

Before he could even question the page he had heard, one of the labor room nurses said "It's the Jason baby."

"What happened?"

"The fetal heart dropped into the mid 50's and we can't get it up. We've turned her to her left side and tipped the bed down into the Trendelenburg position. We've given her oxygen but ..."

"Is there any bleeding?" he quickly asked and did not wait for a response.

Then, "Get me a glove."

Mrs. Jason, panicked about her baby, listened to what was being said.

There was no time for the niceties which he usually utilized before an examination such as, "We're going to do a gentle vaginal exam" or "I'll try not to make you too uncomfortable" or "Is there anything you'd like to ask before the exam?"

His eyes flashed across her bed toward the monitor. The line had dropped in a steady slope from the normal range in the 140's per minute down into the 50's and 60's, where it now fluctuated. It could be one of several things. A separation of the placenta would be the most critical, but some sort of compression of the umbilical cord was more likely.

Jay leaned across the bed and, without saying a word to Mrs. Jason, he lifted her as if she were a feather. At least a portion of his strength was due to the adrenaline rush. He turned her from the position on her side and replaced her on her back so that he could quickly and properly examine her. The glove was on in a flash. His second and third fingers were in her vagina and Joan Jason felt them slide around firmly, but gently.

He withdrew them and saw only a minimal blood stain from the normal process of labor.

"She has a tiny rim of cervix which I can slide over the head. Quickly. Move her into the delivery room and get me a pair of long Elliott forceps."

Mrs. Jason never said a word, though she felt the panic in her heart. She watched her doctor give specific orders. There was no fear in his voice, just authority. Though he moved with great speed, she sensed no panic in his demeanor. She knew fully well that a disaster was imminent, but she also sensed that Dr. Brown was fully in control.

Within seconds Jay was in a scrub suit. There was no time to scrub his hands before this case. He had made an immediate decision. The choice to perform a Cesarean section involved preparation for the operation even with the most rapid induction of anaesthesia. At its ultimate speed, it would be fifteen minutes before the baby was out. Jay believed he could get the child out in less than five minutes if he could accomplish a vaginal delivery.

Not three minutes passed in the move to the delivery table. The nurse applied the sterile drapes while Jay put on his gown and gloves over the scrub suit. Doing a forceps delivery without even local anaesthesia was a technique he never chose, due to the discomfort for the patient. But time left him no choice.

With her legs strapped into stirrups he repeated the examination. The baby had come down to below the pelvic spines. That meant Jay would do a difficult mid forceps delivery.

As her contraction began, Jay said forcefully to Joan Jason, "Bear down and push... hard."

There was a total hush in the room as he slipped her cervix over the baby's head. His hand was high in the vagina. The nurses who assisted him just stood and watched. In the relatively brief time since Jay arrived at Sam Rayburn the nursing staff had come to realize that his manual dexterity was exceptional. They knew he was capable of deliveries that few other members of the staff could accomplish.

Only Jay knew what was the status high in that blind cavity in which he worked to save this child. He turned sharply toward one of the nurses.

"Tell someone to call the neonatologists and get one of them here, STAT!"

With his right hand completely immersed in Joan's body, Jay took a half turn back to his instrument table and lifted the blade to be inserted on the left side of the vagina. He quickly dipped it into the basin of water to allow it to slide more easily. Then he gently slid it between the baby's head and his right hand. As the blade came across the palm of his right hand, his fingers controlled its placement alongside the baby's skull.

He withdrew his hand and the blade maintained its position in the vagina, its long handle projecting out in space. It remained stationary because its distal cupped end was firmly held between the baby's skull and the side of her pelvis.

Now Jay lifted the opposite blade with his right hand. In a flash his left hand disappeared up to the wrist as his right hand had done previously on the opposite side.

All these manipulations were done not without discomfort for Mrs. Jason, but not one utterance was heard from her lips. At least a part of her silence was due to fear. All of her confidence in Jay Brown did not eliminate the feeling that she was about to lose her first child.

The second blade slipped in around the baby's head. In an uncomplicated forceps delivery there would be time to make repeated adjustments of the position of the blades in order to have the best placement. Jay could tell that due to the angle of the head, the blades had been placed on the skull on a slight bias. It was called asynclitism. He made a minimal attempt to adjust them, but he knew that he must get this baby out, now. The heart rate remained frighteningly slow. The handles were so constructed that they fit together where the operator held them on the outside. Now they were on, and Jay began to lift the baby's head out of the vagina.

The fit was somewhat tight, but the head gradually descended and then appeared at the vulvar opening. Jay continued to exert a slow but steady pull and finally the head was withdrawn. The baby was extremely blue and limp. With the head out, the forceps were removed. Jay slipped his finger up over the baby's head and down to its neck, and there was the answer to what had caused this near disaster: Not one, not two, but three loops of cord were wrapped tightly around the baby's neck. In order to get the baby out, he quickly clamped and cut the cord and flipped the loops around the head and off the baby's neck. Once cut, it became apparent that the cord was unusually short. The tension around the neck had become tighter as the baby descended during labor, due to the shortness. The result was the severe fetal distress they had all seen on the monitor.

The cord cut, Jay rapidly delivered the baby's shoulders and then the body of this limp newborn. Gobs of meconium—thick dark green stool—had been extruded from the baby's rectum and immediately followed the child out of the vagina. Some of the meconium was still adherent to the dark blue newborn buttocks of this oxygen deprived baby. The passage of the meconium at that time indicated the severity of the stress to the baby during the rapid and prolonged drop in its heart rate. Jay quickly turned and placed the baby in the hands of Sid Bacon, the neonatologist who had arrived even before the birth was accomplished.

Within seconds three pairs of hands were on the baby under the warming lamps. While one nurse was drying and gently stimulating the body, a second held a stethoscope to the baby's chest, timing the heart rate.

"It's at ninety."

Sid Bacon inserted a laryngoscope and verified that no meconium had gone down into the baby's trachea, the breathing passageway to the lungs. That was an absolute necessity before attempting to resuscitate with positive pressure oxygen. The oxygen mask was now on and Sid began to see a change in the baby's skin color. The pinkness returned first to the face and head. Then one could actually see the change from blue to pink move gradually down the baby's body.

Jay had made a small episiotomy to provide sufficient space to accomplish the delivery. He anaesthetized it locally before he sutured it back together.

Jay's confidence in Sid Bacon was total. Once he handed the baby back to Sid, he did not look back again toward the heated table where the baby was cared for until all his work with Mrs. Jason was completed.

The speed with which Sid Bacon and the staff worked on the newborn was so remarkable, that even before Jay injected Joan, he heard the sweetest sound that could possibly fill the room. It was a diminished, but nevertheless definitive, newborn wail. Jay looked up over the sheets to Joan Jason's face for the first time since entering the delivery room. He smiled at her.

Joan smiled back and said, "Thank you so very much, Dr. B."

By then Mrs. Jason was into a full-fledged cry, a combination of joy and pent-up anxiety.

———————

When the several rows of sutures were completed, Jay walked over to look at the baby over Sid Bacon's shoulder.

"How bad was the forcep placement?"

"Not that bad, Jay, for that kind of speed in an emergency. See the little bruise down there at the corner of the mouth. That's it. No other bruises. Nice job Jay. You earned your keep today. The baby's great. The one minute Apgar score is only three, but the five minute is nine."

The low score at one minute indicated the severe stress the baby had endured just before delivery. But the high five minute Apgar reassured everyone that there would be no permanent effect from that episode.

While he repaired the episiotomy, Jay had asked one of the nurses to call his office and tell Joan Nordstrom he would be about a half hour to forty minutes late. By the time he returned to the office Joan knew all about the emergency and the happy result. As he walked into the crowded office, she spoke without raising her head.

"Decide to have a long casual lunch?"

As he flipped his head around quizzically to look at her, her head rose, they did a double take, and both broke into laughter.

Chapter Eight

Playing With Fire

$\mathcal{B}$y the time Jay Brown was into his third year in Texas, prosperity began to overtake him. Joan could no longer manage the office alone and Felicia Gonzales was now an integral part of the office staff. She assisted in the examining rooms, answered the phone and made appointments. Joan was in charge of the front desk. She was responsible for the collections, balancing the ledger, and dealt with insurance companies. More than anything else, she was the primary public relations person for the office.

Joan Nordstrom was dedicated to the well-being of the women who passed through those doors. Unfortunately, her dedication to simple arithmetic demonstrated less of a commitment.

At the end of the day the Brown-Nordstrom comedy act began. Jay, prepared to leave, would find Joan at her adding machine, mumbling.

"Can't balance the numbers?" he would ask. The question dealt with the one issue in the entire world he did not want to face.

"I know Mrs. Morales gave me a ten and a five. I didn't have three singles to give her, but I found two in my purse. Then I went into Mike Jones' office. They had only four singles. So I gave them the five and took the four singles and I told them I'd come back later to pick up the other. I picked that up later. But I had to give it to Mrs. Acevedo for change. Then I returned my two dollars to my wallet. But I've still got one dollar too many on the books."

Jay looked at her and slowly shook his head from side to side, resigned that his work day had not yet ended, and said, "O.K. move over."

It happened at least once a week. Always after about thirty minutes of review, the answer was found. Though he hated the drudgery of the entire process, Joan had a way that made him finally find humor in the exercise. It could only be assumed that she understood the humor in the process, since she never varied from her approach, and the result was always laughter.

"Dr. B. I don't understand why you make me go through this same mess every day."

"Joan, this is not your home checkbook. This is a business. We are required to account for every dollar or penny that goes in or out of here. Our accountant can't deal with our books in an approximate way."

"But sometimes I have more money and sometimes I have less. By the end of the year I'm sure it will come out almost equal."

With one of his typical puns he uttered, "I'm certain Joan, that the time you spend here can be called countless hours."

"She turned, and with the nose of her face barely an inch from his, she would utter, "Boo!"

The most significant problem that resulted from Jay's rapid expansion was the need to get some help with his practice. At times he worked through the night on consecutive days with active labor patients, as he tried to manage his office hours. It had begun to be a major problem when, out of the blue, an offer presented itself which seemed to be the perfect solution.

A group of three other obstetricians had a loose affiliation. They practiced separately but covered each other at night and on weekends. The decision to add a fourth member to their group meant that each would be on call only one out of four nights and weekends. The idea sounded attractive to them and they approached Jay with the proposition.

Jay asked if he could ponder the offer for a day or two. It presented certain problems which caused him to be somewhat wary. He had practiced long enough to have known a number of groups. From what he had seen, the larger the group, the more the difficulties ensued.

The problems were not primarily medical, although the quality of communications about the status of patients within larger groups did seem to suffer. The main stumbling blocks usually were the different personalities of the associated physicians. For Jay there was another problem that concerned him. The other three obstetricians had no concerns about who delivered their patients on the nights they were not on call. Jay could not imagine practicing obstetrics in an arrangement in which others delivered the majority of his patients. He thought about the women with whom he had built a strong bond. The idea of so many of them delivered by a doctor they had never previously met seemed horrendous to him. Alone he might miss the delivery of an occasional patient. But he could not tolerate the delivery of approximately three fourths of his patients by some other physician.

As part of the group though, he could take off an occasional night or weekend. He could take the vacation he had been unable to even consider since he arrived in Austin. There was no requirement to sign out to the covering obstetrician every night that he was not listed on call. He decided to make use of the other obstetricians only on chosen dates. In that way he could still fulfill the responsibility he felt toward his patients. The extra work he had to accept as he cared for all their patients on the nights he was on call was a fair trade, as it finally allowed him the opportunity to sign out when he felt the need. It seemed like a worthwhile compromise.

One other major drawback deterred him. The offer had been made by Norman Freeman, one of the best obstetricians he had met since arriving in Austin. Jay had become friendlier with Norm than with any other physician on the staff. They had spent many hours discussing issues far from medicine on the nights when they found themselves waiting at the hospital for babies to be born.

Norman Freeman was extremely bright. He had followed in his father's footsteps as an architect and entered his father's firm, as was expected of him. His father's untimely death in an airplane crash, though devastating, had freed him from his career obligation. At the age of thirty-five Norman Freeman returned to school to study medicine. His brief tenure as an architect, a field which he despised and to which he devoted little energy, had left him much time to read. Freeman's thirst for knowledge was quite eclectic. It provided him with a smattering of information on any subject that might arise.

Norman Freeman looked like a college professor. He was almost never seen without a pipe in his hand or on his lips. He and his family were much more orthodox in their religious practices than Jay, but their common religion was an advantage in their friendship. It was the first time in Jay's life that he had lived in a community that was not predominantly Jewish. Even though he had a minimal religious affiliation, the friendship with Norm Freeman provided him with a non-secular bond that was, in some nebulous way, comforting.

If the present group of physicians who made him the offer was comprised of three whom he liked as much as Norm, Jay would have had no qualms about the opportunity, but the other two presented some problems for him. Jay raised that issue with Freeman, but only in a very subtle manner. He did not wish to offend Norm by questioning the quality of the doctors Norm had chosen to care for his patients. Nevertheless, Freeman was sufficiently astute to get the drift of the conversation. He assured Jay that he had complete confidence when he placed his patients in the hands of his associates.

Alexander Stoddard, generally called Alley, was a very quiet physician. Hardly a driving force in the department, he was possessed of a very bland personality. There was no reason for Jay to think poorly of his ability as an obstetrician, or any reason to be impressed either. Alley was never heard from during an obstetrical meeting, or in between for that matter. His one claim to fame was made by others and never by him. This fiftyish obstetrician, who looked like a Bob Cratchett office clerk, was having an affair with a young nurse. No one ever knew, at least not Jay, who that might be.

But the issue involved for Jay was not a personality contest, nor was it Alley's personal life. He certainly was not obnoxious. And, if Norm assured Jay of the quality of Alley's obstetrical skills, that was all that was necessary.

It was primarily the third member of the group who made Jay waver in his decision. Louis Crown presented problems for Jay, some of which Jay understood very well. Some he could not place his finger on, but sensed. "Louie" Crown was no Alexander Stoddard. For, as little as Alley had to say, nary a discussion would ensue, in or out of meetings, in which "Louie" did not possess expertise. It was not just his domineering attitude which seemed to hold sway over the department. His French accent in this land of drawls provided him with an air of authority.

"Louie" Crown sounded as if he had just arrived from France, but in terms of English grammar and vocabulary, it was as if he had lived his entire life in America.

The only obvious variation in his vocabulary from a native born was his refusal to use words like "think" or "believe." In their place he always substituted "suppose."

Crown's manipulation through language did not disturb Jay, for back in New York he had known plenty of doctors who were pompous and overbearing. But in the case of "Louie" Crown, something else bothered him.

If there was a pattern Jay applied to the general approach that Crown espoused at the monthly meetings, it was the existence of an adversarial relationship between patients and doctors. His speeches—for in fact at those meetings they truly were speeches rather than comments—were always very flowery. They extolled the needs and rights of patients. But somehow, after all the crap had effused from him, he finally reached the point of his position. The very special needs of the patients notwithstanding, the action he recommended was always to the benefit of the physicians who "needed to be protected from the hostile environment that gradually grows against the medical community."

Jay did not know whether that attitude was reflected in the manner in which Crown related to his own patients. After all, Brown was pretty much a medical loner, without much access to local gossip. Word had gotten around about the incident which occurred when Jay assisted Ralph Tyson and created something of a rumpus. The result was that Jay had no way to determine who might be doing unnecessary surgery, because almost no one asked him to assist after that. Certainly no one who felt threatened by his presence wanted to have Jay Brown at the operating table.

But one rumor did float around the department. Since Jay was no ol' boy, his access to the rumor mill was very fragmentary. Even so, he heard that Crown had cases regularly brought back to the operating room for secondary operations that resulted from complications which revealed themselves in the post-operative period. But if it were true, why would Freeman and Stoddard work with him in their group?

After he wavered back and forth, several extremely busy nights back to back made him decide he might as well try the relationship.

"Norm. It's Jay. I think it will be a fine idea for me to join the group. I assume it's something you've all discussed in detail already."

"Most definitely, Jay. Can you imagine anything could happen in a group with "Louie" without a prolonged discussion? As far as Alley's concerned, the next time he takes a position on anything, we'll ask him about you. Just kidding. He thoroughly supported the idea."

Jay felt really good about his decision. He foresaw a change in his lifestyle. His social activities up until then had nearly been non-existent.

He saw Alice on a regular basis in the Labor and Delivery suite, but wasn't interested in anything other than a professional relationship with her. At times when they worked, as they watched labor patients, there would be some conversation about their past experiences up north. But they were both committed to a new approach to their lives.

Like everyone else, Jay knew there was a solid relationship between Alice and Jack Marsh. For Alice it was more fulfilling than any she had ever known. She was sufficiently intelligent to know that love is blind and that lovers tend to view the present romance as better than any which had preceded it. She understood that Marsh would not end his marriage and that she could never really claim him as her own. But Alice would block that out of her brain and think, *"Perception is more important than reality."*

Jay, on the other hand, was totally committed to his work and the development of his practice. That is until Alice Crain's inside track with Jack Marsh opened up a can of worms.

Alice never intended to make use of her bed partner to elevate her position within the Department of Obstetrics. For his part Marsh had never been exposed to a woman who so aggressively possessed and pleasured him. Alice's sexual behavior was a natural part of her being. It had not changed to suit Jack Marsh. In bed she made no demands. She would give and give, and if that were not satisfactory, she gave some more to please her lover. As long as her partners allowed her to do that, she made them feel that she was completely satisfied. Whether she wanted it to happen or not, Jack Marsh was so taken by her that he felt compelled to help with her career.

Alice worked as a staff nurse during the day shift from seven in the morning to three in the afternoon. Then a leadership position opened up. Jack knew Alice's background and had no qualms about exerting his influence to be certain that the role of charge nurse for the night shift, eleven at night to seven in the morning, was offered to her.

It was the "dog shift" of the three, but a return to a position of authority, which, even at the bottom, meant she was once again in the administrative chain. It was Alice's chance to move back up to the stature she had known in the past in New York. She accepted the assignment enthusiastically, and was on her way up once again.

"Could life get any better, a devoted lover and a blossoming career?" She thought not.

Conversations between Alice and Jay were warm, friendly and singularly superficial when Alice was a day to day grunt on the day shift. The entire Labor and Delivery suite during the day shift was hustle and bustle, without a break. It was standard for any busy hospital. Every elective delivery or procedure on a maternity patient was done on the day shift. There were constant elective inductions of labor, some for medical indications, but most for convenience. Sometimes the convenience was because the patient wanted to deliver by a certain date, but mostly they were for the convenience of the obstetrician. If the patient could be delivered in the daytime, why give her the opportunity to go into labor during the middle of the night?

There were as well a multitude of elective Cesarean sections, all scheduled on the day shift.

The result was that the evening shift had far fewer patients under care. Some of those were patients were still around after three in the afternoon because their labor was not completed by then. Almost all were delivered by eleven in the evening, if not vaginally then by Cesarean section. But the night shift, without question, had the fewest patients.

On the night shift a basic minimum of nurses were on duty. There were still a sufficient number of patients who went into labor in the middle of the night despite their physicians' best efforts to avoid that by induction. In general the pattern was one of great inconsistency. Some nights there might be five patients in labor, while on others the nurses occupied themselves with maintenance chores. Some read or did crossword puzzles to fill out the night, when no one was in labor. It allowed for long, drawn out conversations and philosophical thoughts about everything from love to marriage, to men or politics, and on occasion to medicine.

On some of those occasions Jay might have the only patient in labor. He did not believe in, or accept as proper practice, the elective induction of labor in pregnant women for convenience.

For the first time in almost five years, Alice and Jay talked about serious matters, at times for long stretches, during the wee hours of the morning. .

Although children are taught not to touch fire or hot objects or other dangerous items, sometimes no matter what they're taught, they put their hands back in the flames.

Chapter Nine

Dissension

*I*n September of 1982, with a rather light schedule of patients due to deliver, Jay decided it was the perfect time to take off for a few days. He checked the schedule and planned his brief trip around the coverage he wanted. On his return, Joan had some distressing information to give him. He confronted Alley.

"Alley, when I left, you and I agreed that you'd be covering me."

"Jay, it's a four man group. We've all agreed to that, and each one of us is an equal. This thing came up in the last minute and I made certain that everybody would be covered. That's all I'm responsible for. Why are you giving me a hard time? Louie covered the practice."

"You call what he did covering my practice?"

"Look, if you've got a problem with him, straighten it out with him. I'm tired of being in the middle of it."

It actually *was* Jay's problem. Undeniably, coverage from Louis Crown left a great deal to be desired, but Jay created problems that none of the three were happy about. It wasn't only his discontent with Crown that caused friction. The truth was that J.D. Brown was meant to practice alone. His devotion to patients was not typical and his behavior, as it related to his associates, was more than frustrating to doctors who worked in close association. It was downright intolerable.

Once, on a weekend when Jay was on call, a patient of Alley's became critically ill. Jay was prepared to manage the patient, but decided that he should call Alley first to tell him of the serious complications that had occurred. Jay felt that if it were his patient, he would want to know.

Alley was about to take off on a weekend with his secret love when he got the call. He was furious.

"I'm off, Jay. What's the big idea of calling me? It's supposed to be your responsibility. Now that you've called I've got to come in to see her. I'm God damn pissed off."

Jay had never heard Alley so angry. He wondered if he had

overstepped the line by assuming everyone else's dedication. He was genuinely sorry he had made the call, but unfortunately, if the situation arose again, he would probably repeat his behavior.

When on call, Jay provided conscientious attention to the patients of all three of his partners. But when they covered him, he constantly checked to see whether similar care was provided to his patients. Often it wasn't.

Almost a full year of conflict passed when it all came to a head.

"Norman," Louie said in his thick French accent, "we've tried very hard, to get along with your friend Jay, but he is extremely difficult. My days, and hours, and weeks in this fleeting life should not be wasted in struggles with him. I suppose he has a complex that makes him feel like he is better than we are. If he feels that way we should split up the group and go back to three."

Crown may not have been the best physician, but he wasn't dumb. He knew when someone was on his tail. He'd been in that position before. It wasn't just his belief that Jay created problems for the group, although that was true. He sensed that Jay, a man who didn't like the way Louie practiced, might someday create a problem for Louis Crown.

"Louie, you're not thinking clearly," his wife Monika told him. "I told you when you added him that it was a mistake. It's bad enough you work with that other Jew. I've told you before, in the long run, they're nothing but trouble. A Jew is a Jew is a kike. But now that you've made that mistake, use your head and get out of it."

"What do you suppose I should do?"

"He's already complained about how you handled his patient. The next thing you know that fucker will make a complaint against you."

Louie smiled and said, "When you talk about Jews your language always becomes very flowery."

"Louie, there'll be nothing funny about J.D. Brown if he begins to attack you. So take the offense now. Don't break up the group. FIRE HIM! Make sure everyone knows. Put him on the defensive. Discredit him. Only then will he be too busy defending himself to be worried about you."

Though he had no one with whom to discuss the problems of the call group, Jay gradually reached the same conclusion. He was unhappy in the group. The only thing that made any sense was to resign. But beyond that other things nagged at his brain. He felt a general sense of depression—a sense that what had distressed him in New York, existed here in spades. The difference was, here he was impotent to take any action. There were a few times during monthly meetings when he made some brief statements about quality control, but the response had been generally to ignore him. The Department leaders flicked him off like a fly during a summer's day at the beach. There was no hostility, only the sense that he was an annoyance.

"Well, let's see what the statistics are for this month."

Randall Royal headed up the meeting. The Department's policy was to have a figurehead Chairman who ran the meetings and the Peer Review Committee in order to relieve Jack Marsh of those responsibilities. Randall really was a decent sort of fellow. Though he certainly was one of the ol' boys, he had no malicious instincts. Essentially, all he wanted during his year at this assignment, was for no one to start any rumpus and for things to run smoothly. As far as Randall was concerned this was not a year for change. If he were to name the year, like the Chinese, he might call it the Year of the Status Quo.

But Randall Royal was smart enough to know that something dug in Jay Brown's belly from the few conversations he had had with him. Randall wanted it to stay there, at least until the next January. If Jay wanted to fuss about the way the Department functioned, let him do it after Randall Royal finished his stewardship.

"Come on, Jay, we all got to get back to our offices and take care of the good women o' Texas. If you'all want to chew the fat about C-sections, we're gonna have to set a special date for such a meetin'. Maybe we could set it up for the beginning of the year, after we all get through the holidays."

Randall thought that was a pretty cute ploy. Alley was the Department Chairman-elect. Let him mess with Jay. Who else was better suited to keep Jay in line than his own partner? But Randall didn't know that status was not to remain for long.

The month of November had half its calendar left when the ax was dropped on Jay Brown. He had no idea that his notion to drop out of the group would be undercut. Louis Crown did his job carefully. Concerned that he might be voted down two to one if they met as a threesome, he decided to talk separately with Norman and Alley.

"I must tell you that I am very concerned about some information which has come to my attention through a source I'm not free to reveal. I'm told that Jay, whom I like very much, had some shady problems bock in New York. If something bad would come out, it would be a reflection on the rest of us. Now that there seems to be some stress among us, I think we should ask him to leave the group."

His cleverly devious way of presenting the matter won over his somewhat naive partners. Before the week was out, they were a three-man group once again. As a gracious gesture to Norm and Alley, he relieved them of the stress of notifying Jay of "their" decision.

"I will be willing to take the brunt of any reaction which would come from Jay by being the one to break the news."

By the time of Louis' meeting with Jay it was presented as a definitive three way decision. But he would couch it in clever terms.

"But I, ESPECIALLY, feel most bad about this decision."

Jay was not nearly as naive as Norm and Alley. He listened to Louis with only half an ear. He had learned, long before, that when Louie spoke, it was only half a truth. He knew that Louis Crown was not to be trusted and that there was no jewel in this crown.

Not really disturbed at all, Jay assumed that the termination was good for all of them. It was agreed that the general story which would be gossiped around would indicate that all sides desired to go back to the original status of the group for personal reasons. But not twenty-four hours passed before Louis Crown quietly whispered to physicians in the Department, and key figures in other departments, that Jay's work had fallen short of expectations.

"I don't feel comfortable telling in detail the kinds of problems we had. Enough said that he is a nice man, but a little too dangerous for us to let him treat our patients."

It was typical Louis Crown—only a few facts and lots of innuendo. Nevertheless, his tactics over the years had been clever enough to bring him to a position of considerable power. The successive figureheads in the Department were controlled by a handful of obstetricians who were the movers and shakers. Louis Crown was one and Jack Marsh another.

Chapter Ten

A Day in the Office

"*R*oom three, Dr. B.," Joan said.

Jay took the chart from her, glanced at the name, and looked up at Joan. He had a wonderful small grin, with a bashful component, that was nothing short of charming when it appeared.

Jay knew exactly how he would find Ann-Marie Strider when he walked in the room. Joan knew, also, because Jay had described the encounters to her in the past. J.D. Brown took a deep breath and held his shoulders erect.

For as long as Jay could remember, there were always stories about gynecologists who had sexual liaisons with patients. Some stories involved patient seduction of doctors. At other times there were tales of abuse by physicians of unwilling patients. There had even been anecdotes of physicians who actually had intercourse with patients who were in stirrups in examining rooms. Jay believed strongly that all these situations were grossly exaggerated. He was also certain that gynecologists who claimed they were constantly the object of seduction, created an atmosphere that was conducive to such behavior. As far as Jay was concerned, he had never been placed in a compromising position by any patient, not even Ann-Marie.

Jay pushed open the door and found what he had expected. Felicia's instructions to every gynecology patient were quite clear. They were told to remove everything except their brassieres, sit on the examining table, and cover themselves from the waist down with the sheet. No one seemed to have much difficulty following those instructions, except for Ann-Marie.

Under normal circumstances Jay Brown began the examination with a check of the patient's ears, eyes and throat. He then listened to their heart and lungs with his stethoscope. The majority of his patients never saw any other physician, so his examination extended beyond what would be considered strictly gynecological. Because of the professionalism with which he always worked, frequently it wasn't necessary for his nurse to remain in the room during the examination. Joan and Felicia wandered in and out as they were needed to assist with Pap smears, bring supplies, etc.

Jay discreetly opened the bra and uncovered one breast at a time to be checked. He re-covered each breast once the examination was completed. He then asked the patient to lie flat and after the breast examination was repeated in the recumbent position, the abdomen was checked. Finally he progressed to the pelvic examination.

The sheet remained draped across the abdomen and down beyond her knees so that the patient did not see any of her pelvic anatomy exposed during the vaginal exam. Dr. Brown worked on the opposite side of the sheet, seated and unseen by the patient. He completed the vaginal portion of the examination as quickly as possible and returned the patient once again to the seated, upright, covered position. That was what happened to the normal, average patient.

Ann-Marie was neither the normal nor the average patient. Jay knew she was not a seducer. But she was an exhibitionist.

As Jay opened the door he received a warm and jovial greeting from a strikingly handsome woman. She turned toward him, threw her arms wide apart, and thrust out her chest so that her quite adequate bosom appeared to stand at attention.

"Hi Dr. Brown. Long time no see."

The first time it occurred, Jay had to admit he was somewhat distracted. But, of course, that was its purpose. By now Jay was prepared for what his approach to Ann-Marie needed to be. It was not yet time to take action.

Jay nonchalantly responded, "Good morning Ann-Marie."

The remainder of her body was completely uncovered as well. Her next step would be repeated every time.

"Oh! Before we start this hateful exam I must show you something I found in the newspaper about proper nutrition."

Completely naked, she bounced off the table and skipped over to the chair in the far end of the room where she had left her purse on the floor. With her back to her doctor, she proceeded to bend over from the waist down, her legs straight, to find the item. While Jay Brown was directly "mooned," he smiled and wondered how many times in the past Ann-Marie had gone through this performance.

With a quick change of position she turned and walked over to him, as casually as any fully dressed person might in a day to day conversation. But she was still stark naked.

As she began to hand him the clipping, Jay was already prepared. In his hand he held a sheet. Without any comment, or being judgmental in any way whatsoever about her state of dress, he simply wrapped the sheet around her like a sarong and said, "Well, shall we get on with the exam? I'll read this in the other room."

It happened that way every time. She may have noticed that the shock value of the first encounter had somewhat diminished, but it was something she apparently enjoyed. Perhaps in a past life Ann-Marie had been Lady Godiva.

———————

The remainder of the day passed uneventfully until he received a beep on the intercom from Joan. He picked up the phone.

"We've got another second opinion request from Greater National Health and Life. And guess what? It's a case of Louie Crown."

She said it with concern in her voice and Jay understood.

More than two years had passed since the problem with the insurance companies began. Jay had openly expressed the idea among obstetricians that it was a good idea for them to participate in second opinion programs.

"How else could there be controls on unnecessary surgery?" he would ask.

Joan, never one to pull punches when she spoke with him, would tell him that she thought he was having a little difficulty with his brain.

"Don't you understand that a significant portion of the staff doesn't want those types of controls?"

That was when Greater National Health and Life, one of the largest companies which sold health insurance, made demands that such a program be initiated. The staff found an easy way out of that. They would refuse to provide any second opinions. For a while that left Greater National stumped. That is until Dr. J.D. Brown agreed to do them. Now some of the doctors on the staff began to view him as a real problem, and dispensable.

Jay had wrestled with the decision for some time before he decided to participate. He illogically thought that he would avoid any problems with the staff if he accepted only a minimal fee, less than half of what the insurance company offered to pay. He was certain that would demonstrate to the remainder of the staff that he did not do it for economic gain. What he didn't understand was that the staff didn't give a damn how much money Jay earned. They just didn't want him to affect their income by the issuance of non-confirming second opinions which could result in the cancellation of their scheduled operations.

As the months passed the problem became more serious. Jay found that he was in agreement with only about half the scheduled operations. However, his rejections fell repeatedly on the same small portion of the staff. Their anger and hostility about what happened, as a direct result of Jay's actions, was hardly subdued. He received angry phone calls from some of those doctors whose cases he had rejected. Louis Crown had been burned by Jay Brown several times already.

Jay Brown was not stupid. But a wide assortment of thoughts moved through his head.

Why am I doing all of this? It's obvious that I'm not making any headway! Even if I changed this minute share of the entire medical community, would it change anything in the big picture? Why do I have this unending compulsion to change the world?

Chapter Eleven

The First Step

$\mathcal{R}$andall Royal's delay tactic had worked. Discussions about Cesarean sections were put off until 1983 when Alley Stoddard took over his role for at least two years. Even then, Jay's attempt to get the staff to look more closely at the Cesarean section rate fell on deaf ears—until late in 1983.

It was inevitable that this day would arrive. The article in the Austin Star was the last straw. Instead of breaking the camel's back, this one cracked open a woman's belly.

Jay was never able to get a handle on the excesses in gynecologic surgery at Sam Rayburn Hospital as a surgical assistant. Only in his early days in Austin had he seen extreme examples of abuse in gynecologic surgery. He had heard occasional references by the more ethical members of the staff about the terrible practices of several of the other physicians, but these were usually in the course of humorous conversations. Even the most reputable of them had no inclination to take action against any other members of the department.

There were many times when he heard about Dr. Crown's reputation for the return of his patients post-operatively to the operating room to control bleeding, later the same day as the surgery. Whenever one of Crown's patients took a downhill turn in the hours subsequent to surgery, Jay heard the banter about Crown's "great" surgical technique.

Now that the group had dissolved, Jay's concerns about Louis Crown were part of the framework of the general quality of the staff at Sam Rayburn Hospital.

Jay was bewildered by how Crown maintained a position of power within the Department, with his questionable reputation as a physician. But his weaknesses as a physician were overpowered by his leadership qualities, his speaking ability and the charm of his French dialect. His greatest protection lay in the nearly non-existent Peer Review at the hospital.

At monthly obstetrical meetings, statistics were reported quickly and ignored. It was a practice to which Jay Brown was accustomed from his experiences in New York. Even if one had any particular interest it could hardly matter. What kind of significance could be applied to: "There were 62 major gynecologic procedures and 74 minor procedures during the month. There were no operative deaths and the morbidity has not been calculated. Now on to ..."

No one had access to the cases themselves. Jay Brown knew that it was impossible to do in Texas what he had been able to do as Chairman back in New York. There was no way he could meander into the Medical Records Department and say that he wanted all of last month's charts pulled from the racks and left in a stack for him to review. He couldn't show up after office hours and spend the entire evening in the Record Room and review whatever he pleased or spend four to six hours in the examination of all the complications in order to analyze them. He would not be allowed to pull the pathology reports on each individual operation and cross check them against the initial history and physical examination to determine whether there was a proper correlation between the indication for surgery and what in fact was found at the operating room table.

Jay often longed for those great days in the past that he remembered so well. He had been trained in his earlier years at the feet of two great and challenging physicians, Dr. Isadore Snapper, world renowned as an internist, and Dr. David Spain as a pathologist. Once a week in front of the entire staff, residents and interns were called upon to present the most important cases throughout the hospital in terms of complications or questionable treatment. It was not Grand Rounds. It was the much more frightening Morbidity and Mortality Conference.

It was not just the members of the staff who came faithfully to hear the combination of medical brilliance, adroit witticism and personal attack, which ranged from the subtle to the outright abusive. Physicians from surrounding hospitals, some quite distant, would regularly attend. For those on the staffs of other hospitals, there was no stress as they ran no risk of being the subject of the verbal abuse. They would attend either to learn or just for the fun of listening to others who faced the challenge of two great medical minds.

Spain and Snapper had tremendous respect for each other, but it was not unusual for them to disagree on a specific point of medical therapy. When the two giants bantered back and forth, laughter rose from everyone in attendance. Dr. Spain did have one tremendous advantage. As the pathologist who treated no one, but was privy to the absolute answers by virtue of the possession of the surgical specimen or autopsy findings, it was difficult for anyone to be able to challenge him. His opinions were based on final and absolute information, which as opposed to everyone else, were never considered theoretical.

Dr. Snapper, already well into his seventies, was seated on the front row and faced the presenter. He or she was generally more than a little nervous, especially so if it was in July when the training year had just begun, and it was the first conference. A young intern presented the case and its conclusion, or if the patient was still hospitalized, the progress up to that day. There was a silence and a long pause as the crowd of physicians, especially the private physician whose case they discussed, awaited the comments of the All Knowing One.

"Dr. Smith," he would say in a long drawn out monotone voice, "did you ever consider doing a Bence-Jones Protein on this patient before you subjected her to all these other studies?"

Smith would clear his throat and then clear his throat once again, "We, uh, we uh,… did do it. I uh, think, uh, twice,… and it was negative, uh, both times."

"Then I would suggest," slowly spoke Dr. Snapper, "that you did it wrong twice. This is definitely a case of Multiple Myeloma."

Dr. Snapper turned to his resident, his personal resident who spent the entire year in the company of this genius. He gave the resident instructions. By this time his speech pattern had turned from slow to authoritative.

"Bring me a urine specimen from the patient NOW and…" He rattled off a list of laboratory equipment he required.

No one flinched or was even surprised at the suggestion that in the very middle of this hospital conference Dr. Snapper would perform a laboratory test to prove his point. There was nothing orthodox about the way he ran his hospital. He did it with authority and fear—fear that if one's behavior as a physician was sloppy, he or she would be openly ridiculed in front of their peers.

In Jay's daydreams about the past he realized that that could never happen today. No one would be allowed to make a private physician appear a fool, as Snapper did. Never would Dr. Spain be able to ask some physician how he could have made such a "dumb diagnosis" when the autopsy findings verified the egregious error. It was unheard of in this medical environment. In this new world, men of that ilk were quickly eliminated from their positions of authority. Hospitals learned to look at the bottom line. Physicians who brought in a lot of cases, surgical or medical, were the ones who kept the institution afloat. If their work wasn't the best, that was a pity. But they were not to be criticized too severely, and certainly not discouraged in their admission practices, which were economically worth more to the hospital than brilliance. The hospitals didn't promote bad medicine. They just turned their heads slightly.

But the article in the Star proved to be more than Jay could tolerate. A young inquisitive reporter, Jack Rappaport, had written a story about the rising rate of Cesarean sections in the Austin hospitals. Unfortunately, he was more acquisitive than inquisitive. Instead of delving into the data directly, he accepted the hospitals' decisions that he would acquire the data as they reported it to him.

"You see, Jack, we have a problem with allowing you to review the data and records yourself. There is an issue of confidentiality involved and we have to respect the rights of our patients. Otherwise, we would have no difficulty. But it doesn't present any problem, because we have all the statistical data collected and we would be glad to provide it to you."

Jay knew better. If they really wanted to, they could present all the information with hospital numbers alone. But it was all so reminiscent of how governments, caught up in a bind they want to keep quiet, utilized the concept that the information could be released due to national security reasons. Jay, who had seen the remarkable hubris of men in power, understood when information was kept under wraps. Somebody, or a lot of somebodies, had something to hide. There was a lot to hide here.

Jack Rappaport accumulated the data provided by the hospitals and reported it on the front page of the Sunday Austin Star as a special investigative report. He was quite pleased. He believed that it would have significant shock value when the public found that the Cesarean section rate had climbed to approximately thirty percent in all the private and voluntary hospitals in the city.

Jay had no knowledge of the ongoing investigation before it appeared in the newspaper. He was the ultimate outsider at the hospital. No piece of information about the administration of health care reached his ears until it was known by the community at large.

Even though the Operating Room data was unidentifiable and irretrievable to him, the obstetrical data was somewhat different. Each month there had to be a report, no matter how quickly it was pushed aside, which revealed the number of deliveries, the number of Cesarean sections, the complications, etc. No one could get information in the O.R. except those working there. The labor and delivery suite, to the contrary, was an open suite. Obstetricians sat around in there, or wandered in and out all day, as they waited for their laboring patients to deliver. The section rate may have been in the range of 30% for the other hospitals in the city, but Jay Brown knew that the rate at Sam Rayburn Hospital was considerably higher. He also had some suspicion about how many were unnecessary.

As he read the article he felt the tightening in his stomach that he had experienced whenever he thought of the abuse that went on within the profession which meant so much to him. In his utter state of frustration he picked up the phone and dialed.

"God damn it Alice. Did you see this morning's Star?"

"What do you want from me, Jay? I read it and I went on to the editorial page, the financial section and the funnies. I read the obituaries and was really upset that Pat O'Brien had died. Didn't you just love, "The Knute Rockne Story," "The Fighting 69th" and… what was that other one?"

"Alice! You do know what you read is a lie… don't you?"

"Jay," plaintively, "Jay, what do you want?"

"Alice, are you going to ignore it? Do want things to get progressively worse because no one has the courage to do anything about it?"

"You know what your problem is, Jay? You think you're still the head of the department. I don't like to talk to you this way, but you're shit here. You're not even shit. Shit is something they have to have. You, they can get rid of completely. You're less than shit."

"Gee Alice, I feel better already."

"Come on Jay, stop kidding. You can't do anything around here except get your ass blown off. Let it lie. Take care of your practice. Do a great job. Keep your nose clean and let the rest of the world go by." And after a long pause, "P-l-e-a-s-e, Jay."

"I can't do it Alice. I've watched quietly too long. I'd like you to help me. I'll make certain not to expose you in any way."

There was agony in Alice Crain's voice as she asked, "What are you planning to do?"

"I want to get accurate data and present it to the department. I'm not going to go to the media. They don't have to be nervous that I'll blow the whistle on them. But I know the rate is much higher. And I know it's that high because some members of the department have unconscionable statistics. I think we can show that some obstetricians here are doing more than half their deliveries by Cesarean section, while others are quite good."

"But they probably already have that data," Alice pleaded hoping to dissuade Jay.

"I also think we can show that there are an inordinate number of cases done just after five in the evening, so that those doctors don't have to wait until the middle of the night to deliver those babies. I think we can show that the sections get done mostly before office hours, at lunch time or right after office hours are over, just for convenience. I'm certain we can demonstrate that a generalized massive abuse is going on with C-sections and that the department needs to take internal action to correct it. Now is that terrible, Alice?"

"No, Jay. And the entire department is going to applaud you because you were able to see through their inadequacies and lead them into an honest and decent life. Jay Brown, you've lost your mind."

"All right, hold it. At first they won't be thrilled. But I want to try to get them to understand that it will not help to tell the press a lie. If the word accidentally leaked out, the Department would really be in a jam. This way the problem can be controlled before it becomes a disaster for the whole hospital."

"That's not the way the obstetricians will look at it, Jay." And then, because he had the ability to reach into her conscience more than she wanted him to, she asked "What do you want me to do?"

———

Jay had decided to tell no one other than Alice, not even Joan. Office hours generally ended late on Friday, as there were always a few women who called in that afternoon and asked to be seen immediately. Whatever their problem was, their concerns about having difficulty over the weekend led them to attempt to get it resolved before Saturday arrived. It was usually close to six o'clock before Jay, Joan and Felicia left.

It was common for Jay to return to the hospital to make one last check of his patients. He usually wandered into the obstetrical suite during that visit. As a result, his appearance at that hour was not considered unusual. Five consecutive Fridays had passed since he started to initiate the scheme he had in mind. Each previous Friday there were patients in labor as he stopped by, either with their doctors in the vicinity or on call to come in once the delivery was imminent. Each time he gave the labor room nurses a friendly "hello" and "good-bye" and went on his way. But today, the circumstances had changed.

Sheila Ryan was sitting in the center of a U-shaped nurses' station. In front of her was a crossword puzzle.

"What's a five letter word for laziness?"

"Try, uh, uh, sloth."

"Hey that looks good. Thanks, Dr. Brown."

"All quiet around here?"

"Yeah... Mary, Barbara, Sally and Liz have all gone down to the cafeteria for dinner and left me here to slave over this puzzle. You haven't got someone in labor, have you?"

"No! There's no one even in false labor. But I do have some work to do here. I've got a recertification application for the Ob-Gyn Boards that I've got to fill out. They require that I provide them with information about all my deliveries for the past few years. If you don't mind I'll just take the Delivery Book back into the doctor's lounge and not bother any of you out here."

"Sure Dr. Brown. No problem. Can I help you in any way?"

"No. Thanks a lot. I've got to review the data myself and sort out my cases. I'll just take the last two years, if that's all right. I'll bring them right back to you as soon as I'm done."

"O.K. Doc. Don't work too hard. It is the weekend. You ought to be out trottin' around the town."

They all knew that he was unmarried, but they knew very little of his social life. Since he was such an eligible bachelor, some at the hospital, who thrived on such conversation, rumored that he was gay. But there were sufficient people who had seen him out on dates with women in the community, so the rumors never caught on.

With two very large journals tucked underneath his right arm, and his brief case in his left hand, he pushed open the swinging back door that exited from the main area of the obstetrical suite. It led him into a corridor into which several other doors opened. There was no lounge area where physicians congregated. Two of the rooms each had a desk and two bunk style beds, an upper and a lower—sleep rooms for doctors who were conscientious enough to stay in the hospital if their patients were in labor in the middle of the night. The layout of the rooms was not very well planned. It was difficult for a physician sleeping in the upper bunk to respond to a telephone call, so the hospital placed a phone on each bed in the corner, alongside the pillow. In that way the physician who slept there would have easy access to the phone. It was, of course, especially convenient to the doctor in the upper bunk.

At the end of the corridor a door led to a shower room and two toilets. There was also an adjacent locker area where doctors could change into their scrub suits.

Jay entered one of the two sleeping rooms and placed the journals on the desk. His next step was to re-enter the corridor. Slowly he pushed open the door to the second sleeping room. It was empty. He wanted to be absolutely certain that no one else was present. Finally, he walked to the end of the corridor, entered the bathroom and checked for legs under the doors of the cubicles. There were none. He returned to the original sleep room.

No female obstetricians occupied this back area. When their numbers became significant, a separate set of facilities was arranged for them on the opposite side of the suite.

Having verified that no one else was in the back area, he sat down on the lower bunk and dialed the phone. If he removed the phone from its base, a hospital operator would answer within a matter of five to ten seconds, unless a hospital extension or a "nine" were dialed to get an outside line.

"Alice, I'm here and waiting. The coast is clear. The place is empty. Come in the back entrance. I'm in sleep room number one. Try to make it as quickly as possible. I'll start without you."

Jay had laid out all the plans with Alice more than a month ago. Each Friday she waited to see if he would call to say that "the coast was clear." As she hung up she wondered to herself, *"How did I get into this position?"*

"We've got to do this as efficiently as possible. I don't believe we'll get a second chance."

Though the description of the procedure Jay wanted Alice to follow was offered in a clear concise manner, Alice could hear the tension in his voice. Anxiety and fear had increased his adrenaline output significantly. It was partly the fear that they might be caught which made this night such a challenge. Alice knew as well that was part of the reason she was there. The tension had overtones related to the never fulfilled personal relationship she had once hoped for with Jay Brown.

Alice had been home all day. She slept for several hours after her night shift on Thursday. Friday night she was off duty and planned to spend the evening in. She had changed into a robe and was preparing dinner. The evening news was on when the call came. She quickly threw on a simple blouse and a plaid skirt. A pair of pink sneakers completed her outfit and she rushed to the hospital.

She parked in the employees' lot and briskly walked toward the rear entry of the Delivery suite. She had not noticed that a car had pulled in just before her. The door opened just as she reached the back bumper and out stepped Stan Byler.

"Hi Alice, coming in for another shift?"

Everyone on the staff knew Alice well. It was no secret that she and the chief, Jack Marsh, were a couple. They knew of Marsh's non-marriage and it was just assumed that Alice was his girl, now and permanently. In the Texas' ol' boy network, it was sort of a matter of possession.

"Oh, uh, hi Dr. Byler," she said with some trepidation in her voice.

"You cain't be comin' back to work in those duds."

"No, uh, not in these. Have a nice weekend."

She walked away quickly and hoped that he was not right behind her. Byler was not one of her favorites. He was a mediocre obstetrician and definitely one of the ol' boys. When she heard obstetricians speak in a derogatory way about Jay, it was not uncommon for Byler to be one of them.

Her relationship with Marsh was so open that at times she would be with him in the company of other obstetricians. Her apartment was now a place where some of them met for poker games. On those nights, when Marsh was the host, he didn't want to bring them back to his house.

She wasn't particularly fond of the games or of some of the doctors who played in them. When they played there it would go into the wee hours of the morning. On working nights Alice would leave and go to the hospital by 10 P.M. If she were not on call, by 10:30 she would say goodnight and go off to bed.

What happened subsequently reflected the outcome of the game. If Jack lost at poker, he would straighten up the apartment and head for home. But if he was a winner, especially a big winner, at about 2 A.M. she would feel a hand under her nightgown as it moved up her thigh, and he would, in a matter of moments, satisfy his needs. She soon learned that it wasn't the sex that was important for him. He wanted to share the evening's victory with her. It wasn't necessary for her to reach a climax, but she understood that there had to be some response. Marsh wasn't into necrophilia. As a compromise, she found that a few deep moans would suffice. Her love affair with Jack Marsh was very important to her. She never turned him down or made him feel unwanted. She assumed that it was one of the reasons he wanted to spend his nights with her rather than with Claudia.

———

Byler had been called about a patient having a miscarriage and had come to the hospital to do a D. & C. That was his custom in every miscarriage, whether or not the procedure was indicated. After he spoke with Alice he walked toward the main entrance of the hospital and headed for the operating suite.

The arrangements had already been made by phone, although Byler had not seen the patient since the miscarriage began. He had received the call from the Emergency Room physician, where he had sent her to be checked. A call from the patient earlier in the day about the bleeding had started the process.

"Dr. Byler, Mrs. Morales began bleeding early this morning. She was about seven weeks pregnant."

"Yes, she called me early this evening, and I sent her in there."

"She developed strong cramps shortly before she came in here. I examined her and there was tissue coming out of the cervical os. I was able to lift it out and the bleeding and cramps have now subsided."

"Good. Get a CBC and a type and cross match of her blood. Admit her and set her up for a D&C as soon as possible and I'll be on my way."

The Emergency Room physician knew that Mrs. Morales had completed her miscarriage and nothing further needed to be done. But the patient belonged to Dr. Byler and he had no choice but to go ahead with the instructions. From their exposure to so many patients cared for by different physicians on the staff, the Emergency Room doctors knew firsthand how many unnecessary operations were done. They also knew which doctors did them. But it never occurred to them to speak to anyone in authority about that. It was just the way the system worked.

They weren't the only ones aware of what happens in the hospital. Certain other physicians had even greater exposure to the abuse. There was always an anesthesiologist present who could clearly recognize when the operation being performed was needless. But their income was tied to the total volume of surgery, necessary and unnecessary. Only a self-destructive anesthesiologist would blow the whistle.

Radiologists were knowledgeable as well. And certainly, no one more so than the pathologists who examined the surgical specimens. But it was not a pre-arranged conspiracy. It did not result from an agreement. It was not even the outcome of a single conversation. It was simply a conspiracy of silence. It was just understood that the system worked that way and no action could, or should, be taken. Stan Byler came to the Operating Room and did his D. & C. It was simple as that.

Stan Byler saw nothing improper in his actions. He had not caused the miscarriage. He hadn't planned it or hoped for it. But on the other hand there was no reason he should suffer economically as a result. The fee for the D&C was about one third of his obstetrical fee. When the separate office charges for the beginning of the pregnancy were added in, it became about 40%. That was pretty good if one considered that the obstetrical care would have involved many more visits, plus all the time during labor and delivery and the course afterward in the hospital.

The D&C took him ten minutes at the most, and he sent the patient home first thing in the morning. Some patients who had their D&C early in the day didn't even stay overnight. He reassured Mrs. Morales that there was no problem and that the miscarriage was just her way of getting rid of a defective pregnancy. He encouraged her to try again in about two months. Stan Byler would then have her back to pay her full obstetrical fee.

There was no thought in Stan Byler's mind about how this had increased his income. There was no plan to abuse the patient for financial gain. The amazing part of the process was that over the three decades he had practiced obstetrics, he had learned to rationalize a number of procedures as being important for the patient's health. The existence in the medical literature of information to the contrary was a non-factor. Stan Byler did not "waste" his time in the study of any medical publications, except for a few throw-away journals. Those publications gave him some insight about new procedures. There was always the possibility that they could be added to his armamentarium.

Even when Stan added a new procedure he had no knowledge of whether or not what he did had been definitively identified as being to the patient's advantage. It was just another new test, another new procedure, another new operation.

About the D&C, Byler actually did not even know that they should only be done for certain indications. He was unaware that invasive procedures in the uterine cavity, though at times necessary, had an increased risk of subsequent infertility, or other non-obstetrical problems. So Stan Byler did his D&C without another thought. The patient felt it was to her advantage. And everyone who knew better, remained silent.

"Powers- Vaginal delivery"

"Marsh- Vaginal delivery"

"Gresham- Vaginal delivery"

"Tyson- Repeat Cesarean section"

"Freeman- Vaginal Delivery"

"Byler- Primary Cesarean section, 5:27 P.M. Failure to progress. Fetal weight, seven pounds, one ounce. Seven hour labor. No stimulation with pitocin. One previous full term vaginal delivery."

"Brown- Vaginal delivery."

"Tyson- Primary Cesarean, 7:04 P.M. Failure to progress. Fetal weight, six pounds, fourteen ounces. Nine hour labor. One hour and twenty five minutes of pitocin stimulation. First pregnancy."

"That's the end of May. O.K. Start a new sheet for June. We're making progress but we've got to move more quickly. We won't get another chance. That's almost one fourth done."

There was tremendous tension in the room. Alice said absolutely nothing. She just wrote as quickly as Jay could speak. More than that, there seemed to be almost an absence of breathing on her part. As would be expected in any situation this stressful, she was riveted to the job at hand and unconsciously held her breath.

Jay looked at her and saw that glazed look of anxiety. "Alice, you're allowed to breath. We don't have to be that quiet."

He remembered a ski instructor who once told him that the

anxiety and tension beginning skiers feel as they slide down the hill causes them to hold their breath. The result was that their bodies received less oxygen and they tired more quickly. The teacher told him to sing on the way down. There was no way one could sing and hold their breath. But, under these circumstances Jay didn't have the nerve to tell Alice to sing.

They were well into July of the second year when they heard the sound of the outer door of the corridor as it opened. Both Alice and Jay remained silent and motionless. Everything stopped as the footsteps began.

Chapter Twelve

Caught

*W*ith great composure, even though his heart raced at more than 100 beats per minute, Jay rose from his chair, leaned toward the door and flipped out the light. At the same time he whispered to Alice, authoritatively, "Stand up."

In a flash he loosened his belt and dropped his pants to his knees. He turned toward Alice, who stood speechless. He grasped her skirt as he pushed her back toward the lower bunk. She offered no resistance. Alice trusted him implicitly. As she fell backward onto the bed, he pulled the front of her skirt up and threw it over her face. Then he came down forcefully upon her. Her head fell back against the bed and hit the telephone in the corner. He wished that he had not been so rough, but there was little time for civility. He quickly yanked down his jockey shorts. The door opened and the light began to slide into the room. The image was of Jay's bare bottom as he thrust himself between the legs of a woman whose skirt had been pulled up.

With his face against hers, and his lips up against her right ear, he whispered, "Moan, loud, please."

Alice, who was in a state of shock, followed the instructions faithfully. Her performance was superb. She had feigned orgasm many times in the past to please an insecure partner.

The light from the hallway did not disappear immediately, as Jay would have hoped. Stan Byler was less shocked than amused at the sight. He enjoyed the opportunity to take a long look. He had no way to know whose behind he saw in front of him.

Only a portion of the skirt had been pulled up over Alice's head. It was sufficiently high so that Byler could not see Alice's face. But the corner of the skirt was folded back on itself so that the plaid pattern could be seen. And, more than that, the pink sneakers were a giveaway. Stan Byler thought, *"That's Alice Crain getting humped."* But it somehow didn't look like Jack Marsh doing the deed.

Byler closed the door and walked back out to the nurses' station.

"Hey, Sheila, is that Dr. Marsh sleepin' out back there in the doctor's room?"

"Oh! Did Dr. Brown fall asleep back there? He was trying to review his records from the delivery book and I guess he just got too tired. Well, he'll bring the books back when he wakes up."

"Yeah, ahm sure he will.... So he needs to review his records."

"Something about recertification I think he said."

Stan Byler turned and walked out the hospital entrance of the delivery suite, while his mind raced. *If Jay Brown was beating Jack Marsh's time with Alice Crain, why would he bring her into the hospital to fuck her? Why wouldn't he just take her back to his apartment or hers? If for some dumb reason he wanted to do that, why would he borrow the delivery room books first, when anybody who might need them would just wander back there and find them together? Maybe something else is going on.*

"Sally, have you got line seven?"

"No Toots, I'm stuck on four. Will you pick it up?"

Toots Schultz had been a telephone operator at Sam Rayburn for twenty three years and had seniority by far over any of the other operators. Now just past sixty, she was matronly and lived alone. Matronly was actually a kind description of her. Her skin was deeply wrinkled. She looked as if she might have spent a considerable portion of her life imbibing excessive amounts of alcohol, but if that were the case, one could not tell from her on-the-job behavior. She was a loyal and devoted employee who never missed a day's work. She was always totally sober at the switchboard. Her dress style, at best, could be called frumpy. And no one who had ever stopped by the small operator's working area had ever seen her without a cigarette hanging out of the side of her lips.

The job itself was very tedious and demanding, as it was an extremely hectic switchboard. Many others had worked there for short intervals of time and quit out of the frustration as they tried to satisfy a multitude of simultaneous caller requests. Not infrequently, operators would suffer the abuse of callers who could not understand the reason for delays as they attempted to reach their party. Even that was mild in comparison to the hostility and verbal abuse Toots was subjected to when someone was accidentally cut off. But to Toots, her job was very special. It was a way to serve a group of individuals for whom she had enormous respect. There was nothing within reason she would not do for "her doctors."

Toots knew just about everything there was to know about these physicians. She was certain they were the best anyone could find anywhere. They were her friends, and she would do what friends do for each other.

"Toots, I don't want anyone to know I'm leaving the hospital, not even the little lady. So if there are any calls just tell them I'm tied up in the O.R."

She had taken many calls such as that over the years. And whatever the request, that was all right with her. Her primary duty was to all those "wonderful Sam Rayburn docs".

Toots had known Jack Marsh from the day he began his residency, more than twenty years ago, when he first started at Sam Rayburn. She was crazy about him. She chose him as her doctor within the first year after he began his practice. Among all the physicians, he was her favorite. It was to be expected because the relationship between a woman and her gynecologist is generally a strong bond. And Toots got to know Marsh better than most women have the opportunity with their physician.

She knew all his shortcomings, especially in marriage, but that didn't change the fact that he was entitled to special treatment.

"Hello, who are you trying to reach?" Toots asked.

There was no response.

"Who are you calling?"

And then in a distant voice:

"Jay, do you think we can get up now?"

"No, just stay still for a little longer. Am I hurting you?"

"Maybe just my feelings. After all that pushing and bouncing, it doesn't feel like you got any erection."

"I don't think I'd exactly call that making love."

"Well whatever it's called, it's the first time I've ever had intercourse with my pants still on."

"Whoever opened that door probably enjoyed watching it more, than we enjoyed the performance. It took him a long time to close it," Jay responded.

"Are you sure it was a him?"

"None of the women come back through here. Oh, but it could have been one of the nurses looking for the delivery room book. If so, she would have known it was me, but not you."

Alice couldn't help saying, "Would she have recognized you by your rear end, Dr. Brown? I know I would have enjoyed it more from the door instead of here with someone making believe they were fucking me."

Even with his sense of humor, Jay couldn't laugh. "You know what I mean. They knew I was back here."

Toots listened with her mouth agape and decided to listen more. Alice's head had knocked the phone off the hook and the line was open beside her.

As he reassured Alice, Jay said, "I'm certain they wouldn't recognize you. They could only see your legs."

Toots could not disconnect. She was shocked. Alice sounded like Alice Crain and she was in the Obstetrical sleep room with Dr. Brown. *Oh my God!* she thought, as she put her finger against her lips for Sally to remain quiet. Sally had never seen Toots' eyes open as wide as they were that very moment.

"Let's hope that the sight of us there kept the attention of our voyeur, so that the books and papers on the desk weren't noticed," Jay added.

Alice gave a slight giggle as she said, "If I saw your ass swinging around like that, I wouldn't notice anything else in the room."

And then her voice turned serious. "There have been times in the past when I hoped that we would be in this situation, but not for some time now. Right now I'm a little shook up. Don't you think we'd better get out of here?"

Jay raised his body from hers, stood still and listened intently. He pulled up his shorts in the dark and then his pants. Slowly he cracked open the door. The hall was clear. The door closed and he turned on the light to find Alice now seated at the edge of the bunk, her skirt back down.

Toots listened as the voices appeared more distant.

"Alice, we're so close to the end. If you've still got the nerve, let's finish collecting this last little bit of data before we go."

Alice didn't answer. She got up and moved back to the desk.

"Laredo- Primary Cesarean section., 11:56 A.M.. fetal distress. Weight 8 pounds one ounce, four hours of labor, Pitocin induction. One previous vaginal delivery."

"Stoddard- vaginal delivery"

"Brown- Primary Cesarean section. 4:21 A.M. Failure to progress. Weight 9 pounds 8 ounces. 21 hours of labor, Pitocin stimulation. First baby.

"Well, Dr. Brown, it appears you did some sections too. Is this one necessary?"

Alice tried to inject some levity into the air that had become much more than just tense. They moved along even more rapidly in the hope of completing their work without another interruption. All the while Toots listened and wrote down the same information while Sally maintained the hospital phone system by herself. Callers found that there were delays in getting an operator to respond, but Toots would not get off that line as long as it was open. Whatever was going on she felt certain that her "Doctor Marsh" would want to know about it.

Within forty minutes everything was completed. Jay quickly glanced out the corridor. It was empty. He sent Alice off and out the back way. Then with the two books tucked under his arm he returned to the nurses' station in the delivery suite.

Sheila was still seated out front, working her crossword puzzle. Several other labor room nurses were there as well. Jay tried to appear totally relaxed and casual as he laid the books down and said to Sheila, "Thanks, now I'll be able to get my application in."

But a dagger went through his gut when Sheila looked up and smiled and said, "You need to get some rest, Dr. Brown. Dr. Byler stopped back there and saw you asleep, when you needed to get this work done. He thought for a minute you were Dr. Marsh until I told him it was you."

"Oh... yes... I guess I dozed off for a few moments. Thanks for all your help."

Jay knew he was dead in the water. Just how much Stan Byler knew he wasn't certain. Jay was absolutely convinced he had to present this material as quickly as possible. He had to be out front before anyone challenged the motivation of his actions .

Did Byler know that it was Alice? Should I tell Alice who had opened the door and that Stan Byler at least knew it was me? What could she do if she knew? He decided it would be better to avoid even greater anxiety and assume that he was the only one who could be identified. Alice was less likely to act strangely in the upcoming days if unaware of what he knew.

Toots listened for a few more minutes after all the voices stopped. She disconnected herself from the line and paged Dr. Jack Marsh. There was no response. She then put in a call to his paging device. Within a few moments her board lit up.

"This is Dr. Marsh. You'all have a call for me?"

"Dr. Marsh, this is Toots on the board. Are you coming back to the hospital tonight?"

"Ah don't have any patients comin' in that I know of. Is somethin' goin' on?"

"It can wait until morning. But, could I PLEASE get a chance to talk with you?"

"Well, ah'm off for the weekend, but if it's important, ah'll come in."

"No, that's O.K. Can I see you on Monday?"

"Do you need an appointment in the office, Toots?"

"No, it's nothing like that. I just need to talk with you. Please don't forget."

"After all these years, how could ah forget you Toots? See you on Monday."

It would be a long weekend as Toots anxiously awaited Monday. Also Stan Byler anxiously awaited the opportunity to tell his buddy that a Jew boy was humping his girl. Or was he? Alice was alone because Marsh was headed out of town to join his friends in a hunt.

Jay Brown spent the next forty eight hours in the examination of the data they had collected. He had lots of experience in the evaluation of statistics. He would learn that just what he had expected was clearly true. The Cesarean section rate was just barely shy of 40%. Five of the obstetricians had rates between 35% and 50%. One was even over 50%. It was only because four of the other doctors, including Jay Brown and Jack Marsh, were between 9% and 14%, that the hospital average was kept below 40%.

Beyond that Jay identified how many "emergencies" were done just after 5 P.M. or just before office hours. He was shocked and angered to see that emergencies almost never occurred in the middle of the night or during office hours.

He thought to himself, *Those emergencies certainly do have a nice way of working themselves into a convenient schedule.*

Finally, he was able to identify the average length of time that labor progressed before a decision was made to perform a Cesarean section, for each individual obstetrician. The evidence was indisputable. Certain members of the staff jumped to that conclusion with much greater rapidity than the remainder of the physicians.

By the time the weekend was done, he was overwhelmed by the evidence of abuse. Fortunately, the Department would meet on Tuesday, so the opportunity for anything to happen about his being identified before the meeting was slight. He reassured himself with the idea that Byler had no concept of what actually happened in the sleep room other than some "illicit behavior with a woman in a semi-public place." If confronted, he would simply apologize for his indiscretion.

Jay tried to think positively. He entertained conclusions that the Department would see the light. He felt even more reassured because Jack Marsh's own statistics stood out as some of the best. Marsh had never befriended Jay in any way, but Jay never assumed there was anything personal about it. *Certainly a fine obstetrician like Jack Marsh would want his department to be the best it could possibly be. Wouldn't he?*

If nothing else, these thoughts would keep Jay Brown from panic now. He needed to work diligently to be ready for Tuesday.

————

Toots looked up from her board.

"Hi. So what did you'all want to talk about to me?"

"Dr. Marsh," with a deep sigh, "can we go someplace private?"

"Sure."

"Sally, could you take care of the board for a few minutes?"

"I've got it."

Jack Marsh looked at Toots' face and thought, *"She looks like she's gonna tell me my best friend died."*

Chapter Thirteen

The Real World

*J*ay and Alice had not been aware of the phone being knocked off its base. Were it not for that accident, things might have turned out quite differently.

By late Monday morning Stan Byler was on the phone with Jack Marsh. Byler had no great love for Alice Crain and he definitely disliked Jay Brown. He relished the fact that the story he was about to tell could very well result in the permanent removal of both parties. Byler knew that Marsh considered Alice to be no less a wife to him than Claudia. He was certain Marsh would treat the entire matter as adultery, with him being cuckolded. The results could be almost anything. At least Byler hoped so.

But, by the time of the phone call, Jack had thoroughly reviewed the word-by-word conversation between Jay Brown and Alice, which he received from Toots. Understanding quite clearly what transpired, he decided he would sit tight and take no action. Everything might work out just fine by itself.

———————

"I know that some of you may be annoyed that a physician who came from another community and was welcomed and accepted by you...."

Jay thought what he said probably sounded like bull. They knew as well as he did, that he had never really been welcomed or accepted. It was now December of 1983. Six years had passed since his arrival. He was as much an outsider on this day as the day he arrived in 1977.

"But I believe that the doctors in this hospital want to practice the highest quality obstetrics. Sometimes that goal can only be reached if we look at ourselves and analyze in detail whether obstetrical practices need to be modified."

While Jay talked about his motivation and the possible value to the Obstetrical Department, the response was quite different from what he had experienced when he put forth a similar challenge years previously as the Director in New York. Then physicians who knew they could be subjected to unpleasant changes, and were fearful of the power he exerted, tried to stop any action before it ensued. Now there was only a silence. A common thought was, *You squeally son-of-a-bitch, we'll put our foot on you like an insect, twist it back and forth, and mush you into nothing.*

When he was through presenting the data and the explanations for his actions, and the assurance that it would go no further, Jay Brown sat down. There were no comments. The meeting proceeded into the next phase. It was as if not one word had ever been spoken. When the meeting ended the obstetricians gradually meandered out of the room and talked to each other about a multitude of matters, mostly non-medical. No one criticized Jay. No one spoke to Jay. No one even acted as if he were present.

––––––––––

"I know you were involved in helpin' Jay Brown collect that C-section shit that he presented to the department meetin' today... I ought to shove my boot up your ass.... First, I don't even like talkin' to you this way. I thought there was no one in the world I could trust more than you.... You really disappointed me."

Alice cried harder than she had ever cried in her entire life. She and Marsh had met back at her apartment after he called to tell her he would come over after his office hours. Not even the deaths of her parents, nor at any time in her broken marriage, had she become so overwrought. Whatever had been left of her sense of security was now shattered. She felt certain that Jack Marsh was about to tell her that their love affair was over. Their shared existence had been the zenith of her life and it was about to end.

Marsh was more than surprised by her response. It wasn't just that Alice cried. He could see the jerks and thrusts of her body with each gasp as she sucked air between sobs. There was no question in his mind about her devastation.

He withheld any support while he asked, "Is there any explanation you can give?"

It was almost impossible for her to respond, her sobs were so uncontrollable. Finally, Jack moved toward her and held her in his arms. It was a long time before she could utter a word. He held her as they sat down on the sofa.

"I... thought... I... was... doing... what... was... right."

"You were just helpin' him make me and the rest of the department look like fools. I'm gonna ask you never to help him again. I want your word."

"I swear..." she sobbed again... "I swear."

"Then I'm gonna forget this day. Like I'm gonna forget it forever. But don't you ever turn on me again. Not ever, do you hear?"

"I hear. I swear."

She held him tightly as the sobbing continued, without pause, for some length of time.

"I'm not gonna be here Thursday night for our poker game, but it's not because I'm mad. Like we're just not playin' this week. We'll be playin' again next week."

She put her hand on his belt and undid the zipper, but this was not going to be a typical sexual encounter for them. Marsh still carried a great deal of anger for her disloyalty as well as the make believe non-sexual incident in the doctor's room, which he never mentioned. She was not to have her time of slow tender foreplay that he always relished. He quickly rose, and for the only time she could remember, roughly picked her up and carried her into the bedroom. Before she knew it she was on her back while he pulled off her panties. And then, for all intents and purposes, she was raped. Marsh felt better. For that matter, Alice did as well. As sophisticated as she was in so many ways, he was her master. It was a sad commentary that she perceived herself as taking her punishment like a woman.

Steve Slack was Jack Marsh's partner. With the exception of Louie Crown, no one had greater disdain for Jay Brown than he. He assured Jack after the departmental meeting that it would be not be difficult to arrange for the destruction of Dr. Brown. Marsh was somewhat concerned about what action Slack planned. Slack assured him there would be nothing improper. It would all be laid out on Thursday at a meeting at Buddy Lane's house.

"John, Stan, Jose, Louie and, of course, Buddy will be there."

Though there was a general concern among all the department members about the action Jay Brown had taken, most of them were good practitioners who understood his point. But they didn't like the way Brown had accomplished it. They saw it as sneaky. The better obstetricians realized everyone in the department wasn't strong, but they did not like it shoved in their faces by an outsider. The general desire was to avoid political infighting in the department, and be allowed to practice medicine without having someone look over their shoulders. However, the handful that Slack selected had a particular dislike of J.D. Brown. They were motivated to utilize whatever power they could wield to get rid of him.

Slack and Marsh were at least well qualified obstetricians, and certainly above average for the department. That could not be said for Crown, Byler, Lane, Candless or Laredo. But they were all shrewd enough to know that all the power was in the hands of the head of the department and the Quality Control Committee.

Over the years that committee had changed its name several times. First known as the Audit Committee, it then became the Peer Review Committee before it was changed to its present title. Any investigation of medical wrongdoing ended up there. What could be safer than to be a member of the watchdogs? No one in the Department seemed to care very much about who watched the chicken house. The Head of the Department made all the appointments to the committees. Of the ten members in Quality Control, these six were re-appointed every year. As the Head of the Department, Marsh was an automatic member.

For several years Jay Brown had requested the opportunity to serve on Quality Control. "I've had a great deal of experience in that aspect of health care from my role as a director in the past."

"Jay, I'd be glad to put you on that committee. But like some of these fellas just enjoy doin' that police work so much, I don't have the heart to take them off. And as far as fillin' the vacant positions each year, so many others have seniority to you that it's difficult to get you on. But, don't give up hope. Like I'll get you on that committee one of these years."

Jay knew, after the first few rejections, that the promise was never to be fulfilled.

That Thursday evening, six of the members of the Quality Control Committee and Jack Marsh met at Buddy Lane's home.

From the beginning it was obvious that Slack and Crown were the ring leaders. The others were natural followers. Marsh would be out front, but he would run the show as Slack and Crown arranged it.

Crown's position was easily understood. He had a realistic fear that Jay Brown, of all the physicians he knew in his reincarnated medical life in the United States, was the one most dangerous for him. Brown and he had worked together in the call group. Crown believed that Jay "mistakenly" perceived him as inadequate professionally. He also saw Brown as the kind of troublemaker who might make his life very unpleasant. Finally, his personal animus against Jews, fueled by Monika Crown's deep seated anti-Semitism, made Brown a perfect target. It was Jay's secret collection of data that helped set all these feelings in motion.

Slack was less easily understood. His Protestant family background had not exposed him to any significant dislike of Jews. He was a handsome young doctor, the junior member of the group that evening. Through all of the years of his training he was considered quite a catch among the women he dated. As a first year medical student he fell head over heels for a Jewish nurse, several years his senior. He sincerely wanted to marry her. After almost nine months of frenzied dating and torrid love making, she told him that she could never marry a non-Jew. Subsequently, she married a Jewish classmate of his. To top it off her husband was at the very top of the class—bright and aggressive. He surpassed Steve Slack in every academic sphere. In subsequent years Slack never completely lost his anger about the loss of his "lover." From that time on he thought of her husband as a "loud mouthed Jew." He applied the same mental image to Jews he met subsequently over the years. It didn't help Jay Brown to be a New York Jew, especially not when he told the doctors at Sam Rayburn what the proper practice of medicine should be.

John Candless was pure Texas, many generations deep in that

state. John wore exquisite carved boots on every occasion. The only exception was during surgery. He was teased around the department. They said he wore them even while making love. But when his friends gave him the needle, "making love" was not the terminology used. He grew up with the belief that everyone and everything worthwhile came from Texas, and outsiders weren't welcomed or needed. Jews for that matter were weird people with strange behavior. They weren't worth much for anything except making trouble and "bein' taught a lesson for the trouble they caused." Even non-Jews not from Texas, weren't any great shakes. Jay never developed any better feeling about John Candless than he had on his first day in the hospital, when from the O.R. dressing room he heard the anti-Semitic conversation with Jack Marsh.

"So who the fuck needs this God-daimed trouble makin' kike down here? Let's string him up by his circumcised prick and send him back to New York."

"John, I'm going to ask you just one time to refrain from that language in my house. It's offensive to me and my wife. And, I've got three children around here somewhere who don't know or hear that kind of talk. You know I feel the same way about Jay Brown as you do, but let's watch the language."

Buddy Lane was a born-again Christian and talk like that was never heard in his household. The only reaction he obtained from Candless was a mumbled "shit-ass fanatic."

Lane did get into a rather strong attack on Jay Brown to indicate his support for the action to be taken. He had a generalized distaste for Brown. He suggested that Jay could threaten the security and practices of all of them. Of course, Lane was correct. Mediocre physicians like him had a realistic fear of Jay. In his condemnation of Jay, Lane made several references to his Judaism.

Stan Byler was not too bright a follower who was just glad to be included in the company that was present.

Finally there was Jose Laredo, by far the weakest of the many Hispanic doctors on the staff. He was an outsider even among them. While all the other Hispanic physicians were of Mexican origin, Laredo came from Colombia. They never took him into their inner circle. His only motivation was to achieve some minimal level of political power in the department. He couldn't care less whether Jay was a Jew or anything else. But he did care about Brown's position on the nature of medical practice and he wanted that threat eliminated.

So the group was formed and a plan was made. All were in agreement that it should be activated immediately and that other members of the staff should be utilized—but unwittingly—to spread the responsibility. Others could be given assignments to move the plan ahead, without any knowledge that any plan actually existed. Finally everyone agreed that unless absolutely necessary no further meetings would be held. And above all, no one would ever mention that this night had ever occurred. It was sworn to by all.

When everyone was gone and the children were in bed, Mary Lane felt compelled to speak with Buddy.

"Buddy, I really want to thank you for speaking that way to John Candless. I don't like that man and I never have. He's a foul mouthed, uncouth, semi-human being, whom I hate having in my house... but more than that," she took a very long pause before deciding to finish her sentence, "I despise having you conspire with him."

Knowing she couldn't leave it with that she added, "I couldn't help hearing all the plans you were making and frankly I don't understand... I don't understand the reason, and I don't understand you."

Buddy kept silent as Mary continued speaking.

"It seems from what I heard, that Jay Brown is going to be destroyed because you just don't like the things he has said. Or am I mistaken? Is it just because he's a Jew?"

"No! It's not that."

"Now I heard you, Buddy Lane. I'm not even talking about all of them. I heard you make repeated references to the fact Jay Brown is a Jew. You know very well we've listened to the Reverend tell us many times that the Jews are the Chosen People and that they are destined to be in the Promised Land. You know that he's given the Jews his support. What's happened to you? Don't you listen to or believe in the sermons?"

Buddy was on the hot seat and he didn't like it at all. He shook his finger at Mary, and spoke forcefully.

"You don't understand, Mary. You don't understand at all. There are Jews and there are Jews. Some are good, but not all of them. Jay Brown is a Jew, that's true, but he's also a... a... a liar. He's... he's dishonest. He's phony and what he wants to do is hurt a lot of good Christians like you and me. That's bad. And he's got to be stopped.... You just don't understand."

"You're right, Blanchard Lane." When she became angry she reverted to his given name instead of Buddy. "I don't understand. I don't understand who you are talking about. Did you forget about that surprise birthday party I gave in your office? Jay Brown was the one who helped me arrange it without you being aware. He wasn't even invited to the party."

Mary knew the reference to the party had no significance whatsoever. But, it was the only way she knew how to express, without actually saying it, that she really liked Jay Brown. She had spoken her piece and said nothing further. There would never be another conversation between them on this matter. But one night, lying alone in her bed, while Buddy Lane was out at the hospital, for a fleeting moment she considered the possibility that she might call Jay Brown to tell him of the background of the conspiracy. No call was ever made.

As a result of the knowledge of what she didn't do, Mary Lane always had a little less respect for herself, Whenever she thought about that night, she would think of herself as an accomplice. She lost more than a little respect for Blanchard from the day of that meeting forward. But there was a family and her three children to raise. The issue of Jay Brown was put aside.

————

"There's a horse fly in here and the buzzing is driving me wacko," Jay Brown called out from his consultation room. He was at his desk with stacks of charts, while Joan was occupied with day to day clerical matters up front. It was Wednesday and there were no office hours.

"I guess it comes with a buggy."

"What does that mean? What are you talking about?" Jay shouted back to Joan.

She sat for a moment, then swiveled her chair and rose to go back to his office. As she stood at the entrance to the consultation room she saw Jay at his desk. His elbow was on the desk, his hand on his forehead. He tapped his fingers slowly back and forth, as he stared at the chart in front of him. His concentration was so complete that he was totally unaware of her presence.

"Dr. B., I've been with you a long time now."

He looked up, quizzically.

"When I came here you were light hearted. Sometimes you were silly. You drove me crazy with your constant puns. You for some ungodly reason loved them. And I loved you for it."

"What is it Joan? What is it that you want?"

"You started fighting this whole damned department and now they've got you so rattled that I haven't seen a smile on you, or heard a pun for that matter, for two weeks. And now, worse than that, you can't even catch someone else's pun. You see it's a horse and a buggy... a buggy. Have you got it?"

By now she was shouting at him. "A fly is a buggy, but a horse fly is a horse and buggy. Dr. B., you can't let them do this to you."

Jay Brown didn't respond for a while. He hated what had happened to him. Out of the clear blue, less than one month after the presentation he had made, he received the letter that brought him to this mental state. He had never experienced such an occasion in his career as a physician.

Chapter Fourteen

The Initial Assault

*I*t all began on January 27th, 1984. No one had gone into labor for several days. No surgery had been scheduled for more than a week. There was, in fact, not one patient of Jay Brown's in the hospital.

With no rounds to be made and no office hours until one in the afternoon, Jay arose somewhat later than was his custom. He was always able to adjust his internal clock to suit the circumstances. A middle-of-the-night call from a patient in labor had no adverse effect upon him. To the contrary, there was an excitement about the trip into Labor and Delivery. Many aspects of the field of obstetrics had drawn Jay, not the least of which was the anticipation of the unknown. Something new and different was always on the horizon with a patient in active labor. Everything was always in a state of flux. The uncertainty of what the next moment might bring was part of the wonder of childbirth.

Of all the spectacular developments he had seen over the years, he disliked most the ability to predetermine the sex of the newborn. Ultrasounds and amniocenteses had brought about great advances in maternity care, but he wished they had not destroyed the remarkable excitement of the discovery of the baby's gender at that moment of birth. For Jay Brown, obstetrics was a delicious mixture of an ultimate joy with the ever-present fear, no matter how unlikely, of imminent disaster that challenged him to perform at his optimum.

When there was early surgery, rounds, or office hours he rose at the crack of dawn. but should a day such as this Friday occur, Jay could adjust his circadian rhythms and sleep right through his normal waking hour.

He was engrossed in that morning's edition of The New York Times, which he read diligently ever since moving to Texas, when the phone rang.

"Dr. B., it's Joan."

Her voice sounded strange.

"Good morning," he said with a jovial lilt. "You sound terrible.

Been out at the bars all night?"

"No, but maybe I'll go tonight."

"Hey, it can't be as bad as all that. What's up?"

"A registered letter just arrived for you from the hospital and…."

"The hospital sent me a registered letter? Across the street? Are you kidding? What's it about?"

"Dr. B., I think they're after you."

———

Jay stared at the letter, and reread it for the third time. He had not uttered a word since he opened it. Joan stood in the doorway to his office and did not say a word. She waited for Jay to say something.

Dear Dr. Brown:

At a routine check of your records several concerns have been raised. There is insufficient documentation of the medical services you have provided and serious questions of improper care in a number of cases which the Committee has reviewed.

I have been asked to request your presence at our next meeting on February 16th, 1984, at 12:30 P.M. to discuss the following cases:

1. Cynthia Morales, #83-048952
2. Wanda Stone, #83-095643
3. Sandra Stanley, #83-024636
4. Delia Guerrero, #83-042957
5. Linda Cavazos, #83-068364
6. Paula Whooley, #83-073645
7. Betsy Venango, #83-025369
8. Lottie Downs, #83-048725

The charts will be available for your review by contacting Genevieve Powell in the Medical Records Department any time between now and then. However, you will not be allowed to remove them from the department.

Sincerely yours,

Christiana L. Forsythe,

Medical Staff Secretary

cc: Alexander Stoddard, Chairman Quality Control Committee

Jay continued to stare at the letter as his mind raced. One phrase hit him like a sledge hammer, right between the eyes, "insufficient documentation."

There was a characteristic about himself that Jay understood very well; his belief that if he did everything honestly and conscientiously in his care of patients, he was never in any jeopardy concerning the quality of care he provided. No one had ever filed a malpractice suit against him. No Peer Review Committee had ever questioned him.

His self-assurance, and even cockiness about his ability, had caused him to falter in a way he had recognized years before. Other physicians, some who practiced extremely poor medicine, got into the habit of writing voluminous notes about their patients. Jay, on the other hand, scribbled bits of pertinent information. He frequently skipped the frills and details. In a way, those less talented physicians were quite a bit wiser than he was. They understood the risks that were faced by physicians who practiced in the litigious environment of the 70's and 80's.

Jay always thought that the time he spent in conversation with his patients and the attention to their care were more important than the documentation. He was certain that no one perceived him as one who provided substandard care. He knew there was almost never even the most minor complication with his patients. But this flaw in his character provided him with the naive belief that he was impervious to criticism of the care he provided.

Of course the Quality Control Committee never did anything anyway. Doctors who were constantly in trouble were never even challenged. As far as he knew the Committee had not taken action on a physician for as long as he had been at the hospital.

As he continued to examine the letter he knew that Joan was right. There was a scheme to try to get him.

A meeting one week previously with Dr. Stanley Howard flashed through his mind. Howard was the Chairman of the Department of Ob-Gyn at the medical school. Jay and Stan had become friendly during his frequent trips to conferences at the school. There was no social relationship between them except for an effort that Stan Howard's wife once made to introduce Jay to a single woman friend, a psychologist in Austin.

Jay had received a message in his office from Dr. Howard. It requested a meeting at his earliest convenience. It all seemed rather strange, since Jay had no official relationship with the medical school. Later that week he went to see Stan Howard. Howard asked his secretary to close the normally open door behind her. Though Jay had no reason for concern with the semblance of secrecy, he felt somewhat anxious about the purpose of the meeting.

"Jay, I like you a lot and that's why I asked you to come in. The school's relationship with the private practitioners hasn't been spectacular. There's a basic mistrust of the ivory tower out there. I'm not going to tell you that none of that is our fault. As a result, I constantly keep my eyes and ears peeled to what's going on outside in the medical community, in the hope that with information I can somehow defuse the level of hostility."

"Are you asking me to be a spy?" Jay asked.

"Ha,... ha, ha, ha!" Stan Howard broke into uncontrollable laughter. The somber atmosphere of the meeting changed for a brief moment.

"No Jay, this is not the CIA... and I didn't call you to help me; quite the reverse."

"Stan, I think I got lost somewhere in this conversation."

"Let's sit down," Stan said as he walked toward the sofa in his office. "I want to tell you about something I've been told."

Jay followed, completely baffled about the direction of the conversation. He sat down at the opposite end of the divan.

"I've known for the past few years that you've challenged the department at Sam Rayburn to upgrade the quality of care. It's a worthwhile effort. But, as I'm sure you'll agree, it hasn't accomplished much." Howard took a long pause. "But it's the right thing to do. A-a-a-and, I would say that it probably doesn't bother anybody very much either. They saw you as sort of a gadfly, or maybe just a nuisance, but nothing more than that."

"What do you mean by "saw"? Has it changed?"

There was another pause before Stan Howard spoke, "It certainly has!"

Howard stood up and walked across the room to his window. Jay waited for him to say something further.

"You see, Jay, it's one thing to be a noodge. It's quite another to confiscate records by which to challenge them. But even more than that, you've gone too far when it involves the money in a man's wallet. The word's around that you've written a large number of negative second opinions which caused cancellations of surgery. Surgery that means money to them, surgery that YOU,... not the insurance companies, have deprived them of."

"Do you mean I should concur with operations that are absolutely unnecessary and present risks to these patients?" Jay blurted out.

Annoyed by Jay Brown's response, Howard countered, "I'm not your father, nor your mother. You do whatever the hell you want to. Don't get pissed off at me. It's just very clear if you continue that, these fellows will cut your balls off. Now it's your life. You do with it whatever you want. I've just provided you with information that's come to my attention."

Jay regained his composure. "I'm sorry, Stan. I know you mean well. But tell me... if you can, how can I watch it and turn the other way?"

"I've seen a lot of horrible things in my career. There were some that I could do something about and some that I couldn't. And as the old saying goes, thank God I could tell the difference. But I'm Chairman of this department, and a damn good one, because I know how to survive. You'll have to figure out for yourself how to survive. I can't tell you what to do."

———————

That meeting now sat front and center in Jay's brain. Forewarned is forearmed, but only if you hear the warning. Jay had put it aside. But today Stan's words had become reality.

Fully five minutes passed before Joan made a sound.

"Can I do something, Dr. B.?"

Jay turned his swivel chair around toward her. He was not one to panic and plans began to take shape in his head. He saw the look of anguish on Joan's face.

"Cheer up Joan. It's not the end of the world... It's just that you can see it from here."

It was an old joke. She had heard him say it before. This time it brought no smile to her face.

"What are we going to do, Dr. B.? I don't even understand this letter. I know these women. Did they have problems that I don't know about?"

"Joan, you know everything I do. I can't tell you for one moment what their game is. I don't know what questions they'll raise or how they want to pull this off.... I do know that I never write enough on my charts."

"But how much trouble can they invent... if there weren't any problems?"

"O.K. Joan, the first thing I want you to do is call Genevieve Powell and find out when I can see all those charts in Medical Records."

Joan turned immediately toward her desk.

Jay called after her, "Tell her I want it to be as soon as possible."

He spun his chair around again and stared at the ceiling. His initial shock was now being converted into positive energy.

He thought to himself, *If those bastards want a fight, I'll give it to them. I'll be damned if I'm going to roll over and play dead for a bunch of bullies. Some of them shouldn't even be allowed to practice medicine, let alone make decisions about who can.*

But Stan Howard's admonition diminished the bravado he felt as he pondered, *How do I deal with this? Should I just back off and let them do what they want and ignore it?... Is this the wrong time and place?*

Then what's the right time and place?... I don't know! I just don't know!

In the outer office Joan was thinking too. *This isn't going to work out well. Jay Brown's got too much pride. He doesn't know when to back off or when to stop pushing people. He hasn't learned that everyone's not perfect. They'll destroy him. Oh God, I don't know what to do.*

———————

Over the next few weeks Jay spent every free hour in the Medical Records Department. He went through each and every chart with a fine tooth comb. He searched for problems and tried to guess what issues they might raise. The lack of proper documentation could not be argued against. He knew that he would have to change that aspect of the practice of medicine for the remainder of his career. Henceforth, he wouldn't sneeze without some documentation of it on the record.

Beyond that, Jay needed to discover on what issues they would challenge him. The request to explain his actions at the upcoming meeting provided no explanation whatsoever as to the nature of their inquiry. Common sense told him that there was something either illegal or immoral about an official challenge without the charges specifically named. *Isn't the accused always to be notified of the charges before being asked to respond?*

Jay Brown would soon learn that this was not a court of law and that these hearings and subsequent ones were not held to any legal standard. There was no standard, that is, except for the rules they set for themselves and those they set for him.

The voice was muffled, "Mrs. Lansford?"

"Yes."

"I'm just a friend who met you once at a party several years ago. I'm so sorry about your baby."

"Who is this? What's your name?"

"I know it's not my business, but I felt so bad that I wanted to be sure that you knew that Dr. Brown has been named in a number of other problem cases. I think you should contact a lawyer."

Carla Lansford began to cry as she thought about her four-month-old son whose diagnosis of severe brain damage left her in a state of depression for the greater part of each day. She understood little about what had caused this terrible outcome. She knew that her baby had been delivered as a breech, its butt coming out first. Beyond that she had been told there was no explanation for what had happened to her child.

He had been released from the hospital less than a month previously. The discharge from the intensive care unit became possible once the neonatologists got him off the respirator, and he tolerated the feedings administered through a long feeding tube into his stomach. The baby's inability to swallow without choking necessitated the tube feeding.

At times Carla wondered whether she would ever be able to survive and get out of her present state of mind. She tried to deal with the disintegration of her life. A state of constant hostility existed between Carla and her husband Fred. Their marriage had not been particularly strong before this devastation. Fred spent a lot of time away from the house with his "buddies." Carla had seen this in her own father and private conversations with her mom had given her the strength to accept Fred's nights out. Sometimes he would disappear several days, when he went fishing before the baby was born. Even though, at some level, there was always the fear that there might be another woman, she blocked that out by the belief that her ready and active sexual availability satisfied his appetite. She was certain she was a good wife, and that he would never desert her.

Everything had changed since the baby. Nights out were more frequent. But even that was more pleasant than the hours Fred spent at home. Neither of them received any counseling. They had no concept of the psychological trauma of the disastrous birth they had experienced. Her dream of a perfect child was destroyed. When that dream died, she progressed through the stages of rejection, anger and depression, as if there had been an actual death. But the death of the dream was even more unbearable.

Fred avoided some of that. He rejected the idea that this poor soul could be his son. It was impossible. Fred's son would be big and strong, an athlete, and yes, a fisherman in his old man's image.

Carla was half angered and half confused. Who was this stranger on the phone who had "met her several years ago at a party?" The Lansfords had only lived in Austin for eight months. She had come to Dr. Brown in the middle of her pregnancy.

Carla blurted out "Who are you?"

"I'd rather not say. I feel so bad about this, just as I did about my own child. Let me just tell you that I've dealt with Carnahan, Davis and Drinan and they are the best malpractice lawyers in Austin."

Carla heard the woman begin to cry over the phone.

"There's no reason you and your baby should have to suffer like this at the hands of a butcher. Call them. You'll feel better."

Carla held the phone and didn't utter a sound as she heard the click. She stared in space for almost a minute. She replaced the phone on its base. Then from somewhere deep in her gut, she burst forth with a frightening shriek and...

"No! No! Nooooooooo! My baby! What did they do to my baby?"

"I've spoken to both Susan Delman and Carla Lansford. It was terrible."

Monika made no reference to her feigned tears. Even with her rather minimal standards of morality, she felt uncomfortable as she revealed the thespian effort to entrap Carla Lansford for their personal advantage.

"Monika, I would have called them myself. But you know that I couldn't disguise my voice. I'm so sorry. I suppose thot was very difficult for you to do."

"That's all right, Louie. I did it for both of us. I'll be glad when Jay Brown's gone. Who's calling the law firm?"

"Steve Slack has been in touch with their office through some source to let them know that the Quality Control Committee is looking into a number of problems with Jay Brown."

"Mrs. Lansford, I want you to know that there's no stone we'll leave unturned to get to the bottom of this matter. If your case has any merit, we will do everything possible to get the people who were responsible for this to pay for their errors. Our only goal will be to do the very best we can for you. You should understand that if we decide to accept your case, we must obtain the very finest expert witnesses to stand up for you, your family and your baby, Robert. That will all be very expensive. But you will pay nothing, unless we win the case for you."

Bill Drinan did not go into the particulars of the monetary agreement which he would have Carla and Fred Lansford sign if the firm agreed to represent them. He briefly explained that all the expenses of the case, with the exception of the fee to the attorneys would be taken off the top of the reward. From the remainder, Carnahan, Davis and Drinan would take 40%.

During the trial, when computations would be made of the cost of baby Robert Lansford's care for the remainder of his expectant life, there would be no provision made for the removal of 40% by a separate source.

But, it wasn't because of their minimal education level that the Lansfords had little understanding of the malpractice game. Jay Brown, who found the entire system of malpractice despicable, knew very few people who understood how it was played, regardless of their educational level. As much as he had battled physicians to clean up their act over the years, he also fought against what he called "the malpractice debacle." Less than one year had passed since he represented the medical community in a major debate held jointly by the local Medical Society and Bar Association.

––––––––

Myron Davis, of Carnahan, Davis and Drinan had been selected to speak in opposition to Jay Brown.

"Let's be honest about the numbers, Myron," Jay said in a very warm and friendly manner. It was a style that he found most successful in debates. It had always appeared to him that he did better with a little honey than with an arsenal of weapons.

Jay continued, "You know as well as I that what looks like 60 cents of each dollar going to the plaintiff is really done with mirrors. Actually only 27 cents of each malpractice dollar spent goes to those who suffered the consequences of an error in practice or judgment. The other 73 cents goes to the insurance companies, the plaintiff's and defense lawyers and the expert witnesses."

Myron was somewhat taken back. "But Jay, if it weren't for the contingency system, all those folks you always seem so concerned about, but who have no financial resources, would have absolutely no access to the system. They would suffer at the hands of inadequate and inept doctors, whom you have agreed do exist and are respons…"

Jay cut him off short, "Myron, give me a break. If a patient has a small claim, he or she could hang upside down from a tree and whistle Dixie before a qualified plaintiff's lawyer would even notice.

It's a simple axiom. No big payoff means no decent lawyer under this system."

"That's not true. I had a case just this year in which..."

Jay cut in again. "Are you going to tell us some wonderful anecdote about once upon a time when a plaintiff's attorney's only concern was for some unfortunate poor soul? You and I know very well what the normal routine is."

"I don't know what normal routine you're talking about, and I absolutely reject your premise."

"My only answer to that is you're just too honest and decent to know what the rest of your fellow plaintiffs' attorneys do. It is, however, very well documented in the literature. What I can say in your behalf is that the defense attorneys for physicians are not that much more ethical. Getting paid by the hour, they'll do anything to build up the hours billed during a case. But I don't want to throw all the blame on lawyers. I know physicians who work by the same philosophy."

But all the rhetoric, all the arguments and debates, all the philosophizing about the malpractice crisis, had been just that, a lot of talk. Until now, for Jay it had been a subject of theoretical analysis. He had simply been a thinker about a difficult problem. With conversations now going on between Drinan and the Lansfords, and even possibly Susan Delman, whom Monika had touted to the same law firm, Jay soon learned of the personal reality and pain of malpractice. He discovered that no one remote from such experiences could ever know the anguish involved for either the physician or the injured party, regardless of whether malpractice was committed or not. It was the process itself that was so demeaning.

Chapter Fifteen

The Pressure Builds

"So Byler gets a call to come to the Delivery Room, stat. I mean on the double. Buddy persuaded one of the delivery room nurses to call his answering service.... Don't ask me which nurse because everyone's been sworn to secrecy."

"Well she tells the service that this patient... you see it's a name they looked up in his advanced list of maternity patients who was only about halfway through her pregnancy... is in the Labor and Delivery suite. Buddy persuades the nurse to tell Byler's answering service that the patient came in and is in active labor."

Jack Marsh listened intently as Steve Slack could barely get the words out of his mouth fast enough. His laughter was unrestrained. John Candless had related the story to him earlier in the day and John certainly had good reason to know all the details. John and Buddy had been stuck in the delivery suite for several hours on that late Saturday afternoon. John Candless had complained about how their whole evening was ruined by these two "slow-assed mommas." Out of their boredom they concocted this scheme.

"Stan rushed into the delivery suite all out of breath," Slack continued. "John stood there in a scrub suit and gloves on, like he just did the delivery. John said in a soft and depressed sort of voice, not typical of him, 'You'd better go in the nurses' work station and see what we delivered before you come in to check her. It's in the big basin covered with a towel.'

"About three seconds after Stan gets in the room, he comes running out of there holding the basin up in the air and shouting 'You dumb fucks!'"

By this time Slack is holding his side, almost unable to finish the story.

"He threw the basin, with all the shit they had put in it, clear across the delivery suite. It missed John and went smack up against the wall. I think they're still trying to get that place cleaned up."

Marsh laughed, then finally said, "Someday John Candless is goin' to go one step too far."

Jack Marsh wondered to himself how this diverse group of physicians would fare in their effort to get rid of Jay Brown. He knew Candless to be a bigoted mean son-of-a-bitch. By comparison Jack Marsh was a pussycat.

Lane was a religious fanatic and Marsh had little time for religion.

Stan Byler was simply a fool who could be led anywhere, as long as he believed his personal inane world would be protected.

Marsh had no illusions about Louie Crown. Crown was bright, crafty, and dangerous. Marsh expected that Crown could be trusted less than any of them. He knew he would not like to be up against him in three card Monte.

And Laredo was a complete enigma.

Essentially, Slack was the only one Marsh trusted. He was bright, aggressive and just mean enough to be out front in this plan, yet smooth enough to appear even handed.

What worried Marsh the most was whether this group would be able to handle Jay Brown, without trying something dumb or crazy. He seriously considered an end to his involvement in the entire mess.

"Is this really worth all this dumb ass maneuvering that has to be done? He never fucks with my cases on second opinions…. But I hate his God damned, smart ass, holier than thou attitude about everything. And I don't like the way that fucking New York Jew looks at and talks to Alice."

All these thoughts traveled through Jack's mind on a daily basis. Then childish pranks like the shit in the basin for Stan Byler made Marsh worry about internal squabbles between them. He couldn't help being concerned that one of them might do something that would prove to be dangerous for the others, out of revenge or just stupidity. Stupidity had no short supply in the group of obstetricians trying to rid themselves of Jay Brown.

"Now, Jack," Slack interrupted Marsh's private thoughts, "I've spoken to Alley Stoddard. I told him that many members of the department are very concerned about Brown, but I didn't say we wanted to get rid of him."

"O.K."

"I asked if he had heard about the possibility of several malpractice cases against him. He seemed shocked. You know they worked together for more than a year and Stoddard thought Brown was very good, if at times a pain in the ass."

"Did he ask what the cases were about?" Marsh asked.

"Yeah. But I told him that I didn't know any details. Then I said there was a general belief the only way to control his behavior was to place some restrictions on him. I gave him the definite impression that we wanted to be fair and just keep him in line. I'm certain he didn't get the significance of all this."

Marsh took it all in. He said nothing.

"If the attorneys can present evidence that the hospital has restricted him, they'll nail him to the cross at the trial, which is the best place for a Jew," Slack snickered.

They had so little knowledge of the law that they didn't realize that such evidence would probably not even be admissible.

"Whose goin' to question him at the committee meetin'?"

"That's the best part," Slack answered. I've arranged it so Candless and Byler won't be there. Buddy, Jose and Louie will all be there, and they'll be fine. I'm not nervous about them. But beyond that I persuaded Alan Powers to take one of the cases. He doesn't even dislike Brown, so that will be great. And I've got George Craft to take another. So we'll hit Brown right between the eyes with at least three people he wouldn't even suspect might give him a hard time."

"Three?"

"Yeah, Craft, Powers and don't forget Stoddard."

Slack began to lick his lips and smile from ear to ear.

"And this is the best part, Jack. I persuaded Norman Freeman to come and sit in on the committee hearing. We'll have our token Jew. But this one won't open up his mouth for anything, I'm sure. He'll watch Brown get fried and we won't hear a peep from him. He's like every other Jew. He's got a yellow streak a mile wide straight down his back."

Marsh was impassive. "Are you'all so sure about Freeman?"

"Trust me!"

"I hope you're right. I hope this resolves it."

"After the hearing the malpractice case should be a breeze. These lawyers are the best. They'll go straight for his jugular. He'll be so wiped out by the two blows, I'm sure it won't be difficult to persuade him to pick himself up and leave even before the second trial begins. It will be good riddance to bad rubbish and the end to anybody looking over our shoulders."

———

On Wednesday, February 15th, two days before the hearing was scheduled, Jay called Alley Stoddard.

"Alley I've got to meet with you before this committee hearing. Can I see you this evening after office hours in Medical Records?"

"Well, I... uh... I'm not sure that we should."

"It's urgent, Alley... and I will not compromise you in any way."

"Well... uh... I... I guess I can. But we've got to be out in the middle of the room where no one thinks it's secret or private."

"No problem Alley. I'll meet you there at five. Is that O.K.?"

Halfheartedly, he agreed.

———

Less than an hour had passed after his call to Stoddard when the mail arrived with another registered letter. It was the first since the letter from the hospital which had advised him of the committee meeting. This one wasn't from the hospital. It was from Carnahan, Davis and Drinan.

It was a form letter which requested the office records of Carla Lansford. As was typical, it ended with a promise to pay whatever minimal fee might be charged by the physician who provided the copies, as if the entire matter was an amicable request between two friendly offices.

The shock of this new development stunned Jay Brown. He had never in his entire career been charged with malpractice. As he sat silently at his desk and stared into space, he wondered how his life as a physician had suddenly come so close to the edge of the precipice.

Over the next few weeks he received multiple letters. He had heard of this before. Every few days, requests were made for every piece of paper ever produced in the care of this patient. Most of it was irrelevant. But Jay understood the significance: This was the beginning of psychological warfare. There was constant harassment. There was no more powerful weapon for the plaintiff's attorney than the creation of anxiety and frustration on a continuing basis. Nothing served them better than to have their opponent angry and aggressive. The last thing the attorneys wanted to face was a level-headed physician who remained cool under fire. The tactics were understood by everyone—the plaintiffs, the defense attorneys and the doctors. But the attorneys continually hoped that enough pressure could be exerted to overcome the physician's ability to remain composed.

Jay reviewed the charts for hours. His concerns about inadequate documentation were well founded. But none, not a single one of these cases, had adverse outcomes. He saw that his choices for treatment in several of the cases were quite the opposite of the standard practice at Sam Rayburn, but that was because the physicians at the hospital were so backward in those specific areas. Certainly they wouldn't challenge him on such shaky ground.

In one case he saw that they might charge him with neglect of a patient. He remembered the incident very well. It had arisen as a result of a misunderstanding between him and an anaesthesiologist. They had received conflicting information about the time that a Cesarean section was scheduled. He could clear that up. It presented no problem for him.

His anger about all of this reminded him of neglect in a case which was not listed in the committee's letter. Jay searched through his records and found exactly what he wanted. In the next several hours he prepared what he hoped would be a minor bombshell. It helped him to defuse some of his anger. It was obvious to him that he was the object of a personal, unwarranted attack. He would not lie down and give in to the assaults.

"Joan, I need to work on these charts some more, now. Please tell anyone who calls that I can't—absolutely can't—be disturbed now. Tell them I'm in the O.R. Tell them I'm in Delivery. Tell them anything you want, but keep me off the phone.... Don't worry Joan. We'll stand up and stand tall. Nobody will push this office around."

Jay called Alley and told him there was something wrong with the manner in which the committee had proceeded... that to be able to prepare himself properly to respond to his accusers in any court of law, he needed to know what the charges were. Alley agreed to see him.

Alley Stoddard felt extremely pressured and nervous about the entire matter. He didn't want to bring up to Jay what he had heard about malpractice actions. On the other hand he didn't want to reject Jay's request and appear to be hiding something.

Immediately after Jay's call, Alley was on the phone with Jack Marsh to tell him what had happened.

"Well you probably shouldn't have agreed to meet with him, but there's no harm. Just don't say anythin'. Let him do the talkin' and say that it's not proper for you'all to speak for the other members of the committee privately. Like you just tell him that you're gonna make certain that he gets a fair hearin'. I feel like that should be simple enough."

"Why doesn't somebody else do this?"

"'Cause you're this year's administrative head of the department, and we know you're gonna give him a fair hearin'. Alley, don't get so upset. Just do your job and everthin' will be fine."

Alley wasn't that dumb. He'd been in the department for many years and seen a lot of bad medicine practiced at one time or another, even by one of his covering physicians, Louis Crown. But, he had never known this committee to call any doctor on the carpet for anything. There had to be more than met the eye in this meeting. He knew that Jay Brown was not among the most popular in the department, but he had no idea that it was such a deep-seated feeling.

Chapter Sixteen

A Misjudgment

*T*he days gradually got longer. At five thirty the sun had not yet set. Jay decided to walk outside on the medical campus instead of down the long corridor between his office and the hospital. The underground passageway was quite an advantage during rainy days when it was necessary to rush from the office to the labor and delivery suite. Many were the days that he had run down that tunnel between his office and the hospital. Others who walked through the corridor supposed that Jay rushed back and forth to see his patients in labor, but the truth was that Jay ran that distance for a totally non-urgent reason. It was a form of exercise.

He remembered a story told about Benjamin Franklin. Apparently Franklin left the light in his study burning all night. The conclusion reached by those who passed by was that this amazing man worked at his desk all night long. Franklin continued the practice because he felt certain their interpretation of his nighttime behavior, though completely inaccurate, served him well among his peers.

The assumption that Jay had so many patients that he had to run back and forth between the two buildings could only enhance his image.

When the architects designed this massive medical center complex, they took an area that had been rather rundown and landscaped it to the nines. On this day, in his somewhat depressed state of mind, Jay decided it might cheer him a little to walk the outside route. It was quite a lovely saunter down the tree lined street with flower beds wherever the eye turned on this cool and refreshing evening. Jay thought, *"It'll clear my head, just to get some fresh air before I meet with Alley."*

Alley, on the other hand had no desire for anything—not a clear head, not fresh air, not anything. He just wanted an end to the meeting, before it even began.

When Jay walked into the Medical Records Department only a sprinkling of evening employees were there. The normal hustle and bustle in the large open room had quieted down by this hour. Two women sat at desks at the far end of the room. A member of the housekeeping department very slowly moved around the room as she collected trash from the waste baskets. Alley was nowhere in sight.

Jay made his way toward one of the occupied desks. He did not know either of the women by name, though their faces were familiar.

As he approached the clerk she looked up and said, "Can I help you, Dr. Brown?"

"Mrs. Powell was supposed to leave some records for me to review with Dr. Stoddard."

With a quizzical look, "Did she say where?"

"No."

"Sylvia, do you know about any charts for Drs. Brown and Stoddard?"

Sylvia was much older, which was probably the subconscious reason Jay had selected to approach the other secretary with the request. She responded, but with some hesitation.

"I think she may have mentioned something. Let me go look."

Sylvia raised herself with great difficulty and walked with a very pronounced limp that made it apparent the assignment she had undertaken for Jay was not an easy one for her. After each step she took with her right leg, she dragged her left leg slowly behind. The sound of her left shoe as it scraped across the hardwood floor could be heard in a definite rhythm as she made her way into a separate room that seemed distant, based on the number of difficult steps she took. That only added guilt to the numerous other emotions that overwhelmed Jay Brown.

In less than five minutes she returned to the main room. She carried an armload of charts which made her efforts on Jay's behalf even more difficult. He rushed over to relieve her of the load and she thanked him profusely. As Jay heard the office door click open, he turned to see a rather somber Alley Stoddard enter the room.

Jay looked at Sylvia and asked, "Is there a good place for Dr. Stoddard and me to review the records?"

She pointed toward another small room off the main area.

"You should find plenty of room and a few chairs in there."

Not a word had passed yet between him and Alley. Jay entered first, placed the charts on the table and by a hand signal alone, invited Alley to sit down.

"Hi, Alley. Thanks for meeting with me."

Alley made a few affirmative shakes of his head and said only, "O.K."

It was apparent to Jay that Alley was going to say and do as little as possible.

"Alley, I've reviewed these charts. I've reviewed them over and over."

Alley said nothing.

"Alley, there's nothing wrong here. I could have made more notes on these charts to document my activities, but that wouldn't have changed the treatment in any of these cases. Every last one of them has an excellent result."

Still there was no comment from Alexander Stoddard.

"The Committee has made no statement... provided no information... told me nothing about what I'm being charged with. What's going on here, Alley?"

His voice raised in volume considerably from the beginning to the end of his questioning.

The two women out front now heard everything and slowed down their activities to listen to the conversation.

Stoddard was angry. He didn't want to be in the center of this mess. He was sorry he had agreed to meet with Jay and angry that Jay challenged him. He didn't know why, but in every conversation with Jay Brown he always seemed to be on the defensive.

"Don't start fighting with me. This was not my decision..." and after a brief pause, "alone."

Jay knew full well this wasn't Alley Stoddard's decision. That was why he had hoped that this meeting would provide him with some support. But he had started off on the wrong foot.

"I'm sorry Alley. I'm just a little pissed off. I really didn't mean to vent my anger at you. I'd like you to look at these charts and tell me where you see a problem, so that I know what to do."

"I can't do that, Jay. Different people have made decisions about each case. I'll just run the meeting. I've got a responsibility and I can't undermine the other members of the department even before they have a chance to be heard."

Jay stared straight into Alley's eyes. For the longest time he said nothing, then, "I'm disappointed."

Alley put his hand up to his forehead and passed his fingers back and forth with his eyes closed and his head slightly tucked, as if he had a very bad headache. After a brief moment he spoke again.

"I'll promise you this, Jay. Whatever is said, I'll give you a fair hearing. But, I can't say anything else now."

Jay did not move or change his expression. Without any inflection in his voice he said, "I'll take you at your word."

Almost nothing else was said as the charts were returned to the evening personnel in the record room and the two men quietly walked out.

"Goodnight Jay."

"I'll see you on Friday Alley."

————

Jay Brown did not think that this day was the beginning and end of his struggle. On the other hand, it did not occur to him that it was the beginning of a three year nightmare.

He arrived at the Board Room, the customary location for small to medium sized committee meetings at Sam Rayburn Hospital. The long table was set up with the simple preparations provided for all these sessions at noon time.

There was a meeting of some sort held there every day, from routine departmental meetings to special events such as this one, planned for Jay Brown. The usual tuna fish, chicken salad and ham and cheese sandwiches, several plates of potato chips, paper cups with large bottles of soft drinks and a few plates of inedible cookies were spread out from one end of the table to the other.

Jay came prepared to take nothing lying down. He had, in his two weeks of review, found what he believed would be a bombshell that would silence his detractors and allow him to practice in peace. But, that was exactly the kind of judgmental error that Jay was prone to make. He usually saw the world in terms of a black and white image. He had difficulty with shades of gray. Solutions he found to resolve a problem left little room for the possibility that other individuals might perceive things differently.

The committee was poorly prepared. They challenged him for the performance of vaginal deliveries on women who had previously had Cesarean sections and stated that in some he had even used pitocin to stimulate the labor, "knowing full well that the woman's uterus had a scar from previous surgery."

"But certainly you must be aware that this is being done all over the country."

He laid out the evidence with article references and dates. They remained silent when he responded.

Alan Powers could only say sheepishly, "You've got more guts than me to try that."

"But Alan, that's the standard of care now at every medical center. It takes no guts to follow the standard!"

The issue of vaginal deliveries of breeches ended up with the same kind of evidence and documentation that caused no end of consternation for Steve Slack. Things did not go the way he had hoped. It was his expectation that the cases would be presented with greater commitment on the part of the members of the committee. He hoped that Jay would leave the meeting with his tail between his legs. Slack thought the malpractice trial, this hearing, and maybe a little more pressure would force Brown to resign and leave Austin.

Even when the issue of inadequate documentation was raised, nothing much came of it. Jay admitted freely that although he had done all the things he should, his documentation of them was terribly inadequate. He agreed completely that, had an adverse result occurred, he had laid himself and the hospital open for serious problems. But none had arisen.

He completed his response with, "I'm grateful to the committee for having alerted me to this before a problem arose."

There was little they could do other than to accept his apology and say that they expected better and more complete recording in the future. He assured them of that and the issue died.

Slack's entire plan might well have fallen apart on that very day were it not for Jay Brown's decision to overpower them, embarrass them and hopefully, as a result, silence them permanently.

"Before we adjourn, I'd like to ask a question about something that confused me."

"What's that, Jay?" asked Alley Stoddard, somewhat wearily.

"Well… I reviewed all my cases for the past few months, not just the ones you referenced for the meeting, and while I could find no problems with the ones you listed, I wondered why another one had not been selected."

The committee was confused by this candor. No one responded.

"You see, my patient #82-056375 arrived in the hospital at 6 P.M. on September 9th in early active labor. The nurses definitely called to notify me of that. By 8:30 P.M. the patient became more uncomfortable. Without having been seen by a physician even once, medication was ordered for her to relieve the pain. The nurse was assured the patient would be seen shortly. The nurses called again at 10:07 P.M. The patient still had not been seen by a physician, although she had been in labor in the hospital for more than four hours."

The silence was such that a dropped pin could be heard. None of the committee members could understand the reason for such a confession.

"At that call, the nurse stated that the patient was in considerable pain. She had checked the patient and found her to be at 5 cm. of dilatation The patient continued to ask for her doctor."

Jay stopped to look at his notes. "Did I mention that more than four hours had passed?" He knew very well that he had mentioned it before.

The members of the committee sat up straighter in their chairs. They were uncomfortable with this presentation. Something was wrong.

Why would he turn this entire meeting around, just when it was all ending in his favor, and be self accusing? was the common thought among the group.

"Once again the nurse was assured that the patient would be seen. No office hours or surgery were in progress."

He paused and then, "At 11:20 P.M. the nurse called for the fourth time to say that the patient had the urge to push, and she had checked her and found the cervix to be almost fully dilated."

This time Jay took a much longer pause and looked up from his notes. He just stared at the group. Incredulous and in a state of complete confusion they stared back at him.

"At 11:55 P.M. the patient delivered, attended by only the nurse."

He slowly looked up and down the table and said, "I would have thought that the committee would be furious about such neglect."... and after another long pause... "but the case was never listed."

The room was absolutely silent. Those who were bright could see clearly that another shoe was about to drop.

John Candless fully understood there was a rat in this story. He finally broke the silence in a very slow Texas drawl, "Ah wouldn't tell anybody if ah did that."

"Well John, you're right. But you see, it turns out this way. She is my patie... but I was away on vacation when all that happened. The doctor who took care of her was... " after a long pause and a very deep breath, "you, Louie." He pointed to Louis Crown.

The room was stunned. Crown was too clever to appear flustered. He calmly looked at Jay, with venom in his eyes and said, "I think you may have distorted the information on this case. I would be glad to review it and discuss it further at a later date."

"The meeting is adjourned," Alley immediately blurted out.

Everyone left. They didn't feel ashamed. They felt ambushed and angry. Jay felt a surge of power. But his analysis of what had just happened completely misjudged and misunderstood the true power brokers on the committee. He had just provided them with the last bit of proof they needed to prod the less aggressive, and certainly the less qualified, physicians into a clear understanding.

"This cocky New York Jew is out to get us."

The only self-protection they had was to get rid of him. Jay Brown's hope that this might be the end was a pipe dream. The battle had just begun.

Chapter Seventeen

A Life in Israel

*I*n the Spring of 1969, just when Label Krause began his less than ethical research project in France, his father Duvid died in Israel. His premature death in his sixties should not have been totally unexpected. Like so many others of his generation Duvid Krause was a heavy smoker. He succumbed to lung cancer after a relatively short battle with the disease.

In 1963, while a doctoral candidate at Hebrew University, Label's sister Esther met Uri Allon. With great hope for their future Esther married Uri in the Spring of 1965, immediately following Passover. On the day of their first wedding anniversary in 1966, Esther gave birth to Itzhak.

In 1967 the State of Israel achieved a remarkable victory in its Six Day War, but Esther Allon lost a piece of her heart. Only 115 Israelis were killed in the entire war, approximately one twentieth of the Arab losses. Uri was one of those who died.

Rebecca assumed much of the care of her grandson, Itzhak, as Esther went through a mourning period that seemed never to end. More than a full year passed before she returned to work in 1968. And then she had to face the death of her father in 1969.

In 1979 Rebecca identified a breast lump which turned out to be malignant. After surgery and chemotherapy she did quite well for several years before it recurred. In 1983 at the age of seventy-seven she succumbed to her illness. Itzhak was seventeen years old and about to go into the army for his compulsory service.

Esther was now 46 years old. Her mother and father were gone. She had been widowed for sixteen years and her only child was about to embark on his own independent life.

All these personal losses drove her more than anything to a thought that came to her now. She had to find Label, the only fragment of her past that still remained. Esther had to find a way to reconnect. She began to search out where Label was; to know what had become of her brother.

Label was now fifty years old. Dr. Jean LaRouche, who had been the Head of his department when Label was in Paris, was now well into his seventies. When Esther found him, it was the first time Dr. LaRouche had heard the name Label Krause in more than a decade. If he had never heard it again, it would have suited him fine.

However, in the telephone conversation with Esther it was clear to him that she was made of a fabric quite different from her brother. He sensed urgency in her voice and felt compelled to tell her the entire truth.

Esther accepted the entire tale with great sadness. It was not as if she did not believe that her brother was capable of such corrupt machinations. Nevertheless, her desire to find some joy in a reconciliation, caused her to feel compassion for the plight which had befallen him, albeit self inflicted. In her despair she fantasized a completely changed person with whom she would re-establish a new and wonderful relationship.

Dr. LaRouche knew that Label had changed his name to Louis Crown and where he had been since he left Paris, but no further details beyond that.

Through the offices of the United Jewish Appeal Esther made contact with the Jewish Federation of Austin to see if she could obtain help with arrangements to be in Austin for about one week.

Separately, Esther contacted Sam Rayburn Hospital and obtained the address of Dr. Louis Crown. Shortly before she was to leave, she wrote to him.

Dearest Label:

It is not the time for either of us to chastise the other for the very long interval of time which has passed without communication. There is much that has happened which we must put behind us. I am coming to see you in Texas.

It will not be necessary for you to make any arrangements for me, as I have done all of that on my own. I look forward to our reconnection and, hopefully, to meeting a fine family that you have established. I am anxious to have you meet my wonderful son, your nephew Itzhak. Presently, since he is in the process of fulfilling his obligation to the military, he will not be able to make the trip.

I cannot fully express to you how much I look forward to seeing you once again.

Your loving sister,

Esther

She sent the letter directly to his office, the only address she possessed, and marked in bold letters on the outside of the envelope, "PERSONAL, TO BE OPENED ONLY BY DR. LOUIS CROWN!!!!"

Crown was less than thrilled when he received the letter. He had no desire to see Esther or anyone connected with his past. He sent a telegram to her at the address on her letterhead.

"Esther, please do not discuss the purpose of your trip with anyone. I will meet you at the airport. Please notify me of your arrival date and time. Louis"

Esther returned a telegram message to him.

"No need to meet me at the airport. All arrangements have been made. I will call you at your office after I am settled. Love, Esther"

So the meeting was set. Esther was nervous, but she knew that she had to make this journey. Louis Crown was nervous as well. His wish, not to ever hear from his family, was not to be fulfilled.

———

Jay Brown was single, charming and the obvious person in the mind of Sally Birnbaum, the Director of the Austin Jewish Federation, to escort Esther Allon during her visit.

At the appointed time Jay was at the airport. He carried a small sign, "Esther Allon." Sally Birnbaum had prepared it for him to make the connection easier.

"Dr. Brown?"

Jay was somewhat shocked and taken aback by the strikingly lovely woman who approached him. He wasn't sure why, but he expected an obese matronly woman to arrive. Esther was tall, somewhat dark, with beautiful features. He would probably estimate her age to be at least ten years younger than she actually was.

"Yes! Mrs. Allon?"

The baggage was retrieved. Jay brought his car around and took her to the Driskill Hotel. As they drove, the air of formality became much more relaxed. They agreed to meet later for dinner.

As Esther unpacked and gathered her thoughts, it occurred to her, *"This is a good beginning to the trip... Dr. Brown is very warm... I'm certain I'll enjoy his company this evening... I guess I can't put off calling Label... But, I'm nervous."*

She stripped down to her undergarments, put on her robe and sat on the edge of her bed and stared at the telephone. Finally, with a deep breath, she picked up the phone and dialed.

"Is Dr. Crown in?"

"Who shall I say is calling?"

"Uh... " for a moment she paused as she almost said "his sister." "Mrs. Allon."

The interval until Louis Crown got on the phone seemed almost interminable. Finally, she heard, "Esther?"

"Yes, Label, I am here in Austin.... How are you?"

"All is well with me."

Esther was more than shocked by the total maintenance of his French accent. To the contrary Esther had a mixture of sounds in her speech. A little bit of French could be discerned. It was mixed with an eastern European dialect so common for most Israelis. But she sounded as if she had lived most of her life in America when she spoke English.

Why had Label's accent remained so constant, she wondered to herself.

"I will pick you up in my car and bring you to my office tomorrow."

Esther had no idea that her brother's accent had been intentionally maintained. It provided an image for him. He was the suave European with great sophistication. It was his greatest source of strength in the local medical community.

"Thank you so much, but it won't be necessary for you to make that trip. Just tell me what time you would like me to be there."

"Will ten in the morning be all right?"

"Absolutely Lab... Louis. What would you prefer I call you?"

"My name has been Louis or Louie for many years."

"That's fine. I shall call you Louis." It was interesting that she selected the anglicized version, although he would have preferred Louie. "I know where you are located as I've checked the map. I won't need any directions. Au revoir, Louis… and Shalom."

She had hoped that her words demonstrated that she bore no anger. But the response to that greeting was dead silence.

Then, after a moment, "I will look forward to tomorrow."

"'til tomorrow." Esther hung up the telephone and sat on the bed for a while, and stared into space.

Momma, have I made a mistake coming here?

Tears poured down her cheeks as she thought, *Momma, Poppa… dearest Uri… I miss you so much. Help me be strong.*

———

Almost three hours had passed since Jay picked Esther up at the Driskill. They went to dinner at Jeffrey's Restaurant on 12th Street. Almost immediately they were extremely comfortable in conversation. So typically of strangers who hit it off, they told each other of their lives, families and problems in great detail. But each consciously, or subconsciously, left out details they did not wish to reveal.

At no time during the evening did Esther mention a brother. She told of her parents and their struggles, her beloved Uri and her son Itzhak, of whom she was so proud.

When Jay asked, "Do you have any brothers or sisters?" her response was quick and certain.

"I had a brother who died when I was very young."

"I'm sorry."

"Oh that's all right. I don't even remember him."

Jay told Esther of his desire to improve the quality of medical care, but never mentioned the difficulties he faced in the local medical community. The name of Louis Crown never came up.

When the evening ended Jay and Esther sincerely agreed they had a marvelous time. She told him she had daytime appointments the next day.

"Would you like to have dinner again with me tomorrow evening? I'm a little uncertain about the hour. It depends on when office hours will end."

Slightly surprised, but very flattered, Esther accepted the invitation.

Jay drove home feeling quite contented. He had not expected to meet such a bright, charming woman. In his mind it had been a duty he was asked to perform for his local community. It could have been a long, dragged out drudgery. It was more than a very special surprise.

———————

Esther stepped out of her clothing once again in front of the mirror and thought, *what a sweet, charming man... I think he likes me... I'm glad he gave me that little kiss on the cheek when he said goodnight.... He's definitely not French. He kissed me on just one cheek.... Tomorrow WILL be a good day.*

Neither one knew of the other's tie to Louis Crown. Neither one knew of the pain they would be subjected to at Crown's hands.

Chapter Eighteen

Confusion in the Operating Room

*T*he nights seemed much longer as Jay spent most of them lying awake—an experience totally foreign to him. Since his earliest days in medicine he had learned to fall sleep whenever the opportunity presented. Now, no matter how many hours of sleep he had missed in the process of delivering babies, sleep had become a major problem. Even the very pleasant evening with Esther Allon could not wipe away the anxieties he experienced.

What's become of my life?

He was challenged on all sides. Never had the thought once entered his mind that a patient would sue him for malpractice. It seemed inconceivable. That kind of thing only happened to incompetent, lazy, careless or uncaring physicians.

It wasn't the money that was involved, nor the inordinate number of hours utilized in the defense of himself that distressed him so. There was something much more basic and devastating. To Jay, it was the very essence of himself that was challenged. He would never again feel the same way about the bond he had thought was untouchable between him and his "mothers." It was as if he had lost one of the closest members of his family. Jay Brown was heartbroken.

Beyond that, he was under direct attack by his colleagues. That in itself, he could handle. It was his choice to take them on, and he understood the possible consequences. At least when he began, he thought so.

The one saving grace was his work. The practice had grown rapidly. Patients were still unaware of what had transpired. He knew that sooner or later the information about the malpractice case would appear in the newspapers and become common knowledge. He didn't realize how bad it would be.

Through a contact, Steve Slack let the word out to a friend at the Austin Star that this was to be a very exciting trial. Steve was assured this trial would get "lots of press."

Jay wondered what the reaction from his patients might be. He came to realize that the loyalty ran very deep. That buoyed his spirits quite a bit as the days went by.

No one understood Joan's "Dr. B" better than she did. She knew the weight on his shoulders. She made a concerted effort to keep his spirits high. Joan loaded his office schedule way beyond what was customary. She mumbled to herself, *"I'll keep him running."*

Jay believed that schedules should not be so heavy that patients had to wait a long time to be seen. He remembered very well Marvin Green's philosophy of "keep the waiting room full of patients, no matter how long they wait," and he hated it. Marvin insisted that was the way to build a practice. "Make everyone feel as if they were in the only place to be."

Jay vowed that if he ever practiced without Marvin, he would change that approach and never leave patients waiting. When he questioned Joan as to why there were more patients than usual, she feigned annoyance.

"Dr. B! I'm doing the best I can with the schedule. I can't help it. These are patients that just have to be seen and can't wait for later appointments. You'll keep up okay. Don't worry."

Joan only hoped that she was doing something worthwhile for him. She was never quite certain whether or not he understood the scheduling game she played. She wouldn't have been surprised to find out that he went along just to keep her happy.

"Dr. B. I know I've got you scheduled up until 3:30, but the O.R. just called. They've got an empty slot and want to move Mrs. Carter into it. They'll be ready in a half hour, so I'll have to change some appointments. Remember you're scheduled to meet with Mr. Parsons…."

"Who?"

"… Mr. Parsons, the malpractice attorney, at 4:30 this afternoon. The tubal ligation will take you thirty to forty five minutes and we'll catch up."

"I haven't spoken to Ingrid since this morning after the delivery. Are all the consents signed?"

"All done! Everything's ready and they don't want to put the case off until later when they'll only have one O.R. crew, in case they get an emergency."

"That's fine. Tell them to call me when everything is ready and I'll run right over, down the tunnel. Until then I'll see as many patients as I can."

Ingrid Carter was a favorite patient of Jay's.

He once said to Joan, "It's like being a parent. You don't want to admit that you might like one child better than another. But some of them make life easy and some of them drive you crazy."

Ingrid Carter made life easy. She never complained, and always had a smile and a warm greeting. She was a doctor's joy.

Jay had delivered the last two of her four children and it was sheer pleasure. At every office visit during those pregnancies, she was on an emotional high. Even the deliveries were easy, not just for Jay, but for Ingrid as well.

He never gave her a single dose of medication for pain relief during those labors. It was always offered and always declined. Jay believed that every patient was entitled to whatever help was needed during labor. But every once in a while there were patients like Ingrid who somehow were able to cope without anything.

Most of his patients required pain relief in one form or another. Even with large amounts some found it difficult to maintain their composure. But Jay accepted each one as an individual and supported them in whatever way was necessary to help them through. Ingrid, on the other hand, was one of those remarkable women who went through labor as if it were a minor inconvenience. It always amazed him.

But if Ingrid was remarkable, her husband was less so. Not once had he appeared at either of her labors or deliveries. For Jay that was even more unbelievable than the way Ingrid handled the process. Almost universally, Jay's patients had husbands who, if not absolutely great in their support of their wives in labor, at least were present for the occasion.

Jay had met Bubba—actually Bernard, but known to his friends as Bubba—on only a few occasions in the hospital, a day or two after the deliveries. Bubba was definitely a good ol' boy. He spent as little time as possible at home, but could always be found with his buddies hunting or fishing for whatever game was in season.

Jay entered the operating room all scrubbed and ready to begin. Ingrid had already received a spinal anaesthetic and the scrub nurse had draped her for the surgery. Her abdomen had been prepped with a cleansing solution. The catheter was in her bladder and everyone was ready to go.

"Hi, Ingrid, feeling fine?"

"Super, Doc."

"That's good, we're all set and I don't want you to be nervous. I've done this operation once before and the nurse has the textbook here to read the instructions to me as we go along."

"That's no problem Doc. If you have any questions about how to do the operation I'll be glad to be of help."

The nurses got a charge out of Ingrid's response. They had heard Jay's nonsense a thousand times and loved it when a patient had a comeback. Jay loved it even more.

Nancy, the circulating nurse, brought the consent form to Jay to verify before they started. He looked for the signature, as he glanced over his mask. It was no longer necessary for a woman to get her husband's consent to have her tubes tied and be sterilized.

"That's fine," he said to Nancy.

Then he looked at Ingrid and added reassuringly, "This won't keep you in the hospital any longer than you would have stayed just for the delivery."

Jay was then gowned and gloved by the circulating nurse. He grasped a forceps from the scrub nurse's instrument tray and pinched Ingrid's skin under her navel. At the same time he looked at the anaesthetist, over the screen, to get any indication from him as to whether Ingrid felt any sensation.

"Feel any pinching, Mrs. Carter?" the anaesthetist asked.

"Nope," Ingrid responded cheerily.

The first thought that came to Jay's mind was, *"She'd probably say no even if she did feel it."*

"You can start, Dr. Brown."

Jay took two Alyss clamps, long scissors-like instruments with fine grasping points at their ends. Each one held the skin at a distance of about one and a half inches apart along an imaginary line transversely across the abdomen, immediately under the umbilicus. With a scalpel he made an incision along that line seen only in his mind's eye. With each step he rarely asked for an instrument. Marguerite, the scrub nurse he had worked with on innumerable occasions, knew exactly what each step was without being prompted.

Nancy wandered in and out of the O.R. suite to get needed supplies for Marguerite or the anaesthetist.

After the initial skin incision, Jay cut deeper. He went layer by layer. The first portion was bloody and yellowish due to the fat in the subcutaneous tissue. Then he incised the major supportive layer for the abdominal wall—the white, relatively bloodless fascia. Within a few moments he had opened the peritoneal cavity where the dome of the post partum uterus appeared. Several small loops of bowel pushed their way out of the abdomen. Jay carefully replaced and packed away the bowel with the gauze packing used for that purpose to avoid any injury. Then, through the small opening, he inserted his finger, and blindly went to feel the tube on the left side. It was so second nature to him that it appeared as if his finger had eyes as he lifted the tube through the small incision and grasped it with a Babcock clamp. That instrument, designed to be non-traumatic at its grasping end, was placed on the tube. The tube was then lifted out of the incision so that the process of ligating it could be done on the outside, where no other structures could be damaged.

"There," said Jay, as he gently passed the Babcock clamp to Marguerite, so that she could hold the Fallopian tube in place while he ligated it.

With her free hand, Marguerite handed Jay a fine suture. He placed two sutures on the tube and with a free piece of suture material, unattached to a needle, he tied the two locations of the previous sutures together, forming a loop of tube between the two sutures he had placed. With a long fine dissecting scissors, known as Metzenbaums, he cut off the loop of tube, which completed the blockage of the passageway for eggs and sperm on Ingrid's left side.

Jay examined the area carefully.

"It looks dry to me," he said after he checked for any bleeding. The remaining portions of the tube, cut and tied, were released and allowed to fall back into the abdominal cavity. Once again, but this time directed toward the opposite side, Jay inserted a finger through the small opening to find the right tube.

All was going as expected, maybe even easier than usual, which was not surprising as that was the customary experience when he treated Ingrid Carter. This type of surgery was generally pretty routine work.

The image for the public about surgery centered around well publicized cases where teams of surgeons worked feverishly to save lives in serious trauma or sophisticated transplant operations. But for the most part surgery was not nearly as theatrical as had been portrayed by Hollywood or television. At least that was usually true before this particular day.

"Stop," Nancy shouted, as she burst back into the operating room.

The operating room was not usually dead silent. There was frequently conversation going on, requests for instruments, discussions between surgeon and anaesthetist, and when things were going very smoothly, not uncommonly a joke might be told. But, a dash into the operating room and a shout of "stop" by a nurse was purely for the movies.

Jay turned toward Nancy. "What? What are you talking about? What are you shouting about?"

"I'm sorry Dr. Brown. We have a problem."

"Is there a fire?"

"No doctor."

"Something related to this case?"

A horrible fear came over him. A surgeon's worst nightmare is that somehow the wrong patient had been brought to the O.R. But quickly his thought processes organized as he said to himself, *This patient's not under general anaesthesia. She's had a spinal. She's awake and it's definitely Ingrid. I've been talking to her.*

"Something related to this case?" he asked once again as Nancy seemed to be having difficulty responding.

"Ye... eh... eh... ess"

"You do know that Mrs. Carter is awake, don't you?"

"Yes sir. But it concerns her as well."

Jay looked absolutely dumbfounded. "What is it?"

"Dr. Brown, Mr. Carter's in the waiting room and... he's... inebriated... drunk."

"Nancy, I know what inebriated means. If he's causing a problem, just get the security guards to handle it."

"Dr. Brown, I don't believe you understand. Mr. Carter insists he doesn't want his wife's tubes tied."

A hush fell over the room. Jay looked at the ceiling, slowly shook his head, and mumbled "Schmuck!" He stared at his scrub nurse, Marguerite, in disbelief and remained silent for what seemed an eternity to the others in the operating room. One tube was already cut and tied.

This was straight out of Hollywood. Jay wasn't certain whether to be angry or just laugh. Laughter seemed to make more sense, but he didn't want to upset Ingrid who must not consider the situation funny. Maybe years later she would... and maybe not.

Marguerite didn't know if she would be able to control herself. She was afraid to look directly at Jay, because she knew that would cause her to break up completely. He looked at her and could tell that she found it all very funny, even if he didn't. Marguerite had to force a make believe cough to avoid laughter. Unfortunately she did it for so long and hard, the next sensation she felt was a gush of urine. For the next half hour she would stand at the table with her panties soaking wet. She only hoped that no one would see the evidence through her scrub gown.

Finally Jay looked over the screen that separated him from the head of the table and said to Ingrid, "Do you want to talk to him?"

Ingrid's eyes rolled and she sighed with frustration as she finally said, "Okay!"

"Take Mr. Carter to the dressing room. Get him into a gown, cap and mask and bring him in here," Jay blurted out in anger.

Everyone else remained silent. All they could think of was how crazy this had all become. Jay thought for a moment that he heard Marguerite snicker under her mask.

In about five minutes Nancy returned. Even as the door opened

Jay heard, "Ah doan wan her tubes tied."

"Mr. Carter…"

"Ah doan wan you to operate on her."

"MR. CARTER!!!!! Be quiet and listen to me or I'll have the security guards remove you from the hospital completely. Do you understand?"

Jay heard a mumbled "Yes."

"The law is very clear. Your wife doesn't need your consent to have this done. But, frankly, I don't want to do this unless you both agree. Unfortunately, because you were NOT here for the labor and delivery…"

And in his mind, but not his mouth Jay thought, *"You good for nothing son-of-a-bitch."*

"… OR the beginning of this surgery, we have already destroyed one tube. At this very moment your wife is neither fish nor fowl. She is half sterilized. Now I need to know from your wife… not from you… what to do."

"Ah doan wan her tubes tied."

"Mr. Carter, please be quiet. We know how you feel… Ingrid, what do you want me to do?"

Ingrid Carter, normally the very essence of sweetness, was fit to be tied, and with good reason. If she had a lethal weapon in her possession, she probably would have done him in right there and then, glad to leave her children fatherless. In her mind she was saying to Bubba, *You dumb fuck, you are really going to pay for this insanity somewhere down the road.*

She looked at Bubba, her pitiful husband. Then she looked at Dr. Brown and looked at Bubba again before she said, "Close me up, Doc! Don't do the other side."

Jay doubted that anyone in the future would ever believe this story, if he had the occasion to tell it, not even physicians. But Nancy, Marguerite, Ingrid, the anaesthetist and possibly Bubba, if he remembered anything from his drunken stupors, knew that it actually happened. It was one of those episodes, though stressful at the time, which would bring on nothing but laughter as it was told many times over in subsequent years. When retold it would probably be embellished each time it was related.

In just over one year, Ingrid became pregnant again and delivered her fifth child. Once again Bubba was gone with his hunting buddies. Jay destroyed the opposite tube surgically after the delivery. But Ingrid was the only member of her family in the operating suite during that second operation.

Chapter Nineteen

A New Friend

*J*ohn Parsons grew up in the upper peninsula of Michigan. At least in Jay's mind, there was something special about the people he had met from the midwest, especially the upper midwest. To Jay, places like Minnesota and Michigan grew their own breed. He wondered if it was the Scandinavian influence.

The people he had known from that part of the country had a strong work ethic. They were self reliant. Honesty and decency were not characteristics they sought to possess; they were inborn and natural.

John Parsons' profession, the law, was not something that Jay necessarily equated with those character traits. The discussions among physicians about the morality, or lack thereof, of lawyers who were involved in malpractice suits had made him wary. Up until this time he had no personal experience to base it on. He just felt it in his gut.

Jay had come to Parsons' office immediately after he completed his office hours and the rather unbelievable tubal surgery. He had been placed in contact with Parsons by his insurance company, once he notified them of the impending law suit. After about a week he received a phone call.

"Hello, Dr. Brown, I've been contacted by your malpractice insurance company about a case that's been raised. They've asked me to represent you. Would it be possible for you to collect all your records on the case and meet with me for several hours?"

Jay wasn't certain why the voice on the phone gave him a sense of comfort and security, but there was one thing he knew for sure. It was a relief to know that there was somebody out there on his side. Jay had definitely developed a siege mentality. It seemed to him that he was alone and under attack from all sides.

"That'll be fine," he said.

On the date set, Jay showed up at Parsons' office with all the records on Mrs. Lansford.

"Have a seat please, Dr. Brown."

"Could we work on a first name basis?" Jay asked, uncomfortable with the formality.

"Absolutely, forgive me. Is it J.D.?"

"Just call me Jay. That's what everyone calls me."

"I've always had great respect for doctors. It just came second nature to me to refer to them formally. My father and grandfather were both physicians in our small town. I'm really John Parsons the third. My grandfather was known to everybody in town as Dr. John. And, believe it or not, my dad was called Dr. Little John. No one ever addressed them without the "doctor" except us kids. Even my mother called my dad Dr. Little John."

"Really!"

"Dr. Little John, can we expect you at home for dinner tonight?" Mom would ask.

They both laughed. A bond had been formed.

About an hour was spent in review of the pertinent information and then the conversation drifted away from the case.

Parsons was much younger than Jay Brown, *probably in his mid-to-late-thirties*, Jay thought. He was big in every way, tall and husky. Some of it was muscle. But, many years had passed since he played college football. Since then he had spent too much time behind desks and too little with exercise. Added to the muscle was now a fair share of adipose tissue. He was married and multiple pictures of his wife and small children adorned his desk. Everyone was blond and fair skinned.

The conversation drifted from subject to subject. It went on for some time. Each one told the other about family, philosophy of life, even hopes and dreams. In a few hours these two men knew they would be fast friends even beyond this case. There is a mutual respect that two people can find as suddenly as a couple who find love at first sight. For Jay Brown and John Parsons it was the recognition in each other of a philosophy that seemed to them to be in the common good for mankind.

"I love the fact that I can spend my life taking care of patients and teaching young people what I have learned. But there are downsides as well. Being here with you to discuss a malpractice claim is one of them."

"Thanks," John quipped.

"John, most of my patients come into the hospital and have an uncomplicated delivery and go home in a breeze. That's the easy part of obstetrics. Then there are others who may be in labor for hours. Sometimes, during that process, a patient may suddenly develop complications. There are times in emergency situations when my pulse probably shoots sky high. My heart's in my throat and I'm quietly in a panic that I'm going to lose a baby or even a mother. In those frightening situations I work as calmly and decisively as I know how. But I know, if everything doesn't come out perfectly, it's not impossible that someone will say that I caused the unfortunate outcome."

John Parsons listened as Jay continued.

"The public doesn't understand that there's one thing called malpractice, and another situation in which no matter what the physician may do, there will be an adverse outcome. They're not synonymous. Of course, improper care can cause a bad outcome. But the reverse isn't true. A bad result may neither have been caused by malpractice nor be avoidable in any way."

"That kind of stress has got to be terrible, Jay. You know that everything you do is seen and you're accountable for it. I can't tell you how many times things go wrong here, or in any lawyer's office, and then have to be corrected. If all that was under scrutiny at all times, I'd probably be sued every week."

"That happens in medicine too. Many more things go wrong in the care of a patient than the public ever sees. Those don't result in malpractice cases because there's no serious adverse outcome, and they go unnoticed."

"Jay, I know this is your first experience in this kind of thing. But primarily, especially now as we start, I don't want you to be too stressed about it. From what you've told me, I can't believe there will be a problem with this case. But... I want you to understand before I make any definitive decisions about it, I need to get an unbiased expert opinion. It isn't that I don't trust you or believe you. I just have to be certain about where we might confront any pitfalls."

"Absolutely! I understand. I can't imagine how you could possibly take any other course."

"You know Jay, unlike you this is not my first case, just the first one today."

Jay smiled, and said, "God, I hope you don't have any more like mine today."

Parsons snickered and said, "I don't expect any, but I do have a problem. After your description of the case, I'm having difficulty. I can't figure out why there's a lawsuit at all."

Jay knew he would have to tell John Parsons about the other things that were a part of his life.

"That may be because we haven't discussed everything."

John sat quietly and listened to Jay relate the details of what happened at the hospital. He started from the late night delivery room search, to the second opinions he provided to the insurance companies with rejections, the warning from Dr. Stan Howard and, finally, his own perception that a concerted effort was underway to have him vanish from the local scene.

"I have absolutely no proof and not one piece of specific evidence that this is true, but I do believe there is the possibility that a tie exists between the harassment at the hospital and this malpractice case."

John sat passively. Jay could tell that his mind was at work a mile a minute.

"We've got our hands full. The review by the hospital will be very treacherous for the case… unless we can make certain it is not admissible. And the malpractice case is bound to cause you problems with the hospital hearing."

"Jay, the coincidence of a baseless case and this hospital hearing is too much to consider accidental. However, I've obviously got a muckraker for a client. Strictly in relation to this case, if I had my druthers, you would not be involved with a fight against the establishment. Whistleblowers are difficult to protect."

"I'm terribly sorry," Jay said. "I wish I weren't here today and it was all a bad dream."

"I'm sure you mean that, Jay. But try to remember as we move through this, it's not like the pregnant woman who suddenly confronts you with a life and death problem not of your making. You've created the background we face today, and we have to face the consequences."

"Will I need a separate attorney to represent me and advise me how to deal with the hospital committee, should that go any further?"

"I'll manage that. We'll just consider it a part of defending against the malpractice action. Which in truth, it is."

Jay felt more reassured with each moment. He then added, "There's something else I've thought about. I've never believed the hospital itself is involved in this. I'd like to contact some of the important physicians from other departments, such as the present and past Chiefs of Staff and maybe the hospital administrator, to discuss the departmental actions. I thought I'd present evidence of the harassment and ask them to take action in my behalf. Do you think that's wise?"

After a few moments' thought, John said, "Yes, I think we should attack this head on and see if we can nip it in the bud. I'd be careful. Don't accuse any individuals specifically... but the point can be made that none of this is good for the hospital. There can be no doubt that the attorneys will be forced to sue the hospital for malpractice on the same case, while they sue you... I'd go for it."

Jay stood and thanked John Parsons for the emotional support he had given and the help he expected in the future. But John sent him off with a less than encouraging farewell.

"I would not be surprised to see other things happen, so be psychologically prepared."

"Like what?"

"I think the committee will definitely pursue this further. And I wouldn't be shocked if another malpractice action is begun."

Jay was somewhat stunned. He had hoped, but was not confident, that his presentation at the last meeting might bring an end to the hospital challenge. It never occurred to him that more malpractice threats might come.

They shook hands and Jay left. On the crowded elevator he was oblivious to those around him, deep in thought about John's final comment. At the street level he walked through the revolving glass doors of the large office tower and aimlessly down the sidewalk. His rather slow pace continued for about two blocks before he realized he had walked away from his car instead of toward it. He quickly retraced his steps back to the car and then drove to his office. He called Esther to see what the arrangements for the evening would be.

I wonder what kind of a dinner partner I'll be after this meeting with John Parsons?

Jay took a deep breath, determined not to lay on Esther all the anger and frustration he felt.

Chapter Twenty

The End of a Dream

"Who shall I say wishes to speak with the doctor?"

"Mrs. Allon," Esther responded to Louis Crown's nurse.

After a conversation on the office intercom, the nurse told Esther that he would be out in a moment.

Esther sensed that her brother did not want her to remain in the outer office for very long, as only a minute or two passed before he appeared at the door between the waiting room and the inner office. Without a single word spoken, he waved her to come in.

Esther did not even recognize the man who beckoned her. He had aged much more than she had imagined. She had somehow expected to see someone who looked very like the brother she had last seen so many years before.

Without any warmth or affection, he said in his completely French accent, "My office is straight ahead and to the right at the end of the corridor."

Esther understood very well that he did not intend to allow anyone from his office staff to conclude that she was a member of his family, or anyone important to him at all for that matter.

As he closed the door, Esther approached him and said with significant warmth, "Hello Louis."

She came toward him as if to make some physical contact, a kiss or even just a hug. Then she became aware that he stood there aloof, and non-receptive. As a last ditch effort, she thrust out her hand. Crown barely accepted it.

"In our letters I mentioned nothing about the family," Esther began. And then after a long pause, "Did you know that Mama had died?"

It was as if Esther had just told him that she killed a fly. Louis looked at her impassively and said, "No... when?"

"This year. Papa has been dead for more than ten years."

Esther wanted so badly to talk to Label, not Louis, about the intervening years. She wanted him to know how much she had loved Uri and what it was like to have to raise Itzhak alone. She desperately wanted Label to know how much she had admired their mother and father for the courage they had displayed over the years. Now, with almost everyone gone, Esther wanted to find a way to bring Label back to her emotionally, even if they had to remain geographically far apart.

But there was no reason to check the thermostat to determine how cold the room had become. Some words passed between these two siblings, but certainly no communication. In the long silent stretches Esther felt compelled to somehow reach her brother.

"I felt I could no longer accept the loss of you. Except for my son Itzhak, you are the last member of my family."

Esther turned her back to Louis and walked a step or two away because she felt tears well up in her eyes that she did not want him to see.

"I didn't feel I could afford any longer to lose you. I want us to start again, and, even if we are thousands of miles apart, be a family once again. My son needs to meet you and get to know his uncle. I ..."

Louis interrupted her and said "I'm afraid that will be impossible."

Esther was somewhat confused. Whatever the past had brought, she had been in no way unpleasant, demanding or rude. She brought love and expected some modicum of love in response. So many years had passed. Shouldn't they find a way to bind up past wounds and seek something better in the maturity of their lives?

"I am no longer Jewish and do not wish to be."

Hurt, but not willing to retreat she whispered, "And your wife?"

"She has never been Jewish. She is Austrian."

"Aren't there a significant number of Jews in this community?" she asked.

"Yes."

"Since I imagine many are doctors, don't you socialize with them?"

"Yes."

"And doesn't your wife have a relationship with these Jewish men... and women?"

She was not one foot away from Crown when he looked her in the eye and said coldly, "She tolerates them."

It was not an action that was preceded by any thought or plan. She merely lifted her left hand and smacked him with all her strength across his right cheek. An immediate pink color appeared.

Louis said not one word and flinched not an inch.

"I am so glad that Mama is dead. I would cry my eyes out if she had heard that.... and frankly, LABEL," she spewed out the name with full force and more of a Yiddish accent than Crown had heard in any of her previous conversation, "... for me, you are dead as well."

Louis Crown remained motionless and stoical as Esther continued her tirade.

"You are the scum of the earth. I could not be more pleased that you do not consider yourself Jewish, because to me you stand for everything I hate. But let me assure you that had your mother and father not saved you from the Holocaust, some Nazi would have pulled down your pants, recognized you as a Jew, and gassed you with the rest. Though you think you have washed away your Judaism, someday those who hate Jews—probably your friends—will find out about you and call you a Jew whether you like it or not. And you will deserve whatever they mete out to you."

In an act that Esther had never done in her entire life, she spat in the face of Louis Crown. She turned to the door, left his office, walked down the corridor, through the outer office and out the door, never to see her brother again.

Back at her hotel Esther called the local Federation office and asked them to arrange for an immediate return to Israel. She told them only that she had completed the matter for which she had come to the United States. She asked them to please cancel her engagement with Jay Brown and to apologize to him for her.

Esther would never again speak with Jay Brown. He would never find out that one of the main anti-Semitic doctors behind the assault on his career was himself Jewish.

Chapter Twenty One

Preparing for the Trial

*T*he sudden departure of Esther Allon was a disappointment to Jay Brown, but no more than that. Sally Birnbaum had made it quite clear that Esther's urgent departure was unrelated to him. As far as Sally could determine something quite serious had occurred in Austin or back in Israel—something that caused Esther to leave. Sally told Jay she believed a very private and personal incident was behind Esther's unexpected decision.

Jay assumed that someday he might meet her again. But all the problems he faced had caused him such stress that he put Esther Allon out of his mind. It had been one pleasant evening and nothing more. Whatever had such a significant effect on her was certainly not a part of his life.

Jay began to understand how concerted the effort was to eliminate him from the Austin scene. Once his coverage group dissolved, he made a decision not to seek any group of obstetricians with whom to share time. Instead, he would, when the need arose, contact individual doctors and ask for coverage which he would gladly repay in more time than he requested for himself.

Even with that generous offer most of his requests went ungranted. Physicians told him it was impossible to make such an arrangement, for a variety of superficial reasons.

The pattern could not be considered a coincidence once the harassment began. It was consistent.

Jay finally made a loose arrangement with Roger Ryan. Ryan was not the physician Jay would have nominated for Obstetrician of the Year, but he was competent. That was the level Jay had found it necessary to reach down to, in order to have someone spell him when it was absolutely necessary. Jay took even less time off than he had in the past. He knew he was under close scrutiny and needed to be certain that everything that happened in his practice was beyond questioning.

One morning, after several months had passed, Ryan asked to meet him for a cup of coffee. Jay innocently thought that Ryan merely wanted to make some arrangements for coverage. To Jay's surprise it was to terminate the arrangement.

Roger was extremely apologetic, but related that he had been contacted and told that the Hospital's Quality Control Committee was about to evaluate a number of his records. When he went to check them out, he found they were all cases that Jay had managed for him during times that he was away. He had spoken to members of the Committee who told him they were concerned about his choice of a coverage physician. They insinuated that Roger had "made an improper choice in Jay Brown of a less than adequate physician to cover him." If he continued to cover with Jay, the Committee would find it necessary to continue to scrutinize Roger Ryan's records, even more closely.

Roger told Jay that the pressure was too great. He felt he had to make other arrangements.

Somewhat angered, Jay asked, "Has there ever been a single problem with any patient of yours that I cared for?"

Roger sighed, "Well, no... I just can't constantly be watched by them. I'm sorry Jay, but I've got to end it."

Jay knew then that it would be almost impossible for him to find anyone else. The vise had screwed tighter. But the conspirators really didn't understand Jay's personality very well. Their actions didn't make Jay more willing to throw in the towel. To the contrary his spine got a little stiffer each time another challenge was thrown in his path.

"To hell with the sons-of-bitches. It'll take more than this to make me fold my tent and slink away from these incompetent bastards."

Jay's reaction was at least part of the problem he faced in Austin. He actually did think he was better than most of them, and they sensed that.

———

The meeting was held in a small restaurant, not far from the Medical Center. Jay had requested three men to meet him privately for lunch.

One of the first things he learned, shortly after they were seated, was common knowledge—but not to Jay. The hospital administrator, Martin Stonisch, who was one of the invitees, had been forcibly retired from his position. Jay had become friendly with Martin shortly after he arrived in Austin. There had been an effort by another hospital to steal away some of Rayburn's obstetricians, which in fact did happen. During that time Jay, with the encouragement of Stonisch, remained loyal and Stonisch had not forgotten it. The news of Stonisch's departure was quite a shock to Jay.

Though Stonisch still held the position for another eleven days before a newly hired administrator assumed the role, it was in name only. Ray Baker, the new wonder boy, who was half Stonisch's age and twice as dynamic, was actually already in charge.

Where Stonisch had been a long, strong and stable force for the hospital, Baker had grand ideas for rapid and explosive changes. He saw a future punctuated by takeovers of smaller hospitals, the purchase of the most sophisticated hi-tech equipment to draw specialists from far and wide, and, most important of all, increases in the patient census. The hospital would achieve that with an environment more physician-friendly. To Baker the hospital was less a place where the community could be served than a massive corporate enterprise to be expanded and developed.

Besides Stonisch, Jay lunched with Dr. Harold Burton, a surgeon who was the immediate past President of the Medical Board, and Hiram Watts, the present President. At the very moment Jay hoped to reach these men in his effort to gain support to stop the powers that be in the Department of Obstetrics and Gynecology, Ray Baker was at a separate meeting elsewhere.

––––––––––

Baker sat with Marsh and Slack in his office. It wasn't their first meeting and Baker was less than thrilled about what had transpired within their department. After several meetings with the two of them, he understood what was at stake. Baker's political sense was just about perfect. He was able to rapidly size up risks and benefits of every issue. He knew exactly when he should be a part of the scene and when he should back off and let others be out front.

Marsh had made it clear that the Obstetrical Department brought in a great deal of revenue to the hospital. If for some reason the Department should take a turn for the worse, there were many other ramifications. No hospital Pediatric Department could sustain itself if the Obstetrical Division vanished. Marsh presented Baker with case histories of several other hospitals in which the Departments of Obstetrics had lost a number of physicians. The result was that the OB departments were closed down and shortly after that the Pediatricians found other affiliations which were more satisfactory.

In their presentation to Baker, Slack usually led the way. An emphasis was given to the possibility that Jay Brown's actions might send the hospital's Obstetrical Department down that disastrous path. Never in the discussion did the issue of the quality of care, which Jay Brown had pushed, ever get raised. Nor was there any consideration of the lack thereof by some of the doctors on the staff.

It soon became clear to Baker that the effort to get rid of Brown was a good idea. He knew nothing of how this was to be accomplished and frankly felt better left in the dark. But, he did make it clear that the hospital was ready to be of assistance in this matter.

Slack told Baker, at this meeting, he believed the hospital attorneys should be brought in to help advise them in the management of the Quality Control Committee's handling of Jay Brown.

Baker sat quietly, tipped his head down toward the floor, and scratched his neck. Then he looked up at the two men in front of him and said "Brown's very sharp. I think we have to be very careful not to take any action that might later be subject to some legal challenge. Are you satisfied that the members of the Quality Control Committee won't do anything to create a problem for the hospital?"

Both Marsh and Slack gave rather modest assurances that everything would be arranged carefully. They mentioned nothing of the strange ending of the previous meeting. Actually, they were not quite sure that some among their group might do something foolish.

Since he wanted to take every precaution, Baker readily agreed, and said he would get the hospital attorneys involved immediately.

"If I had to guess who was behind this, I would definitely think in terms of Dr. Crown," Stonisch said. "He's a bad apple and I've known it from shortly after I met him. Now that the black sheep has jumped over the fence, all the others are following him."

"I don't think we should blow this up out of proportion, Jay. Actually no one's stopped you from doing anything," Burton responded.

Harold Burton was a well respected surgeon and a very likable man. He understood that Jay Brown was something of an outsider while Marsh was a major force in the ol' boy network. Burton was not a lame duck like Stonisch. Stonisch could say whatever he wanted. Burton was right in the beginning of his term of one year. By custom it was always renewed for a second year unless something terrible was done by the President of the staff or illness befell him. Burton was not of a mind to stick his neck out.

Hiram Watts was much more naive than Stonisch or Burton and had difficulty believing that any group of physicians would be involved in a scheme to damage another physician. He especially felt that way in this situation, because he truly liked Jay Brown, and could not comprehend that any group of physicians might conspire against him.

Jay continued trying to persuade them that a real problem existed. He tried to make it clear that the problem was getting progressively worse, and would continue, unless someone took action to stop it. Only Stonisch was willing to understand Jay's plight. His promise to look into it, however, was actually rather empty, because no one was going to allow Martin Stonisch to take significant action on any issue, let alone a hot potato such as this. His last eleven days were to be of significance only to the hospital accountant in terms of days left in his salary. All hospital duties for all intents and purposes, had already been transferred to Ray Baker.

Burton would leave this meeting and not think of it again until he was actually confronted by it in a much larger way.

Hiram Watts, on the other hand, would never quite understand why all of this was going on, even when Jay Brown's predictions of how major this would be came true.

Jay had met with John Parsons now on nine separate occasions in preparation for the malpractice trial. They had reviewed the case over and over. By the time they were through, Parsons knew as much as any physician about the delivery of breeches.

It was the nature of the business for really good attorneys. When a medical malpractice case was being handled, they learned every minute detail about that one segment of medicine. John Parsons repeatedly requested articles from journals. He also wanted text book references to support their positions on every issue, from the most major to the most insignificant. Jay filled John's every request.

Dr. Sidney Sternhagen had been named as the primary expert witness for the plaintiffs. Everyone knew Sidney Sternhagen. He was the foremost plaintiff's expert witness in the country. He was bright, glib and an absolute showman. The word was that plaintiffs never lost cases when they had him in their corner.

John devoted many hours going through all the available records he could find in which Sternhagen had testified. He found three things that impressed him significantly.

The first was that it was not uncommon for Sternhagen to take positions that were completely in opposition to each other in different cases. That made it clear to Parsons that Sternhagen would say whatever was necessary to win a case.

The next very surprising thing he found was that the stories surrounding this man's successes were not only distorted, they were amazingly inaccurate. Parsons thought Sternhagen must have had a super PR person working for him. In actuality, the cases in which he testified were more frequently lost than won by the plaintiff's side. The perception of his invincibility must have accounted for some of his victories just on the basis of fear.

The final piece of data that he accumulated in his review dealt with language. As John Parsons read through transcripts, he found an interesting ploy which Sternhagen used repeatedly. In the midst of his testimony, he would repeatedly use multiple syllabic words which Parsons had never heard. He could only assume that the juries who heard them were also completely dumbfounded by his vocabulary. Through the use of his trusty Webster's dictionary, John found that in fact those words did exist. But—and this really broke up Parsons—they usually meant something totally unrelated to the subject at hand. In other words, Sternhagen buffaloed his juries with malapropisms that no one recognized, not even the opposition attorneys. Parsons doubted that it would have any effect on the way he managed the case. It was his belief that badgering an expert witness too much would antagonize a jury rather than yield support. But he did have a plan that would attack Dr. Sidney Sternhagen in a more subtle way—a way that John believed would appeal to the jury. He did not reveal that to anyone—not even to Jay Brown.

John Parsons knew Bill Drinan, who was representing Carla Lansford, very well. Their offices were in the same building. So it was not surprising for Parsons to receive a phone call asking if they could meet. John agreed and asked Drinan to stop at his office and they would talk over lunch in the neighborhood. Side by side they remained silent in a rather crowded elevator. They walked through the lobby out onto the street and down the block to "Not Your Ordinary Deli." It was not as good as many delis he had been to, but it was convenient.

Some idle chatter passed between Parsons and Drinan walking down the street, but nothing of significance. They were not particularly fond of each other.

They entered the restaurant and sat down at a table handled by John's regular waitress, Annie. She knew him well and was crazy about him. Drinan was also known to her, and particularly disliked.

"Good afternoon, John. Got a new intern working for you," she quipped.

John was considerably over six feet tall. Drinan was only about 5`7`` after a lot of stretching. He was also much younger. So Annie continued her harangue with "Would you like a booster chair?"

John interrupted before Drinan could give her a nasty response, "Come on Annie, let up and give us some lunch."

Annie took their order and left.

"Well, Bill, what's this meeting about?"

"A few things have come up that I wanted to be certain you were aware of."

"You shouldn't end a sentence with a preposition," John responded, to get Drinan a little off balance. It served the purpose of annoying him.

Parsons understood very clearly that when a meeting such as this was held a short time before a trial, it was with the express purpose of trying to frighten the defendants into a hefty settlement instead of going to trial.

Stridently Drinan asked "John, are you aware that your client has been under investigation by the Quality Control Committee at the Hospital for improper management of a number of cases?"

"And?" Parsons calmly queried.

"Well I believe that will make him very vulnerable during the testimony."

Parsons brought his left hand up to his jaw, rubbed it, and said, "Why Bill, I believe that testimony will not be allowed in the trial. We'll just have to have that cleared up at a pre-trial hearing."

"Is that your intention?"

"Well, now that you've brought it up, though I hadn't planned it, it certainly is."

Parsons knew just what was necessary to get under Drinan's skin. He had of course been well aware of everything that was happening, and fully intended to call for such a hearing, but he liked the idea of having Drinan think he was unaware, and wanted him to believe he had accidentally spilled the beans, spoiling the opportunity to bring it up as a surprise at the trial.

"And there is something else you should know…" he went on… "we've been asked to represent another patient taking an action against Dr. Brown. The request for information will be going out to him any day. Even though it won't be brought out at this trial, should he lose this trial, it will probably make it even more difficult for him to settle the next one should he desire to do that."

The attempts at intimidation knew no end, which John Parsons understood very well. He knew that demonstrating any signs of weakness had to be avoided. He calmly looked at Drinan and said, "I guess we'll just have to look at the next case when it comes along.

Quite possibly it might have as little merit as this one, and end up just costing your firm a lot of out-front money with no return under your contingency arrangement. That wouldn't be too grand a result for Carnahan, Davis and Drinan."

The remainder of the brief lunch was just tolerable enough for the two of them to finish their sandwiches.

Annie watched the encounter from the other side of the restaurant and could tell from Drinan's raised voice and annoyed looks that the conversation was an unpleasant one. It bothered her that Parsons was having to deal with this person whom she always thought of as the "little runt."

Seeing that they had finished their meal she approached the table and said to Drinan, "Do you get burped before or after you pay your bill?"

The following day in Jay Brown's office there was a request for all the records on Susan Delman, the other patient Monica Crown had called. The demoralizing effect of receiving the letter was slightly diminished by the advance notice John Parsons had provided to Jay that it was forthcoming.

Chapter Twenty Two

The Trial

*J*ay was somewhat surprised when he entered the courtroom for the first time. It was much smaller than he had expected. The courtrooms he had seen in the past, primarily on television or in the movies, looked much more imposing.

The judge's chair and desk were raised above floor level, as he had expected, with a seat for the testifying witness on one side and immediately next to that a jury box. Out in front of the judge there were two tables. Each held the attorneys for each side, and one held the defendant. Beyond that there were only three rows of seats. Everything was rather close together.

When Jay arrived a number of people were already there. The plaintiff's team of two attorneys—Drinan and Carnahan—had multiple cartons of materials they had brought to the courtroom. Parsons had Sue Slater from his office to assist him. He wanted to provide Sue the opportunity to gain some experience. He planned to have her question one or two of the witnesses. The major characters in this play, however, were in the province of John Parsons.

As Jay stood there staring at the volume of material the plaintiff's attorneys had brought, Parsons leaned his head over to Jay's ear.

He whispered, "Don't get nervous. It's an old ploy meant to accomplish just that. They bring cartons and cartons they will never use, just to intimidate you. There's nothing better they can accomplish than to frighten you. First they would like to force you to make a settlement. That would relieve them of the job of the fight and probable loss in this case. If they can't succeed with that, and have to go ahead with the trial, they want you to be in the most agitated state they can possibly get you once you're on the stand."

"Bastards," Jay mumbled to himself.

"Stay cool."

"Who are all those people in the seats in the court room?" Jay asked.

"I wondered about that myself. I've never seen so many people in the gallery at a malpractice trial before. Apparently they're newspaper reporters. My guess is that they got a tip to come to this trial. I'm sure it didn't come from you, so it doesn't take much intelligence to figure out the source. They've got a full court press against you, Jay. The pressure will be unrelenting. If it's too much for you to tolerate you might as well throw in the towel now, rather than go through the torment only to give up later."

Jay looked John square in the eye. "It will take more than these whores to knock me out."

The trial was expected to last three or four days. The first day was pretty much routine, for everyone but Jay Brown, that is. The jury had to be selected from the panel of individuals called for jury duty. Jay listened intently to the *voir dire*, the process used to determine the juror's suitability by each side. John Parsons was pleased to see Jay so intimately involved. Some of his clients had been in such a panic that they barely stirred during the entire trial.

Once all the prospective jurors had been questioned and a portion of them eliminated for a series of different reasons, John, Sue and Jay retired to a private room to select the defense's recommended jurors. The plaintiff's attorneys proceeded in the same manner.

In the privacy of their conversation, it was just as Parsons had expected: Jay Brown had made his own choices for jurors already. They jointly agreed on the jurors they would like and the list was submitted to the judge. The plaintiff's and defense's lists were then used by the judge to name the jury. By this time it was well into the afternoon, so Judge Gladys Farnsworth closed the first day's session. She told the plaintiffs to be ready to present their case at 10 A.M. the next day.

Once the court was out of session, Jay immediately went to the phone to call Joan. The arrangement they had made was that Joan would remain in the office until whatever hour the court session ended. Jay would not carry his pager. He did not want to be disturbed while he was in court. Every time the court broke for a recess, Jay would go immediately to the public phone and call her. If there were emergencies, or patients went into labor, she would call Roger Ryan. Dr. Ryan had agreed, while the trial was in progress, to cover Jay for any deliveries during the daytime. There was a clear understanding there would be no payback in time. He absolutely did not want Jay's name on any of his charts. Jay was more than pleased, and had worked out a financial reimbursement if Ryan needed to be called.

After the first day's session, John Parsons told Jay there was no reason to meet to discuss any strategy, so Jay left immediately for the office. He spent about two hours there, returning all the calls that had been held by Joan during the day. Joan refused to leave the office until all the work was completed and she was certain that her Dr. B. went home.

"You need to get a good night's rest before you go back to court in the morning. Don't you think it's a mistake not to have Dr. Ryan cover you during the nights as well? If you get called out, you'll go to court completely exhausted."

"I can't do that. I'll be all right," Jay said.

She ignored his tone of voice. Joan understood that it was not the Jay Brown she knew and loved whose voice she heard. The stress was unbelievable. She could see it in every expression of his face, as well as the way he spoke. It seemed that her boss—and friend—had aged considerably in the past year or two.

In the morning Jay was extremely impressed as he watched Judge Farnsworth resolve changes in trial dates and special motions that attorneys raised regarding criminal trials. She then retired to her chambers. After that, the participants in his case slowly began to file into the courtroom.

Shortly after ten the bailiff asked the court to rise as Judge Farnsworth entered the courtroom. She brought in the jury and gave them some brief instructions.

"Ladies and gentlemen of the jury, we are here today to tell you about the very sad case of Michael Lansford, who was born..." Drinan began as he gave his introductory remarks.

John Parsons made a brief statement as well. He chose not to get involved with the details of the case at this point.

During this period the Lansford child was held on his mother's lap so that everyone could clearly see that the poor child was severely brain damaged. It was Drinan's intent to have the child appear several times in court, but not for any extended period. Having the child there for too long a period of time would make the jurors immune to the disaster which had befallen this family. The plaintiff's attorneys had a wealth of experience in cases such as this. They knew very well that no matter how horrible a situation might be, after a while the jurors would become desensitized to it. They brought the child back and forth for brief periods just often enough to refresh the jurors' memories. Carla was not happy with the arrangement. She didn't want them to use Michael, but Drinan had insisted, and she concurred.

Jay occasionally looked over at the family with compassion in his eyes. Carla had difficulty with his gaze, and would look away. But it was not out of anger. It was more the horror that it had all come down to this. All Carla really wanted for her baby was to be well and normal, but nothing she could do through anger, forgiveness or any emotion could bring Michael to the state she so desperately wished for. She remembered how many nights she had cried herself to sleep. This terrible misfortune had, as well, destroyed her relationship with her husband. They sat together that day in the courtroom, but in reality their marriage had fallen apart and was not likely to remain intact much beyond the time of this trial.

After Carla Lansford testified to her memory of the day in question, Drinan brought in Sternhagen and went through the details of the delivery and the "mistakes" made by Dr. J.D. Brown. Once Sternhagen identified Jay Brown as the culprit, Drinan brought in other experts to discuss the child's present condition and what services would be necessary and for how many years. Finally, there was an economist who detailed what the total costs over a lifetime would be to care for this child who would never walk, never speak, and never be able to care for himself, for as long as he lived.

When their turn came, John Parsons also had an expert. Richard Weiss was a well-known obstetrician at the medical school and a casual friend of Jay Brown. His credentials were impeccable and his slow, warm, easy manner made him an excellent witness. Unlike Sternhagen, he had little experience testifying in court. But he was so poised, with so much experience as a teacher, that Parsons felt certain he would do his job well.

The morning had been taken up by opening statements, Carla's testimony, and other administrative business. It was after the lunch break that Drinan again brought on Sidney Sternhagen.

Sternhagen, was quite impressive. In response to a question early in his testimony, he turned toward the jury and spoke to them as if there were not one other person in the room. He addressed them in the smoothest, softest grandfatherly tone one could possibly imagine.

"I've spent a great deal of time looking over these records and the background of Dr. Brown. I can say nothing bad about this fine doctor in the past. But, my dear friends, in this case, unfortunately, Dr. Brown inadvertently did some terrible things that caused the very sad result you have had to see this very day in this courtroom."

Sternhagen oozed his way through the testimony. He repeatedly reminded the jury that, were it not for some mistakes from this fine doctor, the Lansford child would be normal. It was near the end of his testimony about the dangers of a vaginal delivery of a breech presentation that Drinan asked him if there were any other aspects of the delivery that called into question the choice of a vaginal delivery.

"As a matter of fact, yes! Everyone I know today would be terribly concerned about the risk of nuchal arms in this delivery. Unfortunately, that is what happened to Baby Lansford, which significantly increased the likelihood of suffering brain damage. As we evaluate…"

Parsons quickly turned to Jay Brown with a look that could kill. Jay could see that in Parsons' head was the question, *'What the hell are nuchal arms? Why didn't you tell me about this?'*

Without a word to Jay, Parsons scribbled out a note and passed it to his secretary who sat behind him in the first row of seats. She took it, rose immediately, and left the courtroom. She returned in a few minutes. Parsons looked at her and she nodded affirmatively.

Drinan continued to obtain testimony from Sternhagen for another half hour. Frequently, during the earlier part of Sternhagen's testimony, Parsons had looked at Jay Brown with reassurance to let him know there was nothing to be concerned about. Not since the "nuchal arms" shocker did Parsons look at Jay again.

Finally, Sternhagen was done. Judge Farnsworth looked at her watch. It was past four in the afternoon. She decided they had been at it long enough and told the jury they would go into recess until tomorrow at nine A.M. The Judge reinforced her admonition to the jury not to discuss the case with anyone. She rose and left and the jury was dismissed.

Parsons looked at Jay, "Let's talk before you make your calls."

They walked into the outer lobby. Richard Weiss stood there. Parsons walked over to him and said, "Thanks for coming so quickly."

The note he had passed to his secretary asked her to contact Dr. Weiss immediately and ask him to come to the courthouse to discuss an urgent matter.

"Let's find an empty conference room."

Once inside, Parsons opened the discussion. "What are nuchal arms and why hasn't this been raised before?"

Weiss looked strangely at Parsons. "Nuchal arms? Why are you asking about nuchal arms?"

"Sternhagen just said one of the problems in this case was that the baby's presentation included nuchal arms and that it adversely affected the outcome."

Brown and Weiss looked at each other quizzically and smiled. Jay finally spoke.

"John, there were NO nuchal arms. Nuchal arms are arms stretched out over the baby's shoulders and above the head, and possibly pulled back around the neck. They are NOT present in this case. Get the X-rays."

Parsons nodded to his secretary and she was out of the room immediately.

While he waited, Parsons tried to pull all the information in his head together.

"Maybe this is part of the whole pattern of using non-understandable words. He does so many things that make no sense, but in the confusion no one challenges him on it."

With the X-rays in hand, Weiss and Brown pointed out how they could verify that the concept of nuchal arms made no sense.

Parsons, who had been in a blue funk for the past hour, began to get elated.

"Tomorrow is going to be amazing. I've got to get back to

my office and work on my cross examination of Sternhagen in the morning. Thanks so much, Richard. I'm so pleased you were able to come over so quickly. And, Jay... I am TRULY sorry that I got angry with you about this."

Parsons was obviously deeply embarrassed, "I really should have known better than to think if either you or Sternhagen had deceived me, it wouldn't be you. And Richard, we probably won't get to your testimony until the day after tomorrow. We still have the Sternhagen cross, their other witnesses, and Jay's testimony, which may be quite long. That will be followed by their cross of Jay. I'll let you know when the time frame becomes clearer. I hope I won't need to call you to come over unnecessarily again."

Weiss and Brown walked out of the courthouse together and said good-bye. Then Jay remembered he had to go back in and get on the phone.

Parsons began his cross examination with his original plan and left the nuchal arms for later. Judge Farnsworth brought Dr. Sidney Sternhagen back to the stand and reminded him that he was still under oath. He reassured her in his smoothest manner that he understood and would do everything that the court desired. During all that conversation he did not face the judge. He faced the jury.

"Good morning Dr. Sternhagen," John Parsons said in a bright, cheery and friendly tone. Everyone seemed comfortable—the jury, the defense attorney, and especially the witness.

"I understand that you are quite experienced in the area of testimony at malpractice trials."

"I am," said Sternhagen rather proudly.

"You don't take every case that is offered to you, do you?"

Once again Sternhagen appeared very confident in his answer.

"No, you're absolutely correct," he replied. With a question as gentle as that, Sternhagen felt that this might be one of the easier cases he had undertaken. He followed with: "There are far too many cases filed and I am very selective. I want to be certain that there is real merit before I wish to sacrifice my very valuable time. After all, it is more important that I care for my own patients."

Parsons continued, "About how much time does it take you to review a case before you decide you will take it?"

"About two or three hours," Sternhagen said.

"And what would you estimate is the proportion of the cases you review that you agree to participate in?"

Proudly, Sidney Sternhagen replied, "Oh, only about one in three or one in four."

"If you decide to take a case, does it involve a lot more time than if you've rejected it?"

Slowly being sucked in, without his awareness, Sternhagen wanted to demonstrate how thorough he was and said, "Oh yes! To do this properly one must spend at least ten to twenty hours of preparation before the trial."

Parsons then began to come in for the kill.

"What do you charge per hour to review cases?"

For the first time, Sternhagen began to show some slight signs of discomfort. He gave a small cough to clear his throat before he very softly said, "Two hundred and fifty dollars per hour."

"I'm sorry Dr. Sternhagen", John Parsons said, "I didn't hear your answer clearly. Was that two hundred and fifty dollars per hour?"

Sternhagen stiffened slightly. "Yes."

"What is your fee for depositions and trials, Dr. Sternhagen?"

"Five hundred dollars per hour," Sternhagen said in a voice that could be heard. He realized that if he mumbled, Parsons would make him repeat it.

"Does that include travel time to and from the different cities to which you travel to testify?"

"Absolutely not! My fee for that is the lower figure of two hundred and fifty dollars per hour. After all, that is time I am taken away from my own practice."

Sternhagen sat up more erect in his seat. These were not points he wished to emphasize. There was a rather lengthy pause as Parsons slowly walked over to the desk where Jay and Susan sat and made believe he looked for something as he shuffled a few pages on the table. His purpose was only to create a pause for effect. With his back to the witness, judge and jury, Parsons looked up at Jay and Susan. The courtroom was extremely quiet. Then he turned back toward Sidney Sternhagen with a paper in his hands.

"Dr. Sternhagen, the records show that you testified at an average of nineteen cases per year for the past five years. Is that correct?"

"I have no idea. I don't keep such a scorecard."

"But does that sound... right to you?"

"I told you I have no idea."

"Well the record seems quite well documented.... If I might, your Honor, I'd like to bring out this large writing pad."

Farnsworth agreed, and a stand with a writing pad about thirty inches high and twenty four inches across was brought into the side area of the court. It faced primarily toward the judge, witness and jury. With a large black marking pencil Parsons printed a very large 19.

"If I just take the lowest number of cases you might have reviewed and rejected by your estimate of one out of three or four, that would make 57 cases. Let's just make it 55. At the two to three hours per case, which you suggested, that would be a minimum of 110 hours."

As if he had not done all the calculations already John said, "Now let's see 110 times $250 dollars would be... 100 times $250 would be $25,000 and 10 times... I think that would make it $27,500. Is that correct Dr. Sternhagen?"

"I don't know."

"Don't you keep financial records, doctor?"

"No I don't." Sternhagen shot back. "My secretary does all of that."

"O.K. Doctor. In the nineteen cases, I calculated, based on their locations, you traveled well in excess of ten hours round trip to each location, including limousine times in the cities where you testified. That's a minimum of another 190 hours. Let's see, that would be about $47,500. That brings the total up to $75,000."

From this point on, every time Parsons came up with another number he got the same brief, annoyed response from Sternhagen.

"I don't know."

"Well let's look at the cases you do take. You said you spend ten to twenty hours in preparation for each. Let's just take an average and say,

Oh… about fifteen for each. Let me calculate this. My math is so bad."

Parsons spoke like a small country lawyer who wished to find his way, but this very clever attorney knew exactly what he was doing with every word, every movement, every look.

"I believe that comes up to 285 hours at $250 per hour."

He went slowly through the steps of multiplication on the pad.

"That should be $61,250. No, I forgot to carry the "one" over. I guess it's lucky I'm not a math teacher."

The little intentional mistake made him appear even more human.

"That's $71,250. Let's make it $70,000 for round figures. Now let's see. That brings the total to $145,000."

John went back to his table and said nothing. The jury, made up of members whose total annual income probably averaged between twenty and thirty thousand dollars annually, watched the proceedings much more intently now. Sternhagen's testimony yesterday had interested them, but the lesson in obstetrics he gave them was non-confrontational. They sat back and enjoyed it. But today was different. There was a tingle in the air and they were acutely into what transpired.

"That brings us to the nineteen cases you accepted. From what I determined, it looks like you spent about an average of twelve hours per case in the combination of the depositions taken before trial and your time on the witness stand. Is that right Doctor Sternhagen?"

The same terse "I don't know" followed.

"That would make it about 228 hours. Let's just round it down to 225 hours."

Parsons continually lowered the number on each calculation to make it seem that he was giving Sternhagen the benefit of the doubt.

"225 times $500 per hour comes out to… $112,500. That makes the total, now let's get this right, $257,500. Okay, we'll just round that off again and say you make about a quarter of a million dollars a year in malpractice cases. Is that correct Dr. Sternhagen?"

The courtroom was in total silence. Saying a quarter of a million rather than two hundred and fifty thousand seemed to have devastating effect.

Parsons repeated, "Is that correct doctor?"

Sternhagen was visibly shaken. "I've told you repeatedly I have no idea. My secretary keeps those records and gives them to the accountant. I don't know the answer."

"Then I'll leave this subject, Dr. Sternhagen. And if I understand you correctly you don't know how much money you earn every year."

Parsons turned and went back to his table. The case had begun to take a significant turn toward the defense. If the plaintiff's primary witness was completely shot down, the case was certain to be won by the defense. Parsons had just begun.

"I think this might be a good time to take a short break," Judge Farnsworth said. "We'll resume in fifteen minutes."

Immediately after the judge and jury left the courtroom Sternhagen, Carnahan and Drinan went back to the corner of the room, heads close together and obviously distressed, they remained in deep conversation until the recess came to an end.

Jay went to the phone to check in with Joan. Parsons and Sue Slater remained at the table and appeared quite relaxed and confident.

Jay was concerned about his call to Joan. Patricia Martin had called. She complained of contractions, but she was only 33 weeks pregnant. Joan had sent her to the Labor and Delivery suite. There had not yet been a return call from the hospital. Jay told Joan to contact Dr. Ryan and advise him of the situation and the need to start Mrs. Martin on Terbutaline if she showed signs of premature labor.

———

Judge Farnsworth and the jury returned to the courtroom.

"Are you ready to resume your cross examination, Mr. Parsons?"

"I am, Your Honor."

"Are you ready, doctor?"

"Yes, Your Honor."

John Parsons began very slowly. He reviewed with Sidney Sternhagen some of the positions he had taken. The post recess questions demonstrated none of the attack which had characterized the previous discussion.

Sternhagen appeared more relaxed. As far as he was concerned, the worst was over. He could return to his approach of conversation with the jury, as if he were more than an expert. He wanted to appear to be their advisor and friend.

After about thirty minutes, or in other words another $250 charge to the law firm of Carnahan, Davis and Drinan, Parsons walked back to his table and flipped through papers. He once again gave the impression of a novice attorney not completely organized. But Parsons sought nothing more than a long, silent pause for effect. Suddenly, he turned and spoke to Sternhagen again. "Dr. Sternhagen…," and another long pause, "tell me about nuchal arms. I don't know to what that refers. I assume the jurors do not know that term either."

Here was another opportunity to befriend the jury. Sternhagen would go into his favorite role as a "teacher.."

"Certainly Mr. Parsons I would be glad to explain that to you and the jury."

He looked the jurors in the eye with a soft smile.

"When a newborn comes out as a breech, especially if the delivering doctor is not very well trained in his technique…" he then continued his explanation for about five minutes, giving the jury a complete understanding of this complication. "…so you can see, with the arms caught up above the baby's head, the space does not allow the head to come through. The results can be disastrous."

"Thank you, Dr. Sternhagen, for your very clear explanation. I assume from what you have told us that unless there is a description of this complication as it occurs at the time of the delivery, the only way to make the diagnosis would be with an X-ray."

"That is correct."

"Since there is no notation of this in the record, I assume that you saw this on the X-rays that were taken before the delivery to determine if there was adequate space for this baby."

Once again Dr. Sternhagen said "That is correct."

Had he seen the wrong X-rays? Had he just made a mistake as he looked at the right X-rays? None of it made any sense.

"May I show you these X-rays, doctor?"

"Certainly."

"Doctor Sternhagen, could you tell me what this is?" John asked as he handed the X-ray to Sternhagen with his pen at a specific spot.

An X-ray box with a light had been brought into the courtroom and Sternhagen, with the permission of the judge, left his seat to go down to the box. John turned the light on and Sternhagen held the X-ray up to it for quite some time, and said nothing.

Parsons softly said, "Dr. Sternhagen, what is this?"

"A finger. I believe it's a finger," Sternhagen replied tersely.

"And this, doctor?" as Parsons pointed to a spot immediately adjacent to the previous spot.

"A finger."

The process continued five times until Parsons moved his pointing pen to an area just slightly apart from the first area. Once again—this time only four times—Dr. Sternhagen responded in the same manner.

Parsons spoke again.

"I believe in this area we only see four fingers. One must be hidden on the X-ray. It looks to me like there are two hands down alongside the baby's trunk. Now that would indicate to me that if there were two arms behind the head we would need to find about twenty fingers, Doctor."

Sternhagen was visibly shaken and angry.

"I'm not a radiologist. I can't discuss these X-rays any further."

"Well, I really don't need to discuss them any further. I just need you to agree that there were no nuchal arms at this delivery."

"I am not a radiologist. I have nothing further to say."

"All right, Dr. Sternhagen. I think we understand."

He looked at the jury for a moment as if to transfer that understanding to them without a word spoken.

Turning to Judge Farnsworth, defense attorney John Parsons said, "I'm finished with this witness your Honor."

Farnsworth dismissed Sternhagen and recessed court for the day.

———————

When she and the jurors had left, John turned to Jay and said, "Get some rest, you'll testify tomorrow after they finish with their minor witnesses. We might start before lunch. We'll take about an hour and a half or possibly two. They may start their cross examination on you tomorrow late in the afternoon and finish on Thursday morning. I'll let Richard Weiss know that it will probably be on Thursday that he testifies. The case might go to the jury late Thursday or early Friday. Remember, get some sleep."

Jay was ecstatic about the day's turn of events and told Joan what had happened. Then Joan told him the bad news: Mrs. Martin was in premature labor. Jay hung up and went straight to the hospital. Roger Ryan was there.

"Thanks so much, Roger. What's happened with Pat?"

"She definitely in early labor. She came in about three centimeters dilated with contractions every five minutes. Fortunately, she has not yet ruptured her membranes. I gave her subcutaneous Terbutaline to stop the labor and it seemed to help for a while. But now she has broken through the medication."

"Thanks again. I'm free now. So I'll take over."

"How's the trial going?" Roger asked. Every obstetrician, except the conspirators, had compassion for the situation because they knew that at any time it could be their turn.

"Very well… yes, very well. Thanks for asking. If this problem's not resolved by the morning, I may call you back in."

"That's fine," Roger said as he left the Labor and Delivery suite.

Until the wee hours of the morning Jay remained there, trying to find the right combination of drugs to stop the progress of Pat Martin's labor. It took rather large doses of Magnesium sulfate, intravenously, to finally gain control of the situation. Pat Martin got out of the danger of a premature delivery that night, but Jay Brown would not get the rest he needed for the next day of the trial.

———

When Jay took the stand the next morning he should have been totally exhausted. But his adrenaline was at full throttle and it was impossible to tell that the previous night had been almost sleepless.

John Parsons decided to let him begin with how many breeches he had delivered. Jay then described how such a delivery was accomplished. Shortly after Jay began to testify, Drinan jumped up and objected. When Farnsworth asked the basis of the objection, Drinan complained that it sounded like Jay Brown was functioning as an expert witness.

Drinan was devastated when he heard Farnsworth's overrule:

"With that many breech deliveries accomplished, he sounds like he can be considered an expert."

Drinan realized the trial was a lost cause unless he could come up with something dramatic.

Jay continued. "The delivery of a breech is totally different than that of a head-first baby. When the baby's head is the presenting part, which we call a vertex delivery, the largest diameters of the baby pass through the pelvis before any other part of the baby. So we know that if there is room for the head, there should be no further difficulty. With a breech, however, the largest diameters pass through last..." A pause then: "... once the legs are out, then the delivering physician must gently, and yet firmly bring the trunk down with the baby's back facing straight up. That is continued until one can see the scapulae appear. Those are the shoulder blades you can see on your back. At that point the baby gets..."

Every member of the jury was listening intently to each word from Jay Brown. It was obvious to John Parsons that they had transferred their trust to him from Sidney Sternhagen. From the looks on their faces they were enjoying every moment of the description. It was true for John Parsons, as well.

"... and finally the face is lifted out of the back of the vagina and the baby has been delivered. If the choice of cases is made carefully in advance, following the rules that I outlined in the beginning, the results for mother and baby are excellent."

Parsons continued to question Jay about the issues that had been raised by Drinan and Sternhagen, but intentionally left out any mention of the nuchal arms. He believed that issue had been clearly resolved. In one hour and thirty five minutes he was done and turned the witness over.

Now it was Drinan's last chance. If nothing was done at this point it was unlikely that anything would change when Richard Weiss testified as the expert witness for the defense. He was not likely to make a blunder such as Sternhagen had done.

Drinan decided to follow Parsons' lead and come at Jay slowly. After about ten minutes of very benign questions he came out with his cannon fully loaded.

"Have you ever been under investigation at Sam Rayburn Hospital?'

Before Jay barely had a chance to breathe, Parsons was on his feet. He shouted "Objection, Your Honor."

"Objection sustained. Would counsel for the plaintiff and defense come up here now?"

As the two lawyers approached the bench, Judge Farnsworth whispered so that only they could hear.

"Mr. Drinan, this matter has already been dealt with in a pre-trial hearing and the decision was laid down. Your question bears no relationship to this trial and was declared inadmissible. Do you understand that?"

Drinan then spoke in a voice intentionally perceptible to the jurors and possibly the gallery. "But, Your Honor, he has gorked babies left and right."

Farnsworth was furious. "This trial is in recess! The jury will take a fifteen minute break. Attorneys for both sides will meet me in my chambers."

Farnsworth rose and exited quickly. The jurors followed suit, a little confused. The lawyers made their way back to Judge Farnsworth's chambers.

"Mr. Drinan, that outburst for the benefit of the jurors was the type of cheap shot I will not tolerate in my court. Were you present at the pre-trial hearing?"

"Yes, Your Honor."

"Is English not your first language?"

"It is."

"Then you understood that the testimony you have tried twice to insert has been strictly forbidden."

"Yes, Your Honor."

"I could toss you into a cell right now for that action, but I want this trial to end. I certainly could declare a mistrial and start this nonsense all over again. But I won't do either of those things. We'll go back into that room and I'll give you one more chance. Another outburst and I promise you I will charge you with contempt of court and throw the book at you. Do you understand me, absolutely clearly?"

"Yes, Your Honor."

Judge Farnsworth looked at everyone and said as firmly as she possibly could, "Now let's finish this trial without any more nonsense."

When the session started again Judge Farnsworth directed the jury to ignore any of the statements made in the last few minutes before the recess. Jay Brown was distressed nevertheless, because he knew that the judge's statement could not wipe out what they had heard.

Jay was certain that in the back of the jurors' minds sat, *"But he has gorked babies left and right."*

More than anything, Jay wished he could punch Drinan square in the face for the lies about him. It was that type of behavior which had made the reputation of attorneys so bad within the medical profession, or for that matter, in society in general. But, as his mind wondered through all that happened, he could not maintain an attitude of dislike for the legal profession. He constantly came back to the realization that he had met and known few people in his life for whom he had greater admiration than John Parsons. It was not just his remarkable skill as a lawyer. It was his basic common decency and his values that had impressed Jay the most.

The trial progressed with no further disruptions. Although it could not possibly have gone better, the anxiety level gradually rose for John Parsons as the time approached for the jury to make a decision.

These twelve strangers went into a totally private and concealed setting to determine, as far as Jay was concerned, the course of the remainder of his life. It mattered not to him that droves of physicians had lost malpractice cases and gone on with their lives. To Jay Brown, if he was found responsible, it would shatter his ability to ever practice medicine again.

John and Jay met privately for about a half hour before the session began. John knew that before the morning was over the two sides would make closing statements and Judge Farnsworth would charge the jury with her instructions. Then they would go into deliberation. Parsons needed to clarify for Jay what to expect after that.

"The law requires that the jury answer certain specific questions. The first thing they will have to respond to is whether some act of yours was improper. After that, they will be asked whether the adverse result was caused by that improper action. In order for you to lose the case they must say "yes" to both questions."

"Yes to only one or the other has no significance?"

"That's absolutely right, Jay."

"And is that the end of it?"

"No. They will be asked a number of questions relating to the financial responsibility, should the case be won by the plaintiff. The law requires that they answer those questions even if they have already decided that you are not responsible. That's really important to understand. Don't get upset or panicky when they start to rattle off the millions of dollars if you've already been vindicated by the first two questions. Remember, they are required to provide those numbers regardless of the decision about responsibility."

"O.K. I've got it. Let's go in and get this done."

They shook hands with a long tight grip.

"I'm sure you're going to give them a great closing argument. I want to say this now before their decision. I couldn't have had a finer attorney representing me. Whatever happens, I will be in your debt forever."

John Parsons seemed somewhat embarrassed by the praise. They headed for the courtroom.

———

"Ladies and gentlemen of the jury, you may begin your deliberations."

The closing arguments and the judge's charge completed, the jurors made their way to the deliberating room. Jay looked at them carefully as they walked out. They seemed like a decent enough group of people. They were mixed racially and composed of seven women and five men. Jay worried that the women, just based on their compassion for this poor mother and baby, might find against him. As unpleasant and obnoxious as Drinan had been, Mrs. Lansford and her baby made a wonderful impression both as they sat in the gallery and during her testimony. Certainly, if Jay felt so bad for her, the jury could feel no less.

John grabbed Jay's arm and said, "Let's grab a cup of coffee. They'll call us if they need us."

"How long do you expect this will be?"

"Well, it's," as John glanced at his watch, "about one forty-five I guess she'll give them until about four thirty. If she doesn't hear from them by then, she'll probably call them back into court and ask about the deliberation. If they say they are almost done, she'll probably send them back to complete their deliberation this evening. But, if they say they're a long way off, she'll send them home with instructions to talk to no one, and return in the morning. So how long might it be? Anywhere from an hour to two days."

After coffee Jay called Joan from the pay phone to find out if anything important had happened at the office. He knew Mrs. Martin was still in the hospital. This morning, before the court session began, he had spoken to the nurses at the hospital. She did fine on the magnesium sulfate. The contractions had stopped and they had decreased the dose. A low grade bladder infection was found. That was probably the culprit that caused the premature contractions. Mrs. Martin drank too little fluid so she was dehydrated as well, which aggravated the condition. Giving her I.V. fluids and antibiotics along with the tocolytic agents to stop the labor may very well have solved the problem.

Joan had a long list of messages for him and matters to discuss. None was very serious or urgent, but they took up time and got his mind off the trial.

Then Jay felt a tap on his shoulder. It was John.

"They want us back in the court room."

Not even a full hour had passed since the jury began deliberations.

"I've got to go now, Joan. I'll call you later... thanks.... I really appreciate all your positive thoughts."

Everyone stood while the jurors filed back in and took their seats. Then everyone else sat down.

"Have you reached your decision?"

"Yes, Your Honor," responded the forewoman.

"How do you find on question one?"

"Our finding is No."

John, Jay and Susan all grasped hands as joy spread over their faces.

"And on question two?"

"No, Your Honor."

Their hands were even tighter.

"On question three?"

"Zero, Your Honor"

"Question four…"

All the way down through question eight, the answers were "zero."

When everything was done Jay sat for a long while at the table and said nothing. Some reporters came down to question him.

"I'll just go back to work and take care of my patients as before," was his response to what the future held.

When they finally left he sat for a while, quietly, at the table.

Then he turned to John, "What did the zeros mean? I don't understand in view of the fact that you told me they apply a number even though it means nothing once responsibility is relieved."

Parsons looked at Jay with a smile.

"Jay, I've been in an awful lot of malpractice cases and I've never seen that. I can only tell you what my guess is."

"O.K."

"I assume that they were extremely upset about this case, because there was no basis for any action. Then, on top of that, was the folly of the plaintiff's expert witness. I guess they were so annoyed that they said zero, even though there obviously are true massive expenditures for this unfortunate child. It was just their way to thumb their collective noses at the whole process."

"It's really the pits. I love you for all you've done. I'll never forget you."

They rose and embraced. Jay took out his handkerchief to blow his nose. He hugged Sue Slater, picked up his papers and walked to his car.

He slept long and hard that night.

Chapter Twenty Three

Maintaining the Pressure

*F*or a few weeks no one made any waves. Jay wondered if it were possible that the results of the malpractice trial had caused a change of heart. After all this effort, might there have been a decision that the entire battle wasn't worth it? Could they have decided to just leave him outside the inner circle and ignore him?

But the day came when Joan brought him another registered letter. It was her custom to open all the mail and sort it out, but she brought this piece to him, unopened, and watched as he read it.

Dear Doctor Brown:

As a follow-up to the previously reviewed records, the Hospital Quality Control Committee requests your presence to review three additional charts which have been selected by the committee since the last time they met with you.

The Committee would like to meet with you on September 5th, 1984 at 1 P.M.

They would like you to be prepared to discuss the following cases.

1. Anita Martinez – #84-045736
2. Joan Jason – #79-038958
3. Alice Forbes – #84-053098

The charts will be available for your review when you contact Ms. Genevieve Powell in Medical Records at any time between now and then. However, they will not be available to be removed from that department.

Sincerely yours,

Christiana L. Forsythe

Medical Staff Secretary

Jay stared at the letter for some time. He flipped the names of the patients in his mind to see if he could remember a problem that occurred in any or all of them, and noticed that one, Joan Jason, was an old case. Her baby had been born many years before all these challenges began. That seemed strange.

Ray Baker was on top of everything that happened in the Department of Obstetrics & Gynecology. Although his ideas might be imprinted on everything that transpired, his fingerprints appeared nowhere.

He called in Marsh, Slack and, this time, Crown as well. He sensed that things had not progressed as they had planned.

"Your idea that this would all get resolved through a malpractice trial obviously hasn't worked out. Is there some logically thought-out plan, or is this just to be hit and miss?"

When there was no immediate response, he added, "I think we have much to lose if this just drags on. It looks like you're more likely to get worn down than he is."

Louis Crown took the lead in the response, as he felt somewhat responsible for the failed malpractice trial. It had been his original idea.

"It's a little bit more of a problem than we had originally thought. But, I suppose, it will be resolved without too much more difficulty. We have a case which I suppose will end this situation. After the next meeting, if he does not quit, we will ask the Board to remove his privileges."

"And do you believe they will do that?"

"I'm certain," Slack interjected.

Only Marsh remained silent. He was less certain than the other two that everything would go so smoothly. He was confident that the continued attack would sooner or later cause Jay Brown to throw in the towel. He didn't think Jay had the stomach for a prolonged struggle. Marsh found it difficult to accept positive personal attributes in someone he held in such poor esteem, but the expectations of the conspirators seemed to be off the mark due to their inability to evaluate Jay Brown objectively.

"How soon will all of this happen?" Baker came back sharply.

"The Quality Control Committee meets in a few days and then we'll offer him a way out or... throw the son-of-a-bitch out," answered Slack.

Baker said nothing, but wondered if they were a little bit too cocky, a little too sure of themselves. Up until now their track record left something to be desired.

Slack, like Crown, could barely wait for all of the pieces to fall together. The plan they had presented to Baker had been decided upon just a few days previously at Alice's apartment. Marsh had been there, in the midst of a sexual encounter with Alice on Sunday afternoon, when his pager went off at the most inopportune moment.

"Hello, this is Jack Marsh!"

"Jack, we need to talk with you, now!" Steve Slack said with some urgency.

"Now?"

"Yeah. We've got to get a handle on the Brown matter."

"Give me fifteen minutes... I've just come out of the shower."

Because he knew where he could usually find Marsh on a Sunday, Slack asked, "Are you at Alice's?"

"Yeah."

"We'll come there," Slack said and hung up before Marsh had the opportunity to change the meeting place.

As he hung up the phone, Marsh looked and saw that he had totally lost his erection.

"I've got to talk to these clowns," he said to Alice.

"That's O.K. Jack. I'll get dressed and leave."

She didn't really care. Her tie to Marsh had changed. She had less interest in making love, but had not revealed that to Jack Marsh in any way. For his part nothing had changed.

"No, I don't want you to go. We can start again. Just stay in the bedroom with the door locked so no one accidentally walks in on you."

"If you say so, Jack," Alice said. She was uncertain as to how all of this would play out. She was fearful of where it would leave her. She did not cope well with that uncertainty.

————

Marsh was somewhat surprised to see how many of his colleagues had met to discuss the problem. Slack walked in the door with Crown, Candless, Byler and Buddy Lane. They discussed the plan in detail. In her bedroom Alice heard only small bits of the conversation. Though she could not make out any of the details it was obvious that they had come to talk about Jay Brown. Alice felt sick to her stomach about her presence there. She knew that in a little while she would give her body to Jack Marsh, who planned to destroy Jay.

———

On Monday when Jay arrived at the office he called Alexander Stoddard to see if he could get some insight into this new request from the Quality Control Committee. Stoddard, of course, knew about the meeting as he had been advised of it by Jack Marsh. Beyond that he knew nothing. He was not even privy to who would discuss each case. Marsh told Stoddard he would handle that. Actually Steve Slack was the one who made the arrangements.

Just as he got Stoddard on the phone, Joan walked in and passed him a note.

"Excuse me one moment, Alley." He looked up at Joan and said, "Tell her I'll call her right back."

"Tell me, Alley, what do you know about this new request from the Quality Control Committee?"

"In all honesty, nothing, Jay. But I understood after the last meeting that they wanted to review your charts again after a few months to see if things had improved."

"Improved! Improved over what? Those charts were all nonsense," Jay shot back.

"I don't want to get into that discussion. I think you should just come with an open mind. Answer their questions and have it over with."

"O.K. That's fine. But I've got one other question."

"What's that?"

"If they decided to review the charts for a few months after the last meeting, why is one of the charts they've listed more than five years old?"

"I… I don't know. I don't know the answer to that, Jay. I wish I could be of more help, but I really don't know."

The conversation ended on that unresolved note. But, to Jay it sounded like Stoddard was straightforward with him. He never believed that Stoddard was a part of this conspiracy. Stoddard was Chairman of the Quality Control Committee, but others behind the scene had to be the ones who pulled the strings.

Jay looked at the message Joan had passed to him.

It said "Alice Crain is on the phone and it sounds rather urgent." He dialed Alice's number.

"Jay, I've got to meet you... today!"

"All right."

"There's a small coffee shop called Hannah's on Sixth Street. Can we meet there at say... eleven o'clock this morning?"

"Let's see." He looked at his watch. " It's just past nine thirty. I've got rounds to make but no patients in the office this morning. That should be fine.... Are you O.K?"

There was a rather long pause, then, "No... not really.... I'll see you at eleven."

———————

Jay finished seeing the patients in the hospital and then stopped down at Medical Records and asked for Genevieve Powell.

"Gen, do you have the charts for the next Quality Control Meeting pulled yet?"

"Yes, I've got them for you."

"I'll stop in later this evening and review them. Thanks a lot Gen."

In a few minutes Jay was in his car on the way to meet Alice. He couldn't help but be concerned.

Jay didn't know the coffee shop and didn't even know the neighborhood very well, but he found the place with no difficulty. When he entered the shop he recognized the back of Alice's head. He walked past the other tables and booths, and greeted her.

As she turned her head he could see a pained expression.

"Thanks for coming, Jay. I needed to talk with you."

Alice sat still for a while. She said nothing and did not look directly at Jay. She took a puff on a cigarette and then a sip of black coffee.

"Would you like a cup of coffee?"

"I'll pass," said Jay.

Then Alice said, "There is absolutely no doubt there's a conspiracy to get rid of you."

Jay said "I have to tell you that I was just as certain of that fact before I made this trip, and before you told me."

"You don't understand Jay. It's not a gut feeling. I was there. I was there as they made plans.... I heard them... this is actually happening."

"Who's 'they' and what's their plan?"

"I don't know. I was in the next room. But they met about you. I'm not certain of everyone who was there. But Jack met with them and I heard Slack, Crown and Candless definitely. I'm pretty sure I heard Byler and maybe Lane. I don't what their plan is.... Jay, you need to get out of this community. Move on and forget it. They're bad."

"Wait a minute. You're not suggesting I'm in danger, are you?"

"I don't know what I'm saying. It's just not worth it to fight with these people."

"Alice, I can't do that. I've got to stay here and fight. You can be a big help to me. Let me know what that group plans. I'd really appreciate some advanced information. But I can't quit. I just can't."

"I know this is one great big mistake, Jay," she said, somewhat angrily. "I'm really sorry you feel you have to change what's here. I don't think that will happen."

They talked for a little while longer, then Alice asked Jay to leave first. Her anxiety level had reached a fever pitch. He would have liked to tell her not to speak with him anymore, so that she wouldn't be in any jeopardy, but was sure she could help him with information. After he left he begin to feel a little guilty about it. He knew that his request meant that she would be a spy for him. He would use her for his benefit in this struggle. But things were difficult and he needed all the help he could get.

Once again matters had piled up.

———

Jay told Parsons about his meeting with Alice. He wanted to know what action he should take in view of the upcoming Quality Control Meeting and the possibility of a second malpractice case.

"Jay, you need to understand that these committees have been provided with all sorts of protection to prevent action against their membership. The purpose was to get them to function honestly without fear of reprisal from physicians who did bad things."

"Is that what they're doing? Stopping bad physicians from practicing?" Jay fired back.

"No, unfortunately, the system is being abused. Many times hospital staffs have used their immunity to harass physicians for personal and competitive reasons. But you've got no protection. The meetings they hold are not subject to the rules of law. They're pretty much on their own."

"You mean I can go into court and demonstrate that rigged up charges against me in a malpractice case are just that, but I have no rights when it comes to this committee?"

"That's pretty close to the truth. If you could demonstrate that there was an attempt to deprive you of your rights by some criminal action, you might have a case… and then again you might not."

"All of this stinks."

"I know, Jay. But in view of that, why not take Alice's advice and just give in to these people and go elsewhere. The malpractice case is so weak and contrived, I'm certain it will disappear just as quickly as you leave."

Jay rose out of his chair, made a half turn and walked toward the large window that looked down on the bustling city of Austin. He stared down at the traffic. Neither one of them said a word for several minutes.

"Will you represent me in this second malpractice case?" Jay asked very softly and without emotion.

"I will."

"And against these thugs, am I alone or are you with me? I'm not turning back."

"I'm with you.… I just want you to understand the odds and the consequences. They'll try to destroy your whole career."

"Thanks, John. I'll get back to you after the Quality Control Meeting and then we can decide what our next step should be."

Chapter Twenty Four

A Sudden Surprise

"*D*r. Gresham, would you please present the third case?"

Steve Gresham had been a casual friend ever since Jay had come to Austin. Jay had a lot of respect for him as a physician. He worked hard and practiced a level of medicine that was above most of what Jay had seen since his arrival.

Jay was disillusioned with the quality of care he had seen at Sam Rayburn Hospital. He had been taught by mentors whose words lived constantly in the back of his mind. They whispered in his ear that the moral stance of a physician was the one principle that a doctor could not violate. When he saw doctors do things he knew were wrong, he was certain that they must know this as well. He was impressed by those physicians he perceived as honest and dedicated at Sam Rayburn. He believed that Stan Gresham fit in that category.

The presentations of the first two cases were made by Buddy Lane and Slack. The lack of any real problems resulted in a quick disposition of both cases. Except for a verbal encounter with Slack, the two cases might have been completed in no more than five minutes.

Slack began his questions in a supercilious manner that got under Jay's skin. Possibly that was Slack's intention. Though Jay knew from all the advice that had been provided by John Parsons that his best response was to keep his cool, he lost it.

"I would have thought that someone who was ONCE the Head of a Department..."

"Dr. Slack, it wasn't necessary to be the Head of a Department to know what is the correct thing to do," Jay shouted back.

It was only when Alexander Stoddard called a halt that the first two cases came to a close.

Jay knew he had made a mistake and tried to maintain his composure.

The session had started off poorly when Dr. Alfredo Anastasia walked into the luncheon meeting. Anastasia had befriended Jay when he first arrived in Austin. Their contact was somewhat limited as Anastasia practiced only Gynecology. As a result he was rarely in the company of the other members of the department who met primarily in the labor and delivery suite.

Anastasia had recognized Brown as a capable physician. During the early months, when Jay tried to establish a practice in Austin, Anastasia asked Jay to assist him at surgery. It was a tremendous boost to Jay financially, since patients were few and far between in those early days of his practice. As the years passed Anastasia had gotten into a permanent group of gynecologists who assisted each other. As a result the opportunities to work with Jay came infrequently, but they would greet each other warmly whenever they crossed paths in the hospital.

Alfredo had heard that his friend had some difficulty with the Department and decided to come to the meeting to find out what had transpired. He walked in just before the meeting began. Jay saw him enter and was quite pleased.

"You can't come in here, Dr. Anastasia. I'm sorry, this is a closed meeting for the protection of Dr. Brown. The information is privileged and Dr. Brown is entitled to have it remain that way," Jack Marsh informed him.

As Anastasia was in the process of an apology, Jay Brown became angry.

"I haven't asked that Dr. Anastasia not be admitted. I see no reason why as a member of this department he should not be allowed to sit in."

Later, when Jay thought about this confrontation, it occurred to him that the entire conversation and decision on this matter was between him and Marsh. Stoddard never said a word.

Anastasia listened to the argument. He apologized again, and left the room.

"Information has leaked out like a sieve from every one of the meetings you've held with me," Jay blurted out angrily. "I don't know what makes this session any different. Everything that happens here today will be in the doctor's lounge before dinner. The only difference is that the truth of what is said here will be distorted."

Stoddard finally entered the conversation.

"Let's stop all this and try to be civil. Nothing will be accomplished if we're at each other's throats. Jay... everything here is privileged. If anything leaks out of this room it will be my responsibility to find out why and deal with it."

Jay looked at Stoddard and a small sneer appeared on his lips as if to say "Good luck."

During the discussion of the first two cases Jay wondered why Steve Gresham was in attendance at this meeting. He was certain that Gresham was not be a part of this. If Gresham was to be a supporter he would have expected some friendly glances from him. Instead, every time he looked Gresham's way, Steve diverted his eyes from Jay. Now Steve presented the third case.

"The case is 79-038958 and...

"That case is Joan Jason," Jay said.

"You know Jay, we never mention a patient's name to maintain privacy," Stoddard interjected.

"I know, but I have the strange habit. I call patients by their names, and I know Joan well, and can't imagine why she is under discussion today."

To the utter shock of Jay Brown, Steve Gresham blurted out, "Because of your unacceptable behavior in her treatment."

Gresham did not sound like someone who was in the process of some nonsensical type of manipulation. He was truly angered and Brown was confused.

"Let's start at the beginning. Mrs. .... Gresham began his discussion with a force in his voice that sounded like he held a snarling cat he was about to let out of the bag.

"Please use chart numbers," Stoddard interrupted.

"Number 83-038958 was in active labor with no sign of difficulty until the sudden onset of marked decelerations. At that time the nurses put out an immediate call for you. From what I have been able to determine from the records you responded immediately. After you tried different standard measures to correct the stress the baby faced, you decided that the baby needed to be delivered immediately."

No longer having any misconception that Gresham was there as a supporter, Jay shot back, "If you've reviewed the chart, is there any question in your mind that the baby needed to be delivered right then? Even the Apgar scores after delivery made it clear that the baby was under considerable distress. Would you have left it undelivered?"

"Absolutely not."

"Then what is this discussion about?"

"The record also makes it clear that still some cervix remained at that time."

"Is that the issue?" Jay asked incredulously.

"Are you accustomed to the practice of a vaginal delivery through a cervix that is not fully dilated, against the specific instructions of every textbook of Obstetrics?" Gresham asked as the decibels rose significantly with each word.

"Hold it a minute, Steve. There's not an obstetrician in this room who hasn't lifted a small rim of cervix over a baby's head and delivered the newborn. It isn't as if the cervix was only halfway dilated."

"Do you not agree that the textbooks say the cervix must be fully dilated before a vaginal delivery is attempted?"

Furious, Brown stared down Gresham, "Are you a part of this same bullshit, Steve?"

Gresham looked up from his papers. "This is no bullshit. Let me tell you about this baby."

Jay became silent. He hadn't the vaguest notion of what Gresham would say.

"Baby Jas..." he stopped and gave the number, " left the hospital in three days. But he was not intact."

Jay listened intently.

"During the process of this difficult delivery you CHOSE to do by forceps..."

"I did that by forceps because I could accomplish it immediately, instead of the fifteen to twenty minute delay—at least—if the choice had been to deliver the baby by Cesarean section."

"But the baby would have been fine," Gresham responded.

"You don't know what that extra fifteen minutes of stress would have done to the baby. You saw that monitor strip and the depressed Apgar scores even after a delivery that was accomplished so quickly."

Gresham ignored him.

"During the process of this difficult forceps delivery you severely damaged the baby's mouth."

"That's ridiculous," Jay responded.

"Only to you, Jay. The baby went home and had a major problem. Despite the mother's best efforts the baby was unable to eat. He became weaker and weaker. Finally after another week's time the pediatrician found it necessary to admit him to the hospital in order to save his life. He was so malnourished that he was placed on I.V. fluids for several days. Maybe YOU think it's ridiculous, but I'm certain the baby's mother does not."

It was the very first time that Jay had heard any of this information. He was in a state of semi-shock.

"Would you like to explain your actions, Jay?" Stoddard asked.

For a few moments there was silence. Jay was trying to piece this all together.

When Jay said nothing, Jack Marsh decided to run with the ball.

"There was a recent malpractice case in court in which you were the defendant. And it has been rumored that there will be a second one shortly."

Jay thought, *how funny for him to say that it was rumored, when certainly there's no reason for this to be common knowledge, unless there's some relationship of this group to the filings.*

Marsh continued, "These recurrent cases of yours we've evaluated present a significant risk to the hospital. I think you know the hospital was named, along with you, in this past law suit as a defendant. The Quality Control Committee of the hospital has met and discussed the risk you are presenting."

"We think it would be in the best interest of everyone if you would resign your obstetrical privileges."

Jay looked at the group and contemplated what his response to them should be. They waited on the edge of their seats to see whether this would be the end of their problem child.

Jay looked up and down the table. His face was almost completely expressionless. They were uncertain about what was to happen, and totally unprepared for what did happen. They had expected him either to agree or to go into a tirade about their position.

After what seemed an eternity to the group, Jay stacked his papers neatly, pushed back his chair, and quietly left the room. He did not utter one single word.

———

Two days passed before Jay heard from anyone. He was in his office when Joan came in.

"Dr. Marsh just called and asked if he could have a private meeting with you. I gave him an appointment for tomorrow afternoon. Is that all right?"

"That's fine, Joan. Make certain that he doesn't have to wait."

Joan did more than that. She rearranged the schedule so that the last appointment would be completed at least a half hour before Dr. Marsh's arrival.

"I have the gut feeling that my non-response at the meeting will work out fine. They've probably decided that this is all too difficult and he will present some sort of a compromise."

"Will you bend a little, Dr. B., so they have room to save face?"

"I will, Joan. I really will. I won't try to make them eat crow. I really just want to be left alone and to see some change in the way obstetrics is practiced here. It doesn't have to be perfect. But, I'd rather it wasn't the worst, either."

"Good. Maybe if everyone compromises we can get back to some sort of normalcy."

Jay had called John Parsons to tell him about the upcoming meeting and his expectations.

"I hope you're right, Jay. I sincerely hope you're right. If so I'm sure the malpractice case will be over. Then, and don't get me wrong, Jay, I can get back to my other clients. I really like you, but I'd rather we meet on a social basis than go through all this mess. My wife will get you a blind date and we can all go out for a drink together."

"That sounds pretty good to me," Jay said in a lighter voice than John Parsons had heard from him in a long time.

It had become more and more difficult for Jay to obtain any type of information from the hospital since all the problems began to expand. Joan Jason left Austin immediately after the baby was born. He had known that was to happen from their conversations toward the end of her pregnancy.

Her husband received an offer from a company that significantly increased his income and stature. Jay Brown could not remember where they had moved. He remembered only that her husband left even before she was ready to deliver, as the company could not wait. She decided that she wanted Dr. Brown to deliver her baby.

Mr. Jason left and found a new home for the family. He set up a nursery for the new baby and obtained everything to make their new home comfortable for Joan as soon as she arrived. She was thrilled when she talked with Jay about what her husband had done during those last few weeks.

"But, damn it. What city was it?" Jay pondered.

Somehow the committee must have been able to track her down in order to get the information they presented. It suddenly struck him.

"Mike, how are you?"

Mike Zinnser was one of Jay Brown's favorite pediatricians. He had taken care of Joan Jason's other children. Sid Bacon, the neonatologist, had been responsible for this new baby at the time of the delivery, but Jay thought he had probably turned the case over to Mike shortly afterward.

"What's up, Jay?"

"You know Joan Jason. She had a baby last year. It was a difficult delivery and Sid Bacon was there for it. But I assume he turned the baby over to you after that."

"Last year… hmm…"

"Do you remember her?"

"Oh sure, I remember Joan well. She was a sweetheart. But I don't…. Oh yes, now I remember. I never did take care of that baby. She left town immediately. It didn't make any sense for Sid to turn her over to me for just one visit."

"What I wanted to know was whether she asked you for a pediatric referral to wherever she moved?"

"Maybe, but I'll have to look that up. I must have sent the kids' records to someone. I'll call you back."

"Thanks so much, Mike. I'd really appreciate it."

Within twenty minutes a call came back from Mike Zinsser with a name and address in Cleveland.

Jay was just about to dial and stopped. Maybe this doctor was straight as an arrow and would give him honest information, but he couldn't be certain. After all, whatever the committee had found out had come from somewhere. Or was it just concocted?

"Joan."

"Yes, Dr. B."

"Will you see if you can trace a phone number for Joan Jason in Cleveland, Ohio for me?"

Alice's thoughts about Jay had become conflicted. Part of her mind, or even more likely her heart, felt great about the fact that Jay had prevailed in the malpractice trial. But she understood him too well.

In a way, she had hoped he would lose the trial and realize that the battle against these doctors was fruitless. Doctors lost malpractice cases all the time and continued to practice. He could pick himself up, leave the community and start all over someplace else.

Alice's relationship with Jack Marsh had changed. During the dark hours of the night, when the demons crept into her mind, all she could picture were black clouds. She was certain that Jay Brown would never give up this battle to change the quality of medicine. He was too stubborn to back off and realize that the forces that he faced were stronger than he could overcome. Ultimately, he would be destroyed professionally and emotionally by these doctors. What worried her even more was the realization that those very same doctors were a part of her life.

She knew that the time was not too far off when her lover and protector, Jack Marsh, would end their relationship because of her support of Jay Brown. Her thoughts were not baseless; they were already a reality. Jack Marsh's associates had turned their sights on her. They didn't trust her and had made their feelings clear to Marsh.

─────────

"Mrs. Jason... Joan... is that you?"

"Who's calling?"

""Dr. Jay Brown."

"Dr. Brown." Joan shouted. "It's wonderful to hear your voice. To what do I owe this pleasure?... Uh! Oh! Didn't I pay my bill?"

Joan heard Jay actually burst into laughter at the other end and felt relieved already.

"That's really funny. No, as far as I know you don't owe the office anything. To tell the truth I've never made a dunning phone call in my life. If it ever had to be done, I'd definitely make Joan do it."

"Well, then, are you checking to see whether I've gotten my Pap smear done?"

"No, I've made a commitment not to follow all my patients around for the rest of their lives to make certain they behave themselves."

"Then I'm at a loss. You'll have to tell me why you called."

Actually all the bantering and teasing pleased Jay. He was extremely nervous about how to discuss the true issue at hand. Anything that put that part of the discussion off for a few more minutes was all right with him.

"As opposed to the silly things I've said for the past few minutes, Joan, what I've called about is quite serious."

"Oh!"

"I'm going to be right out front with you. Are you aware that for a number of years I've struggled with members of my profession to change the quality of care that is provided at the hospital? My actions to try to improve it have caused some anger among some of my colleagues."

"Oh sure, Dr. Brown, many of us knew that you were a rabble rouser. We saw articles you wrote in letters-to-the-editor in the newspaper. We loved you for it."

"Well some of them have made things a little difficult for me."

There was a long pause. Joan waited to hear something further.

"Your name has come up."

"My name? How am I involved?"

"You're not involved, but your delivery is. You certainly were aware that your delivery was somewhat difficult. In the process, as you remember, there was a small laceration at the corner of your baby's mouth."

Jay paused again.

"Dr. Brown, are you still there?"

"Yes, I'm sorry, Joan. Someone has now said that when you went home the baby was unable to eat because of that laceration and lost so much weight that he almost died. Is that true, Joan?"

"Are you serious?"

"Is that not true?"

"They really are out to get you. Here's the whole silly story. You're not the culprit. I am."

"You?"

"Absolutely. It happened this way…." And she explained.

"I can't possibly tell you how good you've made me feel," Jay told her. "I think that it might be a big help if you could write me a letter and detail that information."

"It'll be in the mail tomorrow. I hope they don't make your life too miserable. I wish you'd move out here and be my gynecologist again."

"Thanks so much for that moral support. Thanks for everything and good luck to you and all the family in Cleveland. I'll say a prayer that the sun comes out this winter."

"Oh, so you've heard about the weather in Cleveland. Well, don't make fun of my new home town now that I'm doing you such a good favor."

"I'll never say a bad word about Cleveland again. Thanks again and good-bye."

"Hang in there, Doctor Brown. You're my favorite."

———

"Hi, Jack," Jay greeted Marsh. "Please have a seat. Can I offer you coffee or a soft drink?'

"No thank you, Jay." Marsh responded as he sat down opposite

Brown, who was seated behind his desk.

The office was empty. After Joan had ushered Marsh back into the consultation room, she closed the door behind her. She didn't want anyone to interrupt the privacy of this meeting.

Jay Brown appeared relaxed, but beneath the veneer he waited anxiously to see whether Marsh had come to end this standoff and allow everyone to return to some normalcy. Neither one of them particularly liked the other, but there was a mutual respect. Of all the people that Jay suspected were a part of this, none practiced medicine at the level that Jack Marsh did.

"We have a bit of a problem, Brown, and we ought to find the least complicated way to solve it."

That sounded pretty good as a start to Jay. But all of that was about to change.

"I'm here in an unofficial capacity, but I've got to give you some official information. Uh… the committee, uh… the Quality Control Committee," Marsh was having difficulty even though he had prepared himself for this meeting. "… unanimously recommended that your obstetrical privileges be removed. Now like I'm supposed, by the official procedure, to go to the Executive Committee of the Hospital with that recommendation. That was supposed to happen yesterday."

Jay felt sick to his stomach. His hoped-for compromise and reconciliation was not about to happen.

"This department is not goin' to continue to have you practice obstetrics. We'll allow you to practice GYN, but that's all."

Marsh then went through a long, rambling speech. He stuttered and sputtered and revealed his own discomfort with the things he was saying.

"I have consulted with some people who have been around here for a long time, not to mention names, but, you know, uh… uh… like I was tryin' to know what others would do in this situation. Uh… uh… tryin' to be fair to everyone. The feelin' was that you needed to know in case you wanted to do somethin' to prevent this from happenin'."

Jay's anger built while Marsh dragged himself through his speech.

"I went to the Executive meetin', and of course, without mentionin' your name, explained what was happenin' and the option we were plannin' to offer to you. Some thought like I was oversteppin' my authority and would get the Hospital in some sort of trouble. But I wanted to be fair to you. You could... uh... uh... you could do somethin' that would stop this from goin' any further."

"The son-of-a-bitch is black-mailing me," Jay thought to himself as he stared coldly into Marsh's eyes.

"If you would resign your privileges there would be no official process and uh... nothin' would appear on your record. If not, I... uh... will have no choice but to submit this to the Executive Committee."

Jay wanted to stand up and hit him in the face and throw him out of the office, but he controlled himself.

"And you support this action?" Jay snarled at Marsh.

"As a member of the committee, yes I do."

"And what is the basis?"

"Well, Jay," he said in a conciliatory tone, "there were these repeated cases the committee has reviewed about you and we just feel like you are too much of a risk for the hospital."

"Listen, Jack, the same damn people sit on that committee, year after year. They are the same doctors who do huge numbers of C-sections and excessive numbers of surgical procedures. What about the risk they present for the hospital? Have you thought about that? They remain untouched. If that's the way you want it, that's OK with me. But there's no way, NO WAY, I'll lie down and let these sons of bitches do what they want to do to me."

Marsh ignored the accusation and turned the conversation around. "I just can't accept the idea that there's a conspiracy out to get you. I know that some people have some animosity toward you, but they're not out to get you."

From the information Alice had already given him, he knew how deceitful Marsh's statement was.

"Well, there's just no legitimate basis for this decision. What does unanimous mean? Is it just the same handful of physicians who have been involved every time?"

"No, there were thirteen."

"But they weren't at the meetings. I guess the same handful presented the same lies and distortions to the others that they discussed with me. If you don't know about the lies you'd better get some more information before you go any further with this. You may be in for quite a shock."

Marsh totally ignored Jay's accusations and repeated himself. "This department is not goin' to continue to have you practice obstetrics. We'll allow you to practice GYN, but that's all."

Once he realized that his hoped for expectations of this meeting were not about to be a reality, Jay responded with marked hostility, "That's not good enough. You know damned well that I have a very small GYN practice. I discourage unnecessary surgery. If I continued to practice honestly there is no way that I could even pay my overhead just with gynecology. I'm basically an obstetrician. That's the work I love to do and that's the way I earn my living."

"Well it's just not goin' to work out here. The hospital considers you a problem and we're goin' to give you those two choices. You can either resign your obstetrical privileges or the Department will bring your name to the Hospital Board and ask them to revoke all your privileges. If you resign, nothin' will appear on your record. If the Board removes your privileges it will be on your record permanently, includin' the notation that gets sent to the National Data Center. It's up to you."

Jay hated being threatened, especially by this group of obstetricians.

"Listen here Marsh"—first names no longer being used—"I practice medicine at the highest levels that I know how. I've done nothing wrong except try to get some members of the department to practice at a higher level than they do now. As the head of this department, and a fine obstetrician, that should have been your job. I won't be the fall guy for some people who are incompetent."

"That's the problem with you. You think you are better than everyone else and a lot of people here are sick and tired of a damned Yankee..." he was about to say Jew and held back "...comin' in here and tellin' everybody how they're supposed to practice medicine. You think you do everythin' perfectly and nobody knows anythin', except you."

"That's a totally unfair accusation," Jay fired back.

Actually Jay knew there was some truth to what Marsh said. He really didn't think much of a number of the members of the staff.

In a much louder voice, and just short of shaking his finger in Marsh's face, Jay retorted, "When I've had problem cases I have sought consultation and there is documentation of that. But I'm not about to seek consultation from some of the members of the department who don't even know how to deliver a breech vaginally, or other things that any decent obstetrician ought to be able to do. I won't discuss Cesarean sections with obstetricians who have never done a vaginal delivery after a patient has had a previous Cesarean section, even though that's what's recommended in every decent hospital in the country. I will not ask people to consult on my cases, when for some of them, half the babies they deliver are done by Cesarean section. That percentage is absolutely unacceptable."

"Well, Brown, those are your choices. Take it or leave it. We're goin' to stop you from doin' obstetrics, regardless of what you say."

Jay wanted to throw Marsh out of his office, but retained enough of his cool to do nothing he would be sorry for later.

"I guess that leaves no more to be said. I will not resign."

Marsh rose from the chair and looked Jay Brown straight in the eye. He said, "I'm sorry you feel that way. Thanks for your time."

Looking at Marsh coldly, Jay barely responded, "You're welcome."

Marsh turned and walked out of the office. Joan looked up as he passed. From the expression on his face she had the sense that things had not gone well. No words were spoken between them.

She was all the more certain as Jay closed his private office door with a rather loud slam.

Chapter Twenty Five

The Maneuvering Begins

Over the next few months, meetings between Jay Brown and John Parsons became a regular part of their lives. Jay's practice began to show the effects of these repeated crises. In the early years of his practice in Austin there was a significant increase each year in the volume of patients and the income he received. But, because of his unwillingness to perform procedures which he perceived to be unnecessary, he never found himself in the financial bracket of most of the physicians who surrounded him. He was, nevertheless, able to sustain himself economically.

His income had reached a level of sixty to seventy thousand dollars annually. At times he thought about the income he had earned before he left his former practice back in New York. It was almost twice what he presently earned. Unmarried, without much of a social life, he had been content to watch his income rise gradually each year.

But now things had changed. The warm, friendly, and always very light-hearted physician his patients once knew was not the same person. He was never rude or unkind to them, but his personality was different; he seemed preoccupied. His lighter side had vanished. Too often, office hours were canceled due to meetings, or preparations for them. Too often phone calls that were urgent in relation to his continuing battle came during office hours. And, too often he responded to them while patients waited for him in his examining room. At times these non-medical phone calls interrupted a conversation a patient needed to pursue with her doctor. Those conversations were important to the patients and the frequent interruptions made some of them feel as if they had become less important to him. He was not the same physician they had known for several years and they wondered what had happened.

The efforts put forth to drive him out of Austin worked in ways even his detractors had not expected. The pressures took their toll. Though never concerned about the accumulation of wealth, Jay realized his practice was smaller. There were factors involved that were unrelated to his problems. The popularity of the area had brought a huge influx of new obstetricians to Austin. There was a new breed of obstetricians who came into the city. They were not just young, they were female, and patients were more comfortable with a woman gynecologist.

Jay understood that these new external factors were significant, but felt certain that the environment he had created in his office was the major source of the problem. His office expenses, malpractice premiums and rental—among other things—all rose due to inflation. Sooner or later the practice would be financially worthless.

But as he contemplated the economic pressures, one thought continued to return to his mind. He could not walk away from this situation and ever feel good about himself in the future.

"I don't know what to do," he confided to Parsons.

"What is it you want out of this life? Are you committed to accomplish something that you know will destroy you? Do you really believe that if you persevere, and succeed, something will change here? Or even more importantly, do you think that your efforts will change more than this one hospital?"

"John, suppose everyone who ever struggled to make something better stopped because they said to themselves, 'Even if I change this, will it have any effect on the larger problem.'... How would anything of value ever be accomplished?"

"Just explain to me what will change if you stop them."

"It's not whether I change this environment. Even if I fail here, a seed will have been planted that others will know about. Some will know that I was right. And someone else will take some action that will move the quality of care forward."

"Here?"

"Yes, here, but not *only* here. I'm certain that things like this happen elsewhere. Others see evidence of the same abuses that I see. If we all give up the fight, then everything of quality, not just health care, is at risk."

"But you seem to be all alone here, Jay. Is it worth it?"

Jay thought for a long time before he responded.

"I said that I believed there are many others out there who try to change the same things I've tried to change. I don't believe for a moment that anyone will ever remember me or my present plight. But there are others who have followed their hearts and their beliefs and became known for them. You can't imagine how important those people are. You can't imagine how much they've motivated me. Many, including myself, who struggle for an issue, continue because their words ring in our ears. In my own field of medicine there was Ignaz Semmelweis. He went to his terrible death in a mental institution. He never knew that his efforts saved the lives of thousands... tens of thousands, no, probably millions of pregnant women. They died of what was called childbirth fever, puerperal sepsis. It caused their deaths because no one understood that obstetricians brought bacteria straight from autopsies to the patients while they were in labor. The physicians moved from the morgue to the delivery room without any sterile technique. Meanwhile the medical community constantly ignored his pleas to change."

"Did he change that?"

"No, no,... and that's exactly the point. He wasn't able to change it. But he laid the seed and others after him changed that. Everything has to start somewhere. Even Edison's work didn't start without any knowledge before he invented the electric light. Others preceded him and provided information. It's like the old expression of standing on the shoulders of geniuses to accomplish one's goals."

"Great! Does that mean I have to stand by and watch you go down the drain in the process?"

"John... I'm not that much of a hero. I'm not Semmelweis. I won't lose my life. The worst thing that can happen is that I'll lose my practice here. But it's a battle that has to be fought. On the surface, the struggle is to have fewer Cesarean Sections and unnecessary operations. But it's deeper than that. The question is whether I, or anyone, can see something that is wrong and look the other way. If nobody ever takes a stand when that happens, then the society, ultimately, is bound to fail. This isn't easy for me. I'd rather it never happened. But there were great people who were much more courageous than I—people I sometimes think about—that force me to try."

"Obstetricians?"

Jay laughed.

"No, not everyone who ever stood up for what was right was an obstetrician. I love the story of Henry David Thoreau who had been put in jail for his beliefs and was visited by his friend Ralph Waldo Emerson. When Emerson saw Thoreau in his cell he asked, 'Henry what are you doing in there?' Thoreau looked at him and said, 'A better question Ralph, would be, why are you out there?'"

"So you'd rather be Henry than Ralph."

"I'm afraid I'm neither. I'm more likely to be Henry Aldrich or Ralph Cramden."

Jay finally brought John Parsons to laughter. John was at a loss to find any way to stop what seemed to be inevitable. The best he could do was help Jay Brown in his struggle. If he attempted to stop him, it would only leave Jay with one less person on his side.

"Based on what we've discussed, I think our only approach is to find supporters. Nothing can help more than the ability to show that your ideas are not yours alone. Are there physicians who will speak out in your behalf?"

"In what way?"

John thought quietly for a while as he stared at the ceiling.

"How about letters? Could we get a number of them to write letters that would support you? Could they write about the type of care you've provided for their patients... maybe patients they've referred to you or some they sent to you for gynecologic consultations?"

"I guess so," Jay answered, not quite certain how that would be accomplished.

He thought for a few moments and followed with, "I could go to their offices and ask them directly. Maybe it would work out. I'm not certain how many might want to stick their necks out, especially if they know that the Department has already asked the hospital to throw me out."

"They haven't exactly tried to throw you out, just to stop obstetrics."

"Just semantics. You know that, John."

"What about nurses, Jay? What kind of relationship have you had with nurses—say the delivery room nurses?"

"Great! I know they like the kind of care I provide to patients. They feel responsible for the patients. When necessary I've seen them act as intermediaries and attempt to protect patients from anything wrong a doctor might inadvertently do. I can't tell you how many times nurses have said to me, in a wonderfully tactful way, 'Dr. Brown, wouldn't you like me to do this or that for the patient?' It happens when I've forgotten something that really should be done."

"We've got to see if we can find those other people who believe in the same things you do, but usually stand by the wayside. We've got to get them involved."

The meeting that ended on a positive tone, partly because John Parsons, for the first time, believed that what Jay Brown wanted to do, had to be done. He expected that it would come to no good end, but he now agreed that wasn't reason enough to throw in the towel.

Jay sensed that John Parsons now truly believed in him. It meant a great deal, because John was not just an unusual lawyer; he was an unusual person.

Both sides weighed all their options very carefully. Marsh, Slack and Crown were now certain that Brown would appeal the decision of the Hospital Executive Committee. The hospital would be forced to set up an Ad Hoc Committee as outlined by the by-laws to hear Jay Brown's case and to judge whether the Executive Committee's actions were appropriate. They met privately with Baker and the hospital's attorney, Teresa Carney, to outline plans. Nothing was more critical than the proper selection of the members of that committee.

They knew that none of those doctors who sat in judgment of him at the Quality Control meetings could hold membership on the committee. There were to be eight members besides the Chairman, who could break the tie, if it were a four-four vote.

Originally plans were made for the meeting to be held in December. But, because of the holidays, Baker decided to schedule the Ad Hoc Committee Meeting for late January of 1986. Baker did not want the choice of committee members to be based on availability rather than on who would best serve the purposes the Quality Control

Committee and the hospital.

Everyone agreed that as the Head of the Department, Marsh, though he had been a part of the Quality Control meetings, could be named a member. A second prime choice was Dr. Candless. He had never served on the Quality Control Committee, and his strong dislike for Brown made him an ideal choice. He was also notorious for his anti-Semitic comments.

But no choice in the entire matter was more crucial than who would be the Chairman of the committee. Actually it was Louis Crown who came up with the idea.

"I would like to suggest a person who I suppose would be perfect. I have seen him socially for a number of years and he is very smart. He does not like Jay Brown. I'm not certain what the reason is. Maybe because Brown is Jewish or from New York or possibly just his personality. I am speaking of Alonzo Brehm, the neurosurgeon."

The others made comments, all of which were quite favorable toward the suggestion. Above all they felt that Brehm, who at times could be quite outspoken, would be pleased at being chosen. A big man with a big ego, he enjoyed the limelight.

Baker suggested that Teresa Carney, as a representative of the hospital executive committee, contact him and ask if he would accept the role of Chairman of the Ad Hoc Committee, should Jay Brown submit a formal appeal.

Marsh, Slack and Crown had already planned out the remaining membership of the committee. They believed they could persuade the Executive Committee that the Ad Hoc Committee should have obstetricians as at least half the membership, since they best understood the nature of the complaints. Candless was their first choice to join Marsh. Slack and Crown wanted to get two weak sisters in the Department who probably knew they were watched regularly by Marsh for the quality of their care. Marsh decided he should select Samuel Brenner and Marie O'Donnell. It was not likely that they would go against Marsh when they were all on the committee together.

"Brenner's Jewish. That will be good because we don't want anyone to accuse us of bigotry."

The next plan was to get four physicians in different specialties who did not have any social relationships with either Brown or any of the other members. They didn't want any cliques to be formed. They chose a pediatrician, a general surgeon, an internist and a dermatologist—two men and two women.

When the meeting was over they were pleased as punch, feeling this would work out just perfectly. Each one went his separate way except for Slack and Crown who left the meeting and headed toward the parking lot together. When they arrived at Louis' car, he asked Slack to get in for one moment.

"I have a concern I wanted to talk about with you."

"About the members of the committee?"

"No, I'm pleased with that. It is something else. It is Alice. I suppose she is not to be trusted."

"What do you have in mind?"

"She shares a pillow with Marsh and I don't know what she hears. Even worse I don't know what she might tell Brown."

"You're right. That could be a problem. What do you propose?"

"I suppose we should hire a private detective to follow her. I suppose it would be a good idea to know what she does or if she sees Brown secretly."

"I'll go along with that. I'll make the arrangements and let you know what happens. I'm glad you thought of it. We don't want something stupid to happen because we got careless and overlooked something."

Slack got out of the car, came around the front, and stopped at Crown's open window.

"You're OK, Louie. We'll get this bastard out of our hair as long as the others don't do something dumb."

———

Jay Brown made a long list of physicians he had known over the years in obstetrics and all other specialties. There were many pediatricians; he had come to know them through referrals of his newborn babies. He reviewed the list carefully. There were thirty five he felt comfortable to ask for a letter about the quality of his medical care.

The meetings went very well. Joan made specific appointments for him, several each day.

The procedure was fairly constant at all his stops. He needed to be absolutely straightforward with these friends whom he asked to stick their necks out. Jay told them what he confronted, and provided a reason for why he believed it had happened. He followed that with the *piece de resistance*—he was about to lose his privileges. He explained that he wanted no one to create problems for themselves with comments about the way the Ob-Gyn Department conducted itself.

"It's as simple as this. If you believe that you have seen me provide care that you believe is of high quality, my request is just to write a note to that effect. I want you to be honest. If you can't write such a note, that's fine with me and there will be no hard feelings. But, if you can, I would like to pick it up within a week or you can just mail it to my office. Regardless of what you decide, please know that I respect your decision and want to thank you for your time."

Jay received more letters than he had expected. Some moved him considerably because they went a great deal further than he had requested. Some went into great detail about how they felt about him as a person. He accumulated twenty six letters, but the one that he wanted most of all did not come. In that one case his promise to have no hard feelings was not fulfilled.

One of the leading people in the Ob-Gyn Department, who was Jewish, was held in high esteem by everyone. Josh Rosen had a rather warm relationship with Jay and they had great respect for each other, but no letter came from him. Jay never understood whether Rosen was concerned about a Jew who spoke out for another Jew, or just wanted to stay above the fray. A number of Jews in other departments were included among the twenty six letters. Jay truly felt no anger toward those who didn't respond, but in Rosen's case, he felt deeply let down.

Jay had already made his formal appeal to the Executive Committee, and a date had been set. It was one day during the time he sought outside support that Joan called him to tell him another letter had come from the Executive Committee.

"They've named the committee to hear your appeal," Joan said in a rather flat voice.

Joan's downhearted comment wasn't due to the choice of any

specific members. It was just that the entire process depressed her. She expected no good outcome from all of this.

When she read the list to Jay, his reaction was quite different. He rarely used profanity and certainly not in front of Joan.

"Those assholes won't get away with this." Brusquely he said, "I'll call you later."

Within a matter of seconds he dialed John Parsons.

"I won't sit back and be judged by Marsh and McCandless. Marsh has been in the middle of this from the start... and McCandless, are they kidding? That son-of-a-bitch is a redneck, dyed-in-the-wool anti-Semite, and everybody knows it just from his day to day conversation."

"You don't have a lot of leverage in this, Jay. You're not in much of a position to choose your judges. I can understand your concern about McCandless, but as the head of the department, and the one primarily responsible for how his department functions, I don't believe you'll be able to get Marsh off the committee."

"What do you suggest I do?"

John Parsons remained silent for a moment. Jay knew John was deep in thought.

"I don't believe in idle threats, but I think it may work here." He paused again, then continued, "I'd contact Baker... no wait a minute, instead of you, I'll contact Baker and tell him that unless McCandless is removed from the committee, due to his previous biased statements, we'll take the hospital to court. I don't believe they want us to take that route. And, I don't believe it's important enough for them to keep him on the committee."

"And you don't believe we should take the same position on Marsh?"

"No, I really don't. I believe they wouldn't back down so easily on that. What about the Chairman, Alonzo Brehm? What do you know about him?"

This time Jay paused. "Nothing!... I really don't know him. I've seen him at some hospital wide meetings. He's sort of blustery and outspoken. But, I've never been impressed with him, one way or another. He could be hostile. But it's not like McCandless. I can't deny everybody on the committee that I don't know."

"No, you can't. But from the way this has progressed over the past years, I think you can feel certain they haven't selected someone who's a supporter of yours."

Jay felt sort of sick in the pit of his stomach about the whole thing.

"Thanks John. Thanks for everything. Will you let me know what happens with McCandless."

"The minute I have it resolved I'll get back to you."

Jay completed the request for physician letters and began the effort John had suggested about support from nurses. He decided immediately not to contact Alice. Many saw her as biased toward him. The simple thing would be to go to the staff nurses he knew so well, and as with the physicians, tell them the truth and ask for their support. Jay always emphasized that he wanted no comments about the problem he faced or any other members of the department. He believed that he could not get any help if he pitted himself against others. He understood the nurses couldn't make negative comments about anyone else.

"It's just if you believe that as you've watched me, that I've provided what you would consider to be truly good care for the patients. If you don't feel that way, that's fine. We'll just forget the entire matter."

He spoke to several and they said they would like to speak to the head of the maternity nursing service and get back to Jay in a day or so. That seemed fine to him. What happened next was not.

Jay waited a few days and then returned to the labor and delivery suite to see if anything had been done. Marge Ryan was there. She asked him to come into the nurses' office to talk. Jay followed.

"The assistant administrator of the hospital came to see us yesterday and said the hospital would not look upon it favorably if we wrote such letters. I'm sorry, Dr. Brown, but our hands are tied."

All sorts of thoughts flashed through his mind. Marge could see that his head was in another place. The rest of what she said was not heard by him at all.

"We would have been glad to…"

She saw that she talked *at* him instead of *to* him.

His mind raced. *The sons of bitches! Isn't there any limit to which they'll go?*

"I certainly hope this will all get resolved in…"

He had ended all pretense of a conversation with her as he contemplated what his next move should be.

"Thanks Marge…. Thanks for your time. I've got someplace important I have to go."

Before she knew it, Jay Brown was gone.

At first he planned to call John Parsons, but his anger and adrenaline level had reached such a fever pitch, he discarded that consideration and headed straight for the office of Bill Hardaway. Bill was a young man on his climb up the administrative ladder. He had had several occasions to meet with Jay Brown and they had been very cordial. Bill had been an assistant under the previous administrator and was kept in place when Baker took over the leadership role at the hospital.

Hardaway's secretary told Jay that he was on the phone.

"Would you like to wait until he's done or should I make an appointment for you?"

"No, I'll just wait."

There was no way that Jay Brown would leave. If he didn't talk with him now he knew his brain would burst. After about five minutes Hardaway stuck his head out the frame of his door and with a smile waved Jay in.

"Do you know why I'm here?"

"I have a fair idea."

"Why did you tell the nurses not to make comments about the quality of my care?"

Hardaway really liked Jay Brown and was obviously quite disturbed by this conversation. He looked half away from him as he said, "Those were the instructions given to me."

"Do you understand the significance of witness tampering? That's exactly what you did."

"I do, Jay, but I don't think that applies here. These are not legal hearings. They're not held to the same standards."

"Standards or no standards, the people who told you to do this, and I don't have to guess who that might be, are on risky ground."

Hardaway saw that Jay's blood boiled, and he wished like crazy he was not standing in front of him.

"I'm very sorry, Jay. I really am."

As he stormed out of the room Jay Brown said in a voice just under a shout, "You should be! You really should be!"

Parsons was concerned when he heard what the hospital had done, but tried to make Jay aware that there was very little action that they could take. He re-emphasized that the courts had taken a rather strong position that they would not interfere with hospital actions in relation to their physicians. The concept persisted that doctors would not take action against bad physicians unless the courts protected the "whistle blowing" doctors from retaliations by those being charged. As a result, the normal protections that an accused had in our legal system were not available to physicians in hospital actions.

The one piece of good news that Parsons had to offer to Brown was about the membership of the committee.

His conversation with Baker had gone quite well. Baker had made no commitment when he first spoke to Parsons, but promised to take the question under consideration. In less than twenty-four hours Baker got back to John Parsons and said that the hospital executive committee was unhappy with being challenged about the choice of the Ad Hoc Committee membership. They felt that it was not Dr. Brown's place to tell them whom it was proper for them to choose. However, in order to demonstrate their desire to be as fair as possible to Dr. Brown, they would make an adjustment.

Parsons then said it had been necessary to control himself at that point in the conversation, because he had the intense desire to say to Baker, "You're full of shit. You just don't want charges of bigotry brought against the hospital."

"That, by the way, is why I'm so glad that I decided to make that call myself. Because, YOU,... YES YOU, Jay Brown,... would have actually told him he was full of shit. And, we don't need to antagonize them any more than is necessary."

Jay laughed and said, "You're right. I would have."

"So this is what they've offered. They're going to replace

McCandless with a new member of the staff who just left the medical school to go out into private practice. Do you know Henry Gerber?"

Jay Brown was actually quite surprised.

"I do. I don't know him personally but enough to know that he had a fine reputation at the school."

He paused for quite a while before he said, "I'm really a little confused. That's a strange choice. He's bright. He's certainly not a part of any conspiracy. He's Jewish.... The only thing I can think of is... they might possibly believe, as a brand new member of the department, he would be too intimidated to go against the head of the department at this early stage of his private career. They might be right. But then again they might not. It's a longer shot than I would have guessed they'd take. I can't say that it makes me unhappy. In any case, as a replacement for McCandless, it can't be anything less than great."

"Have you thought about what you'll say to the Committee?" John queried.

"I've been on it for a while."

"You know that I won't be allowed to say anything. I can't challenge anything or speak in any way. I can only be seated with you and whisper suggestions to you. I'm allowed no active role."

"I know. And I'm so thrilled to know that this is America where every person, except a doctor, is guaranteed a honest and fair trial. Do you want to know what I think? I think this stinks. It's difficult for me to believe that Americans, people who live in this country and believe in its system, want this type of thing to go on."

"You know Jay, over the past months we've talked a lot about why you have to do this. But, in some ways, we actually skirted the issue. We believe in free speech in this country and people frequently take the direction of civil disobedience, which in a sense is what you've done. Of course these aren't the laws of the land you've challenged. But in another sense they're the laws of the hospital. You can do what you've chosen to do.... You can do that... as long as you understand the consequences. You may very well have to pay a very heavy price for such action."

Jay listened attentively and said, "And, John, do you think I don't understand that?"

"The important point is to understand up front how severe the consequences might be. Sometimes I think you don't fully comprehend what you may give up by the continuation this battle. I wonder if you have not fully thought it out. Is it worth it?'"

Jay was silent.

"The way this hearing is run is the only game in town. You need to decide, —and now— whether you want to continue or not."

Jay Brown's brain raged as he said, "Continue!!!"

Chapter Twenty Six

The Crunch

A long, narrow corridor led off the main area of the administrative offices. On the walls there were portraits of important functionaries. Some were previous administrators. Some were Presidents of the hospital Board. Some were photographs; some were paintings. These locally renowned individuals all had the same overly formal poses.

It was just before five P.M. when Jay Brown walked past the receptionist for the offices along that corridor. Beside him was John Parsons. Neither of them needed to stop and tell the receptionist why they were there. She did not have to ask.

Jay walked slowly down the corridor and glanced quickly at the paintings and photographs and turned to John.

"Do you think any of these people would have been involved in this kind of shenanigan in their day?"

John shrugged and said, "I don't know… maybe all of them."

That brought a small smile to the corners of Jay's mouth. It was about all Parsons could expect in view of the tension in the air.

They came to the end of the corridor and pushed open the door to the conference room. There was a very large table of the type usually seen in a high powered attorney's office. It was at least fifteen feet in length and about six feet wide. Only two people were seated at the table—the stenographer, who was in the process of setting up her equipment, and Jessica Rehnquist.

Dr. Rehnquist was a dermatologist. Of all the members of the Committee, it was easiest for her to rearrange her schedule to attend the meeting. Jessica was unmarried and extremely attractive. Like the other non-obstetrical members of the Ad Hoc Committee, she had been chosen because she was identified as having no relationship with any of the other committee members. She was, however, identifiable with several physicians whom she dated on a regular basis. On this particular evening she expected to be free by seven or eight o'clock, in time for dinner in her apartment with one of her most ardent admirers.

She had purchased an especially revealing nightgown for the occasion.

Several of the members who had been named to the Ad Hoc Committee had already arrived. The first thing that caught Jay's eye were four people in deep conversation in the corner of the room— Baker, Marsh, Brehm and Teresa Carney, the hospital attorney.

Not even for one moment, even right before this hearing, can these schmucks stop conspiring, Jay thought. He had nothing but contempt for the process and everyone involved.

"You look like you've already started to get angry. That's the worst thing you can do now. Please try to keep your cool," John whispered in Jay's ear.

"Right, John."

After a few moments the four in the corner noticed that Jay Brown had arrived. They quickly dispersed and Alonzo Brehm approached Jay and John.

"Thanks for being so prompt. Hopefully we can get over this difficult process without taking up too much of your time."

Too much of YOUR time, don't you mean? Jay thought. He knew this process would not be brief, but thought better than to say it.

By this time the other members of the committee, with the exception of Henry Gerber, had arrived.

Ramon Lopez, the pediatrician, had already seated himself next to Jessica Rehnquist. It was not a surprise that men would choose to sit next to her. However, before any of the other men could find themselves on her other side, Anne Weakeley, the internist, took that seat.

Anne was not particularly attractive. It seemed almost by intent. Her clothing and hair were always disheveled. She knew that any man who appeared publicly in the same way would be characterized as wonderfully casual. It was her way to respond to a sexist society. She was married with three children and highly respected as an internist. Jay didn't know her well, but several of his patients used her as their primary care physician. Basically he was pleased that she was one of the committee members.

Finally Ryan Barton, the general surgeon, sat on the other side of Anne—which lined up all the non-obstetrical members of the committee next to each other. Marsh sat on the opposite side of the table, along with Brenner and Marie O'Donnell.

At the head of the table, Alonzo Brehm faced the stenographer who was at the opposite end.

Jay sat next to Ryan Barton. Over his left shoulder, but not actually at the table, a seat had been provided for John Parsons. His position, away from the table, was not by accident. The purpose was to make it perfectly clear that he had no part of this meeting except to listen and whisper to Brown. Up against the wall sat Baker and Carney. They also had no role except as observers. They could be called upon if questions arose as to hospital policies or legal matters. At the last moment, Bill Hardaway the assistant administrator, entered the room and sat with them.

"It's just about five. Let's wait another moment or two to see if Dr. Gerber arrives before..."

At that moment Henry Gerber, somewhat out of breath, rushed in, obviously from some distant location, and took his seat directly opposite Jay Brown.

"Good. Let's get started."

Brehm introduced each of the individuals in the room and provided some simple ground rules.

"We will have a slight problem, and things might get a little out of order, because we have a special expert witness who represents the hospital from out of town. His appearance will be by phone.... But we don't know exactly when. So it might be in the middle of some of part of this hearing and we'll have to interrupt that because..."

"One moment, Dr. Brehm," Jay blurted out. "You have some sort of mystery witness? Aren't you required to notify me in advance of any witness who might appear? Haven't you violated my rights?"

"We've discussed the matter with the attorneys and there is precedent for this and anyway this is not a legal hearing. So..."

"It may not be a legal hearing, but I do have rights. It is my career that's on the line."

Jay's voice was becoming louder and harsher. He felt a hand on his lower arm.

"You can't stop this. Wait and see what happens," John whispered.

Brehm then said "You'll be given all the time you need to respond to or question this witness. We'll be certain that everything is done properly."

I bet you will.

"Let's begin with Dr. Marsh, who represents the Department of Obstetrics and Gynecology, as well as the Quality Control Committee, and in a sense even the Executive Committee which has requested that we evaluate this case. Dr. Marsh, would you present the recommendations that we are to consider and why those recommendations have been made?"

"Well, I mean, like the way this all started was... that there is a system. It's an old system that we have sort of believed would make sure that everythin' was done... so that everythin' would be done right. You know what I mean. We set up criteria. Then the records department would check. You see, they would check to see if the charts meet the criteria. Well sometimes... you know just sometimes, because most everybody was doin' what was right, a chart would fall out. It just turned out that Dr. Brown's charts seemed to be fallin' out too much. Sort of like somethin' was wrong.

"Well, over the past few years we had to call Dr. Brown in to explain just why he was doin' some of these things that we felt like were wrong. Then we were tryin' to do somethin' to help him by sayin' that we were glad to consult with him about these problems. He... sort of... didn't want us helpin' him and refused that.

"Finally we had to bring three cases to the attention of the hospital and ask them to help us protect the hospital... which we thought was goin' to get into trouble if he was not stopped from doin'... sort... of the wrong things."

Brehm interrupted Marsh's rather repetitious rambling and asked, "Can you tell us about these three cases?"

Marsh began with the Jonas case. He described how the committee decided this patient was delivered in too much of a rush and that the baby had been terribly traumatized and almost died because of the procedure that Jay Brown had performed. All during the presentation of the case, questions came from the committee members who represented the obstetrical department. The questions from O'Donnell and Brenner fell right into Marsh's theory that what had been done seemed to be without merit. The questions from Gerber seemed to put a different light on the matter. Marsh did not stop Gerber, but was obviously slightly annoyed.

Not one single question came from the non-obstetrical members of the committee. They seemed to be somewhat lost in the details of obstetrical cases. None of them had delivered a baby since medical school, and didn't like that part of medicine even then.

"And the next case, Dr. Marsh?" Brehm asked.

Marsh then presented a history of a patient who was admitted to the hospital in premature labor. He described Brown's management and suggested the differences the committee had with that management and what they would have done. The baby apparently had been born without Jay Brown in attendance.

Finally there was a case in which they believed that Jay Brown should have done a Cesarean section at an earlier point in labor than he had chosen. Marsh appeared to give that case short shrift as if the complaints were not on as solid ground as the first two.

Through all of that presentation Jay stared directly at Marsh, intent on every word he uttered. Parsons had advised him to diligently follow the course of what was claimed in order to rebut anything he believed to be inaccurate.

He needn't have instructed Jay Brown at all. Jay scrutinized every word and made notes. His brain flashed like a computer. He had placed himself psychologically, for the time being, almost as a third party. He functioned as an attorney representing himself, always on the search for any crack he could find in the presentation by the opposition.

"Dr. Brown, if you are prepared, I would like to give you the opportunity now to respond to these charges. Please understand that it may be necessary in the middle of your defense for us to temporarily interrupt you with our expert witness."

Jay intentionally refrained from acknowledgment of Brehm's reminder of the expert witness.

"Initially, I want to thank all of the members of this committee who took their own very valuable time to perform this service. I can't honestly say that I'm happy to be here. Because, for me, what is at stake is the remainder of my career.

"I have spent the last several weeks in the attempt to research and document the literature which will support my position. The document I have prepared with all that information and analysis would take in excess of six hours to present to you. My presentation tonight will be only a small part of that documentation, but I will provide each of you a packet with all the information, which you can read on your own.

"You have the onerous responsibility of a decision which rests upon you. That decision will reflect on the reputation I have achieved over the past quarter century. I appreciate how difficult that is for you. I will try, with my presentation, to make that an easier and clearer choice for you.

"During those twenty five years I have directed much of my time toward the ethics of medical practice…"

Jay then began to tell the committee of his philosophy of the practice of medicine and the reaction to it by members of the Department of Obstetrics.

"Dr. Brown," Dr. Brehm interrupted. "We don't want to hear about your credentials. Just discuss the case."

"But there is background behind all of this that must be understood in…"

"We're not interested in your credentials."

The son-of-a-bitch doesn't want the non-obstetrical members to know what's been going on.

"O.K. They're all in the packet for you to see."

Brown proceeded to discuss the level of practice in the department that he wanted to change.

"Dr. Brown, we're not interested in your harangue about the department. The rest of the staff is not on trial here."

"There is no way to understand what has happened without some knowledge of the history of these attacks."

"You mean your actions won't speak for themselves?"

Brown was about to lose his calm demeanor.

"My actions in these cases and in cases before, as noted by my peers…"

Brehm, Marsh, Slack, in fact everyone, had heard through

the grapevine of Brown's efforts to collect supportive letters from physicians and expected them to be presented.

"Dr. Brown, this is no beauty contest. We're not interested in letters that say you're a nice fellow."

Jay could feel his body begin to shake. He could see clearly how carefully this was orchestrated. They had planned to cut him down at every turn.

"The case that is made against me attempts to demonstrate that these three cases are only the tip of the iceberg, and it…"

Jay could feel the papers he held in his hand begin to shake. The tremors were not controllable. He had spoken publicly for years with no anxiety, but this was completely different. He felt as if he had lost control.

Please stop! Stop shaking. Get control of yourself!

"May I have a glass of water, please."

Bill Hardaway jumped up and poured the water and handed him the glass. As he took the glass the water sloshed back and forth. His hand trembled as he brought the glass to his lips. He intentionally drank each sip very slowly in the effort to give himself time to regain his composure.

Jay kept trying to provide background; Brehm continued to interrupt. He repeatedly stated they wanted to hear only a response to the three cases. No one else in the room made any comments while they watched this battle between Brehm and Brown. Neither appeared ready to back down until Brown finally realized that the power lay completely with Brehm. Maybe, he hoped, the Committee members would read all this information in the document he gave them. In his heart Jay knew that it was very unlikely that they would take the time.

He flipped forward and backward through his planned presentation, which was now obviously markedly shortened. He appeared completely unsettled as he searched unsuccessfully in his massive document to find the information about the three cases. Finally, he asked for and received a ten minute break.

"You can't win in the effort to overpower Brehm. The effort will sooner or later annoy the committee and reflect badly on you," John Parsons quietly suggested.

"I know. There's probably nothing they'd like better than to see me lose my cool. I'll straighten out. I needed this break."

"You've got a lot of positive data in your defense. Give them that alone, unaggressively."

Parsons understood very clearly who Jay was. He admired his courage and the struggle for what he believed was right. He also knew Jay's weaknesses. He did not tolerate those who were not quite perfect enough for him. He truly did believe that his judges were lesser doctors than he. But even more basic than that, J.D. Brown did not seem to understand the frailties of all humans, including himself. At times he could appear supercilious. John Parsons was afraid that all of these characteristics would be more apparent to his judges than Jay's deeply moral side.

During the break Jay decided he would leave Joan Jason for last of the three cases on which to respond, although it had been the first Marsh presented.

Jay quickly disposed of the third case, about the timing of the C-Section. He was not surprised that neither Marsh, nor the other Obstetrical members of the committee had much rebuttal for him. Marsh was probably glad to see that one done with and out of the way.

Marsh had another plan in mind. Besides Brown's approach to these cases, he would expose him on another front. At all the previous Quality Control Meetings, Jay Brown had made a point of the fact that in all the cases which had been brought against him over several years, each and every one had resulted in an excellent outcome. Marsh waited to throw that up at him once the Jason case was discussed.

"I would like to describe my actions, and the basis for them, in the case of the premature birth. This was a patient I had never seen previously. She was brought to Sam Rayburn from a small neighboring community hospital and, as I had the role of obstetrician on call that evening for emergencies, she became my case. When she arrived her membranes had already ruptured. She was only twenty-nine-and-one-half weeks pregnant.

"Dr. Marsh has told you that these monitor strips show a baby in serious distress. I want to challenge that. They have seriously misread the fetal monitor strips.

"We all agree that these premature babies should receive Betamethasone to bring about more rapid lung maturity before delivery. They have stated that they would have waited only twenty four hours and then done a Cesarean Section. The literature is quite variable on that subject. Just as many authors recommend forty eight hours which I tried to achieve.

"They have accused me of a lack of concern related to whether an infection had occurred. In fact, the record will show that I ordered repeated complete blood counts, but one of the orders was inadvertently missed by the nurses. Beyond that the patient never had an elevated temperature.

"Finally they have accused me of neglect because I was not at the delivery. Actually, the patient had no signs of labor until a call in the middle of the night when the nurse told me labor had begun. I went immediately to the hospital, as I do with all my labor patients, unlike some of the members of the department who wait until delivery is imminent, and..."

"Let's not start those accusations of the other department members again," Brehm interrupted.

Jay seemed to ignore him completely.

"I, on the other hand spend my time completely with the patients when they are in labor, even during the middle of the night.

"This particular patient had her baby about forty minutes after labor began, which was extremely rare. There was no way that I could possibly have known that she would have such a precipitous labor.

"The accusations in this case are absolutely baseless and have been..."

"Excuse me Dr. Brown, I believe our expert witness is on the line from New Haven, Connecticut."

Jay made no comment and slowly sat back in his chair.

"Dr. Mandarino, can you hear me?" Alonzo Brehm asked.

"Not perfectly. But I can hear you."

"Ladies and Gentleman Dr. Armand Mandarino is..."

Jay sat up a little straighter in his chair when he heard the name. It was a bit of a shock. Armand Mandarino didn't know Jay Brown at all, but the reverse was not true. Dr. Mandarino had a fine reputation and his name appeared throughout the literature. About a year before this hearing Jay had been contacted by an attorney friend who asked if Jay would review a possible malpractice case. When Jay heard the details he suggested that his friend contact Dr. Mandarino, who had written extensively on the subject involved in that particular case. The lawyer asked if Mandarino's fees would be similar to those of Jay Brown. Jay had been charging $150 per hour for whatever time was necessary to review a case.

"I haven't the slightest idea what he will charge. But I'm fairly certain it will be more than I do."

The attorney contacted Mandarino and subsequently got back to Jay and asked if he had another suggestion.

"Didn't it work out with Mandarino?"

"It could have if I didn't care how I spent my money or the client's."

"What happened?"

"I asked him how much he charged and was slightly taken back when he quoted $500 per hour, but I was willing to go ahead with that. Then he said that it was necessary for him to receive a five thousand dollar retainer. I told him that I didn't think the material I would send could take anywhere near ten hours. With that he responded that it was my problem and he didn't look at any cases without the five thousand up front. I just ended the conversation there."

That episode flashed through Jay's mind as Brehm proceeded with the introduction of the expert. John Parsons saw a small smile come over Jay's face as Brehm spoke and wondered what in Jay Brown's head caused that.

"… and knowing that you have reviewed these three cases, I wondered if you could give us your impressions of them and Dr. Brown's management."

How cute Alonzo. Asking him as if you haven't the slightest knowledge what his approach to these cases might be. I can just imagine how nervous you are that the famous Armand Mandarino might make a statement in support of lowly Jay Brown.

Mandarino, like those before him, gave little time to the first two cases. Like Marsh, he went straight to the Jason case and talked about the kind of damage that can occur from the "overly aggressive" treatment offered by Jay Brown.

Following that, he took positions that followed completely Dr. Marsh's presentation on the premature baby.

When Brehm asked for questions to be put to Dr. Mandarino from the committee members, only Marsh spoke out.

"Don't you think that Dr. Brown should have…? Like, wouldn't you have expected Dr. Brown to…? If you were managin' that case by the time it reached 24 hours, like wouldn't you…?"

Each suggestion by Marsh brought forth further confirmation by Mandarino that the department had done exactly what it should about Dr. J.D. Brown.

Jay listened intently to everything Mandarino said, and took notes. He had regained his composure. At one point he tried to ask Mandarino a question, but he was rebuffed by Alonzo Brehm.

"Please allow the entire committee a chance to ask Dr. Mandarino questions before you begin."

Jay thought that was quite humorous, because not one member of the committee, other than Marsh, had uttered a sound. He snickered and then smiled broadly at Brehm after that comment. The conversation had been exclusively between Marsh and Mandarino.

Brehm was annoyed by the broad smile from Jay Brown. He knew there was nothing kindly about it.

"Is something wrong, Dr. Brown?" asked Brehm, placing strong emphasis on his name.

"Nothing at all," Jay responded, the smirk still on his face.

Finally, after Marsh had milked every last approval out of Mandarino for the actions of the Quality Control Committee, Brehm asked Jay if he had any questions. He knew fully well there would be many. The hour had reached eight and the Committee seemed to be restless. He noticed that Rehnquist repeatedly looked at her watch.

"Dr. Mandarino, wouldn't you agree that many researchers have advocated that an attempt be made to get forty-eight hours of delay before delivery, once the Betamethazone has been started, and even more if possible?"

"There are some who believe that."

"Then let me ask you about the fetal heart monitor strip that has been repeatedly reported as being indicative of severe fetal distress. What would you consider to be the primary sign of fetal well being?"

"I'm not certain that I, uh, completely understand your question."

"Well, then, let me put it more simply. Wouldn't the beat-to-beat variability and fetal heart rate accelerations be the most important finding we would seek to determine the wellbeing of this baby?"

"I'm certain you know, Dr. Brown, that the evaluation of fetal heart rate variability is only made accurately with internal monitoring, not external monitoring."

"But, Dr. Mandarino, that is all we could utilize. You certainly wouldn't have wanted me to insert an internal monitor into this patient which would force us to proceed with a delivery, when the goal was to gain as much maturity as possible."

"That may be true, but you can't make an accurate evaluation without the internal monitor."

Jay maneuvered his question as if he were a trained and experienced attorney.

"You do understand, Dr. Mandarino, that there is the claim that this baby was in distress. Even if the monitoring system utilized is not the optimum one from which to obtain critical data, I'm certain you'd agree, there definitely aren't signs with what we have available to make the assumption of fetal distress."

"Well…"

"What about the accelerations, Dr. Mandarino? They are constantly present and you absolutely do not need an internal monitor to demonstrate them. Isn't that so?"

Mandarino mumbled some minimal agreement with Jay Brown.

"Let's go back to the case of the forceps delivery and damaged baby."

"All right."

"Am I to understand with your discussion about all the terrible dangers of mid-forceps that there is no place for such maneuvers in modern obstetrics?"

"Well…"

"Specifically, Dr. Mandarino, would you have every mid forceps delivery replaced by a Cesarean section?'

"No, I didn't say that, but there are significant hazards."

"And would you be surprised if I produced literature that states that the procedure fell out of use because residents were inadequately trained and became one of several reasons the Cesarean section rate skyrocketed to the detriment of the patients?"

"No... I wouldn't be surprised."

"One of the hazards you specifically alluded to was the delivery of a baby through an undilated cervix. That, of course, was because your information came from the Quality Control Committee which accused me of that very thing."

Jay Brown then took a very long pause and Mandarino said nothing. He could be as sharp as Jay and wanted to see what Jay's point was. Everyone in the room had stopped any examination of their watches, even Rehnquist. They were sitting at the front of their seats, as if they watched two pugilists in the thick of battle.

"What... what do you consider to be an undilated cervix, one that has not reached ten centimeters? Is it... six centimeters... seven centimeters... eight centimeters?"

Jay pushed Mandarino hard. His voice rose, but Mandarino would not be intimidated.

"Any cervix that I can still feel!" Mandarino shot back.

"Fine, Dr. Mandarino. I assume you've done thousands of vaginal deliveries."

"That's true."

"Have you never done a delivery where you can just feel a rim and pushed it over the baby's head?"

"Of course, that's different. Everybody does that frequently."

"And is this maneuver considered a delivery through an undilated cervix?"

"Absolutely not. I consider that to be fully dilated."

"Then I assume you weren't told that this is what was done in this case."

Jay Brown spoke right over a comment Mandarino was about to make.

"Let me ask you something else." Jay paused with no necessary purpose, but just as he had seen Parsons do in the courtroom. "What would you expect to see as the complication for a mother if an obstetrician delivered her baby through a truly undilated cervix?"

"Probably a cervical laceration or even a tear further up into the lower segment of the uterus."

"I agree completely," Jay said and then waited a few moments and added with significant emphasis, "Mrs. Jason had no problem whatsoever."

Marsh listened and was angered that he had been persuaded by some of his cohorts to get this expert witness. Whenever he let them go out too far on their own, he was always sorry. Mandarino had no ax to grind with Jay. If Jay made strong points, it was because Mandarino had no personal reason to see him tossed out. When Jay made statements of fact that Mandarino could not in good conscience challenge, they were left as winning points for Jay Brown. Marsh wished this portion of the hearing would end, but Brown persisted. He wanted to keep it alive.

"Dr. Mandarino, with no disrespect meant," as he remembered the tactics of John Parsons, "… how often do you testify against physicians?"

"Not that often."

"What about in defense of physicians?"

"About three quarters of the time I am defending physicians and one fourth against."

"So I can assume you do something like this, on one side or the other, quite frequently."

"No."

"How much time DO you devote to this?"

"Oh maybe ten percent."

"So ten percent of all your work is as an expert witness. Thank you. I have no further questions."

The conversation on the phone seemed to end rather abruptly. Dr. Brehm thanked Dr. Mandarino. Immediately Jay Brown asked if he could continue the discussion of the cases. By now it had reached nine in the evening.

Brehm looked at his watch. Like Marsh, he was definitely not pleased with how the phone interrogation had gone. "I think we should take a short break."

At least a third of the attendees headed for restrooms. Dr. Rehnquist went to the phone to call her apartment. Her date was there. He had let himself in. He had made himself a drink and was not in the least bit annoyed. She told him she didn't know when this "damn thing" would end. He said if she was not there by eleven he'd leave and take a raincheck. Jessica Rehnquist had the very strong feeling that her new nightgown would remain in its box for this evening.

Brehm and Marsh met in a small office adjacent to the large conference room. They agreed it was necessary to play more hard ball before this evening was to end, in order to ensure that the non-obstetrical component of the committee would come around.

John and Jay stood alone in one corner.

"I know you've saved Jason for the big punch. I'm certain it will be a shocker for the non-obstetrical members, but I don't believe the attack on you is over. Don't be surprised if they come back hard."

"I think you're right. They can't be particularly thrilled with what has occurred so far."

The group reassembled.

"Dr. Brown, I believe you wanted to discuss the cases further."

"Just the Jason case, Dr. Brehm."

Jay gathered his papers while the group waited to hear what he would say. Brehm hadn't the slightest idea what was about to come. Marsh knew nothing more about the case than the information he had heard at the Quality Control Meeting. The material had been presented by Dr. Gresham who was as honest and straightforward as anyone could possibly be. His information came from the chart and one other source. Slack and Crown had provided him the information about what had happened to the baby after the family left town.

"I believe that I've already made it quite clear in my discussion with the COMMITTEE'S witness, Dr. Mandarino, that Mrs. Jason was not delivered through an undilated cervix."

Jay wanted it to be crystal clear that the very existence of the witness was not acceptable to him.

"The situation was, however, quite tense. The baby appeared to be in serious jeopardy based on the monitor strip. I accomplished the delivery in great haste to ensure that the baby would have a good outcome."

Nothing seemed unusual in what Jay Brown described and the hearing appeared to fall back into a more relaxed state.

"The rapid placement of the forceps was somewhat difficult. When the baby was born, in fine condition, there was a bruise on one side of the lips. Within hours, the nurse's notes reported that the mark was, and I quote, "almost gone." The neonatologist noted just "a superficial bruise."

Jay went back to his notes as if he did not know by heart every last sentence he was prepared to say. The committee waited.

"When the Quality Control Committee met with me they asked, in the most antagonistic manner, 'As the former Director of an Obstetrical Department in New York are you aware of the risk of placing a forcep directly across a baby's face?'

"I immediately took offense with the statement and said that I had not placed the forcep across the baby's face.

"The questioner quickly responded at that time, 'And I guess it didn't hurt the baby very much, did it?'

"I shouted back, 'I'm sure it hurt the baby. Would it have been better if it came out dead without a bruise on its face?'

"Then came the shocker, as the presenter described a baby who was unable to eat due to the trauma to his mouth. He went into a vivid description of how the baby was unable to eat, lost one and a half pounds and almost died except for the intervention of a pediatrician." Brown paused between every sentence. "I was stunned... I had never heard such a thing about the child.... No records were there to review.... I was totally at a loss for words.... The meeting ended and I felt totally dejected and depressed about the information presented. In a state of shock I left the meeting. I told them I am committed to provide the best possible care that I can. But, I was very unsure of myself at that point."

The Committee did not know where this testimony might go. Marsh and Brehm knew there was no way possible that Brown would suddenly fold. It was one of the most important reasons that they disliked him. He was about to outsmart them and they sensed it. The level of tension in the room rose again. There was the sense that there was more to come.

"Mrs. Jason left town immediately after the birth. Due to her husband's job, they moved to Cleveland. With some minimal amount of effort we found her there. I contacted her and related, in complete honesty, what I had heard at the meeting about her baby. I told her that I was terribly distressed. She laughed at me and proceeded to fill me in with the entire story and agreed to send it to me in writing. I would like to read this brief letter to you now.

"It happened this way. Trent, that's my baby, never had the slightest problem eating. That laceration was completely gone by the time we left the hospital. I was deeply committed to breast feeding him, no matter what. I tried to feed him but for some reason I didn't produce any milk. My Mom told me that the poor baby would starve, but I refused to believe her. The baby lost weight and cried all the time, so we went to the doctor who told me that Mom was absolutely right. If I didn't start to supplement him with a bottle or just give up the breast feeding completely he wouldn't survive. I decided to give it up and Trent thrived. You didn't do anything, Dr. Brown. It was all me."

There was a hush over the conference room. Jay slowly piled up his papers. He had made his point. Marsh could hardly believe it. For the second time that evening he had been undermined by the foolish mistakes of those who wanted Brown out, They had shot themselves in the foot once again.

But for Alonzo Brehm it was not quite the same. He would not lose this evening to this snotty, know it all, New York Jew. His back just stiffened for a new assault.

"Dr. Brown, I gather from what Dr. Mandarino said that he thought in this case the mid-forceps were too risky. After all, he read the same chart you've referred to."

"But there was no damage to the mother."

"Well, to me that just means you got away with it this time. It doesn't mean you did the right thing."

Jay started to get angry. "It isn't that I got away with something."

"What I want to know is why are you out of sync with the rest of the members of this department? Are you the only one who knows how to practice here?"

"I didn't say that. I've discussed these three cases just as you asked, and told you why I did the right thing."

"But your peers say you didn't. They say that if they did the things you do, they would get bad results. How come you get good results?'"

"Those who say that are not my peers and I won't be judged by them. The things I do are done by others all over the country."

Jay felt John's hand on his arm. He knew he had gone too far. Brehm couldn't be more pleased. He knew these were the kinds of statements that would concern the non-obstetrical members of the committee.

"I guess you think nobody else around here except you knows how to practice."

"Dr. Brehm, these are physicians on whose cases I have written negative second opinions. They don't want me around here."

"Don't tell me, Dr. Brown, that it's back to your harangue about the rest of the department. They're not on trial."

"But these are the same people who have lied to the media about the C-section rate at the hospital and performed unconscionable numbers of that operation."

Brown had completely lost his cool—everything that Parsons was afraid of would happen. All the good points he had made earlier on would unravel. Alonzo Brehm had fed Jay Brown to the lions. Jay's anger rose as Brehm poured salt into his wounds.

Brehm was not about to let up. He continued to needle Jay for the next half hour. He went back to the other case with questions and comments about why Jay did not make it in time for the delivery. He questioned, in detail, how long it takes to get dressed and off to the hospital; why not another blood count; why he didn't agree with the findings that the baby was in distress. He was relentless, even when his questions seemed repetitive and not pertinent. Jay fell deeper and deeper into Brehm's trap.

"It is almost ten o'clock and it seems this problem is not yet resolved. I'll call this meeting to a close. I'd like to set a date for next week to conclude this hearing. I believe in another hour or two all the issues can be discussed."

Jay Brown sat absolutely motionless. He wasn't certain whether he was glad the evening had come to an end or distressed that it would continue for another day. The committee members were not sorry that Brehm had called this recess. They had been there for almost five hours and fatigue had set in. A date was agreed upon and the room emptied very rapidly. Jay and John were left alone.

John did not chastise. He was certain Jay knew full well what had gone wrong without the need to labor the point. Brown needed emotional support more than anything now. The five hours of constant stress had taken their toll.

"Let's just sleep on it, Jay, and we'll talk tomorrow. I think you need the rest more than you need to discuss anything right now. Do you want to leave your car here and I'll drive you home?"

Jay sat and leaned on the table with his head in his right hand. He didn't ignore John Parsons. He was just deep in thought.

"What? Oh no, John. Thanks for the offer. I can drive myself home."

Jay paused for a moment and then said, "John... I can't tell you what it means to have you here beside me. I don't think I could have done this without you here.... I'm so sorry. I know I must be a terrible disappointment to you."

"Don't be ridiculous Jay. You're not here to please me. You'll do the best you can and that's fine. Let's go home. This is no time to discuss this first meeting. We'll have plenty of time to talk."

The two of them rose, collected the papers, and made it out through the administrative offices which were almost darkened. From there they walked silently out to their cars which were parked side by side.

"Don't be too hard on yourself, Jay. There's another day."

"Goodnight John. Thanks... thanks so much for everything."

They drove off through the night, and John Parsons wondered if Jay Brown would be all right. Some scary thoughts went through his head—like whether Jay, in his distraught state, would or could do something to harm himself. John tried quickly to put those thoughts out of his mind.

Chapter Twenty Seven

A Surprise Meeting

*J*ay barely closed his eyes the entire night after the first session of the Ad Hoc Committee. It was a mixture of a few moments of sleep and many hours of thinking. All sorts of ideas flashed through his head. The demons of the night were working overtime. He imagined terrible scenarios. For each one his brain selected an option to avoid a disastrous outcome.

Whenever Jay Brown decided to do something somewhat rash, he avoided telling John Parsons about it until after the fact. His gut feeling was that John would talk him out of taking the action he had planned, especially if it was imprudent. If he was truly committed to a course of action, foolish or not, he didn't want his mind changed by John Parsons. He didn't want sanity or sensible logic to interfere with his plans when his anger was directing him to do something off-the-wall. The day after the first part of the Ad Hoc Committee meeting was to be one of those times.

By morning he had come to a decision: He would contact Alonzo Brehm and ask if he could have a private meeting with him at his office. He would not tell John.

Along with all the other signs that he was reacting badly to the stresses that were mounting, he began demonstrating some degree of paranoia. Though he knew full well that Joan was on his side, he decided to make the appointment himself, telling no one.

"Good morning. This is Doctor J.D. Brown. I'd like to make an appointment to speak with Dr. Brehm."

"He's in the O.R. this morning. I won't see him until after lunch. When did you want to meet with him?"

"At his convenience. But it should be within the next day or two."

"Can I ask him and call you back this afternoon?"

He didn't want the call to come back through his office. "That... uh... will be a little difficult... due to my schedule. Can I check back with you late this afternoon and find out?"

"That will be fine, Dr. Brown. Can you call about four o'clock?"

"Yes. Thank you. I'll speak with you later."

"He wants to come talk with me."

There was a silence on the other end of the line.

"Well what do you think? Should I talk to him or not?"

"What do you think he wants to talk about, Alonzo?"

"I think he's on the rocks. My secretary told me she thought his voice was rather shaky. I think that god damned troublemaker would like to pull in his tail and just get out of this mess."

"OK. Then why don't you meet with him and see what he has to say."

"Suppose he wants to make a deal. Do I have free rein to accept or reject his proposal?"

"If we don't make a deal, what do you see as the probable decision of the Committee?"

Brehm thought for a moment and said, "I think they'll tell him 'No more obstetrics. You can stay on the staff if you're just going to do gynecology.' Just what the OB department offered him."

"Well if he sees it the way you do, and wants to make a deal, then he'll want more than that. After all, if he can get that from the Committee, why does he have to make a deal?"

There was another long pause.

"OK, Alonzo, let's try this. Tell him you'll try to get the Committee to restore his obstetrical privileges with very rigid supervision. I think that will be enough to get him to throw in the towel. Even if he accepts that, after a while it'll be too much for his ego to bear."

"And if he says no?"

"Then tell him that you'll be in favor of the Committee recommending to the Executive Board that they remove his privileges entirely. You can subtly mention that it would be on his permanent record wherever he might go subsequently."

Brehm agreed and hung up the phone.

Baker sat thinking after the conversation ended. Brown was a constant problem. Marsh had warned him that if Brown was allowed to make life uncomfortable for all the other gynecologists, surgery would gradually shift to other hospitals where the staff had privileges. If second opinions were a fact of life by this time, they wanted them done by someone other than Brown. It would affect obstetrics as well. They didn't want somebody constantly watching over all their decisions about Cesarean Sections. Other hospitals in the area would make it attractive for the obstetricians to bring their patients. Baker knew he had to make certain that Brown didn't wreak havoc with the obstetrical department.

He had left the earlier efforts to get rid of Brown to Marsh, Crown, Slack and buddies. They had not managed it too well.

Baker had great plans for Sam Rayburn. He was going to build it into a medical dynasty, expanding every department. He was planning to bring in super specialists in a number of fields with promises of great rewards. This was to be his monument, his baby.

I don't want some dumb shit, self-righteous Jew screwing up my plans, he thought. *I'm just not certain that Brehm will do any better than Marsh and company did in handling this matter up until now. He seemed to be more impressed with his role as Committee Chairman than in getting the job done last night.*

He realized that he had no better choice. In the long run he would be much better off if he remained ostensibly objective, allowing the process to take its course, being managed by physicians who were charged with the responsibility of dealing with their peers. Baker wanted this to end on a positive note for the hospital. But, success or failure, he didn't want his name linked with the process.

––––––––––

"Thanks for meeting with me."

"Don't mention it. Would you like a cup of coffee?"

Jay was in no mood to make this a social occasion. He wasn't certain what he expected to accomplish. He hoped possibly he could reach Brehm and get what he felt would be a fairer hearing during the next meeting.

"I came here because I had the feeling during the first portion of the meeting that you had taken a position against me. I wanted to understand why and see if I could clear up whatever was causing that."

Brehm saw immediately that his earlier perception of the reason Jay wanted to talk was completely wrong It annoyed him that he had judged Jay inaccurately and even more so that Brown had, in an indirect way, accused him of being biased. The initial warm greeting changed quite quickly. Instead of denying it, Brehm went on the attack.

"You're not completely wrong. I think you're a liar, dishonest, an ego maniac and a threat to our hospital."

Jay knew deep down that his chances of turning Brehm around were close to nil, but this was quite a shock. He had expected Brehm to deny any bias and assure him, though disingenuously, that he would make every effort to have him receive a fair hearing. He now knew that his expectations were far off target.

"Lying about what?"

"I don't believe you were the head of the Ob-Gyn Department of some hospital in New York with a big practice and just decided to leave. I think you were a god damned pain in the ass and they threw you out."

Jay knew that Brehm was half right. He had been a pain in the ass, but nothing like that had happened.

"What do you mean you don't believe me? Why don't you just pick up the phone and call them? What kind of crazy idea is that?"

"Sure. I'd call them and they'd say write. Then they'd write back that why you left was privileged information and all that crap. I'd never find out the truth."

"So instead you just make the assumption that I'm lying."

"Well I reviewed your credentials from that hospital and they said you did 83 laparoscopies. But your application here says you did 500. I think you're some sort of megalomaniac and just lie about the things you do or things you think you're capable of doing."

"I think you'd better reconsider your accusations more carefully before you make them. Eighty three cases was the number of private cases I did there. I also operated at two other hospitals. BUT, besides that I trained every member of the entire department, on an individual basis, how to do the procedure. That meant I scrubbed in with them, each on a number of cases, before they received privileges to do laparoscopies on their own. By the way, I never charged any fees for all of those at which I was teaching. I was also training residents."

"That's just your word. There's no evidence for it in your records. I think you mishandled all three of the cases that were brought up at the hearing and thought you could get away with it by attacking the rest of the department. Well I'm not dumb enough to fall for that trick."

"Fall for what trick, Brehm?" He was completely frustrated with the direction the conversation was taking. "I described in detail everything I did and the reason for it."

By this time the conversation had gotten completely out of hand and Jay realized this had been a terrible mistake.

"Well I think you're a dangerous and lousy doctor. The hospital needs to get rid of doctors like you, not limit their privileges, get rid of them. I really have this gut feeling that they ought to lynch you."

Jay Brown was in a state of shock. He was totally unprepared for this attack. He understood that the terminology of lynching him, although this was the South, was only figurative. But the idea that his judge openly stated that he was out to get him, for whatever reason, completely stunned him.

Just as forcefully as Brehm had attacked, Jay struck back.

"You've made a big mistake. I'm not a lousy doctor. I get into less difficulty than just about anyone on this staff. I'm conservative in my treatment. I stay with my patients in labor, unlike most of the physicians on this staff, and Marsh knows it. As the head of the department he has constantly tried to get other physicians to be more diligent in their management of patients in labor instead of showing up at the last minute.

"You may very well be right that I have been a nuisance for the hospital and for the staff, by being outspoken," Jay bellowed as tears were welling up in his eyes, "but I have not been a lousy or a dishonest physician."

Jay repeated, "You are making a very big mistake."

Somewhat shocked by the force of Jay Brown's counterattack, Brehm begged off by saying, "Well that's the way I see it, and if I'm wrong then I'm sorry, but I don't think so."

It almost sounded to Jay Brown as if Brehm knew what was happening was wrong, but had no way to back down.

"I don't mind saying it, Jay, you are an ass."

Jay sat facing John Parsons and had no response. He knew very well that what John was saying was true. In fact he was quite sure that Parsons would call him much worse if he were not such a gentleman.

"How does this effect everything?"

"Not in any significant way. I mean, I'm assuming you didn't try to bribe him or threaten him or anything like that."

Slowly Jay responded. "No! I'm not that dumb yet, but maybe almost that dumb."

"Did you have the slightest impression after the first Committee session that he was unbiased? What could you possibly be thinking that you could accomplish? The only effect will probably be an even more negative approach toward you, if that's possible, now that he's angry about the accusation."

"What do you think is going to happen, John?"

"I can't imagine anything good. They have to make a recommendation to the Executive Committee. Only a total dreamer would guess they would recommend that everything be dropped. The choices seem to be restricting your privileges or denying them completely. I would guess most likely they'll go along with the Department and recommend denying you obstetrical privileges and letting you practice gynecology."

"I'm sure you're right."

"Then you're left with only two choices. Accept what they decide or take your final appeal to the Hospital Board itself.... Do you understand that appeal is not the same?"

"In what way, John?"

"These are lay people. They don't feel competent or in any position to judge the medical issues. They will only hear arguments about the process. If you can demonstrate to them you've been treated unfairly, they can change the decision. But they will not discuss the management of the cases or anything dealing with your ability to practice medicine."

Sarcastically, Jay said, "Oh I didn't know it was going to be that easy. All I have to do is to persuade them to go against all the staff of their hospital. Is that even possible?"

"Don't ask me Jay. I never thought you had a chance from the beginning. I hoped I made it clear by constantly offering to throw in the towel. I can't believe that you didn't understand from the beginning that this was like spitting in the wind. But I can't change the fact that you think you're Don Quixote. All I can do is try to help you through."

Jay didn't say another word. He sat in his chair, with his head in his hand, in front of John Parsons for about a minute or so, then slowly rose and walked out the door.

――――――

"I'm hoping that this evening's meeting will be much shorter than last week's," Alonzo Brehm said to the members of the Committee.

The next hour and twenty minutes consisted of further questions that committee members, especially Alonzo Brehm, raised for Jay Brown to answer. Not all of the questioning attacked his actions. Henry Berger's questions, though carefully worded so as not to appear supportive, provided Jay with an opportunity to present a more positive side to the cases being discussed.

When everyone seemed to be satisfied that there was nothing more to be accomplished, Jay asked if he could make one final statement.

"These last two sessions we have spent together have been extremely stressful for all of us, I'm certain. I would like to leave you with a few final thoughts before you go into deliberation. I've spent the past fifteen years trying to accomplish some small successes in changing the way America provides health care. None of the writing or speaking I have done has been anti-medicine or anti-doctor. I've always believed that institutions tend to destroy themselves from within. I have hoped that the best qualified in the medical profession would insist on changes that would make the actions of the least qualified less meaningful.

"I have tried, not without some failures, to provide the best care possible to my own patients. Medicine, and especially obstetrics, has been the joy of my life. I sincerely want to continue doing that... and doing that here. I appreciate the time and effort all of you have put into this and thank you for your efforts."

After what seemed like a long moment of silence, Alonzo Brehm said, "This meeting's adjourned. If all the individuals other than the Committee members would leave the room, we will meet in private session."

The private deliberations of the Committee had gone on for about two hours. There was absolutely no discussion about Jay's accusations concerning the reason for the department to be taking action against him. Only the three cases came up for discussion. Berger argued that Brown hadn't done anything that seemed extremely unusual in these cases.

The four non-obstetrical members were almost ignored. They asked rare questions of the four obstetrical members and generally got their answers from Marsh or Berger. For the most part, the other two obstetricians, Brenner and O'Donnell, just chimed in in concurrence with Marsh's comments.

Finally Brehm said it was time for them to reach some conclusions. Marsh presented the proposal that the Committee concur with the Ob-Gyn Quality Control Committee and recommend removing Brown's obstetrical privileges. To Marsh's surprise, Gerber offered another proposal.

Henry Gerber was clever enough to know that he should not go in complete opposition to Marsh. He was mild-mannered and spoke in a soft tone. All during the hearing he had demonstrated his considerable knowledge in the discussions that had arisen about different choices of therapy. Whereas Marsh had made definitive statements concerning his feelings about Jay Brown's choices of treatment, Gerber had taken a completely different approach. Each time Gerber spoke it seemed to be more directed toward the non-obstetrical contingent. He relieved their insecurity in making a decision in an area of medicine in which they felt quite lacking in knowledge. He would explain to them why one choice or another might be made. Neither Brehm nor Marsh really understood what was happening. Berger was ingratiating himself with Rehnquist, Weakeley, Barton and Lopez, while the other obstetricians seemed to ignore their existence, assuming that their votes were either automatic or unnecessary.

"I think we all agree that there is some concern about Dr. Brown that cannot be totally ignored," Gerber began. "Taking away his privileges seems a little harsh to me under the circumstances. Soooo... I'd like to suggest another alternative. Why don't we allow him to continue to practice obstetrics with some specific requirements. We could state that he must obtain consultation with a member of the department for whatever specific types of cases we felt were likely to be a problem. As an example all Cesarean Sections, all high risk cases, all breeches, etc. That could be left up to Dr. Marsh who certainly would be capable of making the decisions as to what types of cases would be included."

Brehm acknowledged that there were two suggestions on the table and decided that he might as well end it there.

"If no one else has anything other to offer, we'll just vote on these," Brehm said, expecting fully well that Marsh's recommendation would be accepted.

"All those in favor of removing Dr. Brown's obstetrical privileges raise your hand."

Up went Marsh, O'Donnell, Brenner and Brehm.

Brehm still didn't quite gather what was happening when he said, "And all those in favor of requiring consultation?"

Berger was joined by Rehnquist, Weakeley, Lopez and Barton.

Brehm had a strange look on his face as he raised his head from the sheet of paper on which he had been writing the results.

"It looks like the Committee has decided to recommend required consultation."

What he said after that came as quite a surprise to the rest of the membership.

"I think this is a mistake. I'm not sure why it happened but I don't think we served the hospital very well."

Without another word he rose, angered, and walked out of the room with no further comment to the group. Marsh sat half amazed, the other furiously angry with Henry Gerber. He actually had no emotions about the other four member's votes, laying all the blame at the feet of Gerber.

His feelings were certainly well merited.

Several days passed before Jay was notified about the decision of the Ad Hoc Committee. He received a formal letter from the Executive Committee which stated the Ad Hoc Committee's recommendation and advised him of the Executive Committee's concurrence. The letter also stated that he would be required to request consultation with members of the Obstetrical Department in cases which would be outlined in a subsequent letter from Dr. Marsh. The Executive Committee required that he fulfill that request for one year in order to maintain his privileges, after which time he could request the elimination of that requirement. It did not make clear to whom that request would be submitted. Jay felt certain that it would go back to the same Quality Control Committee.

The day after Jay Brown received the letter, he saw Anne Weakeley getting into her car in the hospital parking lot.

"Anne, Anne," he called out.

She turned and saw him walking toward her. She was not thrilled to have been spotted.

"Hi, Jay, what can I do for you?"

"Thanks for taking the time to serve on that Committee."

"You're welcome."

She sensed that it wasn't the only reason Jay had called out to her as she began getting into her car.

"There is something I would like to ask you. Since I know that everything in the private session is privileged I won't ask you how you voted. But I have to assume that the non-obstetrical group must have wanted this lesser sanction rather than taking away my privileges. I just wondered why they decided to take that position rather than removing any sanctions."

Anne was obviously very uncomfortable. She thought for one moment and decided that if she didn't deal with this now, later on Jay would still have more questions.

"Jay, I can't speak for anyone else except myself. I'm not an obstetrician. I had to accept the fact that the information was conflicting and we were faced with a decision, when we really weren't qualified to make one. But,... but... it sounded to me like you were being railroaded, so I couldn't go along with them completely. I decided this was the best compromise I could make. That's it. That's the whole thing in a nutshell."

"I understand Anne." Jay gave a deep sigh and said, "Thanks again".

Anne Weakeley got into the car and drove off. When she got about fifty yards away from Jay, she shouted to herself in the car, "Shit!"

"I suppose this was not something we would ever imagine would be the result."

"Louie, that son-of-a-bitch Berger will sure enough be payin' for this sooner or later. Like we should never have put that Jew on the Committee," Marsh responded.

Slack tried to relieve himself of some of the blame for the choice of Berger, which they had jointly agreed upon in the beginning, by re-emphasizing the original belief that a new department member was not likely to make waves.

"Well, like this asshole sort of don't follow the rules we expected," Marsh reminded them.

"What happens now?" Slack asked.

"I'm not sure. I'm just not sure."

Almost a month passed before Jay received a letter stating a list of obstetrical situations for which he was required to seek consultation. It was signed by Jack Marsh and stated that it would be effective beginning April 1st, 1986.

"I can't possibly accept that decision," Jay said to John Parsons.

"Jay... listen to me, Jay... you got the most favorable decision you could possibly expect and the Executive Committee has accepted it. Your approach to this is insanity. It's as if you won't give up until you're destroyed. They've given you the chance to put this all behind you and start over."

"It's not so, John. It's not so. Hear me out. If I accept this, the harassment will not only continue, it will get worse. They'll make my life miserable. The only way I can feel even slightly safe here would have been if the Hospital Board said there was no basis for any of this and kept me in the same stature as the other obstetricians. It can't work otherwise. I've got to appeal to the Hospital Board to throw out the entire thing."

Parsons didn't say it, but he had the feeling this was never going to end. They had reached the last appeal. After this, there was nothing.

"I'll request the appeal and they'll set up a date within 30 days. You are going to lose. They will not overrule the Executive Committee. You're asking a lay Board, that is committed to the staff of the hospital, to turn against them. It's not going to happen, no matter what you tell them. Do you understand that, Jay? You CANNOT win."

Jay Brown didn't respond immediately. They were in the library of the firm. The walls were covered from floor to ceiling with law books. Parsons was sitting at the large table in the center of the room waiting for some response. Jay had his back to him, standing and facing the rows and rows of volumes of law cases. A nervous reaction made him pull one of the volumes off the shelf, a book that had no meaning to him, and flip through its pages. After holding it for a moment he returned it to its place on the shelf and turned to Parsons. Parsons had no intention of saying another word until Jay spoke. For the very first time he found that one of the emotions he felt in his relationship to Jay Brown was anger. He wondered for a brief moment if the annoyance the staff had with Brown didn't have some basis. It wasn't that John Parsons misunderstood that what was transpiring was an injustice. He was just wondering whether Jay was incapable of knowing when there was a time to fight and a time to back off. He wasn't happy with the thought that his client might be committed to being self-destructive.

"I know that you're annoyed with me and thinking that this has now gone too far. I'm not certain whether you realize that your impression is really very important to me. I respect your judgment more than almost anyone I've ever known," Jay finally said.

Jay continued slowly walking around the room. Parsons sat quietly. Jay had said nothing that explained what he wanted to do or why.

"I think you are certainly right that this Board will not go against its staff. Well, let me change that slightly. Under all normal circumstances, I'm sure that's true. But I want to ask you a question. Suppose the Board found that their staff was involved in something that was actually so bad, possibly even criminal, that they couldn't turn their backs on it?"

Parsons listened intently and still said nothing.

"I've never told you about this. I've never told anyone. I know you're aware that Alice Crain is Jack Marsh's... I'm not certain what the term might be. Marsh was at Alice Crain's apartment when several members of the department called and told him that they had to speak to him immediately. They came over to the apartment and Marsh told Alice to stay in the bedroom while he spoke with them."

Brown took a long pause again as if he didn't know whether he should continue. Parsons finally broke his silence.

"And what happened?"

"If things don't work out the way I would like, I would prefer that you not repeat this to anyone."

"You and I always have the attorney-client privilege when we're talking about legal matters."

"John, she heard them, actually heard them conspiring against me. She came to tell me that she was concerned about what they would do to get rid of me. She wanted me to stop all this, just back off."

"And what do you intend to do about that?"

"I spoke with her after I got this last decision from the Ad Hoc Committee and asked if she would testify in my behalf to the Board and tell them what she had heard."

"Is she willing to do that?... Isn't she afraid?... How will she be able to remain in this community?... How will she be able to work?... Have you thought about what will happen to her as she tries to save you?"

"One thing I said in the beginning of this conversation was not completely honest. I told you I could never work again in this community unless all of this was reversed. Actually, nothing can save me any longer in this community. No matter what the Board might decide, I can't practice here any longer."

"I'm sure that's true. But what about her?"

"Things are not going well for her either. They believe that she's supporting me and probably don't trust her. Even more serious than that, her relationship with Marsh seems to be deteriorating. When this is all over, I'm going to go elsewhere... and I've promised I would take her with me to work as my nurse wherever I go."

"Are you also having an affair with her?"

"First of all, I'm not even married now. If there were a relationship between us, I don't think the word "affair" applies to two single people who are seeing each other. But no... we are not going to bed together. We've known each other for many years and have fought together to improve health care. Now we're just outsiders in this community and probably need to move on."

Parsons wasn't certain how to respond.

"John, do you think under those circumstances the Board might act differently?"

"Possibly, but I wonder about something else.... If you are now committed to leaving Austin and Sam Rayburn Medical Center, why not just leave now and not involve Alice Crain? Is it worth subjecting her to this when nothing will come of it?"

"There are two reasons. One relates to the present environment in our society. I'll be a lot better off if all of this is expunged as I go looking for another place to start. But there is something else even more important. If I leave right now it means these hoodlums will have won. Everyone will assume that what they've done was proper and that they got rid of a bad apple. The Hospital will allow them to continue in their position of power in the Department. There will be no effort to change the way medicine is practiced here and everything I've worked for will be lost. I've got to try and make that not happen."

"Isn't Crain nervous about this?"

"I'm sure she is. But she says she'll do it."

"What you're asking of her is way, way beyond the call of duty. If she changed her mind you could hardly blame her."

"I know you're right. And it certainly is possible that when the day comes she might find it too frightening."

"If that happens, what will you do?"

"At that point I'd have no choice. I'd just go in and present my case and after their decision I will leave Austin."

John Parsons had a bad feeling deep down in his gut about what the future held. He could see that there was apparently no way to get Jay Brown to change his mind. He assumed that Jay was probably right. If Alice testified about a conspiracy it would be difficult for the Hospital Board to ignore it. If not, it was just an exercise in futility.

"There is something else I wanted to ask you. Is there any way I can get a hearing in front of the entire Hospital Board?"

"I don't believe so. As I recall the Hospital by-laws, they'd set up a committee of at least three people to hear your appeal. There's no way to know who those people might be."

"I'd like to be able to provide information in advance to those who'll be there. Is that going to be possible?"

"Forget it, Jay. If you're going ahead, I think everything is going to depend on Alice's testimony… and you won't need anything else."

"I hope you understand, John."

John Parsons looked at him, but made no response.

On March 20th, John Parsons sent a formal letter to the Chairman of the Hospital Board requesting the appeal and a delay in the implementation of the required consultation until the results of the appeal were finalized. Before the week was out he received a response. The Board would honor Dr. J.D. Brown's request and hear the appeal on Monday, April 27th at 2 P.M., if the date was acceptable to him.

Jay's acceptance of the date was sent back to Roger Cramer, the Chairman.

During that one month interval, Jay spent every moment he could spare from his practice in diligent preparation for this last possible chance to overturn the condemnation of the ringleaders of the Department of Obstetrics at Sam Rayburn Hospital.

Chapter Twenty Eight

Assignation

*J*ay sat alone in a small vest pocket park. It was bordered on its four sides by Fourth and Fifth Streets on the north and south, and San Antonio and Guadalupe on the east and west sides. He had driven past there more times than he could remember and the only specific physical feature of it he could describe was that he never remembered seeing a single person in it.

Full and lovely shade trees were scattered all about in this square tract of land which occupied a city block. It was surrounded by large buildings of concrete and steel which had nothing serene about them at all. They caused this small square to feel even more like a peaceful little island in the midst of this bustling city. Restaurants, shops and even empty storefronts were found on its four borders.

The city had planted two large patches of multi-colored flowers there. Though the light was very dim, Jay identified these as one of the few flowers he knew by name—Impatiens.

He sat on one of the very sparse benches in the park. Alice had specifically identified the area where she wanted to meet him. The bench was placed so that it faced San Antonio Street with its back to Guadalupe. There were large bushes planted behind the bench and around its side, which diminished its visibility from Guadalupe Street.

With no lights in the park itself, a street light at the corner of Guadalupe and Fifth Streets cast a dim glow. From his location, seated on the bench, the light was behind and to the right of the shrubs which surrounded the bench.

Alice knew this small island of nature, surrounded by the hubbub of the city, very well. Many of the buildings were quite unattractive, but it was in no way a slum area. It was part of the city's central business district. A walk through this part of the city felt relatively safe, and the park was by far the nicest aspect of this section of Austin.

Alice had been there several times in the past, during the daytime, with a friend who was also a nurse at Sam Rayburn. Her friend was married and had a small child she brought there to play. The two nurses spent many hours in that park. They sat and talked about the complexities of their lives, as the child played on the grass.

It was past nine o'clock in the evening now. Jay assumed that the sky was overcast that night, with no moon of any shape to be seen. As he looked into the sky it occurred to him that his knowledge of astronomy was so sparse, he had no idea of what stage of the lunar cycle they had reached. For him the absence of the moon could have reflected either its stage or just an overcast sky. He just didn't know. Actually it was the clouds that totally blocked out the moon that night, as no stars could be seen either. But, due to Jay's depth of concentration, he never even noticed there were no stars.

For a brief moment he felt some anxiety. He realized he was seated in a very secluded area with barely any light. He thought, *what a perfect candidate I would be for a mugging.*

Nine was the hour that Alice had asked that they meet. She was almost fifteen minutes late when Jay heard the sound of a car approach the curb on Fifth Street where he had parked. As he looked over his shoulder, he saw a figure approach in his direction. It was dark and Jay wasn't certain whether it was Alice. By the time she had reached about half the distance to him, he recognized her. As he began to rise he heard her say, "Don't come!" She came around the shrubbery and sat down quietly next to him.

"Do you really think we should act as if this was a novel by Le Carre?" Jay asked.

"For the past few days I'm certain I've been followed," she responded in a tremulous voice.

"Do they have any way to know you'll be there tomorrow?"

"I don't know." Then after a long pause, "I don't know. I'm just frightened."

Her voice quivered and Jay put his arm around her shoulder. The weather was pleasantly warm for late March in Texas, but he felt Alice shiver.

Behind them, parked on Guadalupe Street, not far from the lamp which cast the only light, Harry Manchester sat in his car. His binoculars were trained on the park bench. Harry saw shadows of their figures on the bench through the limbs of the shrubbery. He found it difficult to make out anything clearly.

He had followed Alice. When she parked he continued to drive down Fifth Street and turned right on Guadalupe where he parked. His ultra-sensitive microphone was unable to pick up their conversation clearly at that distance.

Jay spoke softly and very slowly as he told Alice, "I know how terribly difficult this is for you and I won't be upset if you change your mind right now. Marsh has been the love of your life and that will absolutely end after tomorrow. But I promise, when this is over, I will leave here and start all over somewhere else.... And I'll take you with me."

Alice said nothing.

"I promise I'll make certain you have the opportunity to start a new life. You're the only one who knows the whole truth and the only one who can clear up this mess."

Jay understood the pressure he exerted, but he saw no other alternative. He viewed the entire world in terms of his own personal goals.

They sat quietly. Not one word was spoken for several minutes. Jay knew nothing more to say.

Multiple thoughts engulfed Alice. The peace and shelter she had felt with Marsh was her first thought, but that was gone. There was no doubt in her mind that their love affair was at an end. Besides that, there were other thoughts which became entangled. As the days went by she had become more mindful of the admiration and very private love she had felt for Jay for so many years. As she turned her head toward his she lifted her right arm, placed it behind his head and pulled his mouth to her lips. The kiss began warm and full until converted by Alice to sensuous. Jay was by nature socially rather shy. He demonstrated the anxiety he felt. There was a slight shudder as the kiss changed. He knew full well what would follow.

Alice slowly slid her lips away. She moved her mouth across his left cheek until it reached his ear.

Alice asked, "Can we go to your apartment?"

The moment the words left her mouth she felt another shudder in his body. She understood that she had created more anxiety in him than he felt about what was to happen the next day at the hospital.

For a moment Jay said nothing. Then he took a deep breath and said, "Why don't you follow me in your car? I think you're parked right behind me."

They walked hand in hand across the park and toward Fifth Street. Jay got into his car, started the engine and turned on his lights. He pulled away from the curb just slightly, and waited for Alice to do the same, then headed down the street to Guadalupe where the street light was located. Jay turned right on Guadalupe toward the river. Both cars then passed Harry Manchester, slumped down in his seat and out of sight. Jay and Alice drove across the river and made a left turn on Riverside Drive toward Jay's apartment. After they had passed Manchester on Guadalupe Street, Manchester started his car and followed them.

Jay and Alice parked their cars alongside each other in the parking lot in front of his apartment house. Harry Manchester drove past them and quietly parked farther down the street. He went unnoticed. He watched them cross the lot and enter the apartment building after Jay punched out the code on the panel at the entrance.

Alice and Jay took the elevator up to the fourth floor. She followed him to his door. She could tell how nervous Jay was as he fumbled to get his key in the lock. She actually put her hand on his to steady it.

"Having trouble getting it in?" Alice quipped.

They looked at each other and laughed.

"It's been a while," Jay responded with a small giggle.

Alice put her arm around him and squeezed as they passed through the door. She was surprised to feel how little fat there was across the mid-section of this man well into his fifties. She felt like a teenager again.

Alice thought, *I'll take the lead... he'll be awkward... but gentle... it'll be fine.... I'll be the best he's ever known.*

In her wildest dreams Alice never imagined the result of that night.

From the street Manchester saw the lights go on in Jay's apartment. Through the curtains he could see figures move about. They moved to a second room where the lights went on. They appeared to be one figure and Manchester assumed they were in an embrace. Then the lights went out.

Manchester waited. He used his binoculars but saw nothing. After about five minutes he returned to his car and dialed the car phone.

"Dr. Slack?"

"Yes."

"It's Manchester. I followed her to Fifth and Guadalupe. There's a small park there, and Dr. Brown was there. They talked for a while, kissed and left."

"Where did they go?"

"I followed them to an apartment house on Riverside. I assume that's where Dr. Brown lives. They went in and after a short time all the lights went out. You can come to your own conclusions."

There was a long delay with no response.

"Dr. Slack, are you there? Did you hear my report? Should I stay?"

The response was long, slow and drawn out.

"Aah... yeh... you can leave there now."

As soon as he hung up, Slack dialed Marsh's number.

Chapter Twenty Nine

A Very Private Discovery

*I*t all began more than twenty years ago. Jay was in the earliest years of his career. It was a time when he wrote and did research on human sexuality. Actively involved in the Women's Movement, he spoke frequently to multiple organizations about the need for women to better understand their sexuality and their right to equality in the sexual experience.

Jay wanted to understand more about the female orgasm. He wanted to know why men, in a healthy relationship, almost always were successful in achieving sexual gratification, and why women so often were not.

He stood firmly in his belief that women could have the same rate of success and that the "failure" was not based on psychological, emotional or social issues. Time and again he pressed the argument that anatomical realities made it more difficult and sometimes even impossible for women to reach the sexual fulfillment they desired.

As the years passed, and other issues challenged him, Jay's interest in the formal research of sexuality diminished. His interest in the subject dwindled. It all resulted from an incident that took place earlier in his career. J.D. Brown had presented a paper on some of his research to a major society in the field of Human Sexuality. He was surprised, to say nothing of his disappointment, to find only a smattering of listeners in the audience. He had hoped his report on the consequences of artificial insemination in unwed females had some significant value. Apparently not many others were of a similar opinion.

The following morning, when he read the local newspaper, he was astonished by the report of the meeting. Apparently very few members attended any of the formal sessions. The reporter stated that the membership could be found in rooms throughout the hotel. There, they reviewed "educational" films on sexual techniques. The reporter watched them as well, and came to the conclusion that the films were more pornographic than educational.

Jay's perception that there was a lack of professionalism in some of the individuals he had met in the field gradually caused him to disassociate himself from the study of human sexuality.. He did not know, was not even interested in, whether the field of sexual research had upgraded itself over the subsequent years. He never had any further involvement with it.

But one thought hibernated in his mind and was never completely eliminated. He had made a discovery. It was purely by accident. There was no associated research project involved. There was no plan... no format... no protocol... no double blind study... no corroborating proof... but he knew that what he found was true and very important. He had come across a phenomenon of female sexuality that had never been written about, never reported and, as crazy as the idea was to him, had never been realized in thousands, even tens of thousands, of years of human sexuality.

He never revealed his discovery to anyone. Jay remembered reports about the "G" spot. He didn't believe it existed and recalled how many had made very light of it. He suspected the same would be true if he reported his findings. Jay believed that the male dominated society in which he lived would have little interest in a fact that was purely directed toward female gratification. He thought it unlikely that the discovery would get much of a response. It necessitated a conscious effort on the part of males to insure their partner's pleasure. He was certain he would take the discovery to his grave.

Jay could not actually remember when he happened upon this finding. But it certainly resulted from his desire to better understand female sexuality. It was clear to him that there were three ways for women to achieve an orgasm. His earlier research had led him to the belief that the magnitude of the climax of each of these was different.

His collected data revealed that a modest percentage of the female population was able to achieve an orgasm through sexual intercourse. Though he had no absolute numerical proof, he believed the frequency was in the range of one third of the female population, or less. It was difficult to determine an exact number as so many women feigned orgasm in order to please. They usually did not reveal that to their research questioner. Jay's research indicated that for many women, the joy of the intimacy of the sexual act provided them with sufficient pleasure not to be preoccupied with the lack of a climax. Jay was certain the cause of this inability to achieve an orgasm was the anatomical location of the clitoris and the lack of direct contact during intercourse. His theory was that it was not in any way a sign of a defect in female sexuality. Many women, however, came to think negatively about themselves due to their perceived "failure" to achieve an orgasm.

The second method of reaching a climax removed the problem of clitoral location. The female reached her orgasm by direct manual or oral stimulation of the clitoris by a partner. In Jay's study almost all women could reach a climax in that manner. Even though the intimacy of the body- to-body contact of sexual intercourse might be lessened, Jay's research indicated that the magnitude of those orgasms was far greater than those achieved during intercourse.

But the major clue in his discovery came from the third method of sexual gratification. It was quite clear to Jay, from the vast number of women he interviewed in his research who agreed to discuss it, that no climax they reached was ever as strong as that achieved during masturbation. *"But Why? Why?"* It was a phenomena which never ceased to puzzle him.

He accumulated all of these different pieces of the puzzle over years of research with women. But, his discovery did not come through that route. It actually happened to him in the process of making love with Rhonda, his wife.

He always understood that all the signs of sexual excitation were intimately tied to the engorgement of a sexual end organ with blood in both the male and female. Only the least educated believed the humorous idea that a bone was responsible for the male erection. The male erection, the enlargement of the clitoris or the vulva, the swelling of the nipples, no matter what, were secondary to blood flow. Women described a pulsation they could feel in the penis, as the engorgement with blood increased and the level of excitement reached a higher and higher plain. It was no great discovery to realize that there was a tie between orgasm, the neurological aspects of sexual excitation and that engorgement.

But when he thought about that phenomenon his usual conclusion was, *So what? What does it mean?*

He had never given great thought to the blood supply of the clitoris. But, when he became aware of a remarkable finding, he immediately went to his gynecological textbooks. To his great surprise Jay found little to no mention of the blood supply to that structure. It was certainly significantly less than what urologic textbooks described for the blood supply to the penis. But, then he was awestruck as he reviewed his old medical school copy of Gray's Anatomy, for there the answer lay. The book's edges were frayed from a year of constant use more than a quarter century earlier in his first year of medical school. As he read, it astounded him to find that the anatomical data comported with his discovery.

He did not remember when it happened, but it was unscientifically during the foreplay to sexual intercourse. Jay found when he placed the tips of his fingers on the ramus of the pubis of his female partner he was astonished by what happened. The rami were the large bony structures which began at the symphysis pubis, immediately anterior to the clitoris, and extending triangularly down each side of the vagina. They ended at the buttocks. His light touch, approximately midway down the length of the ramus, yielded the pulsation of the internal pudendal artery. It was not any different from a pulse in the wrist. While they made love, it became second nature to him and something he no longer thought about at all. In the process of oral and manual stimulation of his partner, as she became progressively more excited, the pulsation of her internal pudendal artery increased in strength. Then the unbelievable discovery happened.

Jay could not be absolutely certain how firm or gentle the sexual stimulation should be. There was no way to know how slowly or rapidly the progression of the foreplay should take place. He could not know what fantasy might occur in her mind that would make her more or less ready to reach her climax. Until… suddenly… it struck him! If his stimulation became too firm or aggressive, the pulsation slowed down or stopped. If the flicks of his tongue or fingers became too rapid the pulsation slowed down or stopped.

Like a shot in the night, or a light bulb that flashed, the answer became apparent. *A woman reaches her most potent climax during masturbation because she knows where she is in her fantasy. She knows if she should go slowly. She knows if the touch should be lighter. She knows if her orgasm is imminent and she should be firmer and more rapid. She can tell, but there is NO WAY that her partner can. No way, that is, unless her partner could determine what happened to the engorgement of her clitoris.*

Jay realized that there was a refractory time for the female neurological system. The pulsations in her vessels, especially shortly before she reached a climax, had a limit to how rapidly they could occur. If there were an additional stimulation of her clitoris, if his tongue went back and forth too rapidly, if there was not a sufficient interval for the refractory time to pass, one second, two seconds or maybe five seconds, there was no responsive pulsation. The pulsations would not restart until a sufficient period of time was allowed to pass. It might be a second, or five seconds or ten. But nothing happened if the time was not allowed to pass.

Jay learned, from the quality of the pulsations, whether his partner was near her climax. He learned that he could stop completely if he had not allowed her to get too close. She would come off her plateau, and be ready to be started again. The unbelievable pleasure he provided as she went up and down the ladder exhilarated him. He also found that if he allowed the approach to get too close to orgasm, she was not able to stop. Under those circumstances, if he stopped just before she reached her climax, not only would she fail to have an orgasm, the neurological process could not be started again for a considerable period of time. That might be anything from an hour to a day. It explained the clear reason to him why a woman might fail to achieve that pleasure when neither she nor her partner had any explanation, only concerns.

It would essentially be the same as if she had reached a climax, and she needed a refractory period before she could for have a completely new sexual experience.

Jay realized that he had accidentally found a way to understand the needs of his partner. The few women he had made love with believed that something miraculous happened to them, but didn't understand why. He didn't tell them. He told no one. But he felt very good about himself, with the knowledge of how well he had fulfilled their sexual needs.

That evening, when the lights went out in Jay's bedroom, after as sensual a kiss as he could remember, he slowly began to undress Alice. Though she was fully prepared to assume the role of aggressor at whatever point was required, she remained relatively passive except for the passionate level of their kisses.

He proceeded to unbutton and remove her blouse and then her skirt. Alice had kicked off her shoes and within a very short time, after she had unhooked her bra, she was completely disrobed except for her pantyhose. With his mouth now on her breast she felt the need to somewhat equalize the level of their dress. As she removed his outer clothing, he lifted his head from her breast and allowed her to proceed without interference. She was seated on the bed and could discern from the tremulous sound of his voice, as he responded affirmatively to her mock request for permission to continue, that his level of excitation was quite high. When he looked at her half naked body in the very faint light, his one thought was, *My God, how divinely beautiful you are!* Many months had passed since his last sexual encounter and the combination of need and anxiety were quite obvious in his demeanor.

As she removed his slacks there was sufficient street light shining through the curtains on the window so that she could see the obvious projection in the front of his narrow-cut jockey shorts. She decided now that the time had come for her to assume an aggressive role. She lowered his shorts coyly and Jay heard a slight guttural moan from her. Alice had made the sound intentionally as if to demonstrate her approval. But the sight of his penis erect to its absolute capacity had an effect on her that she did not expect. The result was that the moan was half planned and half not.

Alice was about to begin fellatio, when suddenly Jay leaned over, lifted her off the side of the bed and placed her on her back. He then removed the pantyhose.

For the next forty five minutes Jay manually and orally stimulated her genital area and breasts in the manner he had learned by accident. Alice sighed and moaned without pause, this time involuntarily. He brought her level of excitement up and down like a yo-yo, controlling it by the pulsations in her internal pudendal artery.

In all of her sexual experiences, and there had been more than she could ever count, nothing, nothing like this had ever happened.

At times she reached out and tried, sometimes successfully, to grasp his penis. She wanted to hold it, and do anything to please him. In the midst of her ecstasy it excited her even more that he too remained at the height of his passion as demonstrated by the maintenance, continuously, of his erection.

On one occasion Alice grabbed Jay's head, pulled it away from her groin, kissed him deep into his mouth, moaned and then actually begged, "Fuck me. Please fuck me."

Jay whispered "Not yet," as he kissed his way back down her body.

That night Alice reached the most explosive orgasm she had ever known. It was during the process of cunnilingus. She was uncertain how loud the noises were that she made, but later Jay jokingly told her he was fearful of the complaints he would receive from his neighbors.

"I'm concerned they may line up for their turn in this bedroom," Alice quipped.

Rather than her role as the aggressive partner, to which she was accustomed, Alice was physically unable to move after she reached her orgasm. She felt as if she was simply a lump of matter lying motionless on Jay's bed. He tenderly and lightly kissed her abdomen, breasts, neck and finally, non-passionately, her lips. He whispered sweet words of how wonderful the experience had been for him.

She wasn't certain how long she lay there like that. She actually dozed for almost ten minutes. When she came out of her stupor, she was on her side with Jay, sleeping as well, spooned up along her back. Suddenly, she felt massive guilt, as only she had reached an orgasm. Alice quickly reached back and felt his limp penis. Within a few moments he was completely aroused. Before she could turn, Jay had entered her from the rear. Her thought that all her pleasure had been achieved was soon gone. He moved slowly while his arms around her gently stimulated her breasts and then very lightly her clitoris. She was unable to think about what happened to Jay as he slowly brought back her moans and sighs. She was in total disbelief as she reached a climax for the second time that night. She knew on that second occasion that it had happened for him as well. They fell asleep with Jay still inside her.

It was just past two in the morning when she awakened. Though the night had been wonderful for Jay, and she could tell that, Alice felt that he had done everything for her. In her entire life she had never had such an experience. Jay was sound asleep when she leaned down to pleasure him in a way she hoped would in some way equal the pleasure he had given her.

Shortly thereafter Alice said, "Sweet Jay, I need to go back to my apartment."

Jay rose to leave with her, but Alice insisted that he go back to sleep and be rested for what he had to endure later that day. She knew her way quite well and was accustomed to nighttime travel, to and from shifts at the hospital.

She was dressed and he was naked as they stood at the foot of the bed in a long kiss.

Jay whispered in her ear, "I love you."

Alice made no response, which did not go unnoticed by Jay. She had been hurt too many times to make a commitment even after such a night as this. But, in her heart, she wanted to repeat those words.

Jay put on his robe and stood by the window. After a minute or so he saw Alice leave from the front door of the apartment. It was a dark night but he easily saw her under the street lamps. Jay was more positive about the world than he had been in many months. His decision to leave Austin did not depress him now in any way. He had no idea where to go, but now it seemed like a new and exciting adventure. Beyond that he was buoyed by the thought that Alice would be with him. What he had said to John Parsons about his relationship with her was no longer true. Jay was absolutely certain his life definitely had taken a turn for the better.

As he watched her enter her car a thought occurred to him.

What can I do to make her life better than it has ever been before?

He then laughed to himself as he thought, *Can I make a commitment to be the kind of doctor for which I've chastised others? Can I just keep my nose to the grindstone and not try to change the world? After what Alice has done for me, don't I owe that to her?*

Jay wasn't sure that he could change that part of his personality, but he would try.

He was certain that she was safe when he saw her car drive off. He thought, *This will be quite a day.*

Chapter Thirty

The Last Contest

The only thing positive about this day, as far as John Parsons was concerned, was that it was the last time he would be going through this with Jay Brown. The appeal was held in the same room as the previous meeting, but the physical setup of the room was quite different.

Jay had been waiting for the past twenty minutes in the main lobby of the hospital for Alice. They had agreed to meet there. He was uncertain how long this hearing would take, but he was sure it would be much shorter than the two days of the Ad Hoc Committee. Jay's plan was that he would allow both sides to present their positions before bringing in Alice. He believed that would take two to three hours but he wasn't certain. He had some concern that if Alice was not continuously available, and the time was misjudged, she might not be there when she was needed. The entire meeting might be over when she arrived. Alice had agreed and said she would bring a book and sit unobtrusively in the main lobby, waiting for John to come out and bring her into the session.

By two minutes before two P.M. Alice had still not arrived and John thought he and Jay should not wait any longer. He didn't want Jay to be late for the hearing. Starting off by appearing late would not serve him well.

"Don't be surprised if she doesn't come, Jay. Your request is almost beyond what anyone might ask of another."

"I know it's going to make a huge difference if she's not here. But, in a way, I'll be glad if she doesn't come. I know I'll be feeling guilty about this for a long, long time. Maybe forever."

As they entered the room John whispered in his ear, "One last time... stay cool."

There were five members of the Board of Directors rather than the three Jay had expected. Tables were placed in the room, along each of the walls. The Committee sat at one end of the room at a long narrow table, like a panel of judges. On the opposite wall there was a table facing it. John and Jay Brown were placed there.

At the table to Jay's left sat Marsh, Baker and the hospital attorney Theresa Carney. Jay stared at Carney for a few moments. He had worked with her on many occasions including the malpractice case. The hospital, as usual, had been sued along with him. That was almost automatic in law suits against physicians involving incidents occurring inside the hospital. Jay and Theresa knew each other quite well by now and she was aware of his strong feelings about medicine.

She knows what kind of a physician I am and she must know that this is all trumped up. Jay thought. *It's astounding at what price one is willing to sell her soul in order to move up in an organization.*

On Jay's right, at a smaller table, the court reporter had set up her steno equipment.

It was just after two in the afternoon when they began. Jay knew one of the members of the Committee very well. He was one of several physicians who served as members of the Hospital Board. Cyrus Crittendon was a senior member of the Obstetrical Department, who by this time in his career had only a minimal awareness of the current politics of the Obstetrical staff. He had not been involved at all in the assessment of Jay Brown all through the Quality Control and Ad Hoc Committees. Not having participated in the process, while being the most knowledgeable Board member concerning obstetrics, he was an obvious choice for the panel.

The panel was all male. Its other four members were all well respected businessmen and professionals in the community. Jay knew none of them, except by reputation.

All the standard introductory remarks were made by the Chairman of this special Ad Hoc Committee set up for this one purpose. Roger Cramer, the Chairman, advised everyone of what the by-laws required in such circumstances and provided the ground rules for the hearing.

"Each side will be given one hour to present their case. Information, not previously part of the process up until this time, cannot be introduced. Finally specific medical data will not, and in all honesty cannot, be evaluated by the Committee. The only question that can be considered is whether the process has been fairly and properly managed."

Jay immediately became concerned because no specific time limit had been previously provided to him. He had considerably shortened his presentation, but he estimated it would take him about an hour and a half.

"Mr. Cramer."

"Yes, Doctor Brown."

"No one had notified me of the time limit and I have a considerable amount of information to provide. Could I request an hour and twenty minutes?"

He decided on the spur of the moment not to ask for an hour and a half. He didn't know what the atmosphere of this meeting would be like. After the frightening hostility of the Ad Hoc Committee he was prepared for anything. Somehow an hour and twenty minutes sounded like a lot less than an hour and a half. It was like selling an item for $9.95 instead of ten dollars.

In the most friendly and cordial manner Cramer responded.

"Certainly. I'm sorry for any confusion."

Turning to Marsh he said, "You, of course, may have the same option."

Jay was half out of his chair, being pulled down by John Parsons, when Marsh responded, "Like we won't need it. It doesn't take that long to tell the truth."

Cramer saw what was happening and interjected, "We'll be the judge of all that."

It was a bad start for Jay Brown. Although John had stopped him from getting into a squabble, his ire was up and was reflected in the less than calm beginning of his presentation.

He soon calmed down and it all went rather smoothly. A few rare questions were put to him during his discussion, mostly from Cyrus Crittenden, but they were not pointed or hostile. Cyrus Crittenden was the first obstetrician that Jay had met on coming to Sam Rayburn. He had been given the assignment to interview Brown before privileges were granted. That meeting had gone extremely well. From that day on, the crossing of their paths was limited to passing in the hallways and regular departmental or hospital meetings. Jay had a great deal of respect for the manner in which Crittenden comported himself.

Crittenden, on the other hand, had the impression that Jay Brown was a fine doctor, but not someone he would choose as a personal friend. Born and raised in the south, he found Jay to be aggressive and pushy, much as he perceived many of the people he knew from the north.

Jay was given notification of the time remaining on several occasions, as he had requested, and could see that he was going to run over. He began speaking more rapidly.

The last notification was at "five minutes." He was certain that he spoke at least ten more minutes after that, but the Chairman never stopped him. At least in the hearing room he was getting as fair treatment as anyone could possibly expect. These were people of stature who took their responsibility very seriously. He did not know them personally, but he knew their type from his years working with a similar Board when he directed the Department back in New York. They were successful and professional in everything they did. But Jay had met privately just two days before with a close friend who was also a member of this very Board. Before seeing him Jay inquired as to whether he had been selected on the Special Board Committee, so as to not be accused of influencing a panel member.

"No, I'm not on the Committee. They took special care that no one selected was a personal friend of individuals on either side of this problem."

Jay sought advice from his friend which was gladly offered. But the conversation ended on a down note.

"Unless you're going to tell them something that completely negates the previous hearings, I do not believe that they will change a decision of the Executive Committee of the Hospital. They are dedicated and committed not just to the Hospital but to the staff as well."

Jay never mentioned Alice Crain.

During Marsh's presentation Jay became angered and frustrated again. He had understood, from what he had been told in preparation for this appeal, that he was not to discuss medical issues and choices of treatment, only the process that had brought them to this point. He was advised to point out wherever he perceived the process being distorted or manipulated. He followed those instructions explicitly in his presentation.

Marsh, on the other hand, was discussing specific medical details and why he thought Brown had functioned improperly in the treatment he provided.

"He's not supposed to be discussing the medical details," Jay whispered into Parsons' ear."

"Don't interfere," John whispered back.

The other thing that got under Jay's skin was the repeated phrase by Dr. Marsh, "Well, I feel like Dr. Brown is not tellin' you the truth."

Jay sat still but knew deep down that he wanted to stand up, forget about how it would affect anything today, and say to Jack Marsh, *You are a God damned son-of-a-bitch lying dishonest bigot,* and walk out. He sat still.

When Marsh was done, Jay asked if he could have a brief recess which was gladly acceded to by Cramer. He and John Parsons went out to the main lobby to see if they could find Alice. She was nowhere to be found.

"Don't be angry, Jay. It was too much to ask."

They returned to the hearing room where questioning from the Board members then continued for about another half hour before the meeting was adjourned. Roger Cramer thanked everyone, and Jay Brown did as well. The Committee then went into private deliberation.

Jay's first thought after the hearing ended was to call Alice. He wanted her to know that there was no anger about her non-appearance. In fact, he would tell her, he was glad she had changed her mind. He wanted her to know that nothing else was changed. This problem would end in whatever manner the Board decided and then the two of them would make plans to leave. It would be exciting, together, making a new start in life.

He allowed the phone to ring longer than he normally would, but there was no response.

Jay called Joan in the office.

"Good afternoon, Dr. Brown's office."

"Hi Joan. Is everything all right?"

"I don't know. You tell me."

"Why what's happened?"

"Are you kidding? Nothing's happened here. I'm talking about what happened at the hearing."

It was strange how Jay was so completely putting everything behind him that the meeting and the decision were no longer major events for him. On the other hand Joan still felt they were still in the midst of the battle.

"It went fine, Joan. Everyone was very nice to me. I don't know what their decision will be, but I have to assume they will support the Executive Committee and require massive consultation under the watchful eye of those bastards."

"What does that mean for you, Dr. B?"

"I really wanted to sit down in person and talk with you about this, but now that it's come up, I don't want to leave you with anxieties."

"You don't? What about all those I already have?"

"Joan, I'm going to leave. I can't stay under these circumstances and pressures.... I hope you're not angry."

"No, Dr. Brown. I was really expecting it. I didn't know how long you could continue this. When is all this going to happen?"

"Not today, Joan, so you don't have to be out of the office by five."

"You mean I've got until five thirty."

"How about five fifteen?"

"I've really loved working with you Dr. B. Do you know where you're going?"

"No. But I do know that I won't leave until I'm certain you have a position somewhere. Not just anywhere. I won't go until you've got a place where you're happy."

"That's really sweet, Dr. B., but don't worry. I'll have no difficulty getting a good job. I've had at least a half dozen offers trying to steal me from you in the past. I stayed because I like to work in a place where everybody's always in trouble and my job is always in jeopardy."

"Don't complain, Joan. It's good for your moral fiber."

It had been months since Joan had heard him bantering like that. The Jay Brown she loved was back to himself and that made her feel that only good things would happen.

"Joan, did Alice Crain call today?"

"No. Was she supposed to?"

"Not really. I just thought she might be calling about the hearing."

"No. Actually it's been deadly quiet. Maybe they know you're closing shop. Who wants to talk to a lame duck?"

"Well, maybe it's because of you. Maybe they don't want to talk to a lame female duck. Is that a hen, a filly, or madame duck? Whatever it is, I'm going home if there's nothing going on. Have a good night, Joan. You are definitely the best. I'll be on my pager."

"Goodnight, Dr. B. I have the feeling you're going to sleep well tonight."

––––––

Aside from the regular mail in his box, there was an envelope with his name on it, pushed under the edge of the box. It had no stamp and was obviously dropped off, not by the postman. He opened his apartment door, put down his briefcase, placed his mail on the table and opened the unstamped envelope. The letter was handwritten.

Dear Jay:

I know this will disappoint you, but I can't possibly come to the hearing today. Everything has become just too difficult.

I am leaving Austin and do not expect to return. Please do not look for me. This has all become too complicated and I've decided to go away and start all over, by myself, somewhere.

Good luck,

Alice

Jay stared at the letter for a long time. A lot of the excitement he had felt seemed to wane. He put down the note and tried Alice's phone number again. Still there was no answer and he realized something that had not occurred to him when he called earlier; There was no response from her answering machine either.

It was after midnight when Alice pulled up in front of her apartment. She was still feeling the glow from the unbelievable experience she had just shared with Jay Brown. On the way home she already decided that the first thing she was going to do when she got into her apartment was call Jay. She didn't care if he had already gone to sleep. She would wake him to tell him how wonderful that was. And maybe, she wasn't certain, she might say she loved him too.

As she approached her apartment, on the second floor, she noted a light under the door. She didn't usually accidentally leave a light on when she left. She slowly opened the door and was shocked to see Jack Marsh sitting on an overstuffed chair in the corner.

"Pretty late."

"Jack," she responded nervously. "I had no idea you were coming over this evening. I certainly wouldn't have been out had I known. I don't recall you mentioning that."

She walked over to the chair to kiss him.

Just as she approached she saw from the corner of her eye, for a split second, the back of his right hand coming up to her head. At the same time she felt an excruciating pain, first over her nose and then her left eye and remembered hearing a loud crack as she went hurtling backward across the room. She landed on the floor, her butt falling immediately in front of another chair while her back and head were thrust up against it.

For the next few moments she remained still, only semi-conscious. She felt liquid dripping down her face from her nostrils. Her nose had been broken. When she was first struck she had let out a low shriek. Lying on the ground she was making no noise.

"You fuckin' whore," Marsh blurted out.

No other words were spoken for a few moments as Alice's senses were gradually returning. She made no effort to raise herself from the ground. She wiped her upper lip with the back of her hand and saw the bright red blood.

"Like you just couldn't help gettin' involved with him. I was afraid you'd do somethin' dumb like that. And I guess you were goin' to speak to that committee tomorrow for him."

For the first time Alice spoke, somewhat defiantly, "Yes I was."

"You fuckin' dumb shit cunt. The others all suspected that. Do you like know what those assholes wanted to do?"

As opposed to Alice, Marsh was half in tears.

"You dumb cunt, did you ever hear of Karen Silkman or Silk-somethin'? They wanted to get you out on the highway in Austin and force you off the road to kill you like someone did to her."

Alice didn't utter a sound.

"I gave you everything. I was faithful to you and you go around fuckin' a God-damned Jew right under my nose. I ought to rip open your cunt so you'll never fuck anybody again," Marsh shouted through his tears.

Alice remained silent.

"You're out of here. Do you hear me, out of here? Now! Tonight! Nobody in Austin is ever goin' to see or hear of you again. If you ever talk to that Jew again, ever, if I ever hear of you two conspirin' against the good doctors here, I'm goin' to let them bump you off. Like you're not goin' to have a bloody nose. You're gonna be dead."

He walked over to Alice and picked her up by the shoulders. She stood, but rather limply.

"Do you have writin' paper?"

She nodded affirmatively while wiping back the blood from her lip again.

"Get it and sit down at the table and start writin' a letter to Brown. You write it in your words and I want it to say that you won't be there tomorrow, you're leavin' town and you'll never, I mean never, see him again. Do you understand?"

She said nothing and only nodded affirmatively.

"And don't get any blood on that paper. In fact go to the bathroom first and wash your face and hands before you start."

Alice looked in the mirror in the bathroom and saw that her left eye was already discolored. Her nose was not perfectly straight, although it would be difficult to say that it was broken except for the noise she had heard when she was struck. She had not shed one tear. It was as if she was not surprised that this had happened and wondered whether it was all her fault. It was not a strange emotion for her considering the negative self image she had always felt in relation to men.

In a few moments she left the bathroom, sat down at the table, and finished the note.

"Now get your suitcases and pack everythin' you can in them. Take everythin' you can with you and we'll bring it down to the car. Like I don't care what direction you drive in, bitch. You can go East, West, North or South. But don't you stop until you are real far away. Like I mean real far away. When you find a place you're gonna stay, send me your address. I'll ship everythin' else out to you, your furniture, kitchen stuff, anythin' that's left here. But don't you ever come back or call anybody here, or you're dead. I don't want to ever hear your name again."

She seemed almost dead as it was, while she listened to him in a stupor, shouting at her through his tears. Jack Marsh was completely devastated by this turn of events. Had she just wanted to break up their relationship with no aspect of disloyalty, he probably would have accepted that without anger, though he did love Alice. His strange sense of loyalty, though married and disloyal to his own wife, made him feel cuckolded. In his eyes she had cut right through to his masculinity. Alice looked at the state he was in and realized that. Amazingly, she felt bad for him. She had never wanted to hurt him, but Marsh never understood that Alice could not tolerate what he and his cohorts were doing to Jay Brown. The inevitable sexuality was something Alice had not ever expected, and wished that Jack had not discovered it. It was never her intent to hurt him in any way.

It was after four thirty in the morning when the apartment door was locked. The car was loaded to the gills, like families she had seen on highways, transporting every material item they possessed. Not only the trunk and back seat were filled, but the front passenger seat as well. During the entire two hour period of packing everything up, Alice never said another word. When questioned she gave affirmative or negative responses by nods of her head.

Not until she had started her engine did she lower her window and say only two words to Jack: "I'm sorry".

Marsh stood at the front of the apartment house as she drove off and cried harder than he could ever remember having done before.

There were no surprises in the letter Jay received from the Hospital Board. He was notified that his privileges remained intact, but he would be required to seek consultations as requested by Dr. Jack Marsh, the Director of the Department of Obstetrics and Gynecology.

It arrived just two days after the hearing. Even though it had been completely expected, there was still a slight letdown upon reading it. In the back of Jay's mind there was always the hope that they might exonerate him completely. Jay took the letter with him and went to see John Parsons.

"I'll bet you're shocked," Jay quipped as John read the letter.

"Think of it positively Jay. If they had reversed everything you might have had a change of heart and decided to remain here. But the obstetricians' attitudes toward you would not be different, unless it was worse, out of anger for having lost. Then you would have been confronted in some other way by them and your life wouldn't be any better. Now with this outcome you're out of here and finished with them. Have you spoken to Alice? Do you know where the two of you are going?"

"Alice isn't going."

"She's staying in Austin?"

"No, I'm afraid I've driven her out of here. That's why she never came to the hearing. Alice packed up and left Austin. She said she wanted to be on her own and doesn't want to hear from me, or I guess anybody around here ever again. I have no idea where she's gone and don't imagine I ever will."

"You never know," John offered.

Then John asked, "What about you?"

Jay sighed deeply. "I don't know where for certain. I've thought about California or Colorado or just doing *locum tenens*. You know that means working for an agency and filling in where obstetricians are needed on a temporary basis. I'll probably start that way."

"Is closing your office going to be difficult?"

"Just psychologically. I'm going to miss Joan a lot. Next week I'm sending out a letter to all my active obstetrical patients, asking them to come to the office for a meeting in the evening. I'll tell them that I'm closing, how much they've meant to me, and how we'll deal with their records and charts. It's going to be a very difficult night."

There was silence for a few moments and then Jay spoke up again.

"You know John… through all this I still love the medical profession and I wouldn't want you to think I feel negatively about doctors. There are so many wonderful doctors I've known. Another thing is that I'm never going to think about lawyers the same way now that I've met you."

"No, Jay, I don't think you hate doctors. But I believe that you and I don't quite see the world the same way. Doctors are like lawyers. And doctors and lawyers are people, just people. There are some great ones—and I mean really great. And there are some bad ones. And there are some REALLY bad ones. But the great majority fall in the middle, just like every bell-shaped curve. They're not malicious… they're not mean… they're not perfect… they make mistakes. They're human. There is just so much we can expect of them. Somehow we have to find a way to try to make things better while being tolerant of human frailties. I hope… I really hope you have the ability to be able to find an outlook that sees both sides of that equation. You're a good man Jay Brown. Don't self destruct."

With that he put his arms around Jay. Jay responded, and he knew that nothing better had happened to him in Austin than meeting this man of such unusual stature.

Chapter Thirty One

Cicada

*J*ay Brown had already submitted his formal resignation as of the last day of April from the staff of Sam Rayburn Hospital. Joan and Felicia, with heavy hearts, wound down the affairs of the office. Arrangements were made for the patients to have easy access to another physician, especially if they were in the midst of maternity care. Details had to be worked out with insurance companies, providers of supplies, the telephone company, the answering service, etc. Joan was certainly up to the task professionally. But all of that was being accomplished by her with significant emotional strain.

For one brief day, less than one month ago, when Jay thought that he and Alice would leave together, there was an excitement about the closure. Now it was merely an unpleasant chore. As he'd told John he'd do, a letter had been sent to all of his active maternity patients. It asked them to come to an important meeting at the office on Thursday evening, April 20th at 7 P.M. It did not state any specific reason why the meeting had been arranged, but indicated that it was urgent that it be attended.

The office had a morgue-like atmosphere. The number of calls for appointments decreased markedly. Jay assumed that his resignation from the staff was known by everyone and word was passed through the grapevine. All new maternity patients were turned down with the simple explanation that no new maternity cases were being accepted. The day finally arrived for Jay Brown to meet with his patients. By that time most of the details of the closure had been accomplished by Joan.

Jay had not fully realized how badly he felt about the closure. This day—even more than the occasion of the rejected appeal—made it clear that there would no longer be a medical practice that belonged to him... anywhere. He would no longer be the independent physician whom a group of women looked upon as their own doctor. He would no longer be the confidant of women who thought of him as a first line of defense when things went wrong, medically, emotionally or in any personal way. Stripped of that role, he felt lost.

He was still a physician, but not the kind that had always been so important to him. He belonged to no one.

Beyond that, certain facts were clear to him. He had lost the battle at Sam Rayburn Hospital. Ray Baker, Jack Marsh, Steve Slack, Louis Crown and company had won. They set their sights in a totally different direction than he had. Ray Baker had a goal for himself and the hospital, but for most of the physicians the aim was to keep the status quo. There would be no attempt to upgrade the level of care, regardless of what was happening in the world of the best medical care.

The goal for Ray Baker was that of expansion and increased political power within medicine. In time he would gain control of other hospitals, in joint efforts where he was the driving force. His aim always would be to keep his physicians happy. To him, the philosophy of the hospital was to make it as user-friendly as possible for the physicians who admitted patients. The concept of being user-friendly to patients was a lower priority.

Jay looked at that scenario and came to one conclusion—he had failed personally and failed his patients as well. These thoughts caused him to slowly slide into a state of depression.

The outer office was completely filled. Joan borrowed a number of chairs from neighboring offices. Still, only a small portion of those in attendance sat. Many of the wives came with their husbands and some with small children as well. As the numbers of those present increased, the decibel level did as well.

Besides the filled outer office, the crowd extended through the space to the back rooms. The door to that corridor was left open to allow for the flow of the crowd. The nurses' station of the office faced both the outer office and the back section of the examining and consultation rooms. With all the doors left open, Jay was able to stand in the nurses' station and be heard throughout the suite.

It wasn't as if no one knew what to expect. Rumors had been going around for several weeks. Those who did not know the reason for the meeting became aware of it shortly after they arrived, by just the rumors that floated throughout the crowd.

"I heard that something horrible happened to one of his patients and that he was asked to leave."

"I don't believe that for a minute. Why spread stories like that when you don't know?"

"Do you think he did something improper with a patient? You know, sexual, or something?"

"That's a terrible thing to say about Dr. Brown. He's always been so proper."

These comments were heard all over the room. Joan heard them and she became furious. She pulled Jay back into an examining room and shut the door.

"Dr. B. You've got to talk to these people soon. Tell them the truth. You can't believe what some are saying about you."

As she spoke, Joan completely broke down. Jay took her into his arms and held her while she sobbed. All the emotions she had withheld over the past months—and even years— came out all at once. It was difficult enough to have gone through those times. To be forced to listen to the horrendous and totally false rumors was more than she could handle.

"Joan. Thank you so much for all your love and support all these years. Now we've got to go out and deal with this. I promise you I will tell them the truth... I just won't use any names."

He held her away from him and gave her his handkerchief so that she could dry her eyes.

"I'll go out now to talk to them. You can join me whenever you're up to it."

Jay walked into the nurses' station and looked at all the people crowded together. He knew all who were patients by name.

"Thank you all for coming. It was not with any great pleasure that I invited you to come here this evening. Many know the reason I asked you to come. You may have heard some of the rumors that are floating around. Tonight I want to tell you the truth of what has happened.

"I came to this community to practice the best obstetrics that I knew how. I brought into this office a staff of employees who I believed then, and even more so now, were the finest that could be found in Austin. But something has happened in the years since I arrived… "

As Jay continued to speak he saw that a number of the women, especially those who had been his patients for some length of time, began to take out handkerchiefs and start to cry. He continued, but when he saw them cry it made his voice begin to crack as well.

He did not stop even when he seemed to lose control of his emotions. He told of the quality of care and made it clear that he was not satisfied. He told about his efforts and then added that a contingent had seen it as their responsibility to get rid of this "trouble maker." He told them about the lies and his efforts to overcome them and finally his decision that he could no longer practice in this community of doctors.

The response was not uniformly supportive, even from a few of his long time patients. Some openly challenged him. It was not because they didn't believe him. It was their own personal feeling that they were being deserted. Some even lashed out in anger.

"But you took us as patients in good faith. You promised you would care for us. Now because of some personal vendetta we're left alone."

Jay understood, but felt sick inside about those responses.

"No one will be left in the cold. I'll provide all your records to whatever obstetrician you wish to use. I will recommend those who I believe are most suitable to care for you. But regardless of where you go, any payments that you have made to this office which are not credited to you for this pregnancy we will refund to you in full. And, if any of you just want all the money you've paid us for this pregnancy to be refunded now, that will be done with no questions asked."

Almost everyone was supportive and very emotional. Lots of tears flowed. Many of Jay's patients did not leave for quite some time after he had spoken and answered all their questions. The only question that went unanswered, and which had been asked in a number of different ways, was "who were the physicians who were responsible?" Most of the patients, once they finally decided they would leave the office, completed the evening with a long tearful hug of Jay Brown. By this time all eyes, including Jay's, were quite red.

Jay remained in the office, while Joan and Felicia cleaned up the mess created by the crowd. There were still to be a few more days in the office. This would not be his last good-bye to his staff. But this one with his patients had been the worst of the good-byes. The remaining days were anti-climactic.

He sat at his desk alone, and thought about how badly everything had turned out. He wondered where Alice had gone, and hoped that she had found something better than she had known since he arrived in Austin. The thoughts of Alice brought out some self-recriminations. He knew that without him on the scene she probably would still be Jack Marsh's mistress, happy and with no windmills to fight. He had screwed that up for her and that knowledge ate away at his gut.

As he rose from his desk and put on his jacket to leave, he was despondent. He had messed up a lot of lives and accomplished nothing. He didn't even have the heart to talk about anything else with Joan or Felicia, about both of whom he also had guilt feelings. He went straight for the office door.

"Good night. Thanks for everything. Don't stay too late. I'll see you in the morning."

As he walked toward the elevator door, he saw Juan Sandoval.

———

Almost ten years had passed since Jay Brown came to Austin, looking forward to his new life. He had selected a location for his new office in Austin in the building attached to Sam Rayburn Hospital.

On one of the first days after he arrived in his new suite, as he tried to get it organized with Joan, whom he had hired only a few days previously, a young Mexican-American walked into his office.

"I'm one of the custodians in this building. I'll pick up your trash every evening and take care of any problems you have in your suite. Can I help you move in when I'm finished with my regular duties in the building?"

Juan spoke with a slight Hispanic dialect in a slow drawl which Jay would come to find was a common accent in the south Texas area. There was a very pleasant softness to the speech pattern.

Juan proved to be a marvelous addition to those who helped him put the office together. Frequently little odd electrical and plumbing jobs could be handled by Juan instead of an expensive repair service. Over the years he and Jay became friendly. At times, when Jay came back to the office late at night to complete some paper work, he would bump into Juan in his nightly routine from office to office. Sometimes they would sit on the sofa in front of the stack of elevators and talk for a half-hour or so. Jay found Juan easy to talk with in this city where he seemed to have a dearth of friends.

On this particular night Jay saw Juan in front of the elevators as he approached them. It was definitely not a night when Jay wanted to sit down and shoot the breeze. The conversations they had in the past gave Juan some insight into the struggle Jay had with the local medical establishment. Juan was quite proud to consider himself a friend of the doctor who fought for the patients, for Juan's people.

Juan knew about what had happened in Jay's world, including the meeting that had just ended in his office. He understood the pain that Jay felt and he empathized with him. Juan was aware that there were only a few days left in Austin for Jay Brown.

Juan stood in front of Jay at the elevator and pushed the button for him. Then he paused for a moment before he spoke.

"Do not be too dejected about what has happened here in Austin. In Texas we have another way to look at this. To me, Doctor Brown, you are like the cicada. After a time like this you will dig a hole for yourself and disappear from sight for a while, maybe for a long while, like the cicada. And then after some time you will reappear to fight your battle all over again. That is because you are strong in mind and spirit.

"When that happens you will make your loud noise once again, like every male cicada does, and be heard for miles around. Then, like the cicada who hooks itself onto the side of a tree and holds tight no matter how hard the wind blows, you will hang on and fight your battle as long as you can. Finally, you will come out of your shell to fly away once again to some other place. A new cycle will begin for you and I am sure you will not give up."

Jay saw the elevator door open and put his arm out to hold it as he looked back to Juan.

"But Doctor Brown, wherever you go there will always be cicada killer wasps who will try to destroy you. Be careful of them."

"Thank you, Juan. You've been a good friend and I really appreciate all your kind thoughts. But this is the last time I'll fight this battle. Someone else will have to pick up this banner and run with it."

Jay and Juan never took their eyes off each other as the elevator door slowly closed.

Jay thought, *I'll never go back to that life again. It's caused so much pain for me and... and other very special people in my life. I'm through!*

Or not!

Epilogue
Five years later

"Those who cannot remember the past are condemned to repeat it."
GEORGE SANTAYANA, "THE LIFE OF REASON" - 1905-06

"Jay you've been here as a *locum tenens* on and off for four months now. I know this isn't the first assignment you've accepted. Sooner or later you'll tire of moving around so often. I'd really like you to stay here permanently and become my partner."

"I've thought about it, Brian. And it really seems like a fine opportunity…. But, there are things that I've seen at the hospital that cause me to have concerns about permanently settling in this community. Some of those things I've seen—the Cesarean section rate and the unnecessary surgery—really bother me."

Brian responded to Jay with moral conviction in the tone of his voice, "They bother me too, Jay. But stay here… with me… and maybe together we can change what's wrong here. You've got the qualities to lead such a change."

"I don't know Brian. Do you… do you really think we might be able to make meaningful…?"